Advance Praise

The Knowing is a spellbinding story. Patton beautifully weaves together themes of family, romance, and bravery in this knockout book. It was the fantasy adventure I didn't know I needed!

— AVERY VOLZ, AUTHOR OF *GRAY MATTER* AND THE *BROKEN BEAUTIFULLY* SERIES

The Knowing is an electrifying book with many twists and turns that draw the reader in as they journey through each chapter. Just when I thought I understood what the characters planned on doing or what might happen, I was surprised with a path that I hadn't fathomed yet. This book is truly a wonder of new ideas and character development to admire as you the reader also explore this wild and magical world that the main character Lottie travels through.

— ABIGAIL BRANNON, EARLY EDUCATION TEACHER

The Knowing is a supernatural coming of age story that is both charming and captivating. Kimberly Patton's spellbinding debut captures the magic of "Sabrina the Teenage Witch" and the teen angst of *Twilight*. I was taken on an incredible adventure with Lottie as she navigates the newly discovered world of powerful witches, family secrets, and a mysterious enemy that threatens to destroy everything dear to her. Add a dash of romance and teen drama and you have a fun, fast-paced novel that will keep you turning the pages until the very end!

— ASHLEY PHAM

Kimberly Patton perfectly blends "Sabrina the Teenage Witch" with *The Craft* in her debut fantasy, *The Knowing*. This story follows teenage witch, Lottie, and everything that falls into place, or falls apart, when she learns who she truly is in her little town of Munroe Falls. Kimberly skillfully made each character and interaction feel so real and raw. The romance and love between Charles and Lottie were cozy and pure. The natural and relatable dynamic of Lottie's parents was so comforting. With a heart-gripping romance, believable characters, beautiful bonds, exciting magic, the unexpected twists and turns and rollercoaster of emotions, *The Knowing* is a masterpiece in the realm of witch stories.

— MISSY MILLER, AUTHOR OF *UNDER THE GYPSY MOON: LAND OF THEE*

I was instantly hooked by *The Knowing* by Kimberly Patton! This coming-of-age story of a teenage girl who was unaware that she was a witch delves into themes of love, loss, friendship, and teen angst set in the world of witchcraft and the supernatural. I especially loved the references to the power of grounding and crystals. The plot line flowed smoothly, and I couldn't wait to see how the story's villain would eventually be caught. A page-turner for sure!

— CHERI D. ANDREWS, ESQ., AUTHOR OF *SMOOTH SAILING: AN ESSENTIAL GUIDE TO LEGALLY PROTECTING YOUR BUSINESS*

Just before her sixteenth birthday, Lottie is haunted by chilling nightmares and ominous feelings. Lightbulbs shatter without cause, and her thoughts seem to have powers of their own. But although Lottie can sense the coming change, she will be grossly unprepared for the truths that await her. Witches, spells, dark magic, and young love, Kimberly Patton's *The Knowing* is perfect for young adult readers who love both fantasy and the paranormal. Lottie will lose so much that she holds dear, but she will gain more than she can ever imagine.

— CHARISSA COSTA, FOUNDER OF
CHARM CITY READERS

In the sleepy town of Munroe Falls, Lottie uncovers her magical heritage on the cusp of her sixteenth birthday. As she navigates newfound powers amidst eerie occurrences and a series of mysterious murders, Lottie discovers love and solidarity within an unlikely group. With gripping plot twists and witchy vibes like *The Craft* and *Practical Magic*, this enchanting coming-of-age story promises to captivate readers with its blend of magic, mystery, and the power of found family.

— KAITLYN COLLIER

I'm a big fan of magical realism and anything to do with witches and coming-of-age stories. In *The Knowing*, Kimberly Patton has woven those elements into a fresh take on discovering the magic within.

As Lottie approaches her sixteenth birthday, strange things begin happening. The cool girls suddenly take an interest in her. Her old friends are acting chilly. Her parents are being downright weird. Long-buried secrets are exposed. And there's this boy...! With the help of her new friends and the most mysterious woman in town, Lottie races against time to unravel the mystery of her heritage and her future before it's too late for all of them.

Hoping this becomes a series! Looking forward to finding out what happens next for Lottie and her friends.

— ANNE WADE, AUTHOR OF *STORYSHIFT*

The Knowing

The Knowing

KIMBERLY PATTON

EDITED BY
DEBORAH KEVIN AND AMANDA MONTANDO

HIGHLANDER PRESS

Paperback ISBN: 978-1-956442-38-0
Ebook ISBN: 978-1-956442-39-7
Library of Congress Control Number: 2024941898

Published by Highlander Press
A division of Highlander Enterprises, LLC
501 W. University Pkwy, Ste. B2
Baltimore, MD 21210

Editor: Deborah Kevin
Associate Editor: Amanda Montandon
Cover design: Miblart (https://miblart.com/)
Cover layout: Pat Creedon (https://patcreedondesign.com)
Author photo: Marjorie Stallard
Chapter icons licensed from AdobeStock

This book is for those who struggle to find their place in this world and for those who have felt less than. I see you. You are amazing, and the world needs you just as you are. Shine on, magical soul.

All souls are reborn. If it finds its purpose, then that soul moves on. If during a lifetime, it was prevented from finding its purpose, that soul must be born over and over until it fulfills its destiny.

Contents

Chapter One

Lottie moved silently amongst the gravestones. The darkness, like pitch, enshrouded everything before her, save for the halo surrounding the thick clouds covering the moon. She gave a quick wave of her hand, wiping them from the sky, freeing the full Hare Moon from its shadowy veil. She continued weaving through the cemetery, allowing herself to lift and float as she proceeded on her course. Exhilarated, she closed her eyes, letting her inner sight guide her.

Without warning, an unforeseen force pulled Lottie against her will toward the older burial grounds. This part of the cemetery frightened her. Something unseen lingered here, oozing malevolence, and it shrouded the place with a choking bleakness. Unable to fight against it, Lottie was swept past the crumbling headstones until the force stopped her over the ink-black water of the neglected, rectangular fishpond. She hovered, frozen in time, for what felt like an eternity in the awful silence. A tiny ripple moved across the surface of the pond, and Lottie trembled, sensing a foulness. Suddenly, two enormous black snakes shot out of the water, latching onto her bare legs, and dragged her down into the murky depths.

LOTTIE JERKED AWAKE WITH A SCREAM STUCK IN THE BACK of her throat. She sucked in a deep breath, forcing the terror away. Her fingers throbbed and prickled with a strange energy, and a palpable foulness lingering in the room made her shudder as she shook her tingling fingers.

That was by far the worst nightmare Lottie had ever had. She tried to implement the breathing exercises Dr. Williams, her psychiatrist, had taught her as she analyzed the dream. She knew she was in another time recalling the details of the long white night shift she wore, but when? The floating and hovering weren't new. There had been other dreams of levitation. This dream—no, this nightmare, left a nasty residue behind. It felt so real. Lottie shivered as she thought of the snakes pulling her under the water. *Ugh.*

A dull thud came from outside the window, and her heart lurched. She hesitated, wanting to ignore it, but the thought of something lurking unchecked was too much for her curiosity. Flinging the covers back, she fumbled through the darkness toward the silvery shimmer of light coming through her window and peeked between the edge of the curtain. She saw a dark shadow move near the garage below, and fear gripped her with its bony fingers. She released a pent-up breath when a large black dog came into the light. Feeling foolish, Lottie shook her head and got back into bed.

~

BEYOND THE TREES, A MAN EMERGED FROM THE SHADOWS. He turned toward the cloaked woman awaiting him, stiffening at her presence.

"Well?" Her tone was flat and demanding.

"She had another nightmare," the man answered.

"Did you discover anything from it?"

"No, she was only dreaming of snakes."

"Honestly, Matthew, why do I keep you in my service? I explained this to you once. The nightmares make her susceptible to our magic—to gain access to her mind. Her dreams aren't typical human dreams. They're a gateway to something more. Try harder."

"Yes, Mistress," Matthew replied.

The woman lowered the hood of her cloak. "Speaking of Mistress, I need another identity—for the cause. I have a plan. You're going to assist at the Paranormal Investigators' Office. They are always on the lookout for people with...your talents."

"But Mistress," Matthew interrupted. "What if they find me out, figure out that I'm not working alone?"

"They won't," the woman said, waving a dismissive hand. "Do you think I'd be stupid enough to risk discovery? I'm sure even you know the benefits of a cloaking spell. How do you think I've managed so long using this form?" She paused, looking toward Lottie's window. "We must watch her, Matthew. If she's who I think she is, I'll need time to get what I came to Munroe Falls for. In the meantime, we'll do what we can to speed things along."

Matthew tensed. "Forgive me, Mistress, but how do you plan to infiltrate the Paranormal Investigators? There are some legitimately gifted people in that office. They'll know I'm a witch."

The woman shot him an exasperated glare. "How do you think these people solve so many mysteries? They *use* witches. Look, if it makes you feel any better, I'll refer to you as my Medium. We'll cause a few unexplained disturbances in town. As a concerned citizen, I'll come forward, give them a big fat donation, and offer your aid. Now, for myself, I think I look like a Selene, don't you?"

Matthew nodded obligingly.

"For formalities, you may refer to me as Ms. Selene..." she paused, tapping a deep burgundy-lacquered fingertip against her chin. "Sullivan. Yes, Selene Sullivan will do." She lifted a long wavy lock of hair away from her shoulder and let it drop. "I suppose I must do something about my appearance. When I meet these so-called 'investigators,' I need to look the part, more womanly."

She waved a hand across herself, and a ripple in the atmosphere around her shifted. "There." She shook her now straight black hair around her shoulders. "How do I look?"

"Changed, Mistress," said Matthew.

"Good. This new appearance is who you will see when we have to deal with the investigators." She waved her hand once again and shifted back to her former self. She turned toward Lottie's house. "Keep an eye on her, Matthew. I'm certain she's the one."

~

LOTTIE RUBBED HER EYES. EXHAUSTED, SHE STRETCHED AND tried to shove away the remnants of the horrible nightmare still clinging to the corners of her mind. She ran to the bathroom to escape the early morning chill lingering in the hall and considered begging her mother to let her stay home from school.

She heard her parents talking about her as she shuffled downstairs to the kitchen. Sighing, she plastered on a pathetic attempt at a smile before pushing open the swinging door. Warm buttered toast and coffee scented the air, accompanied by the sizzling bacon on the stove.

"Morning," Lottie said in her best, upbeat voice.

"Good morning," her mother replied, glancing up from the pan of eggs. "Oh, Honey, you look tired. Another nightmare?"

"Yeah, I'm fine, though."

"Do you want to talk about it?"

"No."

"Sweetheart, I think you need to let Dr. Williams run those tests she suggested. She thinks they will help find what's triggering—"

"Would you just stop, Mom?" Lottie saw the surprise on her mother's face at her outburst and tried to take it down a notch. "I'm fine. I don't want to go through a bunch of tests. Besides, Dr. Williams said they would most likely go away with age."

"Let's talk about it later, Carol," her father interrupted, looking up from his newspaper. "I don't want to send Lottie off to school upset."

"You're right. I'm sorry, Honey."

Lottie sensed her parents' concern as she poured herself a glass of juice and went over to the toaster. She was beginning to regret her mother's idea of therapy. After all, nightmares weren't uncommon. It had been over two months of regular visits, yet something nagged at Lottie that therapy wasn't the answer.

"Sweetheart, Dad and I were talking. Why don't we go somewhere this weekend? We could drive into Akron for a nice dinner or go shopping in Cleveland if you'd like."

"That sounds good. I'll think about it and let you know."

"Okay. Hurry and eat your breakfast. It's getting late."

Lottie noticed her backpack lying on the floor by her nightstand when she returned upstairs. She gathered her notebooks and saw something she'd scribbled on a sheet of paper: New student Friday.

Right. Mr. Spencer, her biology teacher, had announced earlier in the week that a new student would be joining them. Lottie shook her head. Why anyone would want to move to the small, sleepy little city of Munroe Falls, Ohio, was beyond her reasoning. With a population of roughly five thousand in the two-point-seven square miles it inhabited, she decided the reason must be job-related.

LOTTIE'S BREATH CLOUDED THE CRISP AIR AS SHE STEPPED outside. Everything looked stark under the newly fallen snow. Even the sky was white, with dense clouds covering any hint of blue across the horizon. A swath of black asphalt led a path down the steep driveway from her father's snowblade, and salt crystals dotted the pavement. Lottie said a prayer to any beings out there willing to listen that she wouldn't slip on them as she eased her way down to the bottom.

She was thankful when the bus finally arrived, giving her respite from the biting cold. She stepped on and found her usual seat mid-way down the aisle. The snow swirled around the window, lulling her into the white abyss. The bus made its way, stopping periodically to allow kids to board. Lottie didn't notice. Her thoughts were in another world.

"Care if I sit with you?"

The voice pulled her out of Somewhereland. Lottie looked away from the window. Standing by her seat was a girl she had never seen before. Her long bouncy red hair was damp with fat snowflakes clinging in the strands, and a flush of crimson tinted her nose and cheeks. Her hazel eyes stared with hope at Lottie.

"Um, sure." Lottie moved her stuff to make room.

"Thanks," the girl replied, placing her backpack in the seat between them. "I'm Christy Adams. I just moved here."

"Lottie Jacobs. Nice to meet you."

"What do you know about Mr. Spencer?" Christy asked after their introduction. "I have biology first period, and I hope I'm not spending it with a jerk for a teacher."

"Let's just say he's a bit intolerant," Lottie said.

Christy seemed to mull over the meaning behind Lottie's words. Lottie soon lost interest in their conversation when the bus stopped in front of a white house. She knew everything about this house. At least on the outside. It was plain. The shutters were faded, and some slats were missing on a couple of them from the recent winds. A few trees stood at the side of the house, now brown and void of life, with snow heavy on their limbs. One reached out and touched the glass of an upstairs window like gnarled fingers. Lottie often imagined climbing that branch and looking in that window.

The driver opened the door, snapping her attention to the front of the bus. Charles Lachlan stepped on board. Lottie's heart thumped, and the familiar panic she felt whenever she saw him washed over her. Snow speckled his dark hair, and the black jacket he wore made his deep brown eyes even more somber. Her gaze dropped to his mouth, and she felt a warm flush.

"Are you okay?" Christy asked.

"Oh, yeah...I was thinking about something I forgot to do at home," Lottie said, keeping her eyes on Charles. The pulse in his neck seemed to beat in rhythm with hers.

He walked to the back of the bus to the very last seat, those seats unspokenly reserved for the more popular kids. Lottie pretended to be interested in Christy so she could see Charles from the corner of her eye.

Christy's eyebrows climbed. "Are you sure you're okay?"

Lottie flushed. "I'm sorry, I'm tired and zoning out." *Stupid*. It was evident that she was beyond flustered. She couldn't understand her sudden interest in Charles. She had known him since elementary school but felt drawn to him over the last few months, pulled by some driving force.

"Well, it looks like we're here," Christy remarked.

Lottie peered out her window. Stow-Munroe Falls High School came into view. Its beige, cement-colored facade sprawling across the snow-covered knoll reminded her of a prison. Cold, stark, and unwelcoming. She cringed as the familiar dread settled in her stomach. *Just get through the day.*

"I guess I'll see you in class then," Christy said, zipping her parka up to her chin. She slid out of the seat and merged with those already disembarking.

Her perky voice irked Lottie for some reason. As she gathered her things and stepped into the aisle, Charles followed behind her, setting off a panic storm. She reminded herself he was just a boy—a gorgeous boy with an undeniable energy that drew her in. At least she didn't have any classes with him. She would probably die if she had to speak to him.

As she headed toward the school, Charles and the others from the back passed her. He was even captivating from behind. He raked a hand through his hair giving it a tousled, effortless look. Lottie realized she was gawking at him. She fell in with the rest of the student body, filing into the fluorescent-lit halls of Stow-Munroe High School. Everyone seemed to be in high spirits, presumably due to the coming weekend. Maybe some of that would rub off on her.

She shoved her things into her locker and headed to class. Biology. Room 213. The bell rang as Lottie opened the door. Mr. Spencer was introducing Christy.

"Good of you to join us, Ms. Jacobs," he said, glaring over the rim of his black framed glasses. With piercing dark eyes, sharp features, and an inability to smile, the man was formidable.

Embarrassed, Lottie quickly took her seat. Christy shot her an encouraging smile as Mr. Spencer took a stack of papers from his desk and passed them out.

"I trust everyone studied," he said as he crossed the front of the room. He leaned against his desk, waiting for Lottie to put her things away. She could sense his irritation as she scrambled to get prepared. When she found her pencil, he proceeded.

"You have ten minutes. Turn your papers over and begin."

Lottie stared blankly at the questions. A fog swirled around in her brain where the answers should be. She had studied for hours and knew the material. Panic rose as she struggled through the test.

When the bell rang, Lottie was nearly in tears. She still had six unanswered questions. She quickly handed in her paper and rushed out the door, slamming into what felt like steel.

Lottie bit her tongue as she fell back against the wall, and the taste of blood filled her mouth, turning her stomach.

"Oh, my God. I'm sorry. Are you okay?" a panicked voice asked.

Lottie righted herself to see who her assailant was, only to find his face obscured from the hood of his Stow-Munroe Falls sweatshirt. A sudden anger rushed through her. *No, I'm not okay,* she thought. *You ran into me because you had your stupid hood covering your face.*

"Yeah, I think so," Lottie replied—no need to take out her frustrations from a failed test on someone else.

He yanked off the hood and handed her the fallen backpack.

"Here you go. Sorry."

Bryan Michaels, varsity linebacker for the Bulldogs. Why couldn't it have been a puny freshman student?

When lunchtime arrived, Lottie headed downstairs to the cafeteria to her usual table with her friends, Gwen and Abbey. She was surprised to see Christy sitting with them. She smiled at Lottie as she sat down.

"Hey, Lottie," Abbey greeted. "This is Christy Adams."

"Yeah, we met earlier on the bus," Lottie replied, sliding her chair closer. "How's it going so far?"

Christy shrugged. "Not bad. I have English and History with Abbey. Thank God she was kind enough to help me find my way down here. I'm starving."

Abbey and Gwen burst into laughter, and Lottie wondered what she had missed.

"So, where are you from?" Lottie asked.

"Georgia," Christy stated, uninterested in adding further details.

"Really? Wow. What brought you way up here?"

"Let's not talk about me," Christy said harshly, taking Lottie by surprise. "I'm afraid my story would bore you," she added, recovering her earlier chipper voice. She stabbed at her salad, then let the fork plunk down in an unconscious action. "What does everyone do for fun around here?"

"We mostly go to the movies or hang out at the mall," Gwen replied. "But we're close to Akron, so it's not too far for more fun."

Lottie ate her lunch in silence as Gwen and Abbey interacted with Christy. It was as if they were trying to impress her. Her friends were usually low-key and unassuming. She didn't know what to make of their display. Luckily, Charles Lachlan was a good distraction.

He laughed at something someone had said, and Lottie contemplated whether she saw humor or mischievousness in his expression.

Look at me, Lottie thought to herself. As soon as the thought passed, Charles's head bobbed up as if in obedience. He caught her stare. The air between them crackled with energy. She saw confusion and something else she couldn't describe in his eyes. He wore a slightly shocked expression that he tried to hide. Embarrassed, Lottie stumbled out of her chair and emptied her trash. Was that a coincidence?

She rushed down the hall toward the bathroom to collect herself with Charles's face imprinted in her mind. What had she seen when he returned her gaze? Her fingers were hot and tingling, but this time the prickling began to radiate through her entire body. What was happening to her? Fear and hyperventilation, mixed with nausea, hit her at once.

Lottie pushed open the bathroom door and bent down to look under the stalls. She was alone. She took in some deep breaths to try to calm herself, and the tingling began to subside.

She nearly jumped when the bathroom door swung open, and Wren Wesley strode in. Concern replaced her usual serene, photoshop-likened features as she eyed Lottie. "Are you okay?"

"Yeah, something I ate didn't agree with me."

"Is there anything I can do? Would you like me to get the nurse?"

"No, I...I'm fine, thanks," Lottie said. She turned and left the bathroom, feeling the cool-blue gaze of Wren's eyes boring into her back.

∾

EXCITEMENT HUNG OVER THE PARKING AREA OUTSIDE THE school as students planned their weekend. Lottie shifted her backpack higher as she waited in the bus line and watched as a group of boys got reprimanded for 'unruly behavior.' Charles walked out with the back-seat crew, and his eyes fell on hers. Lottie fidgeted with the strap on her backpack. She'd wanted him to notice her for weeks, but after what happened at lunch, the intensity of his gaze felt heavy.

Christy rushed out of the school, a look of relief spreading over her features, and Lottie was thankful for the distraction.

"I didn't think I was ever going to make it out. I had to check in with the guidance counselor, which took longer than I thought." She paused to zip her parka. "What happened to you at lunch? We were all wondering when you rushed out of the cafeteria."

"Something I ate made me sick," Lottie said, climbing on the bus.

They slid into the same seat they'd shared that morning. Christy placed her backpack on the floor and turned her attention to Lottie.

"Sorry if I got rude at lunch today. I don't like talking about my past. I feel like I can trust you. I'll tell you more if you promise to keep it between us."

Lottie nodded, unsure what to think about this new-found friend.

Christy gazed down at her hands. "I've been in foster care, basically my whole life. Janet, my *mom*," she said the word bitterly, "adopted me out of the system when I was eleven. What a nightmare she turned out to be." She shot a glance at Lottie as she paused to take a breath. "Any-way, Janet is a mess. An addict. And she's had some horrible things happen to her because of it. That's why we had to pack up and move here."

"Christy, I'm so sorry." Lottie flushed, regretting that she couldn't come up with a better response.

"Don't be. Anyway, Janet is clean. For now. Here's to new begin-nings, right?"

"Yeah." Lottie paused, trying to think of something positive to add. "Maybe I can call you sometime. We can go see a movie."

"Thanks," Christy replied. "We'd have to arrange it on the bus, though. We only have a pre-paid phone for emergencies. Janet doesn't want to risk her past catching up to her by being accessible via modern technology."

An awkward silence hung between the girls.

"Let's change the subject," Christy suggested.

Relieved, Lottie searched for something to say. "Do you have much homework?"

"No. The teachers went easy on me, first day and all." Christy picked up her backpack and stood.

Lottie realized the bus had stopped at a service station.

"I'll see you Monday."

Lottie hadn't noticed that morning where Christy had gotten on the bus. She looked out of her window. Christy waited until the bus pulled away and then walked back from where they had just come. *How awful.*

~

A GUST OF WIND PULLED LOTTIE'S ATTENTION FROM HER book. It rattled the old windows, loose in their casings. She took in the bleak, dreary day beyond the panes. A gray billowing fog hung heavy on the horizon now that the rain had stopped, depriving her of even a glimpse of the low mountains surrounding her hilltop home. She sighed with boredom. The fact that it was Sunday only made it worse. She was already dreading the school week.

Her mother's voice broke her trance. "Hand me that lightbulb, will you, honey?"

Her mom stood midway up on a rickety step ladder unscrewing the now-blackened lightbulb Lottie had blown the previous night. She handed the new bulb up to her mother.

"This is the third one this week. I'm going to have your father check the wiring."

Over the previous month, the bursting glass had become more frequent and much more explosive—like last night. Lottie stared at the blackened bulb, recalling the force of energy coursing through her when it had blown out. Her hand had felt warm and tingly—it was almost as if she had caused the bulb to shatter. But that couldn't be possible. It had to be the wiring, as her mother said.

"Okay, all set. I'm going down to make lunch."

"Thanks, Mom."

"No problem, sweetie."

Lottie returned to her favorite spot by the window, to the worn-out pale green and pink tufted armchair that once belonged to her grandmother. She reached again for the book she bought over the weekend and placed it on her lap, but instead of reading, she rested her head against the curved chair back and plucked at a fuzzball instead. She felt pent up with frustration and boredom. Perhaps being cooped up indoors through the long winter had affected her mindset. But that didn't explain the countless odd and unexplained things happening to her, like the nightmares and her knack for blowing lightbulbs—and no matter what, whenever it was 3:33 —night or day—she was drawn to look at the clock. Something gnawed at her insides.

Lottie closed her eyes and let the now familiar feelings wash over her. She scanned through past events, the nightmares. But then there was something different. Glimpses of veiled memories filtered through the blackness, like beams of light. What was her mind trying to show her? She only revealed feelings—longing, despair...missing something or someone.

Frustrated, she opened her eyes to her world again. Munroe Falls, Ohio. There were quaint homes on idyllic quiet streets, but for a fifteen-year-old girl with high hopes, small-town living made her feel trapped.

A bead of water trickled down her window, drawing Lottie's attention to the road below her home. What would her life be like outside of Munroe Falls? She had often dreamt of leaving. Dreaming was the one thing that kept her grounded.

Her dad was outside, clearing junk out of their detached garage. He stacked a cardboard box full of old worn-out wires on top of the trash can before going over to his van. Pausing, he swiped at a smudge above the "J" in Jacobs' Electric, Inc., printed in bold black letters on the door. He was a self-employed electrician—and according to her mother, a darn good one.

"Lottie, lunch is ready," her mother's voice sang out from the kitchen. Chilled, she wrapped her favorite blanket around her shoulders and headed downstairs. Each step groaned and creaked beneath her feet as she descended.

"I made tomato soup and turkey sandwiches. Can you get your father a drink?"

"Sure."

A blast of cold air rushed in as her mother opened the kitchen door to beckon her dad indoors.

Lottie placed a soda on the table and pulled her blanket more firmly around her as she sat.

"Honey, how can you eat with that blanket? Why don't you put on a sweatshirt or something warmer?"

Lottie shrugged." I'll manage."

The radiant heat had its benefits, but in their ninety-year-old house, the cold still found a way to seep into her bones. She took a bite of her sandwich and watched the steam roll around her soup bowl. The kitchen door opened, sucking the steam away.

Her dad hung his coat on a wall peg and lumbered over to the old farmhouse sink to wash his hands.

"Did you get the garage cleaned out?" her mother asked.

He pecked a kiss on her cheek." Just about."

Lottie cringed as her father scraped the wooden chair across the floor. She knew what was next.

"Randy, how many times have I asked you not to scrape those chairs across the floor?"

He shot a contrite glance as he sat. "Sorry, Carol."

Her mother threw up her hands. "I'm going over to the shop. I've got a shipment coming at one-thirty. Lottie, would you like to come with me?"

"No, I think I'll go back upstairs and hibernate."

"Okay. Put a sweatshirt on, for goodness sake."

As a child, driving over to her mother's small flower shop in Akron was a treat. She loved the sign that hung over the door, Petal Pushers. Each letter had a different pastel color and size. She recalled entering the shop, the smell of roses wafting past her nose, luring her closer to touch their delicate petals. Now, they just made her sneeze.

She watched her mom ease the car down the driveway and out of sight.

"Mom said you blew another bulb last night." Her father's statement broke her thoughts. "Are you going for a new record?"

Lottie narrowed her eyes. "Ha-ha."

"I'll take a look at the wiring. Don't think I'll find anything, but if it makes your mother happy...."

Chapter Two

Lottie tucked her book under her arm and grabbed a tray. Glancing across the cafeteria, she noticed Gwen and Abbey weren't in their usual spots at their table. She turned her attention to the mashed potato scoop, raking out a hefty load before replacing it beside the pan.

"You're reading *A Calling*. I love that book."

Lottie caught a glimpse of blonde hair before she turned to see Wren Wesley smiling at her. Her deep blue eyes held a genuine warmth.

"Have you made it to chapter eight yet?" she asked, eying the book.

"No. I'm on six. I'm feeling some strong witchy vibes in the story."

"Well, I'm not going to say anything. You'll have to read more. But trust me when I say it gets much better at chapter eight."

Wren was one of the prettiest girls in school. Her outgoing nature was infectious. Lottie was surprised to be singled out by her as they had never spoken much in the past.

"So how are you feeling? You looked pretty sick Friday."

"Oh, right. I'm feeling better."

Wren nodded. "Abbey wasn't in English this morning, and Gwen got sick and had to check out. I heard they have a stomach flu. You should sit at our table today."

Lottie followed Wren's gaze across the room. Her friends waved.

Was this a joke? Lottie managed to keep her features neutral despite the wariness she felt.

Wren smiled. "Come on, no one should eat alone."

"Sure," Lottie replied.

They worked their way over to the table, which happened to be right across from Charles. Lottie vowed to herself that she wouldn't even look at him today.

Wren sat her tray down alongside Rowen Maxwell and Sunniva Browne. Both girls—like Wren, were at the top of the popularity list. Lottie felt out of place. As if sensing it, Wren broke the ice.

"Lottie, you know Rowen and Sunni."

She gave a small, awkward wave. "Hi, yes, we've had some classes together."

They welcomed Lottie with sincere smiles, and she relaxed a little as she slid her chair toward the table. She noticed Sunni had grown her hair longer and was wearing subtle burgundy highlights that streaked through her ringlets, complimenting her coppery skin, and Rowen now had bangs that swept away from her cherub-like face. She had them styled to mesh into the waves of her ash-brown hair.

"What do you think of the new girl?" Wren asked.

"She seems nice," Lottie replied with a shrug. "I think she must have whatever Gwen and Abbey have since she's not here either."

"Pretty lousy to get sick after your first day," Rowen remarked.

"I love your nails," Wren commented. Where do you get them done?"

"Oh, thanks. I do them myself," Lottie replied.

"Wow. I don't have the patience to blend the different colors like that. Not to mention getting the little beads to stay on longer than five minutes."

"I can polish yours sometime if you want," Lottie offered. She quickly flushed. Why would Wren accept when she clearly had a professional manicure given the perfect look of them.

"Only if you include me, too," Sunni added.

Lottie smiled.

"Seriously, we need to hang out," Wren suggested. "We could do a girls' night. Nails, food...whatever you like."

"Good idea," Rowen said. "I need to get my face scrubbed. It feels super gross. I'm jealous of Lottie over here. You have flawless skin. What's your secret?"

Lottie shifted in her seat. She wasn't used to so many compliments. "Well, nothing really. I guess I'm lucky like that."

"Hmm. Well, some of us have to work a little magic before we can face the public," Wren said.

Sunni winked. Lottie thought the look they exchanged was odd, but she didn't dwell on it. She relaxed more and more as they talked. There was a vague sense of familiarity with them that eased any awkwardness in her. The instant connection with these girls awoke something deep inside of her. The feeling of something missing in her seemed to disappear in their company.

A sudden tingling sensation settled in the center of Lottie's forehead, and an unseen force urged her to look up. When she did, she saw Charles staring intently at her. She held his gaze, and the rest of the cafeteria faded into obscurity. Even the noise was muted. From the corners of her eyes, she saw a hue of color, deep crimson, flaring out as waves of energy between the two of them. Startled, she turned away, knocking her water over. Before it hit the table, Sunni reached out like a blur, straightening the bottle upright before even a drop spilled.

Lottie blinked. "Wow, talk about reflexes. And I thought I was good. Thanks."

Sunni smiled. "No problem,"

Lottie noticed an amused expression spread over Rowen's face as she stared intently at Charles. He met her look with equal intensity, and Lottie could have sworn they were having a private conversation. He shrugged at Rowen before turning his attention back to his tray. Their subtle interaction confused Lottie.

"Do you know him?" Lottie asked. "Charles, I mean?"

"Our families know each other," Rowen replied casually. "They go way back."

Lottie caught Charles glancing at her a few times while she finished eating. She hoped he would talk to her. Soon.

When the bell rang, announcing the end of lunch, Lottie realized in the thirty minutes that she had gotten to know Wren, Rowen, and

Sunni, she felt more at ease, more herself than with anyone else. It was bizarre and a little unsettling.

Wren stood and picked up her tray. "I'm glad you sat with us today, Lottie. It was good getting to know you."

"Yeah, we should do this again," Sunni suggested.

Lottie smiled. "Sounds good."

She gathered up her mess and headed over to the trash bins. An uneasy feeling spread over her along with a strong sense that someone was watching her. Lottie's eyes fell on Jake Putnam. She'd been in a few classes with Jake in the past and had always enjoyed his easy-going nature. She flashed a smile at him, but it quickly fell from her lips as his hollow, empty eyes bore into her.

Strange. Maybe he was just in deep thought and happened to be looking her way. She dumped her trash and hurried out of the cafeteria to finish out the rest of the day.

THE MICROWAVE CLOCK READ 3:33 AS LOTTIE CAME IN THE door. "Well, there's a surprise," she muttered sarcastically at seeing the familiar numbers. Settling at the table, she rummaged through her backpack with a mindset to tackle homework.

As evening approached, her mother hurried through the kitchen door with a pizza. "Hi, sweetie. I'm sorry I'm late. How was your day?"

Lottie smiled. "It was good."

Her mother grinned. "So what's this new optimism I hear in your voice?" she asked, pulling out two plates.

"I met some girls in school today. They were overly nice to me, though I'm not sure why."

"Why do you say that?"

"They're just super popular and pretty, and I'm so...me."

"Lottie, you're wonderful. You are a smart and beautiful girl. You don't give yourself enough credit."

"Aw, thanks, Mom." She put two slices of pizza on a plate. "I'm going up to read."

Settling into her chair with a blanket, she dove into her book.

Halfway through chapter eight, a smile crept over her face. Wren was right. It did get better once the main character discovered her powers as a witch. Hooked, Lottie poured through the rest of the pages until the end.

She stretched and went to the kitchen to get a drink before bed. Fumbling for the switch, she took a jolt. *Pow*. Nice. She felt some serious energy from that one—like *she* had a sense of power. Wishful thinking.

Lottie wondered what it would be like to have magical powers as she headed upstairs to the bathroom. Looking in the mirror, she felt a rush of strange energy. Her eyes were almost black from being dilated. She blinked in surprise.

"Okay, scary."

Something caught her attention in the mirror. A reflection of a shadow moved by the window behind her. Fear tingled down her back, and she felt herself go hot, then cold. She squeezed her eyes closed, hoping she had imagined it. Just then, the bathroom door cracked open. She nearly screamed.

"I'm going to bed, sweetie," her mother whispered.

Lottie let out a breath.

Her mother's eyes were full of concern. "You okay?"

"Yeah. I'm going to bed, too."

She glanced toward the window again before going to her room. The branches blew gently in the wind. She must have imagined something being there.

AS THE BUS NEARED QUICK STOP SERVICE STATION the following morning, Lottie saw Christy sitting on the curb near the entrance. The driver opened the door, and she climbed on, smiling at Lottie before sitting down.

"Hey," Lottie greeted. "Were you sick?"

"Yeah. Nasty stomach virus. Thank God it's over."

Lottie grimaced. "Gwen and Abbey were out sick yesterday too."

Christy gave a sympathetic frown. "Be glad you were spared. It was awful. So, what did I miss?"

"Nothing much."

When Charles's stop approached, Lottie decided she was going to brave a glance at him. As he walked toward her, she thought the words again: Look at me, but he didn't. Too bad those powers in the book weren't hers.

"Are you into that guy?" Christy asked.

"Who?" Lottie feigned ignorance.

"The guy that just walked by. I see how you look at him. Admit it. You like him."

Lottie scoffed. For some reason, a strong sense of denial forced its way into words. "No, I don't." She sat silent during the remaining ride, wondering why she had felt so strongly to deny liking Charles.

When they arrived at school, Lottie pretended to look for something to give Christy a chance to go ahead of her. She wasn't up for any more uncomfortable questions. She grabbed her things and stepped out into the aisle.

"What do you think about that book you've been reading?"

Her heart lurched at the sound of Charles's voice. *Breathe, Lottie.* She turned and met his gaze.

"I love it. Have you read it?"

"No, but my mom has."

She could sense his closeness behind her as she shuffled toward the exit. It was a tangible energy that wrapped around her senses, leaving her giddy. She felt like she was floating down the bus steps. When Charles passed by, he glanced back at her as he walked into the school, making her heart race. His lips twitched as if sensing her emotions. She felt silly, but she didn't care. Nothing could ruin her day now. Not even Mr. Spencer.

~

A TWINGE OF EXCITEMENT RAN THROUGH LOTTIE WHEN THE lunch bell rang. Wren waved as she entered the cafeteria, motioning Lottie to her table. She noticed that Christy was sitting with Gwen and Abbey, so she didn't feel too guilty about not joining them. She felt their eyes on her as she sat down beside Wren. Gwen wore a look of shock that quickly turned to irritation. Lottie gave her an awkward wave.

"So? How was chapter eight?" Wren asked.

"It was awesome. I couldn't put the book down—I finished it last night."

"You know there's a Part Two, right?"

"Yes. I'm going to get it after school."

"Oh, well, why don't we see a movie later? You can pick up a copy before we go," Wren insisted.

"I'll have to ask my parents. They're pretty strict."

"Okay. Let me know. My dad can drive us if you think that will help your parents feel more comfortable."

Lottie noticed Charles wasn't at his usual table. She glanced around the cafeteria but couldn't find him.

"He isn't here," Rowen said.

Heat rose to Lottie's cheeks. Had she been so obvious in searching him out? "I...um...." Mortified, she looked away.

Rowen smiled. "It's okay. I know you like Charles."

Lottie started to deny it, as she did earlier with Christy, but an overwhelming sense of trust and release came upon hearing it from Rowen's lips.

Lottie's gaze fell to her lap. She tucked a section of her dark chestnut hair behind her ear. "I do like him. A lot, actually."

"He's a good guy. I could see you two as a couple."

Lottie met Rowen's eyes. "I thought you might like him."

"Not me," Rowen scoffed. "He's the 'holding out for his soulmate' type of guy. I'm *so* not that girl."

Lottie stared down at her tray. Something about the way Rowen said 'soulmate' triggered that familiar aching in her heart.

She wondered about Charles for the rest of the afternoon. She finally saw him standing in the bus line after school.

"Hey," he greeted.

"I didn't see you at lunch today." She noticed his lips twitch and heat rose to her cheeks. Flustered, she began to twist the straps on her backpack.

"I was making up a test. Did you miss me?" Charles teased.

Mischief flashed in his eyes, and Lottie's blush deepened.

The breeze shifted, and she caught a faint scent from him. It was earthy and something else she couldn't describe. His scent reminded her of something that she couldn't quite put her finger on. It was so familiar.

Charles's voice drew her back to attention. "Some of us are going to see *Snatched* later. You should go."

"Wren asked me, but I'm not sure if I'm going yet."

He flashed her a sheepish smile. "It would be a shame to miss it."

Lottie grinned despite herself. For that smile, she would do anything to convince her parents to let her go.

She noticed Christy and Abbey getting into Gwen's car as she got on the bus. Once again, Gwen scowled at her before driving away. Lottie cringed. Great. Girl drama.

~

LOTTIE LET HERSELF INTO THE KITCHEN AND PLUNKED HER backpack on the floor.

"Well, I think it's safe to say Gwen is mad at me."

"What makes you say that?" her mother asked.

"I sat with Wren and her friends today, and now Gwen is shooting me dirty looks."

"She's probably jealous. Don't be too hard on her. Just be kind, as always."

"I know. Speaking of new friends, Wren invited me to a movie later. Her dad will drive us if that's okay."

"I thought we were doing a family night."

"Please, Mom? I could use some time away from school with friends."

"Friends?"

"Rowen and Sunni might be there, too."

"I'll have to talk to your father."

"Thanks, Mom."

Lottie had it in her mind that she was going. She rummaged through her closet for something to wear, then remembered Charles would be there. She chewed on her lip as she scanned through her clothes.

Her mother knocked and stepped into the room. "I spoke to your father. You can go to the movie."

Lottie squealed. "Thanks, Mom."

"You're welcome. We'll do family night another time."

Closing the door behind her mother, Lottie picked up her phone to message Wren.

-My parents said I can go to the movie.

-Awesome. We'll pick you up at six.

Lottie put her phone on the nightstand and yawned. She glanced at the clock. 4:15. Plenty of time for a nap. She set the alarm for thirty minutes.

∼

The sun melted away, leaving the sky blazing in its wake. Lottie closed her eyes, searing the image of the beautiful scenery into her memory. When she opened her eyes again, she saw a man standing deeper in the woods. She looked away for only a moment, and when she turned back, a large black wolf stood where the man had been. A twig snapped behind her.

∼

Lottie jerked awake, disoriented. Her alarm hadn't buzzed yet. Turning over, she saw the numbers, 5:23 glaring red and angry at her. "Oh, my God!" She jumped out of bed and rushed into the bathroom, realizing she had accidentally set the clock for AM instead of PM. Luckily, her hair hadn't suffered from the nap. She ran her fingers through it and brushed her teeth. At least her clothes were laid out.

Lottie was putting her earrings on when she saw Mr. Wesley drive up to the house.

"They're here," she shouted to her mother.

"Coming."

"Seriously, Mom? Do you *really* need to meet Wren and her dad?" Lottie said as her mother stepped out of her bedroom.

"Of course. I need to know who my daughter is with and that she is safe."

"So embarrassing," Lottie mumbled.

After the awkward introductions, they were finally on their way.

"Your mom is nice," Wren said.

"Thanks," Lottie replied. "She insisted on meeting you both. I told you she was overprotective."

"I think it's sweet she came out to say hi," Wren said. "My mom just throws up a hand from inside the door."

When they arrived at the mall, Wren rushed out of the car, tugging Lottie along with her.

"I'll text you when the movie ends, Daddy," Wren called over her shoulder.

"Don't talk to any boys," Mr. Wesley replied. A smirk played at the corner of his mouth.

"Is he serious?" Lottie asked.

"Who knows? Why? Do you plan to talk to one?" Wren teased.

Lottie hoped that she would, yes.

Wren flashed a bright smile. "Come on. Let's get your book and head to the movie."

They bought their tickets and walked over to the concessions. Lottie noticed Charles and his friends making their way into the movie, and a rush of anticipation washed over her.

"Butter?"

A bored-looking teenager held Lottie's popcorn up and shook the bag slightly.

"Um, sure," she replied.

They paid for their snacks and found seats closer to the back.

"I'm going to the bathroom before the movie starts," Wren said, tossing her jacket over the seat.

Lottie wondered where Charles was sitting. It was too dark to see him in the crowd. She felt something hit her shoulder and ignored it. Then a piece of popcorn landed in her lap. *Seriously?*

"Psst." Again—"Psst."

She turned around. "Really!"

Charles and Bryan Michaels, along with some other guys from school, were laughing at her expense.

"You don't like popcorn?" Charles asked.

"Not when it's flying at me from behind," Lottie replied.

"Would it be better if I moved up and threw it at you from the front?" he teased.

"That's cute," Lottie said sarcastically.

Wren squeezed through the row and sat down. "What's with the popcorn in your hair?"

"Don't ask," Lottie said. She heard a commotion and turned to see Charles and Bryan climbing across the seats into the row behind her. So much for not talking to boys.

The lights went out. Lottie felt a hand tickle the back of her neck, followed by a ghostlike, "Oooooh."

"All right," she fussed.

The movie opened with a possession scene. Lottie's heart raced. Nope. Way too scary. She chastised herself for not watching the trailer before agreeing to see the movie. Too late now. Something jumped out from a closet in the next scene. She screamed, and Wren laughed.

"I've gotta go to the bathroom," Lottie announced.

"Now?" Wren asked.

"Sorry, gotta go."

She climbed over knees and feet until she reached the end of the row, nearly stumbling up the aisle on her way to the door. Looking for the signs pointing to the women's bathroom, she sped off in that direction.

Lottie took as long as she could to avoid returning to the movie. She ran her fingers through her hair and picked out the popcorn pieces for a good fifteen minutes. When she came out, she was surprised to see Charles sitting on the bench outside of the restrooms.

"Couldn't handle it?" he asked.

"That obvious?" Lottie replied with a grin.

"Well, when you weren't back after ten minutes, Wren asked if I'd check on you."

"I'm sorry. I wouldn't have taken so long if I'd known you were out here."

"No problem. I'm not really into the movie anyway. Just something to do."

"Now what?" Lottie asked.

"We can sit here and hang out until the movie ends if you want."

"Sure."

Lottie tried to hide her excitement. Her nerves were a wreck. She had no idea what to say to him.

"So, not a scary movie fan?" he asked.

She was grateful that he broke the ice first. "Well, I am; I just don't like movies about possession."

"It's all special effects," he said with a smile. "It's not real."

She liked how his eyes twinkled when he smiled. She tried not to think about how gorgeous he was for fear of saying something stupid.

"There are definitely some things out there that defy explanation."

"Such as?" He was gazing intently at her now.

"I don't know how to describe it. If you had the nightmares I've had, you'd believe."

A look of concern came over his face. "What kind of nightmares are you having?"

"I'd rather not get into it. I've been traumatized enough for one night."

"Would it help if I throw popcorn?"

She laughed out loud. "Probably."

"So, no more talk of nightmares and possession. I sense your vibes of dislike on these topics."

He could sense vibes, too? Lottie was intrigued. "You're right. Some people put out bad energy."

"Ah, you're a sensitive one. You could join the local Paranormal Investigators with gifts like that."

"No, thanks," Lottie replied. "I've got enough weird things going on without fake entities making it worse."

"They're actually legit. You know they're on a lead right now, don't you? My mom heard they've picked up on a load of negative energy around town. They think someone new is in the area. A person of ill-intent is how she put it."

"Wow, you *do* believe in this stuff, don't you?"

"Absolutely. You don't?"

"No. Maybe. I don't know. I'd probably be open to anything, given how I've been feeling lately." She thought about her earlier dream and how it felt like someone was watching her.

"If you ever need to talk about it, I'm a pretty good listener," Charles said.

His intent expression made her wonder what was on his mind.

"So, what do you do for fun when you're not watching horror movies?"

He shrugged. "Not much, really. I read a lot, and sometimes, my mom and I travel; Electronics and music in my free time. Pretty boring, huh?"

Lottie was surprised at his response. He had a substance to him, and she wanted to know more. "What about your dad?"

"I never knew my father."

"I'm sorry. I didn't mean to be nosey."

"No, it's cool. I like it with just Mom and me. She's a great person."

Lottie smiled to herself. What kind of boy was he? He seemed so much older than his age. She knew that feeling all too well. An odd and yet familiar feeling rose inside of her. It was a sense of déjà vu, as if she had been like this with him before.

His eyes were on hers again, intense and questioning. Uncomfortable, Lottie laughed.

"What?" he asked.

"You make me nervous when you look at me like that."

He grinned. "I'm sorry. It's just; I feel like I've met you somewhere before, like, not at school." He shifted his gaze away, raking his hand through his hair. "What about you? What do you do when you're not running out of scary movies?"

"Well, like you, I read a lot, and I love music. I scour social media for the latest nail art designs. When I'm not doing that, I sit around brooding and planning my escape from Munroe Falls."

He softened his expression, and she found herself feeling sucked in.

The moment had an abrupt ending as the theatre door opened. Lottie scanned the crowd, searching for Wren. Her distinct giggle rang out through the hum of conversations. She and Bryan Michaels were the last ones to exit the movie. There was undeniable chemistry between the pair as they laughed together.

"It looks like Wren had fun," Charles noted.

"It seems so. Thanks for keeping me company."

"No problem. I'm glad we had a chance to talk."

"Me too. I guess I'll see you on the bus then."

Wren strolled over, wearing a scowl. "Oh, my gosh, Lottie. You totally ditched me."

"Sorry. I wasn't feeling the movie."

"She's all good," Bryan said. "I held her hand while she screamed."

"Funny, Bryan," Wren scolded. She turned her attention back to Lottie. "Are you okay?"

"I'm fine. Charles kept me company."

"Well, we'd better go. I see Dad. No boys, remember?"

Charles shot Wren a confused look, followed by a smirk. Once again, Lottie could swear they had just shared a private conversation. *Very odd, indeed.*

On the ride home, Lottie's thoughts were of Charles. He was much more complicated than she thought. He was very caring—which was surprising given his aloof and stony aura. He was soft and sweet but very dark and mysterious. Everything about him drew her in. Mr. Wesley's voice broke into her thoughts, letting her know she was home.

Her mother stepped outside wearing her nightgown and robe. Lottie was horrified to see her worn, hot pink house shoes peeking out. She quickly thanked Wren and Mr. Wesley and jumped out of the car before her mother could come over.

"Mom!" she whispered, mortified.

Her mother flashed a grin as Lottie darted inside. She hung up her coat and dressed for bed. The bulb flickered and went out as she turned on the bathroom light. *Seriously?* She brushed her teeth in the dark and crawled into bed, smiling at how the evening had worked out with Charles. She had never had a boyfriend before, and the possibility of dating Charles was thrilling. She hoped it would come to that. As she drifted to sleep, she thought she could feel his presence.

Chapter Three

The last remnants of light clung to the sky. Lottie's heart raced as she rushed toward the trail that led out of the park. There were rumors of bad things happening in these woods, and she wasn't about to stick around to find out if they were true.

As she topped the knoll, something by one of the picnic shelters caught her eye. A fire smoldered in a nearby pit, and she scanned to see if anyone was there. Then she sensed it: evil.

A feather drifted by, drawing Lottie's attention to the table. She swallowed hard. Blood was everywhere, and clumps of feathers were strewn about on the surface and along the ground. Some floated in the breeze.

A muted swish of a sound came from behind. The hair on Lottie's neck bristled as she turned around. There was just enough light from the embers that she could see a stake sticking out of the ground. Her breath caught in her throat. Hanging dead at the top of it was an owl. Its head hung limply from a broken neck, and someone had cut out its heart. Blood dripped from its feathers, splatting onto the ground below, drip...drip... drip....

The sound of an echoing voice rang through her mind, but the wind's fierceness drowned out the words.

Lottie's scream woke her from the nightmare. Her hair clung to her neck, matted and drenched with sweat. She ran her hands across her eyes. The malevolent presence she'd felt still filled the space of her room. She took some deep breaths and tried to calm herself. It was as if she had seen through someone else's eyes in her dream. She shuddered.

The conversation she had with Charles about the Paranormal Investigators came to mind. He did say they had detected evil in Munroe Falls. Maybe there was some relevance to their findings. But what did it have to do with her or her increased nightmares? Lottie shook her head, feeling silly for thinking there could be a correlation.

A soft knock came at her door. Her mother cracked it open and stepped inside. "Lottie, are you okay?"

"I'm fine, Mom. Just a bad dream. I'm sorry I woke you."

"Don't worry about that, honey."

"Did I wake Dad?"

"No, that man could sleep through a bomb."

Lottie laughed, grateful for her mother's humor.

"If you need me, just come in and wake me, okay?"

"I will."

Lottie sat wide awake against the headboard, staring blankly at the ivory-colored wallpaper. The tiny rosebud pattern long faded with age, blurred as she gazed into nothingness. With a heavy sigh, she slid open the drawer to her nightstand and took out some magazines to keep her mind off the awful nightmare.

Matthew shuddered as Selene came out of her trance. The moonlight highlighting her eyes cast an ominous appearance over her.

"I told you the nightmares would help us to get into Lottie's mind. She's strong, but I'll get through to her. It seems she made a deeper connection with Charles tonight, strengthening my suspicions about her."

Matthew almost felt sorry for Lottie. Selene had purposefully woven the terrible nightmare into her mind. Even now, the foul remnants of it hung in the air between the trees.

"Oh, don't look so remorseful. Lottie was too happy when she went off to Dreamland. I had to cause the nightmare, or else I wouldn't have gotten any information from her night with Charles. Be glad you didn't have to do it for once.

SHEETS OF RAIN PELTED AGAINST THE WINDOW, STIRRING Lottie from her sleep. She put on her robe and went downstairs.

"Morning, sunshine," her mother greeted. She wrung out a cloth and ran it over the front of a cabinet. "Would you like me to make you an egg sandwich?"

"Sure," Lottie replied, pulling out a chair. "Mom, can we go shopping today?"

"In this weather? I thought you hated the rain."

"I do. But for a few new outfits, I can deal with it."

"I guess we could go after you eat."

Lottie dug out a hooded sweatshirt from the back of her closet and pulled it over her head, sending pops of static electricity through her hair. She wound a band around it, loosened the ponytail, and returned downstairs.

It was raining even harder when she and her mother left for the mall. Lottie peered out of her half-fogged window and let out an exaggerated sigh.

"It could be worse," her mother said. "It could be snowing."

"I'd rather it be snowing."

"You really do hate rain, don't you?"

"Despise it. It makes me cold and damp and gross."

"By the way, I saw the bulb in the bathroom this morning. Your handiwork?"

Lottie grinned. "How'd you guess?"

Turning into the mall, it looked like everyone else had the same idea. The parking lot was packed. There were no spaces even remotely close to the door. Her mother steered the car into a vacant spot at the end of the row.

"I must have left the umbrella at the shop," she said, reaching behind the seat. "We'll have to make a run for it."

"Meet you at the door," Lottie replied, pulling her hood up. Her shoes were waterlogged as soon as she stepped out of the car. *Gross.* Sheets of cold rain beat down on her, soaking through the hood. She yanked the sweatshirt off and tied it around her waist when she reached the door.

Her mother stepped up on the sidewalk and shrugged out of her raincoat. "Remind me to buy an umbrella today."

"Definitely," Lottie replied, walking into the inviting warmth of the mall.

"So, where do you want to go first?" her mother asked.

"There's a new store that just opened. I saw it last night on the way to the bookstore."

"Lead the way then."

The latest hit music was playing throughout the store, and the sales associates looked fabulous. Lottie suddenly felt like Julia Roberts in *Pretty Woman.* One of them greeted her and turned her attention back to a clothing rack.

A brown sweater hanging on a mannequin caught Lottie's eye. "What about this?"

Her mother gave a nod of approval. "It's nice. You'd look pretty in it with your dark hair."

Lottie had an armful by the time she entered the fitting area. An associate showed her to a large room at the end on the left. As she tried on the brown sweater and a pair of jeans, she heard several girls in the room across from her laughing and making fun of each other's choice of outfits. Smiling at their exchange, she exited the room to look at herself in the angled mirrors. The door to the other room opened, and she caught a glimpse of Wren, Rowen, and Sunni. They erupted in laughter at the sight of each other.

"Lottie Jacobs, fancy meeting you here," Wren greeted. "You look great in that, by the way."

"Thanks," Lottie said.

"I thought I heard laughter in here," her mother said, stepping into the fitting room.

Lottie introduced Rowen and Sunni to her mother before they said their goodbyes.

"You about wrapped up?"

"Yeah. I found a few things that work."

"Good. Let's get them to the register and check out, and then I need to pick up some things from the craft store."

The rain had ended by the time they left the mall. The road was still wet, with the sunset reflecting fiery hues in the standing puddles. Lottie yawned as she watched the scenery blur by her window. She felt more upbeat and confident these days, and the new clothes only helped. As her thoughts drifted, she saw something from the corner of her eye.

"Mom, watch out!" Lottie said as a cat shot out from a yard.

Her mother tried to swerve, but it was too late. Lottie felt a big bump right before the car skidded and slammed into a tree on the opposite side of the road.

"Oh, my God!" Lottie shrieked as her mother's head hit the window. "Mom, are you okay?" She cringed at the trickle of blood running down her mother's face.

"I think I'm okay. Are you hurt?"

"I don't think so, but Mom, you hit that cat."

"Oh, man. We'd better get out and see if the poor creature has a tag on its collar."

Lottie noticed her knee hurt as she opened the door to get out. She shuddered at the thought of seeing the cat. The thump she'd felt when they ran it over was just too awful to contemplate. She looked under the front wheel, frowning when there was nothing there.

"Maybe it's on the other side," her mother said.

They walked around the car. It wasn't there either. Lottie got down on her stomach to check underneath. The cat had vanished.

"Mom, you hit that cat. I felt it—you heard it."

"Maybe it escaped before I swerved."

"No, you felt it, too," Lottie insisted.

"I don't know…. Oh, the car. Your father is going to be so disappointed. We only had one more payment left."

"I'm sure he'll understand. You're hurt."

"I am? Where?"

"Your head. It's bleeding. We'd better get you looked at."

Her mother slid into the car and pulled down the visor to access the mirror.

"It's just a surface wound; there's no need. I want to get the car home and tell your father what happened. We should already be home, and I'm sure he's worried. Will you call him for me and tell him we're on our way?"

"Sure." Lottie took her phone out of her pocket. "It's dead."

"And I left mine on the charger at home," her mother replied. She pulled on her seatbelt. "I just hope this thing starts. It's smashed in pretty good in the front." She turned the key. The motor hesitated but started. "Oh, thank goodness. Let's get home."

Lottie's father stepped out on the porch when they pulled up in front of the house.

"Well, here goes nothing," her mother said.

Lottie grabbed her shopping bag and gave her mother an encouraging look as she slid out of the car.

"I was beginning to think you two got lost."

"Randy, I have some bad news."

"You went over budget?" he teased.

"No, worse. I crashed the car."

"Are you serious?"

"Afraid so. A cat ran out in front of us. I swerved to miss it and hit a tree."

He stepped off the porch to inspect the car.

"Randy, I'm sorry. It happened so fast. I just reacted."

"It's okay. These things happen."

When they got into the light, Lottie saw her father grimace.

"You're bleeding, Carol. Didn't the airbag deploy?"

"No, but it should have, given how hard we hit that tree."

Lottie, are you hurt?"

"I don't know. My knee feels sore."

"Let's get inside and see if anyone needs to go to the hospital. What about the cat?"

"I think it got away," her mother said.

"No, Mom. You hit it."

"Honey, we looked. We couldn't find it."

"Mom, you felt that bump. I know you did."

Lottie fumed. She knew she was right. Nothing about any of this seemed to add up. She was sure she saw a cat. Was she mistaken?

"Okay, calm down," her mother soothed. "We've had a rather upsetting night. We're both shaken up, and we're tired. Let's get you up to your room to check your knee."

Lottie gave a reluctant nod and went upstairs. She pulled off her jeans, careful not to brush the sore spot, and grimaced at the nasty purple and green bruise already forming. She slipped on a pair of pajamas and opened the door for her father to come in.

"Can you bend it?" he asked.

"I can. It just hurts when I do."

"I think it'll be okay," he said after a thorough inspection. "We'll keep an eye on it over the weekend. In the meantime, I'll get you some ice."

"What about Mom?"

"She's okay. The car got the worst of it." He straightened and moved toward the door. "A cat," he muttered, shaking his head as he left her room.

Lottie tossed and turned most of the night. She thought she heard a cat meowing several times but wasn't fully awake enough to know if it was a dream or real.

SHRUGGING OUT OF HER JACKET, LOTTIE WEAVED AROUND the students rushing in and out of the locker area. She saw Gwen and Abbey talking to Christy and stopped to chat.

"Hey, guys."

"Oh, she graces us with her presence," Gwen said with a disgusted scoff.

Abbey laughed under her breath.

"Why would you say that?" Lottie asked.

"You have completely ignored us the last few days to hang out with those snobs. Why wouldn't I say it?"

"That's not fair, Gwen. First of all, they're not snobs. They asked me to sit with them while you three were out sick, and we haven't had a chance to talk since you and Abbey have been avoiding me."

"Why would Wren Wesley and her little crew want *you* to sit with them?"

Her bitter words stung. "What is your problem, Gwen? I've done nothing for you to treat me this way. I thought we were friends."

"So did I, Lottie."

Gwen slammed her locker shut and stalked off with Abbey close behind.

Stunned, Lottie turned to Christy. "I suppose you're mad at me, too?"

"No. We're cool."

"I don't understand why Gwen would go off like that. She's never been the type to get vicious."

"I'm sure she didn't mean it," Christy soothed. "She's just jealous that the popular girls singled you out. I'll talk to them and try to help smooth things over for you. Come on. We'd better get to class."

By lunchtime, Lottie was regretting wearing new jeans. They hadn't relaxed enough in the knee area and rubbed against her bruise.

"Are you limping?" Wren asked.

"Yeah. We had an accident on the way home from the mall Saturday."

"Really? What happened?" Rowen asked.

"A cat ran out in front of our car. Mom swerved to miss it and hit a tree."

"Did the cat get away?" Sunni asked.

"That's the thing. We hit it. I heard and felt the car run it over, but when we got out to look, the cat was gone."

"Hmmm...maybe it ran off?" Wren suggested.

"No, I'm telling you— there's *no way* that cat could have survived."

Charles sat his tray down beside Lottie, catching her off guard. "What's this talk about a cat?" he said, pulling his chair closer.

"Lottie got into a crash Saturday," Sunni answered. "A cat ran out in front of her mom's car."

"Were you hurt?" Charles asked.

"Just a bump to the knee, nothing serious."

"Did you guys hear about the Paranormal Investigators?" Rowen asked. "My mom said that they caught something on surveillance. Get this—one of the images they captured shows a large black wolf prowling around their office at night. When it got out of view from the street, its shadow changed—as in it transformed into human form. It walked upright around the back of the building."

Wren's eyes widened. "Get out!"

"Charles, doesn't your mom know someone that works there?" Sunni asked.

"Yes." He picked at his food, deep in thought.

Lottie watched him as she peeled her orange. When his gaze landed on her, it was full of concern.

"Did the cat really cause your car accident?" he asked.

"Yes."

"Is your mom okay?"

"Yes, just a scratch on her head."

"You seriously need to have your mom find out the scoop over there, Charles," Rowen insisted.

Lottie shook her head. "That's just crazy, guys. Have these Paranormal Investigators ever proved anything in town to be legit?"

"They helped the police solve a murder last year," Rowen replied, her eyes twinkling enthusiastically. "The dead girl told them where to find her body."

"Ugh, I regret asking. Can we please change the subject?" Lottie asked.

Wren obliged. "I talked to my parents about having a sleepover. They said it was cool. We just need to pick a day."

"If Lottie brings her nail kit, we'll be in business," Sunni added.

"I'll talk to my parents later," Lottie promised. "Hopefully, they'll let me go."

"Are your parents strict?" Charles asked.

"Yes. They've always kind of kept me sheltered. I'm not sure why, though. Maybe it's the only child thing."

Charles exchanged an odd look with the others. Once again, they seemed to share some private comments. Lottie was starting to feel paranoid. She was missing something important.

After the last bell, Lottie hurried downstairs. She smiled, despite herself, at the sight of Charles leaning against her locker. He exuded an image of relaxed confidence with one ankle over the other and his arms crossed. He gave her a lopsided grin.

"What are you doing here?" she asked.

"I thought I'd do the chivalrous thing and carry your backpack."

She shook her head, grinning, and passed her backpack to him.

"Why are you shaking your head?"

"I don't know. You."

When the bus arrived, Charles got on, but instead of going to his usual seat, he stopped a little more than midway down the aisle and gestured for Lottie to sit. She slid in, and he sat beside her, leaving only a few inches of space between them. She could feel his energy, and her body responded to it, flushing with a warmth that rushed through her veins. Even the hairs on her arms reached for him.

"What are your plans after school?" he asked.

"I need to study for an English test tomorrow. What about you?"

"I'm helping my mom cook dinner."

Lottie's brows climbed. "You cook?"

"Guys cook," he grinned.

"I know. It's just I didn't picture you as the kitchen type."

"Yeah...my manliness is overwhelming, but don't let it fool you."

Lottie rolled her eyes, contradicting the spreading grin on her face.

Charles grabbed her backpack off the floor when the bus stopped at her drive. "You need help with this?" he asked.

"I'm okay. Thanks."

He stood to let her get out. "I'll see you tomorrow then."

She sensed him watching her as she exited the bus but didn't look back.

That night, Lottie lay in bed, thinking about the horrible run-in with Gwen. It was so out of character for her to behave like that. At least Christy had been kind enough not to join in on the madness. Maybe she could help smooth things over with Gwen and Abbey so they could all get back to being friends.

Chapter Four

It was 3:33 a.m. when Lottie jerked out of a dead sleep. She propped herself onto her elbows and glanced around the room, wondering what woke her. The distinct sound of a loud meow came from below her window, followed by a crash. She bolted out of bed and crept down the hall, cursing the old, creaky steps as she descended. She hoped that the noise wouldn't disturb her parents.

Lottie heard another meow as she came into the kitchen. Peeking out the kitchen window, she saw a cat run by, and it appeared to be limping. She pulled her robe tightly around her and stepped out into the cold toward the garage.

"Here, kitty."

The light reflected off a shiny pendant hanging from its collar as it moved along the shadows. Lottie inched closer to get a better look and crouched. Stunned, she realized this was the same cat that her mother had run over. Its green eyes suddenly glowed brighter.

"Oh, my God!"

Lurching away from shock, Lottie lost her balance and fell back onto her bottom. Before she could react, the cat hissed and scratched her across the arm, then bounded toward the woods.

She gasped and scrambled to her feet, holding her arm tightly against her chest as she rushed toward the house. It burned like nothing she had ever felt before. Waves of dizziness washed over her, making her feel disoriented as she reached the stoop. Something was very wrong. Her vision doubled as she stumbled inside, and the burning was unbearable. She blinked her eyes against the dense, fog-like blur, not understanding what she saw on her arm. The three long scratch marks were glowing red, but that couldn't be right. Scratches didn't glow. As she reached for the kitchen table, everything went black.

~

"OH, MY GOD, LOTTIE!"

Her mother's voice sounded strange, muffled like Lottie was underwater. Was she dreaming?

"Get her on the sofa," her father urged.

Her mother suddenly gasped. "Randy, look at the red marks on her arm. You don't suppose...no, it isn't possible."

"Look again, Carol. Scratch marks don't shift around like that. You have to call *her*."

"No. There has to be another way."

Her parents' voices reached Lottie from a distance, far away. Who was this *her* they spoke of? Lottie felt her father's arms wrap around her and a vague sense of motion before everything went black again.

~

SELENE REMOVED THE CORDED VIAL AROUND HER NECK AND poured the blood contents onto the map spread before her. The bright red dots pulled together, turning into a thick black sludge as it snaked across the map. It neared the heart of Akron but pushed back as if some unseen force was denying her access to the final destination.

"Very crafty," Selene mumbled. She raked her arm across the table, flinging the map and the other contents crashing onto the floor. She grabbed her phone and jabbed an angry finger at the screen.

"Yes?" Matthew answered.

"The little twit has a powerful protection spell over her. No matter.

I can guess who they took her to. Get to Lottie's house immediately and call me the second she returns. My suspicions might not get confirmed today, but they will."

~

"WHAT HAVE WE DONE? BRINGING HER HERE. *HERE,* TO THAT woman. I can't believe I listened to you."

"Carol, you saw her arm. It's unnatural. We had no choice," Randy replied.

She shoved her hair back from her face, squeezing it tightly in her fists momentarily. "This is just too much. How are we going to keep the truth from Lottie now?"

When he met his wife's eyes, he saw fear and uncertainty. He gave her a reassuring pat on her shoulder. "I don't think we can. I hate it, too, but Lottie's going to ask questions. At this point, I think we have to tell her. We'll do it in the morning after she's rested."

"I still can't believe it's come to this. I never thought I'd see the day Mathilda Longhurst would come back into our lives. Poor Lottie."

She brushed a lock of hair away from her daughter's face. She looked peaceful as she slept. Carol shuddered as she recalled Lottie lying on the floor. Dialing Mathilda had been one of the most difficult things she had ever done.

Her thoughts drifted to when she had once called Mathilda a friend. However, their brief friendship ended when Mathilda revealed she was a witch with powerful enemies willing to eliminate anyone close to her. Being a new mother, Carol knew that kind of trouble was not what she needed, not with a baby to cherish and protect. She still felt confident that ending her relationship with the witch had been for the best.

Her husband's voice brought her out of the past. "Let's just be grateful that Mathilda was willing to help."

Carol scoffed. "Have you forgotten the reason I ended our friendship sixteen years ago? Do you not remember the threats that Mathilda received? She said her enemies would hurt *anyone* she held dear. I don't want Lottie anywhere near that woman. She's dangerous. It's bad luck to even be in her company, and it's best we keep Lottie in the dark about her."

"As long as her witchy 'hoo-doo' fixes Lottie's arm, I don't care what she is. It's nearly dawn," he said, glancing at the clock. "There's nothing else we can do. Mathilda will take care of her until she wakes. Let's go back to the house and get some things for Lottie."

MATHILDA PACED IN THE GRAND FOYER OF HER MASSIVE home, her mind reeling. She never expected to hear from the Jacobs again, let alone that their daughter would need her assistance. She looked up as Carol and Randy descended the curved staircase.

"Tell me what that is on my daughter's arm?" Carol asked accusingly.

"It is a result of magic," Mathilda answered. "You did the right thing bringing her here."

"Oh, for God's sake, Tilda," Carol said, barking a mirthless laugh. "Don't act like you're not glad this day has finally come."

Mathilda was surprised by the spite in Carol's voice, but she understood her fears. "I know we agreed to keep Lottie in the dark about me, but it's done now. It seems someone knows about her. We must be careful until I can ensure this isn't a threat from an old enemy. Having Lottie stay here for a few days will give me time to prepare—"

"Oh no. My daughter is not staying beneath your roof," Carol said scathingly. "You will erase that...that *abomination* on her arm while she is sleeping, erase her memory, and then we are taking her home where she belongs."

"Has Lottie been having any unexplained incidents recently?" Matilda suddenly asked.

"What?"

"Any strange happenings, things you can't explain?"

Randy shot his wife an odd glance.

A worried look crept over Carol's features. "Why do you ask?"

Mathilda sighed. "Lottie is a witch. After she was born, I cast a spell to hide her powers until she came of age. I told you Lottie had no magic in her to protect the three of you. I did this so no one could read your thoughts and discover the truth about her."

Tears welled in Carol's eyes. "What? No. It can't be." Randy moved to comfort her, but she swatted his arm away. "How dare you keep this from us. We had a right to know the truth."

"I am sorry, but I could not endanger Lottie just to ease your mind. When her sixteenth birthday arrives, Lottie will come into her power. I will help prepare her as much as possible, but she will need your support after it happens. As for the rest, I will say nothing until you have spoken to her first."

Carol collapsed against her husband, sobbing.

"Can you not do something to keep her magic hidden?" Randy asked desperately.

"I cannot," Mathilda said. "To do so would harm Lottie. Her true nature would eat away at her, trying to get out until she eventually would go mad."

Randy shook his head, resolved. "We'll go get Lottie's things and come back."

Mathilda nodded and watched with pity as they took their leave.

LOTTIE FOUGHT AGAINST THE FOG IN HER BRAIN THAT strove to keep her asleep. Crackling sounds forced her to open her eyes. Yawning, she became acutely aware that she was not in her room at home. The heavy curtains surrounding the bed made her feel trapped. Terrified, she sat up quickly, wincing at the sudden pounding in her head.

"You must lie back," a woman's voice soothed.

The bed curtains slid back, revealing a large fireplace, the source of the crackling. A strikingly beautiful woman with immaculate blonde hair stood by the bed. Lottie noticed their eyes shared the same shade of blue-green. She momentarily stared at the familiar-looking pendant around the woman's neck, trying to place it.

"How do you feel?" the woman asked.

"Groggy," Lottie answered. "Where am I?"

"My name is Mathilda Longhurst. You're at my home in Akron."

Panic washed over Lottie. "Where are my parents?"

"Your parents brought you here, and they will return shortly."

Lottie relaxed a little. "Why did they bring me here?"

"Do you remember anything, Lottie?"

There was a knock at the door, interrupting her answer.

"Yes?" Mathilda called out.

A woman entered the room. She wore a black blouse and a plain black skirt that reached well below her knees. Upon further inspection, Lottie noticed she was in black from head to toe. A small but ornate silver brooch was pinned at the neck of her blouse, the triple moon goddess symbol. Her expression was firm.

"May I speak to you in private, ma'am?" She had an accent. British maybe?

Mathilda stepped out of the room. Lottie heard them talking in hushed tones outside of the door. The only words she could make out were 'the one', something about her parents, and the cat. *Cat!* She remembered.

"Mathilda?"

She rushed back into the room. "What is it, dear?"

"I remember what happened. I want my parents."

"You mustn't get upset."

"Why? Why am I here? Please, get my parents."

Lottie became aware of a painful burning underneath the bandage on her arm. Gritting her teeth, she pulled her arm against her chest and took a deep breath.

Mathilda calmly turned to the woman. "Please, go down and find out if Lottie's parents have arrived. And Marie, have them wait in the corridor."

"Yes, ma'am."

Mathilda sat on the edge of the bed. "Listen carefully, Lottie. There are things you don't know. Until I can explain everything to you, I don't want you to get upset. I'm about to show you something that might frighten you. Try to stay calm."

Lottie's eyes went wild as Mathilda unwrapped the bandage on her arm. "Oh, my God! What's happening?" The hysterical tone of her voice sounded unfamiliar to her ears. She sank back with a whimper.

"What you're looking at is the result of dark magic. Your parents would rather you not see it, but it is my duty to reveal a secret inside you."

Lottie swiped the tears away and took another look. On her arm, glowing like molten fire, were two initials: C L.

"I'm going to help you. Don't move, and don't scream."

Mathilda waved her hand over Lottie's arm and spoke some strange words. Lottie watched in horror as the marks disappeared.

"What did you do? I... I don't understand."

Mathilda took her hand. "Look at me, Lottie. You are safe with me."

Lottie sensed the truth in her words and nodded.

Mathilda smiled. "I promise I will explain everything after you've had time to visit with your parents.

Lottie stared, dumbfounded, as Mathilda left the room to fetch them.

She sat higher in the bed as Mathilda ushered her parents into the room. There was an unmistakable look of relief on their faces upon seeing her.

"Thank goodness you're okay," her mother said. She sat on the edge of the bed. "How are you feeling?"

"I'm okay, Mom. I just feel exhausted. Why am I here?"

Mathilda cleared her throat and moved toward the door. "I'll give you some time alone. Marie will be outside if you need anything."

"Mom, I don't understand. Why am I here?"

Her mother hesitated. "Lottie, we found you lying on the kitchen floor, unconscious, with a scratch on your arm that was...rather disturbing. I immediately thought of Ms. Longhurst. I met her many years ago at my shop. She once told me she was a natural healer for people with ailments that modern medicine couldn't explain. I always thought it was a bit of nonsense until I saw your arm. I knew I had to bring you to her."

Lottie's head swirled with dizziness. "This is all so confusing." She yawned and leaned back against her pillows. She wanted to know so much, but exhaustion was taking over.

"Oh honey, I'm so sorry you're going through this. Your father and I will let you rest. We'll come back later."

"Okay," Lottie replied.

Her father leaned over and placed a kiss on her head. "You just rest, baby. Mom and I will be back."

She was already drifting to sleep as her parents left the room.

～

It was the perfect day to be out of doors, Lottie mused. She strolled through a wide swath of lush grass, admiring the neat rows of giant oak trees surrounding her on both sides. Beautifully tied bows from the tops of her slippers peeked out from beneath the hem of her pale green gown with each step Lottie took toward the garden bench. She smoothed out the folds of her dress as she sat, ignoring the ivory ribbons fluttering about the sleeves that reached just below her elbows.

She smiled at the heady scent of roses wafting along with the warm breeze and tipped her face to the sun. In the distance, she heard a melodic voice calling her. "Lottie...Lottie...."

～

Lottie blinked and opened her eyes at the sound of Mathilda's voice.

"How are you feeling, dear? You slept through dinner."

"Okay, I guess. I had the strangest dream. I was wearing a beautiful dress in a beautiful place, but it was in the past. I thought I heard you calling me. But I guess that was just you waking me."

"Is this the first time you've dreamed of being in another time?" Mathilda asked.

"No. I always have dreams in different times and places. I can tell by what I'm wearing in the dreams that it's nowhere close to the present. I'm just thankful it wasn't a nightmare this time."

Mathilda frowned. "You have nightmares?"

"Yes."

"What are the nightmares like?"

"Horrible. I sense evil is all around, and something is always trying to get to me—like snakes."

Mathilda looked as if she were mulling this information over. "Have you met anyone new recently?"

Lottie wondered why Mathilda was asking such specific questions. It made her a little uneasy.

"Yes...and sort of. There's a new girl in my biology class, Christy Adams. She started this week at our school. And then this boy, Charles, on my bus started talking to me. I've known him since grade school, but we started talking recently for whatever reason."

"How did it come about that the two of you began talking?"

Lottie bit her lower lip and fumbled with her blankets. "I'm sure you'll think I'm crazy."

"No, I won't. Believe me, Lottie. You can tell me anything."

Lottie met Mathilda's reassuring gaze and felt compelled to tell her. "Well, it was strange. It was lunchtime at school. Charles was at his table, and I was across the room at a different table... watching him." She felt embarrassed but continued. "I sort of said 'look at me' —in my head, and he did."

Lottie searched for any signs of judgment from Mathilda but found none.

"Have you ever had anything happen that you felt you caused to happen?"

Lottie began to fidget nervously with her fingernails, thinking of the strange things happening the past few months. And now she was telling it all to a complete stranger who seemed unfazed by any of it.

She placed her hands on her lap and looked up. "I have this thing with lightbulbs."

"Lightbulbs?" Mathilda asked.

"Yes. I blow them—a lot. And there's this weird thing with the clock. It's always 3:33."

"Interesting. So, this boy Charles, on the bus, and the girl, are the only new people in your life?"

"I met a girl in school last week. I've known her for years also, but she and her friends started talking to me."

"What is her name?"

"Wren Wesley."

"Ah, the Wesley family. I know them well. Young Wren is of age now."

"What do you mean, of age?" Lottie asked.

"There's a lot we need to discuss, and it's very late. You haven't eaten all day. I'll have some food brought up for you, and I promise to tell you everything tomorrow. I'll show you around, too, if you're up to it."

"Okay. I am pretty hungry."

Lottie leaned back against the bed. Their conversation left her feeling very unsettled. Something seemed to tie in with Mathilda. But what? She sensed she was missing something and intended to find out what it was.

THE FOLLOWING MORNING, MARIE KNOCKED ON THE DOOR and entered with a tray. Lottie sat up wide-eyed.

"Good morning, Miss."

She sat the tray on the end of the bed and returned to a rigid stance.

"Do you require anything else?"

"No, thank you," Lottie replied. The woman was too formidable to request anything.

Mathilda swept into the room looking even more lovely than yesterday. She wore a pink cardigan over a crisp white blouse and a beautiful pearl necklace draped below the neckline. Once again, her hair was impeccable.

"I trust you slept well?"

"Yes, I did. Are my parents here?"

"They arrived a half-hour ago. I'll send them up now."

Lottie finished her eggs and set the tray on the cart by the bed. She smiled as her parents came into the room.

"Hi, sweetie," her mother greeted. "We brought you some things from home." She unzipped the bag and pulled out Lottie's favorite blanket. "Look what I have."

"Thanks, Mom. Does this mean I have to stay here for a long time?"

"No, honey. We wanted you to feel comfortable while you're in Mathilda's care."

"How's your arm?" her father asked.

"Much better."

Lottie noticed the nervous glance her parents exchanged.

"What's with you two?"

"Sweetheart, your father and I need to talk to you."

"Ooh, that sounds ominous," Lottie teased. She began to feel uneasy as her parents' expressions remained somber.

"You know we love you very much, don't you, Lottie?"

"Of course. What's going on, Mom?"

"Do you remember me telling you I'd met Ms. Longhurst years ago at the shop?"

"Not really. I was so tired last night."

"Lottie, your father and I tried for many years to have children after we were married. After going through numerous tests, the doctor finally told us that we'd never be able to conceive. One day, I was having a hard time emotionally at the shop when Mathilda came in to buy some flowers. She must've sensed something was wrong. She asked me if I was okay or needed to talk to someone. We became friends from that day on. A few months later, I found out she was pregnant. After the baby was born, Mathilda found herself in a... situation. She couldn't keep her baby."

Lottie's chest tightened as panic rose. Tears swelled and burned in her eyes. "Don't say it...please, don't say it."

Her mother struggled to keep her tears at bay. "I'm so sorry, Lottie."

It felt as if the room suddenly tilted. A tightness squeezed her throat. It burned her lungs until she thought she would choke. "No! *No!* It isn't true."

Her father pulled her close. "We may not be your biological parents, but we love you very much, and you'll always be our little girl."

Anger and hurt surged as Lottie wrenched herself out of her father's arms.

"Why would you keep this from me? All these years, and you never told me? Why?"

"We wanted to tell you so many times," he said, "but we had our reasons. That scratch you got—it wasn't normal. It appeared to be some kind of—I don't know...."

Lottie raked a hand over her cheek, wiping the tears away. "I don't understand."

Mathilda's knock interrupted their conversation. She gave Lottie's parents a strange look.

"Why don't we give you some time to process this information," her mother suggested. "You've had quite a shock."

"I think that would be best," Mathilda agreed.

"We'll come back, Lottie, I promise," her father added.

Lottie stared at the door in disbelief. Her mind swirled frantically around what her parents had said. How could they keep this secret from her? Pulling her blanket up to her face, she sobbed until she fell into a deep and fitful sleep.

Chapter Five

No one disturbed Lottie the following morning. She stared beyond the heavy bed curtains with the shocking news of her adoption weighing on her heart. Her anger had subsided, at least, curiosity now in its place. She needed answers. She took her things into the bathroom to get cleaned up.

When she came out, Marie had made up the bed and straightened the room. Her blanket lay folded at the foot of the bed. Lottie sank her fingers into the plush fabric, thinking of home.

Mathilda knocked on the door and stepped in. "Oh, good, you're up and about. How are you feeling, dear?"

"Overwhelmed, confused. The grogginess is gone, at least."

"The effects of the dark magic have finally worn off. The sleep took care of that."

Lottie felt awkward as Mathilda studied her. A gentle smile touched her lips. "I know you have questions for me. How about that tour I promised you? We can talk along the way."

Lottie nodded and followed her out into a vast hall. A massive stone wall led up to unfathomably high ceilings. The doorways were oversized with thick oak trim, and some of the furnishings looked medieval.

Lottie couldn't help the gasp that escaped. "This place is huge. It looks like a castle."

"That's because it is. It's been in my family for centuries," Mathilda replied.

"I can't believe we are in Akron. It's amazing."

They took their time exploring before going outside. Mathilda settled onto a stone bench in one of the many gardens.

"This is lovely," Lottie stated, looking around.

Everything she saw was well-manicured, from the thick shrubs to the perfectly lined rows of oak trees on both sides. Her fingers flew to her lips as she gasped.

"What is it?" Mathilda asked.

"My dream—I was right here. How is this possible?"

"Anything is possible. Search your heart."

Lottie knew there was meaning to Mathilda's words. She waited for her to elaborate.

"I think by now you've figured out I'm a witch."

Lottie stared blankly. Then, a dawning came over her. "Are you saying that...am I...?" She felt a surge of panic.

"Don't be frightened, Charlotte. It's a gift—and a powerful one at that."

"Charlotte?"

Mathilda smiled. "I named you Charlotte. Your parents shortened it. Don't get me wrong, I like Lottie, but you've always been Charlotte to me."

Lottie shook her head. "I didn't think I could get a bigger shock than, 'Lottie, we're not your real parents.' Now I have 'witch' thrown at me. I don't even know if I believe in witches."

"It's true. We exist; you are proof. Think of all of your unexplained incidents. The lightbulbs, the dreams, the synchronicity of time—all these signs pointed you to your true self."

Lottie closed her eyes as an overwhelming sense of truth washed over her. Everything Mathilda said felt right.

"Charlotte, do you think you could ever forgive me for giving you up?"

"If I knew more about your story, I'm sure it would help me understand your motives."

"I never wanted to give you up, and not a moment has passed that I haven't thought of you."

Tears pooled in Mathilda's eyes and Lottie struggled to fight back her own.

"Why did you then?"

"Our bloodline goes back for centuries. Through the years, I have made enemies. Shortly after you were born, someone tried to kill you."

Lottie blinked with surprise. "Oh my God, are you serious? Why would someone want to kill a baby?"

"Revenge. I've had many encounters with dark witches over the years, especially in the months before I became pregnant. I realized that you'd always be in danger as long as you were with me, so I made a pact with your parents. They would raise and shelter you from the evil intent of other witches, and in return, I would never see you again, per your mother's request. Her fear of the unknown—mixed with the horrible fact that someone tried to kill you because of me was too much for her to risk. And that is precisely why I chose her to raise you. I knew she would protect you at all costs. It has been the hardest decision of my life, knowing you were so close and yet never getting to see you. Believe me when I say I wanted to see you so many times, but I couldn't risk your safety."

Lottie tried to imagine what it must have been like for her mother and Mathilda.

A chilly breeze swept up some dead leaves, scattering them past her feet. Diverted, she watched them dance along the garden path. A flood of questions suddenly raced through Lottie's mind.

"So there are other witches out there," she said, turning toward Mathilda. "Are there many, and are they like you? How do you know when you meet a witch?"

"There aren't many witches left," Mathilda answered. "Throughout the centuries, they have always been hunted and killed. Many quit practicing for fear of being discovered, and eventually, the magic in their bloodline line faded. Those who held fast to their true nature stayed hidden, passing their knowledge down through generations. And, to answer your final question, witches know one another when they meet, as we give off a higher energy vibration. We can use crystals to mask that energy. Most witches are good, but occasionally, we come across some with evil intentions, which brings me to you, Charlotte. You were chosen for a great purpose. Walk with me. I want to show you something in the library."

Lottie was thankful for the fire roaring in the massive library. Although spring was near, the air outside was still crisp. As she sat down, Marie placed an ancient-looking book on the table in front of the sofa. It was quite large and looked to be hundreds of years old. A raised circular emblem of a bent and gnarly tree was carved in the middle, with strange symbols encircling it.

"One of my old grimoires," Mathilda said, noticing Lottie's questioning gaze.

"Will that be all, ma'am?" Marie asked.

"Please ask Cook to send up something warm to drink and a light snack for Charlotte."

Before long, the heavy library door opened, and a tall, lean man of middle years wearing what looked like a butler's livery ushered in another man pushing a cart. The man behind the cart had thick, dark hair that was smashed and curled around his ears from the white hat he wore. A white apron stretched across his impressive middle, and a smile nearly split his face when his eyes fell on Lottie.

"Ah, Miss Charlotte," he said, wiping his brow with a meaty hand. "You're a sight for sore eyes."

Lottie smiled shyly and looked at Mathilda.

"Charlotte, this is Cook and Dabney, my butler."

Lottie watched as they unloaded the cart. After they left the room, she turned to Mathilda and flatly said, "You have a maid, a cook, and a butler?"

"Yes," Mathilda answered, as if that were the most natural thing in the world. She reached for the massive book on the table and settled back with it on her lap, and when she opened it, a wonderful old, musty smell permeated the air.

"There once dwelt a dark and forbidden magic in the land," Mathilda began. "The sorcerer, Aelle, harnessed this magic and became dreadfully powerful. He learned to control the elements, transformed himself into the shape of an animal, and used mind control to name a few of his wretched feats. But there was an even deeper, more sinister desire in his heart. He sought to overcome death.

"Aelle had a daughter named Cassandra, who he loved most, above all things. As a gift to her, he created a spell of immortality for himself and Cassandra. However, it required the souls of the innocent. But as he said the final words of the spell, Aelle's soul was pulled from his body as punishment. Desperate to hold on to his power but unable to keep it, he transferred it all to his daughter before the last of his energy left his body.

"Over time, the daughter became drunk with her powers. Those she wanted to use were turned into animals to do her bidding under the guise of creatures. She convinced them that it was a special gift. However, the pain of transformation made them realize that it was no gift but a curse. Cassandra recreated her father's ritual to make those she wanted close to her immortal. But there was a secret in her spell. These beings could indeed be killed during the peak of a full moon by the blood of five witches.

"These particular witches were beyond powerful. They guarded nature and humanity against dark forces. Over time, the witches watched the balance tip. Nature started to rebel. Creatures turned on humanity, and trees and plant life began to die. Unable to allow such an imbalance, the witches created a spell that bound the daughter and stripped away her magic. Vowing that not one of them should hold such powers, they sealed Cassandra's magic in a stone and hid it away. Five witches to gather. Five witches to steal. Five witches to bind. Five witches to kill."

Mathilda closed the book and reached for her tea. "There's more you should know. The five witches that bound and stripped the daughter of her powers are immortal. As Guardians, their sole purpose is to protect the earth and all of humanity from any witch who would meddle in dark magic. I am one of the original witches. So are Regina Wesley, Trina Maxwell, Ramona Lachlan, and Isobel Browne. Regina's husband, Phil, is also immortal, and though he is not a Guardian, he is a trusted member of this coven. You are already acquainted with their children: Wren, Rowen, Sunni, and Charles. That is why you are a witch, by bloodline."

Lottie stared blankly, unable to find words for a moment. "Do they know they are witches?"

"Yes."

"Why didn't I know?"

"Since I could not raise you and help you understand your magic, I cast a spell when you were born so that no one would know of your powers—a veil. On your sixteenth birthday, the veil lifts, and your true self is revealed. You are coming of age—"

"In three days," Lottie finished.

"Yes. At midnight, your powers will unveil, and you will come into your given name, Charlotte Longhurst."

Lottie looked at her arm, recalling the initials. "C.L.," she said.

"Yes. Now, about that. Someone outside of the coven knows that you're a witch. They must have sensed your power releasing, and now they want to know who you are. That cat was no ordinary cat. It was someone using the guise of one and hoping to reveal your identity through your blood. I have something I was going to give to you on your birthday, but I want you to have it now."

Mathilda pulled an old wooden box etched with beautiful carvings from the side table.

"I had this box carved for you the day you were born."

Lottie opened the lid. Inside was a necklace with a pendant shaped like an elongated triangle hanging from it. It was almost translucent, and the color was difficult to describe. Silvery blue was her best attempt.

"Wow, it's beautiful. What is it?"

"Moonstone. It was forged from the earth during a blood moon to protect our coven. You must wear this at all times now, Charlotte. It will mask any spell you cast and prevent other witches from seeing your power. It has a lot of other cool features, too. You can figure those out with your coven."

"My coven?"

Mathilda smiled. "Charles, Wren, Rowen, and Sunni. They refer to my coven, their parents, as The Elders to keep our two covens separate."

"I'm a little confused about something. If you're as old as you say you are—no offense, then how do all of you have children just born within the last sixteen years?"

"Charlotte, those dreams you've had about being in other times and places were real, including the one about being here. You've lived and died many times. All of you have. When we cast that binding spell, it had a terrible price. As we drew out Cassandra's powers, she set her vengeance upon us. Her curse was that as long as we lived, we would watch our children die over and over throughout eternity. No matter how many immortality spells we cast, we soon realized we could do nothing to save any of you. Eventually, we learned to live with the knowledge that we would see you again in another life."

"But how is it possible? Do I have a father to meet?"

Mathilda chuckled at that. "No, not anymore. It's complicated. Your father was killed in battle right after you were born. Cassandra's curse holds all of your souls to this plane, where they rest in limbo, stretched far enough between rebirth that my sisters and I dreadfully feel your losses. Then, roughly fifty years later, the spell pulls your souls into our wombs, where you awaken, and the cycle repeats."

"How cruel," Lottie stated. Thoughts of the potential causes of death flooded her mind despite her attempt to shut them out. "How did I die over the years?"

Mathilda sighed. "I was afraid you would ask that. All of your deaths have come in the form of an illness, and I will leave it at that. I don't want to paint an image. Just know that each time I was with you in the end, you were always comfortable and at peace."

Lottie shuddered. No wonder she hated death. She had tasted it herself numerous times.

"Why don't I remember anything from the past?"

"I cast a spell to suppress those memories and then blocked you from your coven's memory until the time was right for them to remember you, which they now do. I thought it would be better this way. There's only pain in the past, Charlotte. Plus, for your safety, it was necessary. The stray memory will occasionally break through, but only to guide you toward your coven and your true self, which it now has."

"So, whatever happened to Cassandra's powers?"

"They're trapped in the moonstone from which we made your

necklace, hidden away. None in my coven wanted to be tempted by Cassandra's power, so we let the earth choose the hiding place. It was full of darkness that went against everything we believed in. Plus, Cassandra had a few loyal followers at the time who knew that we took her powers away and that alone was too dangerous for us to keep the stone. For a time, they sought to find it, but none prevailed. Still, we knew how serious it was that such powers were out there, risking discovery, so we decided that whichever one of our children born into the last winter moon would be the one to find the stone and destroy it. You were born again in the third month, on the third day, and in the year 1333. That was your first rebirth."

"Three-thirty-three. I always wondered why I feel drawn to the clock at that time," Lottie mused. "Things seem to happen then."

"That is the way with witches. Nature has a way of telling you what you need to know to uncover anything hidden. You have great power, Charlotte. You are one of us, a Guardian. If there should ever arise a call for you to find the powers, your pendant will grow warm. The closer you are to finding them, the warmer the pendant will get. Before we cast away the stone with Cassandra's powers, I took a fragment of it. Upon your rebirth, I added it to your moonstone to link them together."

Lottie inspected the pendant. She noticed a distinct golden hue in the center.

"In the coming weeks, it's imperative that you wear the necklace at all times. As I said, not all witches are good. You, above all, must be kept secret. Your coven will protect you as you must protect them."

"What kind of power do I have? How do I use it?"

Mathilda stretched out her hand toward the rose garden beyond the window. Lottie watched in amazement as the dead flowers from last year's blooms suddenly burst into beautiful color and withered away as Mathilda withdrew her hand.

"Whoa! So, I'll be able to do that?"

"Yes. You'll discover that you have many talents, and I will guide you. Your gift of controlling the elements is quite impressive. But you'll find out soon enough. Be patient, dear."

"This is so surreal. I can't imagine how I'll go on acting like myself —like my old self, knowing all of this."

"You'll know what to do, especially after you come of age. Speaking of which, I've arranged a small party here at the house to honor your big day."

"Oh, I don't know...."

"Just the coven members," Mathilda assured. "It will allow everyone to get to know you again and welcome you back into the fold."

Lottie thought about Charles. It would be nice seeing him outside of school again.

"I guess it would give me a chance to ask questions and get to know everyone."

Mathilda flashed a beautiful smile. "It's settled then. I'd call your parents and let them know you're ready to go home."

Lottie's eyes widened. "Do my parents know about any of this?"

"Yes. I told them the truth after your incident with the cat. I had to. I knew it was only a matter of time before your magic started showing, and from what I've heard from you about the exploding lightbulbs, it's coming on stronger than any of your previous lives, which means I will need to help you control it soon. Your mother is uncomfortable with witches and magic, given that a witch attacked you as a baby. So, I want you to promise me that you will not practice magic at your house out of respect for her.

"Understood."

Lottie folded her blanket and shoved it into her bag. She wondered if her parents would accept her now that they knew the truth. She didn't think she could bear it if they treated her differently.

THE MOON HAD RISEN OVER THE TREES WHEN LOTTIE'S parents arrived to bring her home to Munroe Falls. It had been a relief when they embraced her warmly, easing her fears of nonacceptance. She looked back at Mathilda's house as her father pulled around the circular driveway. She couldn't believe she'd actually been inside. As a girl, when her parents drove by, she always admired the house from afar. During the winter months, she could see parts of the turrets standing tall through the bare trees, which gave her a peek into the world beyond the woods.

"Are you okay, Lottie?" her mother asked.

"Yeah, Mom, I'm okay. Thank you for telling me everything."

"You're welcome, sweetie. I'm sorry about the way it happened."

"It's fine. Honestly, I feel better than I have in a long time."

Her parents exchanged a look with each other.

Lottie kept quiet the rest of the ride home, turning her thoughts to her birthday instead. What was going to happen at her coming of age? Would she be like the girl in her book? Would she wake up and know what to do and how to use her power? If only it were as simple as that.

HEADLIGHTS SHONE THROUGH THE TREES, CATCHING Matthew's attention. He pulled his phone from his coat pocket and raised his binoculars, watching Lottie and her family enter the house.

"Mistress, I thought you'd like to know she just returned home."

"Good," Selene replied. "Everything has been set into motion."

Matthew hesitated. "You should know there's a protection spell around the property now. I can't get past the ridge in the woods."

"Of course. No matter. I've broken through these types of spells many times. Bring me some of the earth near the border of where the spell begins and meet me at the Paranormal Investigator's Office. I'll find a way around it."

Chapter Six

The morning sun poured into the bedroom, chasing away the shadows from the night. Lottie became aware of the necklace Mathilda had given her resting against her chest and lifted it to inspect.

"What exactly will you do?" she whispered, studying the moonstone.

She twirled it and watched in amazement as brilliant light sparkles danced along the walls. Tiny waves of blue-white energy streaked out from the center of the stone, shifting into ornate patterns. Lottie wondered what other secrets the pendent held. Tucking it into her shirt, she bounced down the steps with the resolve to find out later.

Stepping outside, she noticed the air was warmer, the sun finally strengthening. Everything looked different in Lottie's eyes now...clearer. She found promise in the day. As the bus approached The Quick Stop, she wondered if Christy, Gwen, or Abbey would find her any different. The driver waited a moment and drove away without Christy getting on. Gwen must have given her a ride.

A shiver of anticipation ran through Lottie when Charles's house came into view. As soon as he stepped on the bus, his eyes immediately found hers. He had never looked at her with such intensity before. That same intensity burned inside her as he made his way closer; she couldn't pull her eyes from his no matter how hard she tried.

A smile touched his lips as he sat beside Lottie. "Welcome back."

Her heart pounded. There were so many things that she wanted to say. But where to start?

His smile broadened. "I know. You don't need to say anything."

Lottie didn't know how to respond. He knew what?

"You and I are connected," he gently said. "Once your birthday comes, you'll understand."

The frustration of not knowing her past gnawed at Lottie. What did Charles know that she didn't? She reached into the depth of her mind but hit a wall—the blackened void of Mathilda's veil concealing all. She suddenly felt vulnerable.

"How long have you known about me?" she asked, meeting his eyes.

"The second you told me to look at you in the cafeteria."

Heat rushed to Lottie's cheeks. "You heard that, huh?"

"Loudly," he teased. "That's when I remembered you."

"What do you mean, 'remembered me'?"

"As I said, you'll find everything out on Friday."

Charles grabbed Lottie's backpack as the bus slowed at the school entrance.

"I can get that, you know."

"Sorry, can't have you re-injuring your arm."

"Very funny."

By lunchtime, Lottie had caught up on most of her work. She loaded her tray and headed over to the table she shared with Wren, Rowen, and Sunni.

"She's ba-ack."

Rowen's loud, singsong greeting drew stares from the other students. Wren and Sunni further added to her embarrassment by cheering. She giggled until she noticed the looks Gwen and Abbey were giving her. At least Christy was smiling. Lottie waved and turned her attention to her tray.

"I'm sorry about what happened to you, and I'm glad you're okay," Wren said. "But, I'm so excited that you're back with us, where you belong. Mathilda told my parents that you know everything. It's going to be so much fun now that we don't have to hide it from you that we are witches."

"What's it like? The transformation, I mean?"

"It varies," Wren replied. "I had a blinding light come over me that took my vision for a few moments, followed by this extreme ringing in my ears, but I wasn't afraid. I felt in control of what was happening. There's no need to worry. You'll be fine."

"What was it like meeting Mathilda?" Rowen asked.

"Strange, but in a very familiar way, if that makes any sense."

"It does," Rowen replied. "A part of her has always been with you."

Lottie spotted Charles in the lunch line. She watched him methodically fill his tray from the salad bar.

Sunni caught her staring and smirked.

"What?" Lottie asked.

"Just wait until Friday."

Lottie shook her head. "I'll be glad when I'm up to speed."

"Me, too," Charles replied, placing his tray beside hers. "Care if I sit?" he asked.

How could I possibly say "no" to that smile?

His lips twitched in amusement.

"And you heard that, didn't you? Of course you did," Lottie said, shaking her head.

He leaned close to her ear, and she shivered at his warm breath on her skin.

"Don't worry, you'll get payback," he whispered.

Lottie glanced over to her old table as she took a bite of salad. She hated that things were sour with Gwen and Abbey. How could she make everything right again?

"Are you okay?" Charles asked.

"Just girl drama. Gwen and Abbey are upset that I haven't been sitting with them."

"They can join us," Wren suggested.

"I don't think that's a good idea. At least, not until I work everything out between us."

"Speaking of drama," Sunni spoke up. "Charles, did you ever ask your mom about what's happening at the Paranormal Investigators office?"

"I did," he said, wiping his napkin over his mouth. "Shelly, her acquaintance who works there, told her 'off the record' that an anonymous donor came forward a few days ago. A woman named Selene Sullivan felt it necessary to install her Medium at their office to help with the disturbances happening in town."

"Wait a minute," Lottie interrupted. "What disturbances?"

Charles hesitated. "While you were at Mathilda's, a nasty storm came through, and most of Munroe Falls lost power. Some residents reported seeing strange, floating orbs of light in multiple locations. The following morning, a bunch of dead birds were found in the park. Witnesses said they just dropped out of the sky."

"My mom thinks there is a new witch in the area," Wren added.

"She's right," Charles said. "I overheard Mom talking on the phone to Mathilda this morning. It seems the Medium, a guy named Matthew, is a witch. Not a strong one, but he has some small powers that Ms. Sullivan felt could aid the investigators in locating the source of the disturbances."

"No way. How did they find out he's a witch?" Lottie asked.

"Shelly is also a witch. She knew what Matthew was the second he was introduced to the staff. The coven is keeping tabs on him. I'm sure they'll fill us in soon enough."

Rowen shook her head. "Wow. This place gets weirder every day."

"I'll say," Lottie agreed.

~

WHEN THE LAST BELL RANG ON FRIDAY, LOTTIE BOLTED FOR the door. She got in line with Charles to wait for the bus, her fingers tapping anxiously against her arms.

"Everything okay?" he asked, eyebrows arching.

"I guess. I'm ready to go home and lock myself in my room for the rest of the day."

His laugh caught her off guard.

"What's so funny?"

"I promise you'll laugh, too, when this is all over."

They boarded the bus and found their seat.

"You look tired," Charles remarked. "Have you not been sleeping well?"

"No, not really. Between the nightmares and thinking about tonight, I'll be glad when this is over so I can stop worrying and get back to normal life—and sleeping again."

Lottie felt Charles's eyes on her for most of the ride home. She wished she knew what he was thinking. As they approached her stop, he reached for her hand. The energy that pulsed between them was powerful. The pull drew her heart to his, and she wondered if he felt the same pull from her.

"Don't worry about anything, Lottie. I promise everything will be okay."

Warmth flooded through her at his touch. She didn't want to let go.

"Thanks. I'll see you tomorrow."

Her parents stood by the kitchen table with their jackets on when she came through the door

"Going somewhere?" she asked.

"Your father and I want to take you to your favorite restaurant for an early birthday celebration."

"Aw, thanks. Let me run my stuff to my room, and I'll be right down."

When they arrived at Tip Top Restaurant, they were led to a window seat table facing the woods. Lottie grinned at her mother as she eyed the bobbing balloons with curling white and pink ribbons.

"I might have stopped by here earlier."

"Thank you. This is great." She shimmied out of her coat and asked the waitress for the fried chicken dinner with macaroni and cheese.

"Did you have a good day at school?" her father asked.

"It was okay. I'm glad to be out of there."

"Did anything happen?"

"No, just a boring day."

After they finished their meals, the staff brought out a cake with candles flaming on top. Lottie burned with embarrassment as they sang "Happy Birthday" to her.

"You guys are too much."

"Make a wish," her father urged.

Lottie closed her eyes. *Please let everything be okay.*

Tiny sparks danced all around the cake as she blew out the candles. She jumped, knowing she had caused it. Glancing up, she expected to see looks of horror on her parents' faces.

Her mother flinched. "Oh, my. I've never seen candles do that before. I must have picked up trick candles by mistake."

Lottie let out a nervous laugh. "I guess so."

Her father reached into his jacket pocket and pulled out a rectangular box wrapped in pale pink paper with darker pink ribbons curling around it. "Happy Birthday, honey."

"Thanks, Dad." She tore off the paper and opened the box. Inside was a gold link bracelet with a heart pendant hanging from the center. "Oh, it's beautiful. I love it."

"Look on the back of the heart," he said.

She turned it over and read the engraved calligraphy.

Love you always,
Mom & Dad

"Just a little reminder of how much we love you," her mother added.

Tears filled Lottie's eyes.

"No tears—" her mother urged. "Or you'll make me start."

"Thank you both so much. It's been a great night. Just what I needed."

Her father patted her hand. "Let's finish up and get you home. The birthday girl needs her sleep for her big day tomorrow." He suddenly paused, his mouth twisting as he realized the magnitude of his words.

Lottie sighed. "Yeah. The big day."

~

MATTHEW WATCHED AS NANCY, THE RECEPTIONIST, WALKED across the parking lot. The dim flicker of the streetlight across the road highlighted the custom paint job of Slimer, The Green Ghost, on her Pontiac Bonneville.

He drummed his fingers on the windowsill, waiting for her to pull away from the building. Finally alone, he went to Shelly's office to discover what she had been secretly working on all week. He was sure Shelly had a lead regarding the disturbances Selene had been causing in Munroe Falls, and he had to be sure she wasn't a suspect.

He fumbled for the light switch. Shelly's desk was tidy, with a large amethyst geode as the only decoration. A few file folders sat by the keyboard. He carefully skimmed through each one, but nothing stood out. A blue three-ring notebook underneath a magazine caught his attention. He flipped through the pages. Pretty cursive handwriting with absent-minded doodles filled about half of the notebook. Then, staring at him on the last entry was his name. *Matthew.* Shelly had circled it several times. He read on.

Teacher...Defiance...???

He had sensed a lack of trust from Shelly, and now he knew why. She was suspicious of him. He heard keys jingling at the front door. Startled, he dropped the notebook on the desk, knocking over a cup of pens. His heart raced. Gaining composure, Matthew stretched out his hand and used magic to put the room back in order. He darted back into his office just as the main set of lights turned on.

"Matthew, what are you still doing here?" Nancy asked.

"Just finishing up with this last case," he managed to say in a calm, even voice. "I thought you were going home?"

"I forgot my purse." She pulled the denim patchwork bag from underneath her desk. "I'm leaving this time. You should do the same. It's getting late."

"I think that's a great idea. I'll lock up shortly."

As he walked to his car, Matthew let out a pent-up breath. He hated sneaking around, but Selene expected answers. The notebook held Shelly's innermost thoughts, and it was only a matter of time before she put the pieces together. He shuddered at the thought of having to snoop through her office again.

He came to the end of the building, wishing there was better lighting in the parking lot as he fumbled for his key.

"Well, Matthew, how was your first week at work?" Selene asked, stepping out from the shadows.

Already unnerved, Matthew let out a startled shout. He quickly recovered. "Mistress, you scared me. Where is your car?"

"Across the street. I trust you found out what the Paranormal Investigators think is going on?"

"It's been difficult. The witch, Shelly, is suspicious of me. She has—"

"Enough," Selene shouted. She put her hand out as if she was squeezing something.

Matthew grabbed his throat, trying to free the invisible grip that choked him. Selene raised her arm higher, lifting Matthew off the ground. His legs kicked wildly as his face turned from crimson to blue. She flung her arm downward, and he crashed to the ground, gasping for air.

"No excuses, Matthew. If the witch is causing a problem, then get rid of her. Isn't that why you're here? There's an evil lurking somewhere," she gestured to herself. "I'm sure the paranormal riffraff would gladly accept your input should some tragic incident occur. You know what I'm capable of doing. Your job is to make sure no one suspects me. Everything is hanging by a thread."

"Yes, Mistress," he said roughly, massaging his throat.

"Now that we understand each other let's get over to the Jacobs' house. We'll find out tonight if Lottie is who I think she is."

~

THE EVENING HOURS QUICKLY BECAME TEDIOUS. LOTTIE sighed, having watched the clock for the last two hours, her anxiety mounting. She had no idea what would happen when her birthday arrived at midnight, and the thought of sitting and staring at the clock for three more hours was maddening. She decided right then that she didn't want to find out. Reaching over, Lottie turned the clock around and got into bed. She would let her magic come while she was sleeping.

A soft knock came at her door.

"It's open," she said, rolling over.

Her mother stepped into the room. A nervous smile tugged at her lips, and she swept an apprehensive gaze over Lottie. "Everything okay?"

"I'm fine, Mom. There's nothing to worry about."

"Are you sure? I could keep you company, just in case...," she broke off suddenly. When she spoke again, the words came out in a rush. "In case you get scared."

"Mom, I appreciate it, but I would rather be alone when...*it* happens."

She noticed her mother's expression tighten and suddenly felt awkward. Their eyes met in that uncomfortable silence, and her mother quickly pulled Lottie into a tight embrace.

"You know I love you, right? No matter what?"

Her hair rested against Lottie's cheek, and she caught the flowery scent of her mother's shampoo. She smiled with relief at her words.

"I know, Mom. I love you, too."

Her mother leaned back and looked Lottie over with a bright smile.

"If you get scared even for a second, just yell or come to get me, okay?"

"I will. Thanks, Mom."

~

Midnight.

Burning hot, Lottie woke with a start, feeling disoriented. Her hands tingled. Tiny sparks spread up her arms, reaching up and down the length of her body. The flashes crept their way up her neck, then her face, and finally to her head. Her eyes widened as she noticed her hands. She held them out, inspecting the glowing light emanating from them.

She took a deep breath to calm the panic. The lamp on the nightstand came on and began to flicker. Faster and brighter it went until it exploded in a blinding light.

Everything suddenly stopped at once. Light particles from the exploded bulb hung suspended throughout the room. Lottie looked around. She felt as if she was frozen in slow motion as if someone had paused her life and started it back in super slow mode. A section of her hair moved where she had turned her head a moment ago. It floated in mid-air, slowly making its descent. A ringing pierced her ears. She clamped her hands over them at the shock. Insects buzzed and flittered outside in the distance; their sound magnified tenfold. A twig snapped somewhere in the night. The light particles slowly started moving around and around in circles, surrounding her. They seemed to fill her as they spun even faster. Her senses became heightened like never before. She felt grounded. All at once, time sped up, and the particles instantly fell over her. Then it happened—the knowing.

Charles. His name pounded in her brain. His face was all that she saw.

Flashes of memories of the two of them together flooded her mind; age after age, the memories came like the flipping pages of a picture book. Their love had endured over the centuries. She tried to grasp onto one of the many memories, but something prevented her from seeing them, and they drifted into mists of nothingness. She knew one thing with complete certainty, however. She loved him with every fiber of her being. The realization of it shocked her. The depth of their love was beyond what someone her age would feel. She closed her eyes and let the emotions wash over her.

I need you.

As soon as the thought came into her mind, she heard a sound at her window. She pulled the curtain back to see Charles down below in her yard. He was about to toss another pebble when he saw her. She unlocked her window and slid it open.

"Can I come up?" he asked.

"I'll be right down."

Before she could reach the door, he was standing in her bedroom. "Oh, my God, how did you get up here?"

He closed the distance between them. "Magic, Lottie. Happy Birthday." He reached into his pocket and handed her a small box. "Open it."

A gasp came when she saw the ring inside. She ran her finger over the large amber stone, mesmerized by the dark flecks that seemed to swim within the golden depths. Somehow, she remembered it.

He held up his hand. "I have the same ring."

"It's beautiful, Charles, thank you."

He took it out of the box and slid it on her finger.

Shivers went through her body as his fingers grazed hers. He gazed at her with such intensity that her soul burned for him.

I love him so much.

As I love you, he said without speaking.

Lottie flinched at the sound of his voice in her head. "Oh, my God."

"Now, you understand. We're connected, you and I."

He pressed his palm gently against hers. Soft light surrounded their hands. The feel of his touch sent heat radiating through Lottie, and she pulled away at the intensity of the feelings.

Charles leaned in and kissed her cheek at the corner of her mouth. Then again on the other side, and finally, her lips. She felt a spark and jerked back, touching her fingers to her lip.

"What was that?"

"Energy," he said, walking to the window. "Happy Birthday, Lottie." And with that, he was gone.

～

Selene lowered the binoculars. "I knew it! The daughter of Mathilda Longhurst has come into her power."

"How can you be sure?" Matthew asked.

"Because I know Mathilda, and I know her magic. Call it a fingerprint, if you will. I felt the weaves of her spell unravel when Lottie's magic came alive. The little fool doesn't even realize how powerful she is. It seems a shame to waste such a gift on someone so undeserving."

Matthew ignored her comments, still amazed at witnessing Lottie's magic awaken. Like Selene, he questioned whether she knew the full extent of her power. He noticed the window lift.

"Mistress, Charles is leaving."

Selene raised the binoculars again. "So he is. Charles's magic is quite strong, too, you know. I can feel it from here." She inhaled deeply as if savoring it. "How easy it would be to take his power for my own," she mused. "Be a dear, Matthew, and collect more earth. I'm going to get through this protection spell one way or another."

Chapter Seven

Gray early morning light filtered through Lottie's bedroom window. She lay in bed recalling her visit from Charles as she studied the ring that he'd given her.

"We're connected, you and I...."

Could she really communicate with Charles telepathically?

Are you okay?

His response was immediate, startling her.

Never better.

She grinned. This could be fun.

When she arrived at school, Wren, Rowen, and Sunni were waiting at her locker. They all wore pointed party hats and blew wildly into the noisemakers in their mouths.

"Happy Birthday!" Wren shouted.

"Thanks, guys," Lottie said, flushing with embarrassment. She tried to ignore the odd glances from the passing students.

"So, how did it go last night?" Wren asked.

"Insane, but so cool. I woke up with these sensations pulsating through my body, and I literally felt the power inside me come to life. The best part, of course, was when the memories of Charles came rushing into my mind. And although I hate to admit it, you guys were right; I was worried for nothing."

"See, I told you everything would be okay," Wren teased. "And now you finally know what you've been missing."

"Yeah, this telepathy thing with Charles will take some getting used to."

"What did your parents say about the party at Mathilda's?" Sunni asked.

"I haven't told them yet. I'm afraid they won't let me go, so I've been putting it off until the last minute."

"Well, we've been talking about it, and we have a pretty good plan," Wren announced. "My parents said we could have a sleepover at my place after the party. Dad and I will pick you up later and drive you to Mathilda's. Afterward, we'll all crash at my house."

"That's a good plan."

"I see you had a visit from Charles last night," Sunni said, noticing the golden amber stone.

A grin spread over Lottie's face as she eyed her ring. "Yeah."

"Oh," Rowen said, her eyes gleaming with mischief.

"Nothing happened," Lottie scolded, reaching for her lock.

"Wait—what's your combination?" Wren asked.

"Five, seventeen, thirty-two. Why?"

"Rowen, you and Sunni stand guard. Check this out."

Wren focused intently on the lock. The dial spun by itself: Five, then seventeen, then thirty-two. The lock popped open.

"There," she beamed. "One of the many fun things you can do now."

Something fell out of the locker when Lottie pulled open the door. A note with a black satin ribbon tied neatly around it lay at her feet. She picked it up and turned it over. "Doesn't say who it's from."

Rowen snorted. "It's probably a sappy note from Charles, stating what a *special* night he had with Lottie."

"Knock it off, Rowen," Sunni chided.

Lottie ignored the comment as she pulled the ribbon off the letter, half-expecting it to be from Charles.

Don't think for a moment that you are safe.
I know who you are.

An ominous fog seemed to fill the locker area as Lottie read the words, leaving her with a heavy sense of foreboding. "No...I'm pretty sure this isn't from Charles."

"What is it?" Wren asked. "You're shaking."

Lottie gave the note to her. Wren read it aloud to the others.

"Oh, my God," Sunni said, glancing around. "Who would have done this?"

"I don't know," Lottie replied.

"Can you think of anyone who might know about you?" Wren asked.

"No."

"Are you wearing the necklace Mathilda gave you?"

"Yes."

"Good. We're protected together, see?"

Wren and the others pulled their pendants out from underneath their shirts.

"They're the same as mine," Lottie acknowledged.

"Each of our pendants is the point of a pentacle," Wren continued. "We protect each other. Mathilda keeps the center part of the pentacle at her home as a linking stone to all of us."

Wren folded the letter and shoved it into her pocket. "I will hang on to this and show it to my parents. They'll know what to do. Be careful in the meantime."

Lottie nodded and hurried out of the locker area and into the stairwell. When she rounded the second set of steps, she ran right into Jake Putnam. She nearly lost her balance but managed to catch herself before falling backward. He stared at her with hollow, empty eyes.

"Are you okay, Jake?" Lottie asked.

He smiled, but it wasn't the kind smile she remembered him having. It was chilling. An odd sense of danger tingled up her spine. He proceeded down the lower stairs, gazing at her as he walked out the door. She shook off the feelings and rushed up to Biology.

~

LOTTIE KEPT HER THOUGHTS OFF THE LETTER BY FOCUSING on the party instead. She ate an early dinner with her parents, filling them in on her plans for the sleepover, then went up to pack after getting their approval.

Wren had a huge smile plastered across her face when she arrived an hour later.

"Oh, my gosh, Lottie, how are you not dying of excitement?"

Lottie grinned at her friend. "I am a little. I'm mostly nervous."

She said hello to Mr. Wesley and tossed her bag in the car before sliding in beside Wren.

"We'll need to change clothes when we get to Mathilda's. I didn't want to be dressed for a party when we picked you up."

"Oh, good idea. Only, I didn't bring anything appropriate for a party. I wasn't thinking."

Wren flashed a bright smile. "No worries. You just have to show up. The rest is taken care of."

"Very mysterious."

"So, any other run-ins with Jake?"

"No, thank God. That was insanely weird."

"Well, don't worry too much. Sunni stole a pen from his desk to give to her mom. She'll let us know if she finds anything you need to be concerned about in her spell."

Lottie's stomach tensed with nervousness as they turned onto the tree-lined driveway. She gazed out her window, quiet in her thoughts. What were the other members of Mathilda's coven like? Was Charles inside?

Mr. Wesley parked, and Wren bounded out of the car.

"We'll go in the side entry."

"Okay. Thanks, Mr. Wesley. I'll see you inside."

"You can call me Phil now, Lottie."

She smiled. "Thanks, Phil."

Wren led her up the back stairway to the upstairs bedrooms. Marie was waiting by the door to the same room from Lottie's previous stay.

"Happy Birthday, Miss. Everything you need is in the armoire. If you require anything else, I will be out here."

"Thank you, Marie."

"Well, what are you waiting for?" Wren urged. "Get in there."

Lottie pulled open the doors to the armoire. "Whoa."

Hanging inside was a beautiful black tulle dress with crystals and gold beading around the bodice and mid-section. Tiny black beads formed little floral patterns across the sweetheart neckline of the bust. Lottie was afraid even to touch it.

"Go ahead, try it on," Wren said. "My dress is in the room across the hall. I'll go change and meet you back in a few minutes."

Lottie noticed a note on the table by the bed. She opened it and read:

I hope you like the dress. There are some toiletries in the bathroom and some jewelry in the box—they are yours.

— MATHILDA

Lottie rushed into the bathroom, opened the jewelry box, and pulled out the antique-looking chandelier earrings. They were the most beautiful things she had ever seen. The crystals sparkled in the light. *Diamonds?* She put them back in the box and walked into the bedroom.

There was a knock on the door. "Can I come in?" asked Wren. Hearing Lottie's response, she stepped inside. "Lottie, you're not dressed."

"I know. I feel a bit overwhelmed."

"Why?"

"I'm not used to all of these fancy things."

"But it's okay. It's your birthday—and a welcome-back party from the coven. Come on. Please try the dress on."

Lottie sighed. "Fine. You look amazing, by the way," she remarked, taking note of Wren's red, one-shoulder taffeta dress.

"Thanks. I love an excuse to get dressed up." Wren took the black dress off the hanger. "Here. Put this on."

Lottie stepped into it and pulled the straps up. The tulle brushed against her thighs, and she twirled around, fanning the dress about her. She couldn't help the giggle that escaped.

"Okay, I see why you like to dress up. This is pretty great." She glanced toward the bathroom. One more thing. The earrings... are those...?"

"The real deal, baby. They were yours in some lifetime or another."

"Wow. Okay then."

Lottie slipped on the strappy heels she found in the armoire and headed out into the hall with Wren.

The conversations from below drifted up to her ears. She listened for Charles's voice but didn't hear him. When she stepped onto the lower landing, everyone got quiet. The grand foyer was full of smiling faces looking up at her.

"Happy Birthday!" everyone shouted.

She inhaled deeply and descended the rest of the curved staircase, gripping the thick mahogany railing as she searched the room.

By the table.

Her heart raced at hearing his voice in her mind, and the usual feelings of excitement rose whenever he was near. Charles smiled at her from the back of the room. Everyone else disappeared. The distance between them closed, her eyes on him with each step. A figure from the corner of her eye diverted her purpose.

"You look lovely, dear. Happy Birthday." Mathilda kissed her cheek.

"Thank you for everything," Lottie gestured to herself.

"You are very welcome. How was your coming of age?"

"Scary, exciting...I'm glad I met you before it happened. At least I had a heads up."

"That's true. I hope you have a happy time tonight."

"Thank you, I will."

Mathilda followed her gaze over to where Charles stood. "I see Charles gave you the ring."

Lottie looked down at her finger. The amber stone surrounded by antique silver filigree accents looked even more beautiful against her black dress.

"You two always find each other," Mathilda mused.

Rowen rushed toward Lottie, a huge smile etched across her face. "Lottie, you look amazing."

Sunni nodded in agreement.

"Thanks."

"Squeeze in, guys," Rowen said, holding her phone to take a photo.

Lottie felt Charles's eyes on her. She glanced up to find him smiling as he watched her. He seemed very much at ease, his arms crossed and leaning against the carved antique console table.

"I'll be back." She quickly skirted around the edge of the room to avoid any other delays getting to him.

"Happy Birthday," he greeted. His eyes swept over her. "You look beautiful."

"Thanks. You look nice, too." Her gaze dropped longingly to the hollow of his neck, showing between the top two buttons of his shirt.

"I'm glad you're here," she said, willing her gaze to meet his.

"I wouldn't have missed this for the world, Lottie."

His eyes blazed into hers, leaving her breathless. He leaned closer and softly kissed her lips. Another spark.

"Ooh, good one," Rowen said as she took their picture.

Charles scowled at her. She winked and walked away.

"Is it always going to be this way when we kiss?" Lottie asked.

A corner of his mouth lifted. "It'll stop. Eventually."

"Can I have everyone's attention?" Mathilda announced. "Thank you all for coming out to celebrate Charlotte's special day. Let's make our way into the dining hall, and we'll continue the festivities."

"After you," Charles said, gesturing.

The two massive Baroque chandeliers hanging from the wooden arches in the vaulted ceiling cast a soft glow over the room, warming the dark walnut tones of the raised paneling on the walls. Crystal stemware sparkled down the length of the enormous tortoiseshell inlay dining table, and the place settings looked fit for royalty, not a birthday party. Mathilda seated Lottie at the head of the table, then went to sit at the opposite end. Charles sat by her left, and Phil was at her right, followed by his wife, Regina. She was quite beautiful and full of smiles and a ready laugh. Her hair was a light blonde, like Wren's, and brushed the tops of her slender shoulders. Lottie saw a strong resemblance between mother and daughter. Wren had her father's piercing blue eyes, however. Phil was also blonde, though darker; he was handsome, trim, and as easygoing as Regina seemed. They were a very nice-looking family.

A serving staff began to pour drinks around the table before sweeping out of the room again.

"You seem nervous, Lottie." The voice came from her left. Charles's mother, Ramona, gazed intently at her.

"I guess I am a little nervous."

"Relax, dear. You're surrounded by love."

Lottie studied Ramona for a moment. Her hair was darker than Charles's. Nearly black. It was pulled back in a neat chignon held by a sparkling clip. She had an overall look of sternness, but her eyes were soft when she spoke, and the hard edges seemed to fade away.

"So, Lottie," Phil said, turning to her. "What would you like to do as your first test of magic?"

"Oh, I don't know. I'm not even sure what I can do."

"You can do anything you want. Just focus and do it."

"Okay...."

She noticed the candelabras on the table still unlit and pictured a fire dancing on the tips. Immediately, tiny flames shot up on each candle. The fire flickered and swelled, and Lottie burst with excitement, but the flames grew, and the heat and light became alarming. She panicked as the wax dripped onto the table, setting fire to Rowen's napkin. Mathilda's hand clenched into a fist. There was a high-pitched whistling sound like the air sucked from the room. Lottie watched the flames choke out across the table in a horrified numbness. The room was utterly silent, adding to her embarrassment.

Phil's sharp whistle startled her. "Well, what's that saying? Go big, or go home?"

Nervous laughter broke out, easing the tension in the room.

"The key is to relax and trust your magic," Phil added with a wink.

"You'll have to be careful with your magic," Mathilda warned. "Your's is powerful. You wouldn't want to hurt anybody."

"No, of course not." An uneasy feeling crept into her stomach as she considered the possibility.

"You won't," Charles said softly. "We'll help you learn how to use it."

Lottie nodded, thankful for his assurance.

After dinner, a fire roared in the fireplace, and the adults gravitated toward the sitting area around it.

"Why don't we go explore?" Sunni suggested.

"I'm in," Wren volunteered. "It's been a while since I was here."

"You want to go, too?" Charles asked Lottie.

"Sure, I could use a breather."

They wandered down the halls and into the formal sitting room. Lottie's eyes fell on the piano in the corner. She ran her fingers across the keys and sensed she had been here before.

"Play something, Lottie," Sunni said.

"I don't know how to play the piano."

"Yes, you do," Charles added. "Beautifully."

"Seriously, guys, I don't know how."

"Lottie, focus on what your mind is telling you right now," Wren said. "Do you sense it? That feeling you've been here before? None of us knew you could play the piano, but we knew as soon as we entered this room. Listen to your feelings."

Lottie sat on the bench and looked at the expanse of black and ivory. A flash of light came into her mind. She saw herself in the past, perhaps around the 1700s, going by her dress. It was lavender with a floral design in a darker shade of purple, and her hair was done up in a riot of curls and ribbons. Charles leaned over the piano, watching her. Several people mingled behind her in the room, listening to her play. Then, the memory vanished.

Lottie closed her eyes, and without thinking, she began to play. The music was familiar to her. She felt like someone else—like her body was no longer hers. How she knew how to play was beyond her reasoning, but she couldn't stop. Charles sat down beside her, his back facing the piano. He watched her for a moment, then lifted her hair away from her neck and kissed it.

There was an obnoxious clearing of throats behind them.

"Don't mind us, but we'd better get back to the party," Wren suggested.

~

"Did your spell turn anyone up?" Mathilda asked as she poured more wine into her glass.

"No," Regina replied. "Not even a trace of magic was left behind on the letter."

"Whoever sent it seems bent on discovering more about Lottie," Trina added. A wave of her long golden-brown hair tumbled over her shoulder as she sat, and she casually brushed it away. "I worry about the incident with the cat. Our mystery villain has a good bit of power to have shape-shifted to get to her—and they knew how to create a blood-revealing spell. I hope that Lottie got away before the initials on her arm became clear."

"It's only a matter of time before whoever it is does something care-less," Regina pointed out. "Then we'll know who we're dealing with."

"What about Jake, the boy from school?" asked Trina. "Rowen mentioned that he's been watching Lottie. Apparently, she had an uncomfortable run-in with him today."

"Sunni told me all about it," Isobel said. "She has a class with that boy and brought me a pen from his desk. Nothing turned up in my spell other than a lousy home life."

Mathilda's forehead knitted. "The kind of magic we're dealing with here requires a great deal of power and many years of practice. I don't think that a mere teenager is the one we seek."

"What do you suggest, then?" Regina asked.

"I say that we keep our focus on the Paranormal Investigators. Ramona, what does your contact over there say about Matthew Alcott, the new witch?"

"Shelly doesn't trust him. If she is suspicious of him, I think we should also be."

"Very well," Mathilda replied. "Stay in touch with her—and while we're at it, let's see if we can pick up on any ill intent from the anony-mous donor who brought in the witch. I want to make sure this woman isn't a threat."

"What about Lottie's magic?" Regina asked. "You saw what happened at dinner."

"Yes," Mathilda said. "It's coming on too strong. I need to teach her how to control it, and I can't do that if her mind is clouded by fear. This should be a happy time for Charlotte. She and Charles only just found each other again. We must uncover whoever is behind this and keep Charlotte safe."

"Charles won't let her out of his sight," Ramona assured. "You know the bond they share. He will know if anything happens."

"Who's watching her house?" Trina asked.

"I've got this weekend covered," Phil replied.

"Make sure she doesn't know you're watching," Mathilda added. "I don't want to alarm her."

"Don't worry. I'll use animal form."

Mathilda nodded. "Keep me updated if anything happens on your watch."

"I hear the kids coming," Regina said. "I think we'd better end our talk for the evening."

"Where did all of you end up?" Isobel asked, glancing at her daughter. Isobel was a near-mirror image of Sunni, but with more warmth in the coppery tones of her skin. There was a soft, rosy glow to her cheeks that wasn't there before, likely caused by the wine she held between her long fingers.

"The sitting room, mainly," Sunni replied. "Lottie discovered she knows how to play the piano."

"Ah, yes," Mathilda smiled. "And quite well, might I add."

Lottie noticed the black ribbon on the table and shivered. "Did you discover who wrote the letter?"

"There wasn't a trace of magic found," Mathilda answered. "Whoever wrote it masked themself very well, but know that we've got this under our eye, Charlotte. Keep your guard up, and we'll all look out for you. Oh, and I heard about your strange encounters with that boy in school. Isobel didn't find anything suspicious about him in her spell when she used the pen Sunni took from his desk. Now, enough talking. Go on up and get changed to go to your sleepover."

Chapter Eight

The Wesley's house was about a mile from the main road, and from what Lottie could tell in the dark, it was surrounded by dense woodland. Lights shone from the windows on all three floors of the modern Tudor-style home, piquing Lottie's curiosity about the charm that awaited her inside.

"You girls go on up and get settled in," Regina said as they pulled into the garage. "I'll get some food rounded up in a bit."

They thanked her and headed inside.

Lottie could tell that no expense had been spared as she followed Wren through the house. The main living area boasted a massive stone fireplace and lavish furnishings. Tapestries, some looking centuries old, hung from the walls, and ancient-looking artifacts were scattered throughout the room, from old vases to weapons artfully placed over the fireplace.

Lottie's eyes widened as she turned toward the leaded-glass windows. A full suit of medieval plate armor stood in the corner of the room, complete with a sword resting in the gauntleted hands. She noticed the sword's intricate carvings on the rounded pommel and guard gleaming beneath the accent lights, and her small gasp caught Wren's attention.

"It was my grandfather's armor," Wren stated. "My dad preserved it for my mom to remember her father."

"Unbelievable," Lottie murmured as she trailed behind her friend.

Wren's bedroom was equally impressive. It was bigger than most rooms in Lottie's whole house. Even with two queen beds, there was no sense of crowding. She eyed the sitting area by the bowed windows and fireplace on the opposite wall, but the main feature was the tapestry of a giant tree hanging behind the beds. The threads were expertly woven to give the tree depth and an overall look of ancientness.

"I love your room," Lottie said. "That tree is awesome."

Wren glanced up. "The tree of life. It represents the connectedness of everything in the universe. For us, it serves as a strong correspondence between Mother Earth and our ancestors. Mathilda actually made the tapestry a long time ago."

Lottie flinched with surprise. She tore her eyes from the tree and tried to imagine what life was like for Mathilda all those centuries ago as she settled into a chair and pulled her favorite comfy Bulldog sweats from her bag.

"Watch this," Wren said. She turned toward her dresser and made a beckoning motion with her hand. The drawer slid open, and her clothes lifted and floated over to the bed.

"You can do that too, you know. Try it."

"Okay." Lottie focused on the clothes that she had just taken out. They lifted off the chair and flew over with such force that they knocked a lamp off the bedside table.

"Oh, my gosh! Wren, I am so sorry."

"No worries, you'll get the hang of it. You should spend more time with Mathilda. She can help you learn to control your magic."

"I would love to, but I don't see that happening. My mother doesn't care much for Mathilda."

"Why?"

"She doesn't understand anything past what she can't see. Witchcraft and magic are on her list of bad things."

"Oh."

"So, what keeps our powers in check? What if I get angry and hurt somebody? Then what?"

"One word," Sunni chimed in. "Grounding."

"What's that?" Lottie asked.

"It's a sort of spiritual meditation if you will. Mother Earth removes any ill feelings and provides renewing energy we draw from. It's very peaceful. Witches do it every day to keep our sense of calm. We never, ever intentionally harm another living thing. With practice, you'll learn to control your emotions. Once you become one with the earth, it takes root into your whole being. You won't want to cause harm once you get that down."

"That's good to know. I've been uneasy about using magic ever since Mathilda made that comment at dinner for me to be careful."

"That's understandable," Wren said, smiling sympathetically.

"Guys, let's take this conversation to the kitchen," Rowen suggested. "I'm starving."

Wren glanced up at her. "Now that you mention it, so am I."

Regina was finishing up with the snacks when they came down. "You girls help yourselves. I'm going up to bed."

"Goodnight, Mom," Wren replied.

Lottie munched on some chips while her mind turned over a horde of questions.

"Lottie, I swear if you think any harder, your head will explode," Sunni teased.

"I know. I've been wondering about our past. Do any of you guys remember anything?"

"Not much," Wren replied. "The spell the Elders cast over us blocks most memories from coming through. Only the occasional good ones filter in."

Lottie sighed. "Sometimes, I get these urges or vague memories. I can't see what they are, but I can feel things from them."

"We all have certain feelings from our past, and we remember things from time to time, like you, playing the piano, for example. It helps us guide each other toward who we're meant to be," Wren explained.

"I think it's a good thing," Rowen added. "I don't want to know how I've died throughout centuries."

"How *do* we die?" Lottie wondered aloud. "Mathilda was vague on the details."

"Our parents won't divulge much either," Wren said. "They say it's too painful to talk about. I know that you and Charles die fairly close to one another. Broken heart syndrome takes the remaining lover. From what I understand, we never live to be that old," Wren added.

"This is depressing. I'm sorry I asked."

"Look on the bright side, Lottie. We always come back," Rowen said, grinning.

"Do we all talk telepathically, like Charles and I?"

"That's just you two," Wren answered. "We all can, but there are helpers we use to access each other's thoughts easily. Crystals are handy to keep on hand. We each have one in our locker just in case we need to keep in touch."

Lottie's eyes widened. "I *knew* it. I knew I was missing out on some secret conversation between you guys at school. I thought I was crazy at the time."

"Nope, that was the crystal at its best."

"You mean *my* incantation," Rowen huffed. "Without it, those crystals would be useless."

"Yeah, yeah," Wren droned. "Rowen's spell linked us to them."

"How did you figure out who I am?"

"When you released your magic to Charles that day in the cafeteria, he remembered you instantly. When he told us, it triggered us to remember, too. Mathilda veiled you from us until the right moment. That's how I ended up in the bathroom when you were upset. I wanted to make sure you weren't freaking out."

Lottie stared at the table, recalling the incident. "I remember Charles's face so clearly when it happened. He looked shocked."

"He was beyond shocked," Wren added. "And a bit too stupefied to find the words to explain what happened. I got impatient and read his mind. I was given a very personal experience of what he saw. I'm telling you, girl, the bond you two have is solid and unbreakable. There were so many memories—much more than I could read at that moment."

Rowen let out an exaggerated yawn. "Guys, I'm going to bed."

"I'm pretty tired, too," Wren admitted. "Let's call it a night. We'll do some grounding first thing tomorrow."

Lottie lay awake long after her friends slept, watching leaf shadows dance over the fireplace along the far wall.

Charles's voice came clear in her mind. *A penny for your thoughts?*

How did you know I was awake—or thinking, for that matter?

I can feel you. When we connect, we sense things going on with each other. So, what's troubling you?

It's not that I'm troubled as much as overwhelmed. I have so much that I feel I need to do— and then I realize that I don't know what to do. It's frustrating. Wren and the others are going to teach me grounding tomorrow.

Good. That's the best start. Don't worry so much. Everything will fall in line now that you've taken your chosen path.

I hope so.

Did you have a good birthday?

Yes. It doesn't seem real, though. I'm afraid I'll wake up and find it was all a dream.

It only gets better from here.

I can't wait. Lottie hesitated for a moment. *Charles, I'm glad you came tonight. I don't fully understand us yet, but I'm happy we're together. We are together, right?*

There was a second of silence, and Lottie sensed that he was smiling through their bond.

We're together, Lottie. Get some sleep, okay? I'll talk to you tomorrow.

Goodnight, Charles.

～

A PILLOW SMASHED ONTO LOTTIE'S HEAD, JERKING HER awake. "Ow! What the...." Another whack. This time to her legs.

Rowen giggled.

"Wake up," Sunni shouted. "Grounding day, wakey-wakey."

The covers moved as Wren rolled over. "Ugh... go away, you crazy people."

"Nope, it's time for Lottie's lesson," Rowen protested.

Lottie pulled the covers over her head, only encouraging her friends further. Pillows bashed over her body. She giggled and grabbed her weapon, and soon, feathers flew all over the room.

~

THE RAIN THAT CAME THROUGH IN THE EARLY MORNING hours left a chilly and uncomfortable dampness to the air that seeped into Lottie's bones. Wet blades of grass brushed her ankles as she followed the others toward the tree line. Crossing onto a well-trodden path, Lottie wondered how many years of foot traffic had passed to cause the earth to be so worn. Eventually, the path opened up to a clearing. Five giant oak trees that had to be centuries old had been purposefully planted in a perfect circle, and sunlight through the mists above them gave the area a sacred, mystical appearance.

"Shoes off, girls," Wren said, disturbing the silence.

"Seriously? It's cold," Lottie whined.

"You won't even notice after a few minutes," Sunni promised. "Trust me."

Lottie's sigh came out in a misty puff as she slipped her shoes off.

Rowen smiled. "Socks too, girlfriend. Do what we do and absorb the energy."

They each went to a tree. Lottie followed suit and chose the one standing to her right. She flattened her back against it as the others had done, taking note of the soft, damp moss under her feet. It felt cool but inviting. Copying everyone, she closed her eyes and wrapped her arms around the sides of the tree. She took in a deep breath, letting go of her thoughts. On the exhale, she felt the life-force energy travel down the length of her body, exiting through the soles of her feet. The ground suddenly felt very warm. Noticing her feet were tingling, Lottie glanced down and saw a shimmery light enveloping them. She closed her eyes again, and the heat crept up her body, seeping into her limbs. It was exhilarating. A sense of well-being settled over her, yet something distracted her concentration. She screamed as a centipede crawled over her arm. She shook it off, squealing again. The others laughed as she fought to regain her composure.

"That was *not* funny," Lottie shouted.

Sunni giggled again. "Oh, but it was. You should have seen yourself jumping around."

"Come on, Sunni," Wren scolded. "How many times have you had the same thing happen?"

"Okay, true. I'm sorry," Sunni apologized. "You'll get used to it."

Lottie shuddered. "I don't think I'll ever get used to that."

"Before the centipede attack, what did you think of your first grounding?" Wren asked.

"It was amazing. The peace I had was unlike anything I've felt before."

"I like to always keep something from nature with me, usually a piece of bark or a twig. Whenever I'm stressed or upset, I hold onto it and have a small, quiet moment to recharge."

"What a great idea."

"Let's head back to the house," Sunni suggested. "Lottie promised me I could have the first manicure."

"Yes, I did."

Around late afternoon, Lottie gathered her things and headed outside to Phil's car. She sighed as they drove up the hill to her house, wondering if she could pretend her life hadn't changed since she was last here.

"Are you okay?" Wren asked.

"Yes. I dread the boredom that lies ahead."

"I'm sure it won't be easy bottling up your magic around your parents, but you'll adjust—and we'll do this again soon. I'm glad you were able to come over. I had fun."

Lottie smiled. "Me, too. Thanks for everything and for allowing me to stay, Phil."

"Anytime, Lottie. Take care."

She shut the car door and went in through the kitchen. A wonderful scent greeted her.

"Hi, Mom. What's that yummy smell?"

"Potpie. It'll be ready in fifteen minutes. Why don't you go up and unpack your bag, then come back down for dinner. You can fill me in on your sleepover."

"Okay."

Lottie twisted the wand on her blinds, shutting out the view from outside. It was strange being home. It was still comforting, but she no longer felt like she belonged. Guilt swept over her. She loved her parents deeply, but returning to her old life was hard. She unpacked her bag, preoccupied with her thoughts. She missed Charles already. A deep longing for him ached inside her chest. Whenever he was with her, she felt this immense love that completed her, but now that they were apart, she felt adrift. She wanted to know more, feel more. She wanted to learn everything about him. Lottie shook off the thoughts and headed down for dinner.

~

"I'm going to go set up, Marie," Mathilda said, taking the weathered skeleton key from the mantel. "Please send everyone in when they arrive."

"Yes, ma'am."

Mathilda tucked the key in her pocket upon entering her keeping room. The darkened circular room brought to mind an old memory of an ancient forest floor. Letting the memory wink out, she inhaled the organic scents from the earthen-packed walls, the only room in the house not modernized to remind her of her girlhood. Plus, being surrounded by the very earth itself connected her more directly, allowing her to draw in more magic when needed. Iron brackets hung against the walls, and candles rested in them that sprang to life with a wave of her hand. She gathered her herbs and prepared the room while she waited.

Regina sauntered in with the others in tow. "What's going on?"

"I came to check on everything and discovered this," Mathilda said, lifting a jar of dirt. A thick haze of smoke circled inside the glass. "Someone has been trying to remove the protection spell over Lottie's house, and I plan to let them."

"You can't be serious," Ramona protested.

"I'm quite serious. I have a plan."

"Well, fill us in on this plan," Regina insisted.

"Just for tonight, I'll lower the spell. How do you feel about a little adventure, Phil?"

"I'm listening," he replied.

"I know you didn't see anything at Lottie's house last night, but I'd like you to head over there again. Use animal form, say an owl. I'll channel you when the spell has been lowered, and you see what comes through. Hopefully, we'll finally know who we're dealing with tonight."

"And what if something goes wrong?" Trina asked. "Are you willing to put Lottie in danger?"

"It won't," Phil assured.

"I hope you know what you're doing," Ramona chided.

"Oh, I do...." Mathilda said. "I do."

❧

LOTTIE REVIEWED HER BIOLOGY STUDY SHEET AND attempted an early start at bedtime. Stepping into the bathroom to brush her teeth, she felt for the light switch. The bulb was spared. Since coming of age, her bulb-blowing knack had stopped. She noticed her reflection in the mirror and flinched. She could swear her eyes looked brighter, her skin too, for that matter. Everything about her appearance was... enhanced.

Once settled in bed, Lottie fought off the weird feeling of being alone. She reached for her book as a distraction, but before she could open it, she heard Charles's voice in her head.

Are you awake?

Yes.

Good. I'm on my way to your house.

Okay. I'll watch for you.

An owl called from the trees outside the window. Its haunting sound soothed her. She stood, listening, but was jarred from the peaceful solitude by a loud clang near the garage. Rushing to the window, Lottie opened the curtains just as the owl swooped into the darkness in pursuit of prey. A cat screamed out just as the owl disappeared into the shadows. She spun around and rushed for her door.

Stay where you are. I'm almost there.

Charles, I heard a cat. What if it's the one that scratched me?

Don't leave your room, Lottie. I'm at your driveway now. I'll take a look around before coming up.

Lottie watched Charles disappear behind the garage. It was several minutes before he emerged from the shadows. She raised her window, and he rose effortlessly to her.

"I didn't see anything. I felt a lingering magic and followed it to the ridge, but it disappeared beyond there. Whoever it was is gone."

Lottie shivered, and Charles placed a kiss against her temple. "Let's go for a walk. The moon is beautiful."

She shot him a questioning glance as she took in the view of the dense clouds. "Um, can't see the moon."

"You doubt me?" He faced the window and made a swiping motion with his hand across the sky. The clouds pushed out of the way, revealing the glowing orb. "Like I said."

Lottie's mouth fell open. "I cannot believe you just did that."

The corners of his mouth lifted. "Get your coat. It's cold outside."

"Are you sure it's safe?"

"Yes. We aren't going far. I saw a bench swing by the side of your house."

Charles helped her into her coat and pulled the collar around her neck.

"Ready?" he asked.

"Yes."

He took her hand and led her to the open window. Together, they floated down to the ground below. Charles looked up with the intent of closing the window.

"Let me," Lottie said. She flicked her wrist. At her unspoken command, the window slid shut. "Awesome."

As they walked by the garage, the owl flew over their heads into the trees again.

"I heard that owl earlier. It swooped down, and that's when I heard the cat scream."

"Did you see the cat?" Charles asked.

"No."

"If you see it again, will you promise me you won't go out after it?"

His concerned look and protective nature were endearing to Lottie.

She bit back her smile as they walked around the house. "I promise. So, did you miss me, or is there another reason for your visit?" She flashed him a wicked grin.

"I missed you. I didn't get much time alone with you over the weekend, and I wanted to do this." His hand pressed against the small of her back, urging her closer, and then he kissed her.

Lottie met his gaze and saw something like a fire blazing right through to her soul. Everything stopped around them, and the only sounds she heard were their beating hearts and their breath, quick and uneven. The intensity was too much. Emotions exploding, Lottie flew into him. Her hands wound in his thick hair, and she deepened their kiss. Her lips moved to his jawline before savoring his mouth again.

Charles pulled back, conflicted, but then he grabbed her again and kissed her fiercely. He jerked away on a jagged breath. "We'd better stop."

She nodded breathlessly. He took her hand in his, and she noticed how the light reflected in his ring as they settled onto the swing.

"Do our rings do anything special?" Lottie asked, pushing the swing into motion.

"They block anyone from hearing our private conversations. You know how nosey Sunni can be. She wouldn't hesitate to get into our heads if she had a chance."

Lottie giggled. "True."

"How do you feel about not riding the bus anymore?" Charles asked.

"What do you mean? I have to ride the bus—too far to walk, you know."

He smiled at her sarcastic tone. "I thought I would start driving you to school if you'd like that."

"Since when do you drive?"

"I've had my license for a while. I felt the need to ride the bus, but now that we've gotten together, I'm ready to ditch the bus."

"I'd really like to ditch the bus." She paused, frowning. "I haven't told my parents about you. So much has been going on, and I didn't want to add more to their plate. They're super protective over me now, and after what happened, I don't want to put them over the edge again. Give me a little time, and I'll tell them."

"No rush. I'm happy wherever you are."

Shafts of silvery light through the trees cast long shadows around them.

"Isn't the moon so beautiful?" Lottie asked, gazing up.

Charles's eyes widened with surprise, and a smile crept over his face.

"What is it?" Lottie asked.

"Can I show you something?"

"Sure."

"Close your eyes," he said, taking her hands.

Lottie was caught off guard as the memory flooded her mind. She saw herself walking with Charles in another time, not much older than she was now. They stood on a path in a wooded area, gazing up at the moon. He turned toward her and brushed the back of his fingers along her cheek. "I love you, Lottie. I didn't realize until tonight, but I truly love you."

Charles let go of her hands, and the memory ended. She was speechless for a moment. "Wow...."

"Your reaction to the moon tonight must have triggered the memory, and I wanted to share it with you."

"It must have been our first lifetime together. What do you know about our lives before?"

He shrugged, seeming to mull over her question. "It's hard to explain. That day, when you summoned me in the cafeteria, it was like a floodgate opened in my mind. All these feelings rushed through at once, and all I could see was your face, hear your voice, smell your scent. At that moment, I felt alive like never before. It was like pouring life into a shell of a body. I knew we had always been together, but I couldn't just walk over to you and say, 'Hey, I'm your long-lost love; wanna run off into the sunset with me?' It was frustrating wanting to be with you but being unable to tell you everything."

"So that's what I saw on your face that day. You looked so shocked and confused. I was terrified. I had no idea what was going on."

"Yeah, I figured you were. I sent Wren to make sure you were okay. That was a big day for all of us."

"It's so weird knowing we have this intense past but not having access to all the memories."

"It is, but I'm enjoying getting to know you and making new memories."

Lottie smiled. "That's a very nice way to put it."

The owl's hoots greeted them as they came back around the house. Lottie searched the bare branches. "It's still here. I'm glad."

"Good. This one seems to like your tree."

She opened the window, and they lifted to her room. "I enjoyed the walk."

"Me, too." His eyes held hers. Not a word was spoken between them. Lottie's heart felt so full of love for him that she thought she might cry.

"I love you, Charles. At times, it's like I can't breathe because of it. I've tried to make it slow down, but I can't help myself anymore."

As he pulled her close and held her, a warmth spread through Lottie's whole body. Charles tilted her chin toward him and kissed her. It was soft and intense, like an all-consuming love. His thumbs gently brushed the column of her neck as he gazed at her. "You're so beautiful."

His lips were on hers again. She didn't want it to end.

Lottie heard her father's coughs and froze. "You'd better go before he wakes himself," she reluctantly said.

Charles kissed her head and slipped quietly out the window into the night.

～

PHIL WAITED UNTIL CHARLES WAS OUT OF SIGHT FROM Lottie's window before he changed himself out of owl form. Charles quickly turned at the sound.

"Phil? What are you doing here?"

"I could ask you the same thing."

The awkward silence loomed for a moment.

"Listen, the coven lowered Lottie's protection spell tonight. That's why I'm here. I was waiting to see who came through, or in this case, what. They used the form of a cat. Your arrival distracted me, and whoever it was got away."

"Wait, you all *allowed* Lottie's protection spell to lower? You put her at risk?"

"Charles, I know you think it was reckless, but we know what we're doing. Why don't you get back home and let your mother explain the details."

Charles's jaw clenched. "Fine." He stalked toward the edge of the driveway and turned back. "Phil?"

"Yes?"

"Sorry, I screwed up the plan."

"Don't sweat it. We'll get our villain. We always do. Goodnight, Charles."

Phil ran a final perimeter check and touched his fingers to his pendant, turning his mind to Mathilda.

Raise the spell again.

What happened?

Things got a little interesting. The 'cat' showed up again. I almost had it, but it slipped out of my grip. I was distracted by Charles's unexpected visit. It escaped through the woods before I could see it shift out of form.

Is Charles still there?

No. I waited until he left and checked the place over—no sign of anything.

I doubt our shifter will attempt to come back anytime soon after this. The spell is up again. Thanks for your help in this, Phil.

Not a problem.

He glanced back at Lottie's house once more before vanishing into the darkness.

~

"WELL?" RAMONA ASKED, HER EYES INTENT ON MATHILDA.

"Charlotte is okay. But someone did come to the house. They used the form of a cat again, so Phil didn't get to see who it was."

"So, he didn't get the cat?" Isobel asked.

"No. As Phil made his move, he was interrupted by Charles's unexpected visit to Charlotte. He got distracted, and the cat ran off before transforming back to human form."

"Oh, dear," Ramona said.

"Since the plan was foiled, Ramona, I'd like you to call on Shelly tomorrow. I want her to thoroughly search her system for any witches used to aid the Investigators in the last year. Find out if there were issues with any of them or if she simply had a bad vibe from one. I also want to know if they are powerful enough for what we're dealing with."

"I can do that," Ramona said.

"Let's call it a night. I don't think our shifter will try anything else for now."

~

MATTHEW PACED AROUND HIS OFFICE, WAITING FOR SELENE, his fingers clenched tightly around Shelly's notebook. She had finally put the pieces together. With trembling fingers, he flipped the pages to her latest entry and placed the notebook on his desk. The truth, written in red ink. *Selene—the dark witch.* He had kept a close watch on Shelly the past two days. He knew Selene would want every detail, and the thought of anything missed was too horrible to contemplate. His heart lurched at the sound of the door. He took a deep breath and braced himself.

"Well, Matthew," Selene said, strolling over to the desk. "What did you find out about the witch, Shelly?"

"Mistress, you're bleeding."

She waved the comment away. "Just an unexpected incident. I'm fine. What did you learn from Shelly?"

"She knows it's you. She's planning to tell the committee tomorrow that you are the dark witch they've sensed. I followed her. She communes with the dead witch, Eliza Duprey. Her grave is on the outskirts of town. Shelly is going there tonight."

"Good. I know the place. We should be there within the hour if we hurry."

~

THE SCENT OF SAGE AND SMOKE LINGERED IN THE AIR OVER Shelly as she sat cross-legged in the middle of a thick salt circle. With each incantation, the candles surrounding her flickered as more and more energy was channeled into her.

"Oh, this is perfect," Selene commented as she watched. "I can get two birds with one stone."

"What do you mean, Mistress?"

"This is the gravesite of one of the most powerful dark witches this area has ever seen—well, since me, that is. Shelly must be drawing from her power to enhance her own. That explains how she discovered me. Nice going, Matthew. I couldn't have planned this better if I had set it up myself."

"Thank you."

"You keep watch while I do what I do best."

She left Matthew in the cover of the woods and made her way to the tomb.

"Well, well, well, what do we have here?"

Shelly broke her trance. "Ms. Sullivan? What are you doing way out here?"

"Looking for you. I'm afraid you have something I need."

Shelly quickly muttered a protection spell.

Selene barked a laugh. "You're wasting your time and effort," she said, coming closer.

"You can't get through my circle," Shelly said defiantly.

A contemptuous smile twisted Selene's lips. "Don't be so sure of yourself, my dear. *I* am the All-Powerful One. You should know this by now. No one...not you...and certainly not some dead witch will keep me from getting what I want." She waved her hand, scattering the salt and breaking the circle.

Shelly's eyes widened. "How did you...what do you want?"

Selene's smile deepened. "Your power, of course."

Shelly scrambled away, clawing, desperate to get to her feet, but she only made it past the front of the tomb before a powerful force inched her back, dragging the tops of her feet along the sharp rocks. She let out a cry of pain, feeling the warmth of her blood seep from the gashes. The force deposited her mere inches from Selene. A single tear escaped from the corner of Shelly's eye as she realized her fate.

Selene's smile broadened at her terror. She held out her hands.

Shelly tried to resist as her power streaked like a blur into Selene's body. She slumped over as the last of it was drawn out.

Selene peered down at her. "I thank you for your gift, but I'm afraid I will need a lot more." She made a twisting motion with her hand, breaking Shelly's neck at once, then knelt and touched the ground. "Did you know there are secrets in the earth, Matthew? Not that you'll ever be strong enough to learn them for yourself." She closed her eyes. "Just as I suspected, a protection spell over this tomb prevents me from entering. It seems Ms. Duprey was dabbling in the dark arts and was killed because of it. Guess who had a hand in that? No matter. Ms. Duprey claimed she would rise again. She was right."

Selene stood and raised her arms toward the sky. She drew a streak of lightning into her hands and flung it down to the tomb's entrance, exploding the stone doors open. Her voice, unnatural and otherworldly, boomed, splitting the silence: "Eliza Duprey, come forth."

The air turned foul, like sulfur and fetid earth. Matthew looked on in horror at the creature that came crawling up the stone steps. The woman Selene called out had long been dead. Her burial gown was in tatters and hung from her remains. She wore a black, faded veil over her head, but he could still see the dark hollows of what used to be her eyes. The gurgling, raspy sounds she made as she climbed closer to the top made him cringe. He turned his face away.

"Stop," Selene commanded. "There's no need for you to come any closer."

She began to pull the power from Eliza Duprey, the same as she took Shelly's. Horrible screeching sounds came from Eliza as her magic streaked into Selene. As she took the last of it, Eliza turned to dust and scattered into the wind.

"That's more like it," Selene remarked. "Not as strong as I'd hoped, but better than any I've taken recently. Matthew, fetch the dead witch and throw her down into the tomb."

An ominous presence shadowed Selene. Her face seemed altered somehow, more frightening, and he dared not go against her. He grabbed Shelly underneath her arms and pulled her over to the edge of the tomb's steps. He hesitated, considering what Selene had ordered him to do.

"Oh, for God's sake, Matthew." Selene put her foot on Shelly's back and shoved her down. "Now, to erase this."

She swiped her hand across the opening of the tomb. The broken bits of stone gathered up, piece by piece, until the door was again intact.

Selene's lips twisted into a sneer. "There. Tomorrow, I'll see you take Shelly's place as the lead investigator at the Paranormal Investigators."

Matthew shuddered. "Thank you, Mistress."

Chapter Nine

Monday morning came with a clear sky and the promise of a sunny day. Lottie stepped onto the bus and found the seat she now shared with Charles. She gazed at the orange and pink-streaked sky and thought about the weekend. It all seemed too good to be true. She recalled how she felt lighting the candelabras, the excitement before her magic had gotten out of control. The energy that flowed when her magic was released was similar to the many lightbulbs she had blown. Her hands tingled at the thought. Lottie shook them and rubbed them against her thighs. She needed Mathilda's help to learn how to use her powers or, more importantly, control them.

The driver pulled over at The Quick Stop and opened the door. Christy stepped on and smiled at Lottie before sitting down.

Lottie moved up to the seat behind her. "Hey. I thought you were riding with Gwen and Abbey now?"

"Gwen said she was giving Jake Putnam a ride this morning and that it would make her late if she picked me up, too."

"Wait—what? Why would she give Jake a ride? She doesn't even like him."

"Gwen and I went to the mall this weekend and ran into him. He started talking to us, and apparently, Gwen is into him now."

Lottie shook her head in disbelief. "What is going on with her? She's acting completely crazy these days."

Christy shrugged. "I wouldn't know. She seems normal, but I've just gotten to know her."

"Trust me— this is not normal for Gwen. Or Abbey, either, for that matter."

Christy gave her a look that said she didn't know what else to say, and Lottie returned to her seat. Something wasn't right, but what?

～

"YOU'RE QUIET THIS MORNING," CHARLES REMARKED AS they headed towards their lockers. "Anything wrong?"

"I don't know," Lottie answered with a sigh. She filled him in on what Christy had told her.

"I'm sure she's fine. We'd better get to class," Charles said as the bell rang. He pecked a kiss on her cheek. "See you at lunch."

Lottie's mind wandered during Biology. Her intuition was screaming that something was going on regarding Gwen. The odd vibes Lottie sensed were strong.

"Ms. Jacobs, would you like to pay attention?" Mr. Spencer asked in his usual sarcastic tone.

Lottie cringed. "Sorry."

Why that man decided to be a teacher was beyond her reasoning. He clearly hated it. It would be too easy for her to cause his chair to roll back as he sat, but that wouldn't be right. As soon as the thought passed, Lottie watched in horror at the scene unfolding before her.

Mr. Spencer turned toward the whiteboard; he seemed to lose his footing. *Did his chair just move?* She was sure she saw it move. A loud crack sounded as he staggered and fell into an awkward position. His screams of agony prompted the students to erupt.

"Oh, my God!" someone shouted.

Lottie's mind reeled. Did she cause the accident to happen? She would have known it—would have felt it. No, she couldn't have. Someone called out for help. Principal Andrews and several teachers rushed in to see what was happening.

"Call an ambulance," Principal Andrews said to another teacher.

Lottie realized someone was calling her name.

"Lottie? Are you okay?"

Christy eyed her with an odd expression as she waited for a response.

"Y-yeah, I'm okay." Was that her voice replying? It sounded strange.

"Did anyone see what happened?" the principal asked.

Lottie felt Christy's penetrating stare. Paranoia gripped her.

Christy turned around. "I don't know," she answered. "He turned to write something on the board and fell over his chair."

"Quiet!" someone shouted over the noise.

Lottie's mind swirled amidst the chaos. The paramedics rolled the stretcher alongside Mr. Spencer and carefully loaded him on top before pushing him out the door.

"Class, calm down," Principal Andrews urged. "I will remain with you for the remainder of the period. You may read or talk quietly until the bell rings."

Lottie pulled out a book and pretended to read to avoid having to talk to anyone.

By the time lunch arrived, Lottie felt as if she would burst with anxiety. She sped off to the cafeteria and sat beside Charles with a heavy sigh.

"What the heck happened to Mr. Spencer?" Sunni asked. "We heard he broke his leg."

"You heard right," Lottie replied. "I have something to tell you all, so lean in." She looked nervously around the room, ensuring no one was listening in. "Before Mr. Spencer's accident, he made me really mad. I had a moment where I wanted to roll his chair back so he would fall, but I swear I didn't do it, or did I? God, I'm so confused."

Charles put his hand over her shoulder. "Calm down. You would have known had you caused it. It was an accident."

"Are you sure?"

"Yes. You'll find out once you start practicing magic. You can feel its energy release from your body."

The others nodded in agreement.

Lottie let out a pent-up breath. "Thank God. I've been sick all morning thinking I caused it."

"Girl, you need to get some lessons in with Mathilda," Rowen suggested. "Why haven't you started yet?"

"It's my mom. I'm afraid it will upset her if I ask to spend time with Mathilda."

Wren gave a sympathetic smile. "You should ask her, Lottie. Look at you. You're a wreck."

"I know, you're right. I'll do it tonight."

"How do you guys feel about switching tables?" Sunni asked. "It's a bit too crowded here to have the type of conversations we do."

"You think?" Charles remarked.

"How about by the window in the corner, then?"

Rowen let out a snort. "Dude, you know Harvey Mitchem—that mega jerk and his crew won't willingly give up their table without a fight."

"Who cares?" Sunni scoffed. "It's not like I can't handle Harvey."

Lottie pictured Harvey as she followed the others over to the table. He was one of the more obnoxious football team members and had a reputation for getting what he wanted, no matter who it caused a problem for. He was not going to appreciate them taking over his table.

Sunni pulled out a chair and flashed a smile to the others. "We've staked our claim."

Rowen looked outside. "Nice choice."

"I'm willing to fiercely defend my territory, too," Sunni joked.

Charles cleared his throat. "Well, brace yourself because it looks like you're about to have to."

"This is our table," a voice behind her said.

The corners of Sunni's upturned eyes pinched. She plastered a serene smile on her face before turning.

Harvey wore a menacing scowl. He stepped closer to her. "I said, you're at our table. Move. Now."

Sunni's smile broadened. "I'll tell you what you're going to do, boys. You're going to decide you want another table. You're going to go over to that table by the door right now, and you're going to sit down. But before you go, you're going to apologize."

Lottie widened her eyes toward Charles. *Is she insane?*

Just watch.

Harvey took a step back. "I'm sorry. I made a mistake. We're going to sit by the door."

The group turned and obediently walked away.

Lottie stared in disbelief. "Sunni, that was awesome. What did you do?"

"Mind control," she casually said. "Those meatheads were easy prey."

"Do they know what happened?"

"Nah, I made them think it was their choice. Typical men."

Charles shook his head.

DESPITE THE BUMPY START TO THE DAY, LOTTIE WAS IN HIGH spirits when the bus dropped her off at home. Having mentally rehearsed her speech about wanting to visit Mathilda, she took a deep breath as her mother stepped through the door.

"Hi, Mom."

Her mother responded, placing a tulip and hyacinth arrangement in the center of the kitchen table.

Lottie leaned over to smell the hyacinths. "Mom, can I talk to you about something?"

"Sure, honey. What is it?"

"Would you and Dad be open to letting me spend time with Mathilda?"

Her mother's back stiffened, but she didn't seem upset.

"I wanted to ask sooner but feared it would upset you. I...need some advice on magic. How to control it and keep it hidden, to be specific."

Lottie saw the conflict in her mother's eyes and prepared for an argument. She was surprised when it didn't come.

"I can see how learning to control your magic is important. I suppose you'll want to go to Mathilda's house to...well, practice."

"That would be best, yes," Lottie said. She would be glad when the awkwardness of talking to her mother about magic was over.

"Okay, then. Let me know when you want to go—and Lottie, you can always talk to me about your magic. I won't be upset."

The tension went out of Lottie's shoulders. "Look at us, treading unknown territory like pros."

Her mother grinned. "If I am to get over my fears, I must understand them, right?"

"I guess so," Lottie said. She wrapped her arms around her mother. "Thanks, Mom."

"You sure have been wearing that smile a lot lately. What's got you beaming these days?"

Lottie tucked a section of hair behind her ear, averting her mother's gaze. "Well, there's a boy at school that I like—a lot, actually. We've been talking for some time now, and I think he feels the same about me."

"Wow. Way to throw everything at me all at once," her mother teased. "Who is this wonderful boy who captured my daughter's heart?"

"His name is Charles Lachlan. He rides the bus with me."

"So, when do I get to meet him?"

"How about after school tomorrow? He's driving now and wants to take me to school and back if that's okay."

"How about I meet him first, and we'll go from there."

"Deal."

A THICK FOG HUNG OVER THE FIELD SURROUNDING THE crypt. As the dawn gained strength, dense clumps slowly began to lift, floating away like reluctant ghosts. The old mausoleum, with its cracked pillars and mossy steps, cast an ominous shadow despite the sun. Mathilda gazed thoughtfully at the apotropaic marks in the doors. She touched her fingers to the daisy wheel carved superstitiously to ward off evil as she recalled the disturbance she had felt about this tomb. She reached for her phone and pressed it to her ear after dialing.

"Good morning," Ramona answered. "I was just about to call you. Have you been sensing anything odd?"

"Yes. I sensed something was off Sunday night. Then, in meditation this morning, I felt a strong urge to visit Eliza Duprey's tomb. I'm here now, in fact. When I first arrived, it felt like the protection spell was somehow tampered with, but it is still in place; however, something doesn't sit well."

"No," Ramona agreed. "I've been seeing Shelly's face in my mind since last night. I spoke to Regina this morning. She and I will head over to the Paranormal Investigator's office to see if she's turned up anything that may be of value to us."

"Good. Keep me posted, then."

LOTTIE WAS DRESSED AND WENT DOWNSTAIRS BEFORE HER parents. She smiled as the swinging door pushed open to reveal her father.

"Hi, Dad."

"Hi."

He shuffled over to the coffee pot. "You're awake early this morning."

"I wanted to talk to you before I head out." She took her bowl to the sink and rinsed it out. "Hey, thanks for agreeing to let me see Mathilda."

"You're welcome. We just want you safe and happy."

"I am Dad. Life is pretty good for me right now."

"Yeah, your mom mentioned something last night about a boy."

"Charles. That's what I wanted to talk to you about. He's planning to come by after school today. What time do you think you'll be home? I'd like you to meet him."

"I'll be home after lunch today unless I get a call."

Lottie nodded. Hopefully, it wouldn't be too weird later.

RAMONA PULLED UP IN FRONT OF THE PARANORMAL Investigators Office and led Regina inside. A heavyset woman with dull shoulder-length brown hair sat behind a desk with a telephone wedged between her ear and shoulder. She smiled and mouthed 'just a minute' as she vigorously took down some notes.

Regina settled awkwardly down on a metal folding chair alongside Ramona and glanced around the room.

Wood paneling came up about mid-way on the walls, and a banged-up trim piece separated it from the worn-white paint along the upper half of the room. A potted plant with stringy vines trailed over the gray filing cabinets along the back wall. She noticed a door half-opened to a small room filled with what she determined to be ghost-hunting equipment.

"Do you think that crap works?" Regina whispered.

"Who knows?" Ramona replied, following her gaze.

"Crotchety old fart," The receptionist muttered as she slammed the phone back on the base. She plastered on a smile as Ramona glanced her way. "I'm so sorry, ladies. How can I help you?"

Ramona stood and walked over to the desk. "Good morning. I'd like to see Shelly White."

"I'm sorry, but Shelly isn't here. Would you like to leave a message for her?"

"My name is Ramona Lachlan; I'm a friend of hers."

"Oh, Ms. Lachlan, Shelly has mentioned you. Look, I don't want to alarm you, but no one has heard from Shelly since Sunday. She said she had found something relevant to a case we've been working on. She planned to talk to a few of us first thing Monday morning but never showed up. We all agreed that if she didn't return today, we would notify the police. I don't suppose you've spoken to her?"

Everything that Shelly had told Ramona was in confidence. She wasn't about to betray that now.

"What is your name?" Ramona asked, diverting the conversation.

"I'm sorry," the woman said, shaking her head. "I'm Nancy Withers. I run the office here. I've been scatterbrained since Shelly's absence. As you know, we rely on her talents, and things have gotten a bit backed up without her."

Ramona nodded. "I understand. Who have you called in to assist in the meantime?"

"We didn't have to call anyone," Nancy said. "One of our donors has 'loaned' us her medium. He's trying to learn the ropes of what Shelly does around here. I'm afraid we've thrown a lot at him."

Ramona feigned surprise. "Is that so? Who is this man?"

"His name is Matthew Alcott. He's in the back if you'd like to meet him."

"Indeed, I would."

"One moment, I'll go find him."

"I don't like what I'm sensing here," Regina whispered.

"Neither do I," Ramona agreed.

"Shh. Here he comes."

Matthew gave a warm smile as he approached. "Good morning. What can I do for you, ladies?"

Ramona reached her hand out to him. He briefly hesitated but shook it.

"Matthew Alcott, at your service."

Upon reading him during their handshake, Ramona noticed his overly nervous state. She gave a slight smile. "Ramona Lachlan. Is there somewhere private we can talk?"

"Certainly, my office is this way."

Matthew picked up a stack of files from the chair. "My apologies for the mess. I've gotten a little behind."

He dropped some of the files as his nerves escalated. "I'm sorry. I'm a bit exhausted and not at my best today." He bent down to pick up the papers.

"Wouldn't it be easier if you used magic?"

He froze, feigning a look of confusion.

"I know what you are," Ramona acknowledged. She swiped her hand, and the scattered papers slid neatly back into the files. "We witches must stick together, wouldn't you agree?"

He laughed nervously.

"Relax, Matthew. I only want to ask you some questions."

He sat down behind the desk. "Sure."

"How well do you know Shelly White?"

"Not very well at all, I'm afraid. I'm new to the area."

"What brought you here, if you don't mind my asking?"

"I was a teacher in Defiance before I moved here. I started getting these odd vibes from Munroe Falls. I felt I could be useful here, so I handed in my notice, packed my bags, and made the drive. I do some side work as a medium for a non-magical woman; Ms. Sullivan is her name. She bases her life around the cosmic rules. Ms. Sullivan hired me to guide her in making decisions. She also happens to be a donor to the Paranormal Investigators, although she wishes to remain anonymous if you don't mind keeping that under wraps. The woman is obsessed with all things magical, and she likes to assist them in obtaining the most up-to-date equipment so that she can be a part of their work."

"So, her wallet helped get you in," Ramona stated.

"Don't judge me too harshly for bending the rules. I've waited my whole life to do something good with my magic. I've had to hide it for so long, and Ms. Sullivan gave me a way to be useful."

"I understand. Maybe you can be useful to me. You have access to Shelly's files, I presume?"

"I do have a lot of her files here to go through. What would you like me to do?"

"See if she was working on anything before her disappearance—anything to help us find her."

"I'd be happy to help find Shelly. Her files might hold what we need to locate her."

Ramona nodded. "For now, why don't you convince the rest of the office not to report her absence? If the public were to discover that witchcraft is behind the good this office provides...."

"Say no more. I'll do what I can."

"Very good. Regarding Shelly, I will let you know if I find anything."

"I would appreciate it." Matthew rolled his chair back and stood. "Please excuse me," he said, noticing the clock. "I have somewhere I need to be."

"Of course. Good day, Mr. Alcott."

Ramona studied Matthew as he walked out ahead of her. Nothing he said earlier contradicted what she read in his mind. Yet, something about him seemed wrong.

~

"MORNING, BEAUTIFUL," CHARLES GREETED.

Lottie beamed. "Good morning to you."

He reached for her hand as the bus accelerated. "Are we still on for later?"

"Yes. I reminded my parents this morning."

"Good."

"Are you nervous?" she asked.

"No, I'm looking forward to it. I'm glad your parents know about us. Maybe they'll let me drive you now or, better yet, take you out on an official date."

"That would be nice."

Lottie's attention was diverted out the window as a flock of birds burst into a flurry of motion, startled by the bus's screeching brakes. She watched them disappear into the hazy morning mist.

"That's my mother's car at the Paranormal Investigators office."

She followed Charles's gaze through the opposite windows. "Do you think something bad has happened?"

His brows drew in. "I don't know. I'll message my mom to fill me in when she can."

Lottie stepped off the bus and hurried through the mesh of students toward her locker. She smiled at Bryan Michaels on her way down the aisle.

"Hey, Lottie?"

She paused, hearing his questioning tone. "Yeah?"

"What's up with your friend Wren? Is she seeing anybody?"

Lottie tried to hide her surprise as she could tell he was uncomfortable asking. She put him out of his misery. "Nope."

He smiled. "Thanks."

Lottie wondered if Wren would mind that she had just given out the status of her love life. Shrugging out of her jacket, she hung it in her locker, then headed up to biology.

She noticed the whiteboard the moment she stepped into the room. Typically cluttered with Mr. Spencer's notes, today it gleamed white with only one thing written in big, tidy letters: Mr. Lawson.

A cheerful-looking man entered the room as Lottie got settled into her desk.

"Good morning, class. My name is Mr. Lawson. I'll be your new biology teacher for the remainder of the year."

Chatter broke out across the room.

"How's Mr. Spencer?" someone asked.

"Recovering. That's all I was told. Please take out your books. Today, we'll be starting DNA and RNA."

Lottie didn't know whether to be happy about the much-improved classroom atmosphere or feel bad that Mr. Spencer was hurt.

After biology, she found Wren standing outside the classroom door, arms folded and wearing a scowl. *Uh-oh.*

"Well?" Wren asked.

"What do you mean?" Lottie said innocently.

"I've sensed it all morning. You've got something on your mind that has to do with me."

Lottie slid back into an alcove by a water fountain. "Okay, don't get mad. Bryan Michaels asked if you were seeing anyone, and I might have said no. Was that okay?"

Wren's expression was guarded. She glanced at the fountain, pressing a slender finger on the button. "He did? Hmmm. Did he say anything else?"

"No, so was it okay that I told him you weren't seeing anyone, or...?"

Wren's gaze remained fixed on the fountain. She repeatedly pressed the button, unaware of her actions. "What did he say when you said no?"

Lottie watched the arc of water come up and over, up and over.

"He said okay. So, are you cool with me saying no?"

"How was his reaction?"

"Wren, focus," Lottie said, giving two sharp snaps from her fingers.

"Oh, sorry. I don't mind."

Lottie laughed. She had never seen Wren this flustered.

"Bryan was nervous when he asked. He visibly relaxed and smiled when I said you weren't seeing anyone. I saw the dimple. Now, is that enough detail?"

Wren grinned and patted Lottie's cheek. "Yep. Good job."

"I take it you like him?"

Wren shrugged. "He's cute. I had fun at the movies with him. I think he'll do."

~

AFTER SCHOOL, LOTTIE RUSHED THROUGH HER HOMEWORK and straightened up while waiting on Charles. The reverberating buzz of her father's new saw echoed from the garage below. She glanced at the clock. Four-twenty. Charles was coming at five to meet her parents. After that, thanks to some outright begging on her part, they would grab some pizza. She swiped on some lip gloss and went downstairs to watch for him.

"Are you excited," her mother asked.

"Yes. I've never been on an official date before. I'm not going to have to watch Dad tackle Charles as we try to leave, am I?"

"Now, Lottie, I think your father can handle meeting a boy. You've been through a lot recently, and you've handled everything quite responsibly. You're growing up whether we like it or not."

"Yes, I am."

The saw buzzed again, drawing her mother's attention out the kitchen window. She sighed.

"I'd better get your father. I bet he's lost track of time playing with his toys."

Charles promptly pulled up at the house at five in a black BMW coupe. Lottie walked outside to meet him.

"Wow, I can't believe you rode the bus all this time when you could have been driving this."

He smiled and kissed her cheek. "I prefer you any day."

She led him around to the kitchen door, noticing how he seemed so relaxed. His eyes were lively, his smile infectious. She swept through the entry, and he followed her in.

"Mom, this is Charles Lachlan."

Her mother beamed, and Lottie sensed the instant liking.

"Hi, Charles. I'm Carol. It's very nice to meet you."

"Nice to meet you too, Mrs. Jacobs."

The kitchen door opened, and Lottie's father came in, wiping his hands on an old towel. He glanced apologetically at her mother, who gave him a scolding look.

"Hi, Charles. Randy Jacobs."

Charles reached out for a handshake. "Nice to meet you, sir."

"So, you guys are going out for pizza?" Lottie's mother asked.

"If that's okay with the both of you," Charles replied.

"That's a nice car you have," her father interrupted. "How long have you been driving it?"

"Thank you. My mom got it for my birthday in December."

Realizing her dad was trying to assess if Charles was a responsible driver, Lottie gave her mom a pleading look.

"Randy, why don't we let the kids get going on their date."

Lottie met her father's glance with raised eyebrows. He turned to Charles. "You two, be safe and have fun."

"Thank you. I'll have Lottie home by nine."

Her mother's smile got even bigger. *Good grief.*

Charles opened the door for Lottie. She got in and put her seat belt on. It felt strange leaving with him as her parents stood by watching.

"That went well. Don't you think?" Charles asked.

"Yes, oddly enough, it did. My parents have eased up a bit. I think they feel bad for waiting so long to tell me I was adopted."

He reached for her hand, pulling it to his lips as they drove away from the house.

Charles turned onto South Main Street and into the Munroe Falls Plaza parking area. Gionino's Pizzeria shared a building between Subway and Hair and Nails by Jenny. The parking lot was crowded with parents trying to round up their children from an obvious after-soccer-game dinner. Lottie noticed the grass stains on the shorts of several boys.

She squeezed out her door, careful not to hit the minivan beside her. As she went around the back of the van, one of the boys ran out into the road, not paying attention.

The noise that caught her attention afterward sent a chill through her. A truck speeding from Munroe Falls Avenue ran a red light and screeched onto South Main straight into the boy's path. Panic struck Lottie's heart. Without thinking, she stretched out her hand and screamed, "Stop!"

Time froze as the truck abruptly stopped to her will. The boy hovered nearly a foot off the ground, his legs mid-stride and eyes wide with terror. The silence of the place was deafening. Lottie struggled to breathe, fighting against the hysteria that squeezed her lungs. The sheer panic on Charles's face made her grasp the magnitude of what she had just done. People gaped at her in horror, and Lottie felt their fear as it was palpable. She'd shown her magic in front of them.

Oh, God! Do something.

Charles was holding onto his pendant. His lips moved, but his words never reached her ears. Rooted in fear, Lottie remained where she was, watching him. Before she could blink, the boy was gone, and the truck had vanished. Parents gathered their children, totally oblivious to her. Suddenly, one of the boys ran out into the road, not paying attention. Charles rushed over, grabbed and returned him to the parking lot.

Lottie heard a loud motor coming their way. A truck sped from Munroe Falls Avenue, ran the red light, and turned onto South Main Street. It was the same truck. Her mind reeled. Seeing her confusion, Charles grabbed her hand and led her back into the car.

"I—I don't understand...the truck, I saw it almost hit that boy. What's going on?"

"I turned back time a few minutes. Lottie, you have to be careful. People would never understand what happened just now. You have to control your emotions and be discreet with your magic. Spend some time with Mathilda. She can help you. She can help you control it."

Lottie wiped the tears spilling from her eyes. "I'm sorry. I saw that little boy, so small and helpless. I just reacted."

Charles pulled her close. "I know. Come here. You have such a big heart. You're capable of great things. Once you get help with your magic, you can control anything, and the rest of the world will never know."

Lottie nodded against his chest, replaying the scene in her mind. "Time reversal," she said thoughtfully. "I didn't think that was possible. How did you do it?"

Charles hesitated. "You know how when you reach into your mind, to the place where you sense your magic," he said, touching Lottie's forehead between her eyes. "Well, I went beyond that. I delved into the blackness beyond the void where our magic lingers. My mom once told me dark magic resides in the void, but I didn't think of that when I went there and envisioned time reversing. I wasn't sure if it would work," he admitted. "And I don't think I'll try again. It was a chaotic form of magic."

His eyes held an uneasy, faraway glaze that snapped to the present when Lottie squeezed his hand. He smiled warmly at her. "You ready for dinner?"

"Yes. Thank you. I don't know what I would have done if you hadn't been here."

"Don't think about it anymore, okay? Let's enjoy our date."

THE PORCH LIGHT WAS ON WHEN THEY PULLED UP AT THE house. Lottie guessed her parents were spying from somewhere inside.

"I'll walk you to the door," Charles offered.

"Thank you for everything. I had a fun night, despite the rough start."

"I did, too. I'll pick you up in the morning unless I hear otherwise."

"Sounds good."

She hung her coat on the wall peg and entered the living room. Her parents sat on the couch, sitting in their usual spots, watching TV.

"Hi, honey. How was your date?" her mother asked.

"Good. What did you think of Charles?"

"I like him very much. He was very respectful."

"He shook my hand," her father added. "He has my approval."

Lottie smiled brightly. "I'm glad you like him. Oh, I picked up some cupcakes on the way home."

"You wonderful girl," her mother said, eyeing the box greedily.

"So, can Charles drive me to school tomorrow?"

Her mother's smile twisted into a feigned scowl. "Randy, we have a devious daughter. Bribing us with cupcakes...."

"He can drive her to the moon if there's a lemon cupcake in that box," her father quipped.

"Of course there is. I know how you love lemon, but I'm not bribing you."

"I'm joking," her mother assured. "I think it will be okay for Charles to drive you. Will he be driving you home as well?"

"Yes."

"Okay. Want to watch *Criminal Minds* with us?"

"You go ahead. I think I'll go up and polish my nails."

Lottie thought about her incident with the truck as she struggled with shaking hands to put on the topcoat. She picked up the phone and dialed the number, trying not to smudge her polish.

"Longhurst residence," Marie answered.

"Hello, Marie. It's Lottie. Is Mathilda busy?'"

"She just finished her bath. One moment."

Lottie blew on her nails while she waited.

"Charlotte, how are you, dear?" Mathilda's honeyed voice asked.

"Not so great. I need to see you. I did something terrible tonight in front of a lot of people. She proceeded to tell Mathilda about what happened with the boy.

"Oh, Charlotte, I'm sorry. Thank goodness Charles was with you. Would you like to come over on Saturday morning for breakfast? We can spend the day together."

"I'd love to, but I don't know how long my parents will let me stay."

"We'll work with whatever time we have. How does that sound?"

"Good. Thank you, Mathilda. I'm looking forward to it."

Lottie hung up the phone and checked her nails. She was safe to get into bed. She flipped the TV on to *The Originals* and settled into her covers. There was a knock at her door.

"It's open."

"I just wanted to say good night," her mother said, stepping into the room. A scream from the television caught her attention. "Oh, honey. That's just brutal. I don't like you watching that stuff. You know you get nightmares."

"It's just a show, Mom. Besides, I haven't been having nightmares lately."

Her mother's face went into a sort of blank contemplation. "You haven't, have you? I didn't even realize."

"I guess Dr. Williams was right about me growing out of them. Speaking of Dr. Williams, I don't think I need to go to therapy now, Mom."

"Why do you say that?"

"Well, ever since my birthday, I've felt better. The nightmares are gone, and I no longer feel like I have anything bottled up. I think it's because my magic was released, but I can't very well tell Dr. Williams that."

"No. No, you can't. Let's keep the next two appointments to ensure you're okay dealing with your magic, and if so, then we'll figure out how to phase out."

"Thanks, Mom."

Chapter Ten

"A re you ready for day one of ditching the bus?" Charles asked when Lottie got into his car.

"I'm *so* ready."

A few vehicles trickled into the parking lot after they arrived. Several students got out and sat on the hoods of their cars, chatting across from each other. Charles nodded to some guys a few spaces down.

"This is like some cool little hangout spot, isn't it?" Lottie remarked.

"It's interesting."

Lottie jumped when a silver car pulled into the space beside them, horn blaring. The window rolled down, and she smiled.

"Charles Lachlan," Wren said, lowering her sunglasses as if verifying what she saw behind the lenses.

"Look at you, driving again," Rowen called out from the passenger seat of Wren's car. "It's about time."

"Good morning, Wren, Rowen," Charles replied, ignoring the sarcasm.

A big, black truck rumbled into the parking lot, drowning out their conversation. Lottie couldn't see who it was through the tinted windows, but it was apparent that Rowen knew, given her smirk. "There you go, Wren. Look who just got here."

Wren shot Rowen a defensive scowl. "Would you shut up, please?"

The door opened, and Bryan Michaels stepped out. His shirt fit snugly across his arms, showing off thick muscles that flexed when he moved to grab his backpack. He tossed his head, sending a soft curl of his long brown hair away from his face. Lottie noticed the way he carried himself. His walk reminded her of a prowl, and confidence exuded from him. No wonder Wren was nervous around him.

"Charles, what's up, man?" Bryan greeted. "Rocking the BMW again?"

"You know it."

He slapped Charles's hand as they exchanged bro words.

Wren leaned in close to Lottie's ear. "God, he gets more gorgeous every time I see him."

"Has he talked to you since he asked me about you?"

"No."

"Well, go say something to him."

"I can't."

Rowen rolled her eyes. "Oh, good God, Wren."

"Hello, ladies," Bryan greeted. His eyes lingered on Wren before he turned to go inside.

Charles raised an eyebrow. "Oookay."

"You shut up, too," Wren scolded. She flung her backpack over her shoulder and stalked across the parking lot.

"What was that about?" Charles asked.

"Wren likes Bryan, but she won't admit it," Lottie answered.

Charles grinned. "I think it's time for another movie weekend, don't you?"

"I think that's a great idea."

The school buzzed with conversation and high spirits. The coming spring was a mood lifter for everyone. Lottie noticed Gwen and Jake standing by the stairwell door as she entered. He leaned down and gave her a kiss that quickly turned disgusting as far as Lottie was concerned. They broke free from their embrace as she approached.

"Oh, look, Jake. It's the newest member of the snob society."

Lottie stiffened. The comment went in like a dagger, then twisted for added insult. She took a deep breath. "Seriously, Gwen? What is wrong with you?"

"What's wrong with *me*? Let's try; what's wrong with you, Lottie."

"What have I done to cause you to be so angry with me?"

"You have to ask?"

"Yes, Gwen. I do."

"Now, you're a stupid snob."

Anger boiled inside Lottie, but she quickly remembered Mathilda's warning of how she could hurt someone with her magic. She let out a jagged exhale and tried to speak calmly. "Look, I'm sorry if I did anything to upset you. I hate this ridiculous drama between us."

"I'm sure you do. God forbid your perfect new life should have anything inconvenient going on in it. You know what—screw you. I'm late."

Shocked, Lottie could only stare after Gwen as she stalked out of the stairwell. She pushed the ugly scene out of her mind and tried to make the best of her day.

After school, she made her way to the student parking area, where Charles stood against his car, waiting for her.

"You all set?" he asked.

"Yeah. Did you ask Bryan about the movies this weekend?"

"I did."

"You didn't tell him we're trying to set him up with Wren, did you?"

"What, and risk retaliation from her? No, I'd rather stick with your idea of the coincidence of us being at the mall simultaneously."

"This playing cupid thing is fun. I need to convince my mom to let me ride with Wren, and it'll be all settled."

A TRICKLE OF SUDSY WATER RAN DOWN THE STEEP DRIVEWAY when Charles pulled up to Lottie's house. The hose stretched from the garage to her father's van, and he ran a soapy sponge over the windows, eying Charles and Lottie in the car.

Charles threw up a hand to him. "I don't guess I'll be kissing you today," he said.

"Yeah, better not. Dad might turn the hose on us. I'll see you tomorrow."

She grabbed her backpack and got out.

"Hi, Dad."

"How was your day?"

"Good."

"Has Charles been driving responsibly?"

"Dad, seriously? Of course, he has."

"I'm kidding," he said, reaching for the hose.

"Mm-hmm. So, Wren and I talked about going to a movie this weekend. If you think you can handle another irresponsible driver, she'll be picking me up."

"Fine by me," he said, spraying the soap off the windows. "See if your mother can handle it, though."

"Speaking of handling it...." Lottie hesitated.

"Uh-oh."

"Mathilda invited me to come over to her house for breakfast Saturday and to spend some time together. Can I go?"

"I'm okay with that, too, I guess. Better clear it with your mother."

"Already have. Thanks, Dad."

She made a cup of tea and ran upstairs to message Wren after running the movie plans by her mother.

My parents said I could go to the movies with you. Want to try that On The Run that just came out?

It's supposed to be pretty suspenseful. Do you think you can handle it this time?

Lottie grinned at Wren's response. *Yep. No bailing out.*

Filled with sudden excitement, a surge of energy rushed through Lottie, and there was an overwhelming need to release some of it. She noticed her hairbrush on her nightstand.

"Let's get you back on the dressing table, shall we?"

She focused on the brush, smiling as it twitched, but her excitement abruptly ended as it hurled across the room, crashing into the mirror. Shards of glass flew all over, one grazing Lottie's cheek. *Oh, no! Too much energy.* She wiped away the streak of blood on her face.

"Lottie? What happened?"

Footsteps came pounding up the stairs, and Lottie quickly yanked her hair out of a bun to hide her face. It was only a nick; no need to alarm her mother. Besides, Mathilda could heal it later.

"Lottie?"

"I'm okay."

"Oh, honey, what happened?" her mother asked, looking around at the mess.

The truth was on Lottie's tongue but given her recently disastrous result of using magic, she couldn't bring herself to worry her mother.

"I'm sorry, Mom. I spun around and accidentally hit the mirror with the phone."

"Are you hurt?"

"No, just feeling stupid."

"It's all right. Run downstairs and grab the broom and dustpan. I'll clean up."

"I'm so sorry, Mom."

"Don't worry about it. Just be careful when you come back in here."

Definitely no more magic in the house, Lottie vowed to herself.

FRIDAY EVENING FINALLY ARRIVED, MUCH TO LOTTIE'S delight. She was looking forward to playing matchmaker with Charles. She grabbed the money her mother had placed by the entry table and headed outside to Wren's waiting car.

Wren's long blond locks shone from a heavy dose of hair oil. She flashed a pink glossed grin at Lottie. "I'm glad your parents let you ride with me. Mom and Dad had a dinner party, so this worked out perfectly. So, what's Charles doing tonight? I tried to message him about a math assignment but never heard from him."

"I'm not sure. He said something about helping his mom do some stuff."

Wren sniffed in response. "Are you *sure* you want to see On the Run?" she asked, wheeling out of the driveway.

"Yes, I'm good with that one," Lottie said, grinning.

The previews had already started when they came in, and Lottie scanned the darkened room.

To your right.

She looked over and feigned surprise. "No way. There are Charles and Bryan."

"Lottie Jacobs! Did you set this up?"

Was Wren angry? It was too dark to see her expression.

"Because if you did, I'm good with that."

Lottie grinned. "Come on, let's go over. There are still some seats open."

"Oh, hey," Charles greeted. "I didn't expect to see you here."

"Nice try, Charles," Wren said flatly. She slapped his shoulder as she squeezed by him.

Lottie couldn't help but overhear as Bryan leaned close to Wren. "Let me know if I need to hold your hand during any scary parts."

She scoffed. "I think I'll be fine."

"Good job," Charles whispered. "Wren is down with the setup."

"Are you sure?" Lottie asked. "She seems mad underneath that smile."

"She's good. Trust me."

After the movie, Wren and Bryan stood talking in the parking lot. Lottie noticed how she tried to control her smile with little luck.

"I think our plan was a success."

"It seems so," Charles agreed, eyeing the pair. "Here they come; I'll see you tomorrow."

Wren sauntered over, still wearing her grin. "You ready to roll?"

"Yep," Lottie replied. She got in the car and turned to Wren. "Well?"

"Oh. My. God! I have his number. Bryan asked me to call him tomorrow. He wants to take me to dinner."

Lottie's smile broadened. "That's awesome."

"Maybe. He makes me all nervous—in a good way."

"I'm glad you didn't get mad at me for going behind your back."

"No, it's cool. I'm glad you got the ball rolling."

Back home, Lottie turned the light off and settled into bed, pleased with her matchmaking self. Beneath the blankets, her fingers tingled. She pulled her hands out of the covers, examining the soft glow coming from within them. She sighed, wondering what Mathilda could do to help her. Her powers were growing more each day. What if she were to reveal her magic again or, worse—accidentally hurt someone? She shut her eyes against the horrible thought and slowly drifted to sleep.

~

CHARLES SAT AT A RED LIGHT, WAITING FOR THE GREEN. His music was loud, and he tapped his fingers impatiently on the wheel along with the beat. The light turned green, and Charles floored the gas pedal, merging onto the highway so he could drive even faster. He felt good, looking to burn off some energy. Flashing lights came on from the side of the road. Charles glanced in the rearview mirror at the police car coming up fast behind him. He pushed the pedal down to the floor and put distance between himself and the cruiser. Once he was sure he was far enough ahead, Charles used his magic to change his car and plates. He now drove a red Porsche with fake numbered plates. He slowed down enough to let his car come into view of the pursuing officer, then, with more speed and magic, he sped off in a blinding light.

~

LOTTIE WOKE WITH A START. WHAT A STRANGE DREAM. IT was too late to talk to Charles. She would tell him about it tomorrow.

~

MATHILDA PULLED INTO THE DRIVEWAY AT LOTTIE'S HOUSE promptly at eight.

"How are you, dear?"

"Excited," Lottie replied.

"Good. I have Cook working on breakfast. He should be finished by the time we get to the house."

"Sounds good. What is Cook's name, anyway?"

"Wilfred. But he insists I call him Cook."

"Interesting."

"You'll find my household is run in an old and traditional manner. Dabney insists on keeping with the British aristocratic ways. It keeps him happy, and I admit I rather like the routine."

When they arrived, Dabney greeted them and took over the preparations in the breakfast room. Tea was set out in the most delicate porcelain Lottie had ever seen.

"You still like tea, I'm assuming?" Mathilda asked, holding the gold-trimmed handle of the antique hand-painted pot. She balanced the spout over Lottie's cup, waiting.

"I love tea. How did you know?"

"You've always loved it," Mathilda said, pouring. "Afternoon tea was your favorite time of day in most of your previous lives."

Cook came in, pushing a serving cart loaded with silver platters and trays. He turned to Mathilda. "Will there be anything else, ma'am?"

"No, everything is perfect. Thank you."

Mathilda sipped her tea and placed her cup on the matching saucer. "Well, my dear, what would you like to do today?"

"I don't know. I need a good starting point for using my magic responsibly. She filled Mathilda in on the incident with the hairbrush.

A disapproving look swept over Mathilda's delicate features. "Charlotte, we talked about this. Using magic is forbidden at your house."

She grasped Lottie's chin in her fingers, turning her head to inspect the scratch and tsked. A cool healing tingle swept over Lottie's skin as Mathilda's thumb brushed across the wound.

"We can work on that, but no more magic at your house, okay? We should let your parents have the non-magical side of you."

After breakfast, Mathilda led Lottie out into the side garden.

"Go ahead and remove your shoes. We'll do some grounding."

Lottie toed the canvas slides off her heels and followed Mathilda onto a path lined with boxwoods. It arched around into a circle where a massive water feature trickled peacefully. The oversized, clear gazing ball affixed on the top of the fountain reminded her of a giant crystal ball. Sunlight filtered through it, casting light all around the circle. The energy that was within the area was both tangible and self-contained. It seemed to draw from the elements around.

Lottie settled down on the grass.

"Close your eyes and breathe. Listen to nature. Feel her presence in everything. You only need to relax into your magic, trust the gift you possess, and your powers will settle in with more of an ease."

Mathilda's voice was soothing. Lottie took a deep breath and cleared her mind. She felt warmth under her legs and the same sensations as the first time she connected with the earth at Wren's house. Her body felt so charged that her hands and feet tingled. As she moved her hand over the grass, the blades pulled to her like a magnet. She laughed, exhilarated by the sensation. She loved this connection she shared with the earth. It made her feel in control of herself.

"What are you feeling?" Mathilda asked.

"A raging torrent of energy. It's beyond amazing—like I can do anything."

"Good. Direct that energy into moving those stones."

Lottie turned her attention to the stones surrounding the circle, each stack deliberately thought out in the design. She focused on the set of three that were closest to her and pictured them moving. They lifted off each other one by one, stacking themselves back up inside the circle. She continued with the remaining stacks until her magic came naturally.

Mathilda nodded in approval. "You have such a connection with the earth, Charlotte. More than any other member of your coven. It responds to you—and you to it, like a harmonious force."

"Has it always been like this with me?"

"Yes. Your deep love for Mother Earth began in Europe during your second rebirth. There were so many sacred sites that you often visited. I can remember it as clearly as yesterday. You'd return with your basket brimming with the chamomile and yarrow you collected along the way. I've always called you my little hedge witch. You were most content outside the coven, out in nature, gathering your herbs and pieces of the forest. Keep your connection with the earth. When you are at peace, you are at your best. Before long, you won't have accidents with flying objects anymore."

Lottie smiled. She settled back into the grass and let the sun wash over her limbs. Her contentment soon faded. "What happens if I lose my peace, like if I get angry?"

Mathilda's expression sobered. "Come sit in front of me." She patted the grass as she spoke. "Remember at your party when I said you had to be careful with your magic?"

"Yes."

"Close your eyes and relax. I'm going to show you something."

Lottie inhaled and closed her eyes, waiting. A jolt slammed into her mind as soon as Mathilda's fingertips touched her temples. A scene from the past began to unfold.

The angry mob shouted as a man paced before them on a wooden platform. He pounded his fist against his palm as he continued his speech.

"We will not tolerate these unholy creatures. They must be burned and sent back to hell where they belong for all eternity!"

The crowd roared in agreement.

"Bring forth the one whose witchery started the ruin of this village."

Three men emerged from the barn behind the platform. One wore a sack over his head and had thick ropes binding his hands. The large man to the right gave a hard shove to the bound man. He stumbled, nearly falling to the ground. The crowd erupted with shouts of approval.

The man on the platform raised his arms to quiet the noise. "Fasten him to yonder stake, and mind ye now, be not tricked by his witchery."

The men tied more ropes around their captive, binding him to the stake.

"And now, remove the sack. This evil one shall see thy faces. The faces of those who lost crops and livestock, and finally, thine own loved ones to the pestilence. May God hasten him to hell for eternal damnation."

One of the men yanked off the sack. Lottie screamed. It was Charles. She fought to release herself from the vision, but Mathilda held firm, and so it continued.

Thick, dark clouds rolled over the crowd, and a fierce wind rose from the north. Lottie saw herself walk out of the forest, dark hair whipping wildly around her. She held up her hands and screamed in a fury, pulling lightning from the atmosphere. She flung the ball of light toward the crowd, consuming them in flames. Screams of agony and burnt flesh filled the air.

"Lottie, no, stop! Lottie, STOP!" Charles shouted.

But it was useless; her rage had taken over. She did not stop until the flames had consumed every living person.

Mathilda removed her fingers and touched Lottie's hand. "Are you okay, my dear?"

Lottie stared at the ground, reeling from shock. "I'm not sure. What was that?"

"I allowed you to see the only time you completely lost control. You and Charles lived outside that village in the forests of Lancashire, England, in the early 1600s. People began to talk because you dabbled in herbs and the healing arts of natural things. Rumors soon spread that you were a witch.

"One summer, a drought came, and the crops and surrounding landscape died with it. The livestock began to die off, and disease spread. You learned that the people were suffering, so you gathered what you could and set off to the village to help. The villagers, hungry and desperate, saw you in perfect health. They tried to seize you, but you escaped into the forest.

"Charles went out to search for you. They took him as soon as he reached their border. Shortly after, you learned of his fate and returned to save him. Charles could have saved himself, but he knew showing magic to the villagers would only validate their accusations and give them the drive to come after you next. No one understands the unexplained, Charlotte. That's why we stay hidden with our magic. We have our safe places, and we keep to them. That's why I don't want you practicing until you get complete control. Today was the start. We'll meet here often until you have control of all the elements as you once did."

Lottie nodded.

"Let's go inside. I have some things I want to show you."

Mathilda's gait was as graceful as ever. She appeared to float over the stone corridor on her way to the library. Pausing by the fireplace, she pulled down on one of the sconces. Lottie's eyes widened as the wall opened, revealing a secret passageway. "Whoa, no way."

"Follow me."

They went down a narrow corridor until Mathilda stopped at an ancient-looking wooden door. She pulled a skeleton key from her pocket and slipped it into the lock. The room inside looked like something straight out of a cult horror movie. Lottie's gaze fell on the large pentagram on the floor surrounded by hundreds of candles. She imagined what the room would look like with all of them lit. Mathilda went over to a large antique cabinet. She removed one of the many books housed within and pulled out a box from underneath a cabinet.

"What is this place?" Lottie asked.

"This is my keeping room. There's something about me and the coven that you don't fully understand. I didn't tell you everything when I told you that our line goes back for centuries. Our line goes back to the beginnings of humankind as a coven of five. With dark witches roaming freely at one time, someone needed to keep them in check. That is how we came to be. Our powers became magnified beyond belief when we promised the Goddess, Hecate, to keep her ways and protect the balance within the earth. Each line produces one daughter to carry on the traditions. It has been the way of things until you."

"So, that's why our powers are so strong then."

Mathilda nodded. "No other witch has ever had the power that our coven holds. Not even Cassandra could stand against us; her powers were quite strong."

Lottie's forehead furrowed as Mathilda's words sank in. "How did Charles come to be if it's only women in the line?"

Mathilda's eyes took a sad, faraway look. "Ramona met with a great tragedy once, and the Goddess took pity upon her. She granted Ramona's request for a son as long as he promised to remain in the coven and protect it during his lifetime."

"I see." Lottie paused, looking around. "So, what do you do down here?"

"Occasionally, there are dark forces that we have to deal with. When that need arises, this is where we meet. Plus, it wouldn't do for me to keep my sacred items scattered around the house for just anyone to see."

"No, it wouldn't. What's in the box?"

Mathilda opened the lid and took out several stones. Each one differed in size and color.

Lottie recognized a few. "Quartz, and oh, my gosh. Is that a real emerald? Look at the size of that thing." She gasped at one in particular. "Oh... this is so pretty." She ran her fingers across a rough edge of the cluster. Its coloring was a milky green that went transparent toward the outer edges on one side. "What is it?"

"Prasiolite. This one has been your favorite since you first saw it."

"Really? I guess that's why I felt drawn to it. It's lovely."

Mathilda smiled. "These stones all have certain properties. You will want to learn their meanings and uses to enhance them with your magic. Once you've mastered these, we'll move on to the herbs. Grab the box, and we'll have lunch. I'll review some things with you and leave my notes for you to peruse."

Lottie spent the rest of the afternoon digging through the stones. It was nearly four when Mathilda came into the library for her.

"I'd better get you home. I don't want your parents to get upset with me on our first visit."

She followed Mathilda out to her car. "What do you have planned for the rest of the afternoon?"

"The coven is coming by to have dinner and catch up."

"Is there something going on? Charles told me about the missing woman at the Paranormal Investigators' office. Has she turned up?"

"No, Shelly seems to have disappeared without a trace. We're all going to my chamber for some channeling later. It's the end of the lunar cycle, perfect for dark moon magic."

"I hope you find her. Could the person behind the cat that scratched me be involved?"

"So far, there's no indication that it could be the same person." Mathilda gave a reassuring smile. "Don't worry over any of this, Lottie. We know what happens; if not, we always find out."

LOTTIE LET HERSELF IN AND WENT TO CATCH UP WITH HER mother.

She thought about Mathilda's vision afterward as she headed to her room. She felt sick over the thought of anything happening to Charles. She turned her mind to him. *Hey. Are you busy?*

No. How did it go today?

It was amazing.

Do you think your parents will let you go out for a bite with me?
I'll ask. You should probably call to ask me.
Right.

After Lottie hung up the phone with Charles, she returned to the living room.

"Charles just called. Is it okay if we grab a bite for dinner?"

"Lottie," her mother sighed. "We haven't seen you since Thursday."

"Mom, please?"

"I suppose you can go, but you'd better pencil Dad and me in for tomorrow."

"I'm all yours," Lottie promised. "I'll even get up early for breakfast at the diner."

~

WHEN CHARLES REACHED THE BOTTOM OF THE DRIVE, OUT of close view, Lottie leaned over and kissed him.

"Wow, what was that for?" he asked.

"I missed you."

He grinned, pulling onto the road. "Are you okay with a drive-thru? We could ride over to the lake."

"That's perfect."

Settling on burgers, they ate on the way. Charles turned off the road and found a secluded place to park near the water. He noticed Lottie's faraway stare out the window. "What's going on? You seem troubled."

"Mathilda showed me a vision today. It was from the past, about you and me. Small-town villagers thought I was a witch. Like a soft-hearted idiot, I tried to help them during hard times, but it went bad. You went out to look for me; they captured you, tied you to a stake...."

"Really?"

"Yep. Then I came back onto the scene to save you and burnt them all in a horrible, agonizing fire. Each-and every-villager. Burned. I understand now why the elders blocked our memories from us. But, on the bright side, that's the only time I've ever lost control and hurt people."

"That's good to know." Charles gave her a sidelong glance. "How did you sleep last night?"

"Strange that you should ask me that. I had this weird dream about you."

"I know. I gave it to you. I knew you were worried about everything and felt terrible about the accident with magic on our date. I also wanted to show you something from the past that happened to me. The week that I transformed, my life turned unbelievable. I had this energy I had never felt. I saw everything in a whole new way. I was suddenly able to do amazing things, and I let it get out of control. When that cop radioed headquarters, he reported a black BMW. I read his mind. When I changed the car, he was almost frantic in his confusion. He kept repeating, 'I know what I saw,' 'I know what I saw.'

"Anyway, the Paranormal Investigators found out. They went on a massive search for answers. That's how my mom met Shelly. She knew right away that Shelly was a witch. She explained that I had just come into my power and convinced her to let my case go. My mom grounded me, took the car, and hid it at Mathilda's house until everything died down. That's why I've been on the bus all this time."

Lottie took his hand. "Charles. I'm so sorry."

"When I think about what I could have done...exposed me—my mom and the rest of the coven in such a negative way. It was stupid. But I'm much wiser now and a lot more cautious. I just wanted you to know you're not the only one with thoughts of losing control."

"You always were cautious," Lottie added.

"How do you know that?"

"In my vision, you tried to stop me from killing those villagers. You were willing to die rather than reveal yourself as a witch and expose me." She blinked away the tears swirling in her eyes. "Ugh, sorry. It's unbearable to think of anything ever happening to you. I don't know what I would do without you."

He pulled her close. "Nothing is going to happen to me, Lottie. You won't let it," he teased, brushing the back of his fingers along her jawline.

Lottie shivered at his touch. His mouth replaced his fingers.

"I love you," he said against her lips. "I hate the thought of having to take you back."

Lottie sighed. "Me, too."

Chapter Eleven

The diner bustled with the early morning breakfast crowd. The smell of coffee lingered as a waitress skirted between tables, filling cups. Lottie glanced up as a woman exited the kitchen, balancing a tray of fresh-baked donuts. She slid it into an empty slot in the donut case.

"Man, those look good," Lottie's mother said. She tore her eyes away from the donuts and grinned at Lottie. "You guys want to go over to Kent after breakfast?"

"Spare me, please," her father said, burying his head in his hands.

"Now, Randy, we just want to browse in a couple of places. No heavy shopping this time."

"Uh-huh...that's what you said the last three times."

"Look on the bright side, Dad; all the spring landscaping and gardening stuff will be in the stores."

WHEN LOTTIE GOT HOME, SHE WENT UPSTAIRS AND DIALED Wren.

"So, how did your date with Bryan go?"

"Pretty good. We went to dinner and just talked."

"And…"

"That boy's lips were made for kissing!"

Lottie gave a fake gasp. "You're wicked."

"He makes me feel wicked. But I had everything under control, like a good witch."

"Good for you."

"He asked me to go out with him again."

"What did you say?"

"I said I'd think about it."

"No, you did not."

"What? I didn't want to seem too eager."

"But Wren, you are eager. And Bryan seems sweet beneath all that bravado. You should go all in."

"Hey, we all can't be Charles and Lottie."

"I'll take that as a compliment."

～

RAMONA REACHED INTO HER BAG FOR HER RINGING PHONE. Unknown caller.

"Yes?" she answered.

"Ramona, this is Matthew Alcott. I found your number in one of Shelly's files."

"What is it, Matthew?"

"I had a vision while going through some of Shelly's things. I saw an old tomb in a secluded area. Large stone steps led down to its entrance, and the doors to the tomb had these strange markings carved into them. I saw a crescent moon above the name Duprey. Does any of this make sense to you?"

"Yes. I need to go, Matthew. I'll keep you informed."

Ramona channeled her coven. *Meet me at Eliza Duprey's tomb.*

～

"WHAT'S HAPPENED?" MATHILDA ASKED, JOINING EVERYONE by the steps.

"I received a call from Matthew," Ramona replied. "He had a vision of this tomb while going through Shelly's files. I want to go inside."

"Of course." Mathilda joined hands with her sisters.

As the veil lowered, a mist of glittering light fell about the tomb.

One by one, they descended into the crypt. The darkness was damp and heavy with foul intent. Ramona waved her hand, and flames danced along the stumps of the yellowed candles inside the room's rusted iron lanterns hanging from the walls.

Regina gasped. "Look at her...." She eyed Shelly's crumpled body along the side wall in horror.

Blackened streaks ran up Shelly's neck and into her jawline.

"Dark magic," Trina stated. "Her neck is broken."

Mathilda leaned over the body, frowning deeply. "Hmm." She walked back into the deepest part of the crypt, where Eliza Duprey's casket rested atop a stone wall. Her eyes fell to the covering of moss surrounding the lid from a century of dank darkness. Water droplets fell from the roof, landing in muted drips along the moss, sounding loud in her ears compared to the silence lingering in this place. Mathilda waved her hand, and the lid to the casket slid open.

Isobel gasped. "She has escaped her death."

"No, she's here," Mathilda replied. She bent down and scooped up some dirt in her right hand. She cupped her other hand over it and closed her eyes. "She has been disintegrated into the very earth. Someone stripped her of her powers before doing this—"

"Which means they gained a good deal of power," Trina interrupted.

Mathilda placed her palm on Shelly's forehead. "Her powers are gone as well."

"Why would Shelly have come to this tomb?" Ramona asked. "We must find out what went on here."

"I'm afraid we won't find anything here," Mathilda said. "Someone did an impeccable job of cleaning up after themselves. Not a trace of magic has been left, not a trace of anything outside of what we just discovered."

Isobel shook her head in awe. "Who are we dealing with?"

"I don't know," Mathilda replied. "But I intend to find out."

~

Lottie fell asleep watching television. When she woke, Charles smiled at her from the chair. Startled, she sat up higher in the bed. "What time is it?"

"One-thirty."

"How long have you been here?"

"Since midnight."

"Is something wrong?"

"No, I just missed you. I hope it's okay that I let myself in."

Something was off with him. Lottie could sense it.

"Charles, what's going on? I can tell you're keeping something from me."

He sighed, raking a hand through his hair. "I'm sorry. I hoped to avoid alarming you. I'm sure it's just me being overprotective—"

She cut him short. "Charles, tell me."

He sighed again before relenting. "The coven has regularly been meeting at Mathilda's. Mom says it's nothing to be concerned over; however, I've never known them to meet like this, and I can't help but wonder why."

"What has she said?"

"Not much at all. She told me that the coven was trying to locate Shelly and for me not to worry. That's pretty tight-lipped info for Mom. I don't like it. So, I started coming here late at night to make sure you were okay. At first, I was content in the shadows by the garage, but tonight, I let myself in. I needed to see for myself that you were truly okay."

Charles leaned forward, placing his elbows on his knees. "There's one more thing bothering me, too. I came across Phil leaving your house when I got here earlier. I surprised him by the look on his face. He told me he was only checking in on you, but I felt his magic lingering."

Her stomach fluttered with a sense of unease. "Why was Phil doing magic here?"

"I'm not sure. I'd like to know what the coven is up to, but I don't want to question my mom."

"I asked Mathilda about Shelly. She said the coven was practicing dark moon magic tonight to try to locate her. I'm sure they'll tell us something soon."

Charles stood and placed a kiss on Lottie's forehead. He lingered for a moment before leaving her side. "Yeah. I'm sure you're right. I'd better get going."

Lottie watched her window lower by itself after Charles slipped through it. His obvious concern left her feeling ill at ease. She stared at the swaying limbs outside her window until she drifted back asleep.

❧

"What was Charles doing at Charlotte's house at this hour?" Mathilda asked Phil.

"That would be my fault," Ramona replied. "Charles asked about our meetings, and I'm afraid my lack of details has him on high alert. What did you tell him, Phil?"

"Just that I was looking in on Lottie. He didn't buy it, though. The boy is smart, and I know he sensed my magic. I'm sure Lottie knows something is going on by now."

"It's just as well," Isobel said. "We need to tell the children we found Shelly. Sunni has been pecking away at me for information regarding her disappearance."

Mathilda nodded in agreement. "Were there any signs that anyone had been near Charlotte's house?"

"No. The woods were undisturbed, and there was no sign that anyone had been trying to tamper with the protection spell."

"Good. So how do we proceed with this Matthew person?" Mathilda mused. "Is it wise to share this information with the rest of Shelly's co-workers?"

"I say we keep it to ourselves," Regina said firmly. "Considering the nature of how we found Shelly lying on the floor of a dead witch's magically concealed tomb with a broken neck will only create unwanted attention on our part. And we were seen at the Paranormal Investigators office asking about Shelly. That doesn't bode well for any of us."

"Ramona, what do you say?" Mathilda asked.

"I say we tell Matthew. The receptionist at the investigator's office was planning to notify the police if Shelly never turned up. I managed to convince Matthew to have her hold off a couple of days until we had a chance to find her and avoid any unnecessary attention to Shelly's true nature. Seeing how he is also a witch, I'm sure Matthew will think of something to tell the others at the office."

"Yes. I think this is the wisest course," Mathilda agreed. "I suggest we tell the children in the morning that there needs to be a coven meeting."

"Let's hope this doesn't blow up in our faces," Trina said.

"Look at those guys over there by the door," Sunni remarked, scraping her chair up to the table.

Wren scoffed. "Don't tell me you feel bad for the banishing mind control act. They are jerks—especially Harvey. They deserved it."

"Did you get details about why the Elders want to meet with us?" Lottie asked.

"No. I tried all morning to get my mother to give me a hint, but she wouldn't budge," Sunni replied.

"It must be serious," Rowen added. She looked toward Charles, who was in deep thought, seemingly oblivious to the conversation. "Hello? Charles—input would be excellent."

"I don't have anything to say," he said curtly.

Rowen shot daggers at him. "Well, that's harsh. Excuse me for being concerned."

"Look, I'm sorry, Rowen. I didn't mean to be rude. I have a lot on my mind and am not up to chit-chat. Don't take it personally."

"Okay, geez. Lottie, I guess it comes down to your parents as to when we get to meet."

"I plan to ask them if I can have dinner with Charles tonight. They may not let me go out until the weekend, though." Lottie gazed over at her old table. Jake and Gwen were touchy-feely, while Abbey and Christy were in deep conversation. Christy noticed her stare and waved. Lottie waved back. Abbey pretended not to see her. Nice.

LOTTIE ENSURED SHE HAD ALL HER WORK FINISHED BY THE end of the day. With no homework, maybe her parents would let her go out. She made her way through the throng of bus riders toward the parking lot. She nearly jumped out of her skin when Bryan Michaels squealed his tires as he passed Wren.

"Nice, Bryan. Nice," Wren shouted.

He honked his horn in response.

"Oh, Bryan..." Charles muttered. "He does know how to irritate Wren."

Lottie smiled. "I'm pretty sure she likes it."

After she got approval from her parents to go out with Charles, Lottie sent a text to him to pick her up at five, then headed upstairs to scroll through Instagram—anything to keep her mind off worrying about the meeting with the Elders. Finding a cute nail art design, she sat down at her vanity and removed the polish she had on. A change of color would be a good distraction. As she reached for her box of polish, the words Paranormal Investigators whispered in her mind. It was so subtle she wasn't even sure it was said. It was more like a feeling. Lottie didn't know what to make of it. She would bring it up later at Mathilda's house.

THE EVENING SUN SLIPPED BEHIND A THICK, BILLOWY CLOUD, and Lottie gazed at the sunbeams pouring from beneath it as Charles pulled around the drive. She couldn't help but notice the muscles along his jaw tighten as they headed through the foyer toward the library.

"Are you okay?" she asked. "You seem distracted."

"Yeah. Just anxious to find out what the Elders are keeping from us."

"Ah, good, you made it," Mathilda greeted. "I know you kids have been wondering why we called this meeting, so I'll get right to it. We found Shelly White."

Sunni perked up. "Is she okay?"

"No," Mathilda responded somberly. "We found her body inside the tomb of Eliza Duprey, a dark witch whose burial ground was under our protection. Someone found a way to get around our spell and enter the tomb. Shelly had a broken neck, yet there was no sign of visible harm on her body. We also discovered that Eliza's remains had been disintegrated."

Shocked, Lottie sat back against her chair. "What does that mean exactly?"

A troubled look spread over Mathilda's features. "Someone took her powers. They were intact when we sealed her tomb over one hundred years ago, but when we checked her remains, there wasn't a trace of magic left. Shelly's magic was also stripped."

"Do you think Shelly lowered the spell and entered the tomb?" Wren asked.

"No," Ramona replied. "She wasn't strong enough to attempt a spell of that magnitude. Tampering with it alone would have killed her. She knew that. Only a witch with powers to match ours could do that. It's disturbing and cloaked very well."

"We're trying to find a way to get around the cloak," Mathilda added. "In the meantime, we want you to be careful and look after one another."

"What were you doing at Lottie's house, Phil?" Charles asked.

"I knew you'd be concerned over that. I was checking beyond the border of the protection spell. After what happened at Eliza Duprey's tomb, we just wanted to ensure no one had been near Lottie's house."

"Had anyone been there?" Charles asked.

"No."

Satisfied, Charles turned to Lottie. "Why don't you tell them about your vision."

"You had a vision?" Mathilda asked.

"I wouldn't say that exactly. I don't know what I had. I was polishing my nails earlier today, and I thought I heard the words Paranormal Investigators whispered in my mind, but it wasn't a true whisper; more like I was suddenly made aware of them. Does that make sense?"

"It does. Your powers are getting stronger. It could be that your intuition is trying to tell you something, or maybe you're overwhelmed with the thoughts of everything going on with Shelly. I'll send you home with some stones to use during meditation. Perhaps you can gain some clarity from what you heard."

"What about Shelly?" Charles asked. "Does anyone outside of the coven know what happened to her?"

"Yes," Ramona replied. "Matthew Alcott, the new witch who took her place."

"Are you suspicious of him?" Charles asked Mathilda.

"Until now, nothing has given us reason to be. Shelly kept your mother up to date on Mr. Alcott before her death. She never mentioned anything indicating that he was involved with dark magic, and your mother didn't pick up on anything negative when she met with him. However, something doesn't sit well. I think we should focus more on him. Especially after finding Shelly dead."

Lottie shuddered. She moved over to the fireplace and sat closer to Mathilda on the corner of the bench. "What did Mr. Alcott tell Ramona?"

"While going through Shelly's files, he had a vision of a tomb and could give Ramona enough details that we knew it was Eliza's tomb he saw. That's how we discovered Shelly's remains. Ramona asked him to keep this information to himself. If the police get involved, the coven could be put under the heat. Since he is also a witch, he agreed to convince the rest of the office staff not to say anything to draw too much attention to any of us."

"Will they do that?"

"Yes, I believe they will. Their office relies on the aid of witches. They wouldn't want to lose that connection. Now, let's fetch those stones so you can get home."

Lottie followed Mathilda through the dim corridor into her keeping room.

"I asked you to come with me for another reason," Mathilda admitted. "I wanted to get into your head without alarming the rest of your coven."

"Get into my head? Why?"

"I simply want to see your vision for myself. Is that okay?"

"Yes."

"Good. Come closer."

Mathilda rested her fingers against Lottie's temples. The words, Paranormal Investigators, were in her mind, hanging on a shroud of darkness. Abruptly, a cloud-like fog ended the vision. Mathilda removed her fingers and stepped back.

"What did you see?" Lottie asked.

"You were correct. The words are in your mind, and you are stronger than you realize. Your intuition picked up on something, but whatever it is was blocked before it could come to fruition."

"What do you think is going on?"

"I'm not sure. It could be something regarding Shelly's demise."

"Is there anything I can do?"

Mathilda placed a small pouch in Lottie's hand. "Just keep close to the others and use these. The tourmaline will help ground you, and the Apatite will aid you toward clarity in what you seek. Use them both during your meditations and if you find anything from them, let me know."

"I will."

"Are you okay?" Mathilda asked, studying her. "You seem out of sorts."

"I can't help but wonder if there's a connection between my incident and what happened to Shelly. Not to mention the fact that someone is stripping witches of their powers. That alone is terrifying."

"I know you're worried. Keep close to your coven. You have a protection spell over your house. And it's been brought to my attention now that Charles has been watching over you."

Lottie blushed.

Mathilda arched an eyebrow. "Am I to read more from that look on your face?"

"No!" Mortified, Lottie shifted her gaze to the floor. "He's just worried about me, that's all."

"I believe you, Charlotte. Don't fret."

Mathilda stood by the window watching Lottie say her goodbyes. Regina stepped alongside her, two wine glasses in hand. She gave one of them to Mathilda and followed her gaze outside.

"What did you and Lottie discuss in your keeping room?"

"I wanted to see her vision for myself."

"And?"

"Charlotte was blocked out from seeing anything tangible. Either Matthew Alcott is quite powerful and able to mask himself from us, or someone else is masking him. And with Shelly dead, we've lost our link to the Paranormal Investigators."

Regina watched Wren and the others drive away. "Not entirely. The receptionist knows Shelly and Ramona were acquainted. We may still be able to get some information."

"Let's hope so."

~

Lottie let out a pent-up sigh as Charles turned from the tree-lined drive. "What did you think about the meeting?"

He shrugged. "I'm a little uneasy still, but I feel better now that I know what's been going on. What about you?"

"Honestly, scared. The idea that someone is strong enough to get past a spell that the coven placed freaks me out— and what do they want?"

"I know you're scared. The Elders know what they're doing, Lottie. They'll figure it out. Just try not to worry. I'll watch out for you as much as I can. So will the others."

"Poor Shelly. I wonder if she had any family?"

"Mom told me she was a loner. Her parents threw her out at a young age once they found out she was a witch. I doubt anyone would come searching at this point. My biggest fear is if the police get involved. My mom was seen at the investigators' office asking about her."

"I'm sure Matthew will think of something to say to keep them from reporting about Shelly."

~

"I wasn't expecting you home so early," Ramona said, looking up from her iPad. "How is Lottie?"

"She's worried—with good reason. I get the feeling you and the others are keeping something from us. Am I right?"

Ramona sighed and leaned back in her chair. "Look, I wish I could tell you what you want to hear, but the truth is, we don't know what's going on yet. Whoever killed Shelly is strong enough to remain hidden from our view."

"What about Lottie? Is there a connection?'"

"We can't find any. It doesn't mean there isn't one—or that there is," Ramona added after his look of concern. She stood and took Charles's hands. "Son, I know you're worried about Lottie, and it's hard to accept this, but please try not to let it consume you. Our coven is strong. It's only a matter of time before this comes to light."

"I just want everything to be out in the open. I sense this constant darkness, and it's killing me to think that Lottie could be hurt."

"We will protect each of you, Charles. We always have."

Selene strode into the Paranormal Investigators' office and rolled her eyes when she saw the receptionist and the smile spreading over her face. She braced herself for the usual bombardment of gratitude and enthusiasm that was to come. As she approached the desk, Nancy sprang from her chair, sending it careening back into the filing cabinets.

"Oh, son of a...." she muttered as a picture frame fell and broke. With her smile replaced, she turned toward Selene. "Ms. Sullivan, good to see you again. I was just getting ready to head home. What can I do for you?"

"I'm here to see Matthew," Selene answered flatly.

"Of course. He's in his office. Come on back."

Selene followed her into the hall. *Here it comes...*

"I can't thank you enough for sending Matthew to us," Nancy began. "He's been such a huge help in Shelly's absence. And let me mention how your generous donation has helped this office with—"

Selene cut her short. "I'm glad he's been able to assist."

Nancy paused by the door. "Here we are. I'll leave you to your business. Have a good evening."

"Thank you, Ms. Withers."

"Nancy, please."

Selene forced a smile. "Very well, Nancy." She turned away, letting the smile drop, and jerked open the door. "Stupid, tiresome woman. I swear I will make that receptionist choke on her tongue."

Matthew scrambled to his feet at Selene's entrance. She plunked down into one of the chairs in front of his desk. "How did your conversation with Ramona Lachlan go?"

"As you expected, Mistress. I did as you instructed and told her of my 'vision' of the Duprey tomb. I offered to assist in finding Shelly, and she said she would inform me of what she discovered."

"And did she inform you?"

"She did. Ramona told me she found Shelly and that dark forces had a hand in her death."

Selene retorted with a half-snort. "You don't say?"

Matthew ignored her sarcasm. "She asked me to sit on the information until she can learn more."

"Perfect. We're in." Selene splayed her elbows wide on the desk and clasped her hands together. "Now that Ramona trusts you, she and her little coven will search elsewhere for answers. And in the meantime, Lottie's powers will grow stronger."

Chapter Twelve

Being on guard throughout the school day was mentally exhausting. Lottie was relieved when the bell rang at the end of the day, giving her a change of scenery at least. She tossed her things into the backseat of Charles's car as he pulled away from the school.

As they approached a small hill with a stop sign at the bottom, Lottie noticed a look of alarm spread over Charles's features. "What is it?"

"Something's wrong with the brakes," he said.

The car gained more speed as they went through the intersection. Frantic, he stomped the pedal over and over.

Lottie's scream was cut short as the car went over a ravine, smashing into the trees.

Lottie....

Charles's voice in her mind was the last thing she heard.

~

Her head hurt. Lottie groaned as she regained consciousness. Disoriented, she turned and saw Charles slumped over against the door.

"Oh, my God, Charles!" *So much blood.* She nearly choked at the sight of it.

"No, no, no, no...Charles, wake up." He didn't move when she touched his face.

Lottie glanced up toward the ridge. "Help! Someone, help us."

The shout made her head throb. She rummaged around in the car, searching for her phone, but couldn't find it. She noticed Charles's phone was on the floor by his feet.

"Please, please, please...." she begged all of the good forces in the universe as she dialed with trembling fingers.

"911. What is your emergency?"

Relieved to hear the voice, the pent-up terror whooshed out in a jumble of words. "Please help us... our car crashed over a ravine. My boyfriend is hurt badly, and I can't wake him. Please hurry."

Silence.

"Hello?"

The call had ended. "Oh no." Frantic thoughts ran through her mind. What if 911 couldn't locate the GPS? She tried calling Mathilda. No signal.

"Charles, hold on. Please, hold on. I'm going to try to walk up to get a signal."

Lottie had to push hard on the door to get it open. It finally gave way against some brush as it swung open. She stumbled and crawled to the top of the hill, scraping her cheek on the briars. Still no signal. She didn't know what to do. She couldn't leave Charles.

Tears blinded her as she made her way back down the hill. He hadn't moved. She checked to make sure he was breathing. His chest rose and fell beneath his pendant. *The pendant!* She held his hand and reached for her necklace. "Find us. Please find us." She chanted over and over.

Charles still hadn't moved, and Lottie noticed his chest no longer rose with his breath. She checked to see if he had a pulse. It was too weak. She could feel him slipping away.

"Oh, God, no...you can't die!" Lottie sobbed. She stretched her arms over him instinctively. "Pain, be mine...pain, be mine. Take the pain...pain, be mine...."

Her body shook as the pain swept over her. It was more than she could stand. She screamed and slumped over onto Charles.

~

A MUFFLED VOICE CAME FROM SOMEWHERE FAR AWAY, stirring Lottie awake. Had she imagined it?

"Lottie!"

She bolted up and looked around. "Help! Down here."

Rowen came into view at the top of the ridge. "Lottie, are you both okay?"

"No, Rowen, call 911. Charles isn't moving."

Rowen began to make her way down the hill. "Sunni called them, but they were already en route from your call. We saw the car when you channeled us and got here as soon as we could."

Rowen slid as she neared the car. She righted herself and scrambled over to them. "Oh, God! Charles...has he moved?"

"No," Lottie sobbed. "He has to be okay."

"They're coming," Sunni shouted from above.

Lottie held tightly to Charles's hand until the emergency crew reached him. Tears rolled down her cheeks, and she squeezed her eyes closed. *Please, don't leave me. Please....*

She watched Charles numbly while a crew member checked her over, flinching at the sting as he cleaned the cut on her cheek. After being cleared, she answered all his questions, vaguely aware of her responses until he mentioned he would have to call her parents. Her stomach knotted at the thought of her mother's reaction to hearing about their crash. Not wanting to deal with that right now, she shoved the thought aside.

When the rest of the EMS crew finally secured Charles on the stretcher, they carried him to the waiting ambulance. Rowen found Lottie's phone and grabbed her backpack, and they hurried up to her car.

"I'll call Mathilda," Sunni said as they raced for the hospital.

When they finally arrived, Lottie jumped out before Rowen stopped the car and ran to where the ambulance had just pulled up. She watched anxiously as the EMTs carefully unloaded Charles and rolled him into the emergency room entrance. Her throat clenched when she saw him looking so lifeless.

Mathilda wheeled into a parking space. Her expression was mixed with anguish and relief as she ran toward Lottie. "Oh, thank goodness you're okay. What happened?"

"Charles and I were leaving school. His brakes weren't working, and we went over a ravine. It was awful," she broke off in a sob.

Mathilda wrapped her arms around Lottie. "Let's go in and find out what we can about Charles."

Inside, the hospital was chaotic. Nurses rushed around, and orders were shouted out. Ramona stood by the doors to the trauma unit, and Lottie ran over to hug her.

"Thank you for staying with him. I know he felt your presence."

Ramona's voice sounded strained. Lottie noticed tears streaming down her face and slipped further into helplessness.

Mathilda placed a reassuring hand on Ramona's arm. "What can I get you, Ramona?"

"Water. Coffee. Anything."

Lottie went over and joined her friends. "I'm so glad you found us. I was terrified in that ravine, not knowing if Charles would make it."

"Did you see or feel anything strange today?" Wren asked.

"No, not a thing. Are you suggesting someone purposefully did this?"

Wren shrugged. "I don't know. So much has been going on. Maybe?"

Lottie pondered her words. "It seems like I would have felt it. I think this was a true accident."

She turned her mind to Charles, silently talking to him.

"Are you getting anything from him?" Sunni asked.

"No. This is killing me. I hope he can hear me."

Lottie jumped when her phone rang. She took a deep breath and pressed the talk button.

"Hi, Mom."

"Lottie? I called you three times. Are you okay?"

"Sorry. I didn't have a signal for a while. I'm okay. I'm here at the hospital with Charles."

"I'm on my way now. I'll be there as soon as I can."

The doors to the trauma unit whooshed open. A doctor walked over to Ramona, and Lottie held her breath. Tears of joy sprang to her eyes when she saw Ramona sigh with relief.

"Oh, thank God. He's okay."

After talking to the doctor, Ramona made her way over to them.

"Charles is going to be just fine. He has several broken ribs, a concussion, and some nasty cuts and bruises." She reached for Lottie's hands. "I don't know how you made it through that crash with only a few scrapes. You were fortunate."

Lottie didn't feel lucky. She felt guilty that she was okay while Charles nearly died. "Can we see him?"

"Yes. He'll be moving into a room shortly."

WHEN RAMONA FINALLY CAME OUT FROM VISITING WITH Charles, it was noticeable to Lottie that she had been crying. Her stomach knotted. What would she see when she went into his room? She couldn't bear the thought of Charles being in a fragile state. He was so strong and carried her through all of her weak moments. Now, she had to be strong for him. She took a deep breath and opened the door.

Charles lay there motionless, wires attached to his chest amidst the angry red and purple splotches covering his skin. She noticed the IV in his hand, along with deep cuts and bruises. Her eyes followed the injuries up his arm, pausing at his neck, also severely cut and bruised. Fear of what else she might see kept her gaze fixed on his throat. She closed her eyes briefly before willing herself to look at his face. She couldn't help the gasp that escaped. The entire left side of his face was swollen with black and purple bruises. There was a gash under his eye that had been stitched. She felt the tears coming but stopped them.

Settling into the chair by the bed, Lottie took his hand. She held it to her face and kissed it.

"Charles, I'm so sorry."

At her voice, the heart monitor beeped a bit faster.

"Can you hear me? Squeeze my hand if you can."

He didn't respond.

A nurse came into the room. She looked into Charles's eyes with a light.

"Why isn't he awake?" Lottie asked.

"He has a concussion. He'll come out of it," the nurse assured, checking the fluids and making her notes.

Mathilda knocked on the door and stepped in. "Your mother is here. She's asking for you."

Lottie nodded and followed her out into the hall.

"Would it be okay if I stay with you? Just until Charles can come home. Your house is closer to the hospital."

"It's okay with me. You and your mother will have to hash out that request."

Her mother stood quietly talking to Regina when Lottie entered the waiting room. Her features were taut with emotion as she rushed over and embraced Lottie tightly.

"I've been so worried. What happened?"

"Something happened to Charles's brakes, and we crashed through some trees," Lottie said, sparing her mother the worst of the details. "I called 911. He's been unconscious since it happened." Tears sprang to her eyes as she recalled the accident.

"Oh, my God. When I think of what could have happened...."

"I'm fine, Mom," Lottie said, wiping the tears from her cheeks. "That's Charles's mom, Ramona, over by the nurses' desk."

"He looks very much like her, doesn't he?"

"Yes. Mom, would it be okay with you if I stay with Mathilda for a few days—or however long it takes for Charles to get out of the hospital? Her house is so close to here, and I can visit him longer."

Her mother's hesitation sent her into a near panic. "Please, Mom? I can't be away from him. Not like this," she broke off in a sob.

"Oh, honey, you must be so scared for Charles. It'll be okay if you don't get behind on your schoolwork."

Lottie nodded. "Thank you. Have you told Dad about the accident?"

"I did. He should be here soon."

"Okay. I will let Mathilda know I'll stay with her and then sit with Charles for a while."

~

STEPPING INTO THE FOYER, LOTTIE WAS NUMB WITH WORRY. She was barely aware of Mathilda guiding her up to her bedroom.

"Marie has a hot bath ready for you. That should soothe any soreness you may be feeling. I'll bring food up to your room after you're finished."

Mathilda's words went unnoticed.

"Are you okay, dear?"

The wall of emotions finally came crashing down in a burst of tears. "I don't know why he isn't talking to me. I keep trying to contact him, but I only get silence. And I hurt. Everything hurts."

"Here, let me help you undress."

Mathilda gasped as she removed Lottie's sweater. A deep purple hue with strange red streaks ran from her chest to her stomach.

"Charlotte, what did you do?"

"I had to help him," she sobbed. "I took the pain."

"Oh, honey. What you did was very dangerous. You can't just take on a spell like that without having a consequence."

"I love him. I had to."

Mathilda's features softened. "I know you do. I'm so sorry for both of you. Come on, get into the tub. I'll gather my things, but I can only help so much with this."

Easing into the water, Lottie rested her head on the back of the tub and closed her eyes.

Charles, please be okay. I need to know you're okay.

She started drifting to sleep when she heard him.

Lottie.

Charles! Are you okay?

Yes. What about you?

I'm fine. I'm so glad to hear your voice.

The nurse is here now. Come by tomorrow. I need to talk to you.

Okay. I love you, Charles.

I love you, too. And Lottie, thank you.

Mathilda came in with a large wooden box. "You look happy. I'm assuming you finally heard from Charles?"

"Yes."

"How is he doing?"

"He seemed okay. He wants me to come by tomorrow."

"Not until after school.

"What about before school? If I get up early, will you take me to see him?"

"I guess that will be okay."

"Thank you. What's in the box?"

"Comfrey, Calendula, Aloe, and some other things. Dry off, and I'll work my magic."

Mathilda crushed the herbs with a pestle, whispering in a language unknown to Lottie. Orbs of light swirled over the bowl, taking the shape of tiny butterflies as they floated down into the mixture.

"Here you are, rub this in."

Lottie dipped her fingers in the bowl and smeared on the mixture. It tingled, and as the paste began to warm, it took on a bright glow.

"There," Mathilda said, taking the bowl from Lottie. "It's absorbed most of your discoloration. Wipe it off and get dressed. You'll need to do this for three more nights until the color is gone. But the pain you will have to deal with. Spells that alter the natural order of things have side effects. I can't take those away. And Charlotte, think twice the next time you try something like this. You were fortunate the results of your ill-conceived spell weren't worse."

THE FIVE O'CLOCK ALARM WASN'T AS BAD AS LOTTIE HAD imagined. She flew through her morning routine, noting how much the color had faded on her chest. Each movement was a chore, but she kept her mind off the pain by thinking of Charles.

She pressed the elevator button to the second floor. When the doors opened, Ramona stepped off. A broad smile crept over her face. She pulled Lottie into a hug and kissed her on each cheek.

"Good of you to come so early."

Ramona's boisterous greeting took Lottie aback.

"How is he today?"

"Much improved. He's looking forward to seeing you. I know you don't have much time, so I'll be on my way."

"Thank you, Ramona."

Lottie was surprised to see Charles sitting up in bed, looking alert. He smiled and motioned her in.

"Wow. You look so much better." She ran her fingers over his hand, careful not to touch the cut along the knuckles.

"Lottie, I know what you did. I'm grateful, but it was way too risky. You could have been hurt." He shifted higher in the bed, grimacing from the movement. "Thankfully, Mom knew how to fix it."

Lottie looked up from his hand, confused.

He smiled. "Your spell. It took away my pain and reversed the damage to my body, but I started healing too fast. Mom had to work a different spell to stop the healing process until I get out of here, at least."

"Oh. I wasn't exactly sure what would happen using my magic like that. I just knew I had to try to save you."

"Yeah, my mom said as much."

"Thank God she stopped the acceleration. I can only imagine the doctor's reaction over your lack of scrapes and bruises in one day."

"Thank you." He kissed her head and pulled her close.

Lottie winced, trying to hide her discomfort.

"What's wrong?"

"It's nothing. I'm fine."

He searched her eyes. "Show me."

Lottie knew by his dour expression and tone that he wouldn't be put off. She unbuttoned the top of her shirt and pulled it open.

His jaw clenched. "Don't ever put yourself in danger because of me. *Ever.*"

Charles's words stung. He had never spoken to her that way. She felt tears coming and looked away, but he turned her toward him again. He gently cupped her face, wiping a tear with his thumb.

"I'm sorry. I didn't mean to upset you. I don't know what I would do if anything were to happen to you. I love you more than anything. What you did was so selfless and loving...and crazy," Charles said, shaking his head. "But I understand. I would have done the same for you." He rebuttoned her shirt and kissed her. "How are you otherwise?"

Lottie shrugged. "I'm okay, I guess. Maybe a little car-shy now."

Regret swept over his features. "I'm so sorry. We can ride the bus again if it makes you more comfortable."

"No, I'm fine. Time will take away the ill feelings." she kissed him gently and eased off the bed. "I'd better get going. I promised Mathilda I wouldn't be late for school."

~

A GNAWING SENSE OF EMPTINESS HAD SHADOWED LOTTIE throughout the morning. She missed Charles.

Are you out of class yet?

The jolt of his voice made her smile. *Yeah, I'm heading to lunch. Are you still in the hospital?*

I'm on the elevator, getting ready to leave. I'll pick you up after school. Mathilda already knows.

Wow. Are you healed enough to drive?

I'm fine, I promise. I'll be in my mom's car.

Okay. I'll see you soon.

The smile still lingered on her lips as she walked to the lunch table.

"Have you heard from Charles?" Rowen asked.

"I just did, actually," Lottie replied, sliding her chair up.

"Mom said he would be released today," Sunni remarked, shaking her head. "I still can't believe he's recovered enough to go home. He was in such bad shape yesterday."

"I know. It's odd," Rowen said.

Lottie shifted uncomfortably in her seat.

Wren eyed her. "What is it? You know something."

"No...." Lottie said, shaking her head.

"Yes, you do. Fess up, Lottie."

"Okay, fine. Charles almost died yesterday. I felt him slipping away, so I took his pain."

"You did *not* do that, Lottie," Sunni said, drawing stares.

"Shut up, Sunni," Wren scolded. "Someone will hear."

"I love him. What would you have done?"

"What were the consequences?" Wren asked.

"Just some bruising," Lottie said innocently.

"And?

"Pain. Lots of pain." Lottie slumped back in her chair, allowing herself to acknowledge the discomfort in front of her friends.

"Oh, my God. Are you *insane?*" Wren retorted in a loud whisper. "Do you know what could have happened doing that type of spell?"

"I don't care. I would protect Charles—even if it means giving up my life for him."

"Come on, guys, "Rowen chided. "This is Charles we're talking about. You know you would have done the same thing for him."

The bell rang, interrupting the conversation. Lottie dumped her trash and left the cafeteria.

As promised, Charles waited in the parking lot at the end of the day. The spell Ramona cast had worn off. His face was no longer swollen, and the cuts were mostly healed.

Lottie hugged him tightly. "I'm so glad to see you. How do you feel?"

"I'm fine. What about you?"

"Still sore, but not as bad.

"Good. I need to go to the office to get my makeup work."

"Okay. I see Christy. I'll meet you by the doors in a bit."

Lottie headed down the sidewalk to the bus line. "Hey. Sorry, I didn't speak this morning. I was a bit preoccupied."

"No worries," Christy replied. "I'm glad to see Charles is okay. I overheard Bryan Michaels talking about the wreck. What happened?"

"I think something went wrong with the brakes," Lottie answered, averting her gaze as she recalled the horror of Charles repeatedly stomping them before their crash.

"Wow, thank goodness you weren't hurt."

"Yeah."

She saw Charles leave the school and followed him to Ramona's car.

"So, what happened to your car?" Lottie asked.

"Well, for peace of mind, Mom had it checked out for suspicious tampering since she couldn't sense any magic involvement with the crash."

"Was anything tampered with?"

"No. There was a worn hose that had a small crack. It caused the fluid to leak out."

"Do you have plans for another car?"

"Actually, I do. I went to test drive an SUV when I left the hospital. Mom and I signed the papers. She's there now finishing up the sale."

Lottie shook her head.

"What?"

"You get into a crash, nearly die, and you go buy a car the minute you get out of the hospital. So warped."

He grinned. "Yeah, I guess it is a little warped."

"Do you want to work on homework with me? I'm sure Mathilda will be glad to see you."

"Sure."

Charles pulled along the circular drive and opened the door for Lottie. She grimaced as she turned to get out of the car.

"Let me help you." He took her arms and helped her stand. "I'll get your backpack."

"Charles, are you sure you don't hurt anymore?"

"Yes, I'm fine. It's you I'm worried about."

"Hello, Miss Lottie," Dabney greeted with a welcoming smile. "Mr. Lachlan, glad to see you are on the mend."

"Thank you, Dabney," Charles replied to the faithful butler.

"The Mistress is out running errands and said to make yourself at home."

"Will you ask Marie to send some tea and fruit to the library?" Lottie asked.

"Certainly."

Charles lifted an eyebrow. "Fruit?"

"What? I can be healthy...sometimes."

Marie left a tray on the table, and they soon settled into a comfortable silence as they worked.

Lottie glanced up as Charles tossed a grape in the air and caught it in his mouth.

"I never could do that," she said.

"Really? Try one."

She tossed a grape, which bounced off her cheek and rolled onto the floor. "See, I stink at this."

"Try it again."

"You're making fun now."

"No, I'm not. Try it."

Lottie tossed another one. As it came down, the grape stopped, suspended in mid-air.

"Hey! That one was going in," she said, scowling at him.

His eyes smoldered as he took the grape between his fingers and put it in her mouth. He leaned in, and Lottie met his lips. She wound her arms around him, pulling him tight, then jerked away with a gasp, forgetting her soreness.

"Lottie, I'm sorry. I wasn't thinking. Can I see it?"

She raised her shirt. "The redness is pretty much gone."

Charles's eyes turned almost black with desire. He leaned over and gently kissed her chest and ribs, then lower to her stomach. She trembled at his touch.

He eased her shirt down. "We'd better stop, or our homework won't get finished—or worse, Marie will come in here and flog us."

Lottie giggled at the thought.

~

AFTER DINNER, MATHILDA MADE UP ENOUGH OF THE healing paste to last two more nights. Lottie watched in amazement as the sparkling lights hovered over the bowl.

"Will you teach me to do spells like that?"

"Absolutely. But not until after you finish the school year. Some of these spells take lots of practice before you get them right, which means time spent perfecting them. You don't have that kind of time with studies."

"Oh, fine." Lottie knew she was right.

Mathilda handed her the mixture. "Here you are. How is it working so far?"

"It's helped the bruises a lot."

"Good."

"Thank you for making me better and letting me stay."

"You know you're always welcome here, my dear. Come on. Let's get you home."

~

LOTTIE CLIMBED INTO BED, EXHAUSTED. THE EVENTS surrounding the accident and her worry over Charles had taken all her energy. She fell asleep, her mind swirling with the fear that he could have died.

~

LOTTIE! LOTTIE, WHAT'S WRONG?

Charles's frantic voice came through, waking her.

Oh, God, I had a nightmare. It was horrible.

I know; you called my name over and over. I'll be there soon.

When Lottie got out of bed, nausea hit her at once. She rushed to the bathroom and vomited. When was the last time she had been this upset? She cleaned herself up and then crept back to her bedroom, careful not to wake her parents.

I'm here. Can you open your window?

At the sight of Charles, fresh tears sprang to her eyes.

"Hey, it's okay. That must have been some dream."

"I was in the solarium at Mathilda's when suddenly I knew someone had died. That's when I heard your voice waking me. What if something happens to you? I couldn't bear it."

He pulled her into his arms. "You've had a traumatic couple of days. That has to be the cause of your dream. I'm fine. Look at me; nothing is going to happen."

She lifted her head from Charles's shoulder and met his eyes. Emotions soaring, she kissed him. All of the fear faded away, consumed by passion as his lips moved over hers again and again.

Their desire burned. Charles tightened his grip, and in one frantic movement, he shifted her onto the bed. His lips trailed along her neck and lower to her chest. She felt his fingertips graze over her belly and then up her arms. His eyes squeezed tightly, and Lottie felt his reluctance to stop as he let out a ragged breath. When he opened his eyes, her breath caught at the intensity of his gaze. He pressed a gentle kiss to her lips. "I love you."

Lottie didn't have any words. She just let him hold her for a while. It felt good having his arms wrapped around her. She felt safe. Her eyes felt heavy as the blackened void of sleep began pulling her into unconsciousness. After a few minutes, she vaguely became aware of Charles tucking her in before his warmth left her.

Chapter Thirteen

When Charles pulled up at her house the following morning in his new SUV, Lottie grinned. "I like it."

"Thanks. Me, too. You ready to get going?"

"I guess so."

Abbey was at her locker when Lottie came down the hall. She smiled with hope.

"Hey, Abbey."

She closed the locker and walked away as if she hadn't heard.

Lottie sighed. "Enjoy your morning, too."

Abbey turned on her heel. "Why do you bother, Lottie? You have your own life— without us."

"Not by choice. I still want us to be friends, but you won't talk to me. I don't even know what this stupid fight is about anyway. Maybe you can fill me in, please?"

Lottie sensed her turmoil, sensed that Abbey wanted to talk.

"Hey, guys," Christy greeted.

Lottie watched with disappointment as Abbey put the wall back up and left.

"Um, did I interrupt something?" Christy asked.

"It's okay. I was trying to convince Abbey to explain why she and Gwen are so angry with me after all this time."

"Did she tell you?"

"No. I thought she would for a minute."

"And I had to go and ruin it. I'm sorry."

"Hey, no worries. See you in a few. I need to drop off my things."

"You okay?" Charles asked as he turned the corner.

"Yeah, stupid girl drama."

As she walked toward her locker, she smelled something foul. Charles grabbed her by the arm and stopped her before she could go further.

"What is it?"

"Stay here. Hey, Rowen?" he called.

"*What?*" she shouted back sarcastically.

"Get the others, now."

"Charles, what's wrong?" Lottie asked.

Rowen turned the corner and clamped her hand over her nose. "Oh, God. What's that awful smell?"

"I need you and Wren and Sunni to keep anyone else from coming down the hall."

Charles stood before Lottie's locker and used magic to open it.

Lottie sucked in a gasp, keeping her scream from escaping as the door swung open. She squeezed her eyes shut, trying to block out the bloody sight, but it was too late. The image of the owl hanging by its feet with its entrails spilling out was seared in her mind. Bile forced its way to her throat with every plip of blood that dripped into pools at the bottom of her locker.

Leaning against the row behind her, Lottie took a deep breath and opened her eyes. She saw a note attached to the owl's foot. Charles yanked it free and shoved it into his pocket. "Lottie, I need you to do something. Do you think you can stay calm and clear your mind?"

"I...I think so."

"Guys, come here, quick," he called to the others.

Wren paled when she saw the locker.

"We need a vanishing spell now," Charles said.

Wren nodded, pulling herself together. She formed a circle with the others.

"Lottie, repeat this with us," he urged. "Let the seen be unseen. Clear your mind quickly, or this won't work."

She closed her mind against the awful scene before her and chanted with the others.

"Let the seen be unseen... let the seen be unseen... let the seen be unseen...."

She felt an energy come out of their circle.

Charles let go of her hand. "It's done."

"I still see it," Lottie said, opening her eyes.

"Don't worry; it's just an image leftover from the magic and only visible to us. It will fade in a few minutes. Hurry and help me, guys. See if you can pick up on anything before it fades. A familiar smell, energy —anything that will give us a clue as to who put this here."

"I got nothing," Sunni said.

"Same here. I'm sorry," Rowen and Wren said.

Lottie closed her eyes again. "I sense something."

"What is it?" Charles asked.

"I don't know."

"Clear your mind, Lottie. Focus."

"It's blocked. Someone cast a spell. I can't get around it. Something is familiar to me, though. The energy, maybe, but I can't be sure."

"It's okay," Charles said. "Let's get out of here. You guys grab your crystals. If you pick up on anything, let me know."

They nodded and filed out of the locker area.

"Lottie, come with me. There's no way you are going to school. You're a wreck."

She followed him out the side door and into the parking lot, her legs weak and trembling.

"Would you mind taking me to Mathilda's? I want to let her know what happened."

"Sure."

~

MARIE LED CHARLES AND LOTTIE TO THE SIDE GARDEN, where Mathilda sat meditating on the grass.

She opened one eye. "Aren't you two supposed to be in school?"

"I'm sorry to interrupt your quiet time," Lottie said.

"What's wrong, Charles? I can read your energy."

Lottie noticed his clenched fists, which he released upon Mathilda's question.

"Someone decided to slice open an owl and hang its bloody carcass in Lottie's locker."

"You're sure it was an owl?"

"Yes."

"Message received."

"Clearly," Charles agreed.

"Wait a minute," Lottie interrupted. "What am I missing?"

"Right after the cat attacked you, my coven took turns watching your house at night," Mathilda replied. "Phil thought it best to use animal form so he wouldn't alarm you."

"Remember that first night after your party when you heard the owl? That was Phil," Charles added.

"No way." Lottie shook her head. She began to put the pieces together. "He went after the cat. That's why I heard it scream. Oh, my God, Phil...."

"The owl wasn't him if that's what you're thinking," Mathilda assured.

"So, why was it in my locker?"

"To send us a message," Charles said.

"What message?"

"That they are onto us, and they know we are onto them. Basically, let the games begin. Was there a note this time?" Mathilda asked.

"Yes. I grabbed it before we did the vanishing spell."

"Quick thinking, Charles. I can only imagine what would have happened had anyone seen that. May I have the note?"

"Sure."

Mathilda took it and closed her eyes. "Someone was careful. I sense no magic."

"That's what I thought," Lottie replied. "My mind picked up on something familiar, but it vanished when I tried to grasp onto what it was."

"Have either of you read this?"

"No, we came straight here," Charles replied.

"Do you mind if I read it, Charlotte?" Mathilda asked.

"No, I'd rather you do it."

Mathilda untied the strings of the black ribbon, letting it drop to her lap. Unfolding the paper, she read: "Time to play."

A chill ran down Lottie's spine, settling as a sick pit in her stomach. "Oh, no."

"What's wrong?" Charles asked.

"When Mathilda read the words, I felt something unleash."

"I felt it too," Mathilda said, rising. "You two follow me inside." She opened the French doors and placed her sun hat on the table. "Marie, see that we're not disturbed."

Charles chuckled when Mathilda pulled down on the sconce and led them down the corridor into her keeping room. "So this is the secret spell room I've heard my mother mention. Very creative entrance."

"Thank you," Mathilda said. She waved her hand, and every candle lit at once. "Charlotte, please sit in the center of the pentagram. Charles, kindly fetch the agrimony from the herb cabinet."

He handed it to her, and Mathilda set it to flame. As she walked around the circle's perimeter, the incense from the agrimony surrounded Lottie with a cedar-like scent. She couldn't understand Mathilda's words, but she sensed their power. After the third walk around, Mathilda abruptly stopped. A vacuum-like energy sucked the flames from the candles into the circle above Lottie, forming tiny golden orbs of light that slowly trickled over her.

"There you are, dear. How do you feel?"

"Oddly at peace. What did you do?"

"I cast a banishing spell to ward off the dark energy. Charles, will you hand me that small dustpan and hand broom?"

"Sure."

"Charlotte, sweep the debris from the Agrimony and come over to the cabinet—careful not to spill a single ash."

Mathilda took out a small vial and a funnel. "Gently pour the ashes into the vial."

Lottie gripped the funnel and carefully tapped the ashes in.

"Now. Cork it and you're finished," Mathilda said. She cut some wire, wound it around the vial, then attached it to Lottie's pendant. "Wear this every day until the moon waxes full again."

"Okay. Now what?" Lottie asked, pulling the necklace over her head.

"Pick out the Fluorite stone and tell me its properties."

Lottie rummaged through until she found the dark purple stone. She ran her fingers over the rough edges, recalling what she had learned.

"Stone of higher awareness," she began. "It increases psychic development, stimulates the third eye, aids mystic visions, wards off negative energies, and accesses information."

"Very good. Keep it in your pocket and meditate at some point. If anything comes to you, let me know immediately."

"I will. Thank you, Mathilda."

"Now that you're feeling better, I'm going to head back to school," Charles said, grabbing his keys. "I'll swing by at the end of the day to pick you up. If anybody asks, I'll say that you got sick."

"Okay. Thank you."

Mathilda absentmindedly tapped her pale-colored oval nails on the back of her phone case. "Well, I don't like going behind your parents' backs, but I am glad to have you here. I need to better prepare you with your magic, which will take some time. That being said, I need to work my magic and call the school to tell them you won't be back the rest of the week."

Lottie paced as she listened to Mathilda speak in her mother's voice. Her magic captured the exact tone perfectly.

"It's settled," Mathilda said, hanging up. "They have it on file that 'your mother' called in your absence."

"Thank you. I'm sorry I put you in this position."

"Let's not think about it. This is a perfect time for us to complete some of your spell training."

"Can we start now?"

Mathilda smiled. "Sure. We'll go out into the woods today. Why don't you run upstairs to your room and change out of that dress? I'm sure you can find something suitable to put on. There should be some appropriate shoes in the bottom of the armoire."

Lottie pulled on an oversized shirt and a pair of leggings. She slipped on the canvas shoes from the back of the armoire and headed down to the foyer.

"All set?" Mathilda asked.

"Yep. What are we doing with the basket?"

"We'll forage along the way. The henbit should be blooming now."

The manicured path they started on got narrower and more natural-looking as they went along. Lottie took in the wild beauty of her surroundings, pausing from time to time to pick wildflowers.

Mathilda stopped their pace. "Do you sense it? Close your eyes."

Lottie obliged, opening her ears to the world around her. The chittering of birds overhead was the first sound she noticed. Then, she heard it.

"There's water here, but I don't see it."

"That's because it's underground. Your magic is deeply ingrained, Charlotte, and the more you use it, the easier it will be to call forth. Use your power to draw the water out. You can do this."

Lottie focused all of her energy on the ground beneath her feet. She could hear it bubbling and rushing.

"Listen to it, Charlotte. It comes up for you."

Suddenly, the ground burst open, shooting water high into the air. Lottie laughed as the water fell over her. She raised her arms above her head and slowly lowered them, causing the water to go into the earth back to its natural flow.

"That. Was. *Amazing!*"

"Yes, it was," Mathilda agreed. "And you just completed your first lesson on controlling one of the elements—and without my help."

Lottie grinned. "I guess I did."

"Why don't you return to the side garden and practice more water magic by the fountain? I'll check on you in a bit."

∼

JAKE PUTNAM WALKED PAST LOTTIE'S LOCKER JUST AS Charles turned the corner. Something seemed off about him as he stared Charles down with empty eyes, clipping his shoulder as he walked by.

Charles's jaw clenched. He grabbed Jake's arm, forcing him to stop. "What's your problem, man?"

Jake's gaze was bold as if daring Charles to try something. He gave a twisted smile in response, never breaking eye contact.

"Stay the hell away from Lottie, you hear me?"

Jake smirked and walked away.

"I mean it, Jake."

MATHILDA PLACED HER BASKET ON A GARDEN BENCH AND watched Lottie practice her new-found skill of water magic. "How's it going?"

"Good." Lottie made a spiraling motion, causing water to flow around the circle. Tiny droplets beaded along her wrist, cool against her skin and sparkling in the sunlight. She waved her hand, manipulating the water back into the fountain. "What's next?"

"You're quite eager, aren't you? Since you now control water, we could try drawing from the earth for the rest. Come on. Let's go for a drive into the forest."

"Why don't we go back into the woods here?"

"Because we're too close to civilization. What you will attempt requires a place far away from humankind."

An hour's drive east, Mathilda turned the car toward the forest reserve. She took a single-lane road until she came to a gate blocking a seldom-used service entry. A rusted white sign threatened prosecution to trespassers.

"What now?" Lottie asked.

"Watch and learn."

As Mathilda flicked her wrist, the chains dropped to the ground, and the gate swung open.

Lottie's eyes widened. "Okay, then. Breaking the law, it is."

They drove another twenty minutes up the rugged, winding mountain road to a clearing. Mathilda grabbed her satchel and opened the door. "Off we go."

Lottie followed her out into the center of the clearing.

"All right, my dear, fetch a sturdy stick whilst I cleanse the area."

"You know you just said *whilst*."

"I did, didn't I? Sometimes I forget myself."

Lottie held out a stick she pulled from under some brush. "I found one."

"You're going to do circle magic. Use the stick and etch your circle into the ground. Remember what I taught you: breathe and connect with the earth. Draw in the power of the elements."

Pulling off her shoes, Lottie lowered the stick. A flame sparked as soon as she put it to the ground. It blazed behind her, leaving a blackened trail in its wake until the completion of the circle. There was a shift in the air, a tangible thickness, causing the hair on her arms to rise suddenly. Centering on the energy within the circle, she closed her eyes. With careful focus, she drew from the earth below and the air around her.

Lightening began to form outside the circle, streaking in jagged forks, and Lottie reached out, drawing the energy into herself. Enveloped in light and electricity, she stretched out her other hand and sent a blazing white fire around the blackened trail she had drawn with the stick. Feeling more in control and balanced with nature, she released the lightning back into the earth.

"Excellent, Charlotte. You accomplished more than I hoped. You'll do just fine. Now, let's finish up and get home before Charles arrives for you."

～

ANTICIPATION SWEPT OVER LOTTIE, ALMOST ELECTRICAL, sending tingling sensations up and down her arms and fingertips. She clenched her hands and smiled as she entered the library, recalling the sheer force of energy she felt from the lighting.

Charles sat in a leather wingback chair, reviewing his homework. His profile was graceful in the light pouring in from the windows behind him, and his presence sent myriad emotions running through her. He looked up from his book and smiled.

"I didn't expect you to be here this soon," Lottie said, approaching the chair.

He pulled her onto his lap. "I cut out before seventh period since Mr. Taylor was giving a math review, and I'm already prepared. I can see you had a productive day," he said, suddenly grinning.

"You can? How?"

"There's something different about you. Your aura is brighter. You did some serious bonding with nature, didn't you?"

"How can you possibly know that?"

"I told you, Lottie, we're connected. I am in you, and you are in me." He pulled her closer and kissed her.

She eased back, sensing something weighing on his mind. "And you're troubled. What's going on?"

"I had a run-in with Jake by your locker. You were right; he has some issues."

"What was Jake doing at my locker?"

"I don't know. I felt his bad vibes, but I didn't sense any involvement with the owl incident."

Lottie shook her head. "Jake's acting super weird. I'm worried about Gwen. She's not at all herself. Abbey, either, for that matter."

"We'll keep our eye on them."

The alarm on Charles's phone went off. "School just let out," he said, stopping the alarm. "I'd better get you home."

Lottie eased off his lap. "I'll let Mathilda know we're leaving. Let's hope my parents don't find out about me missing school. I don't want to worry them with any of this."

Charles wheeled around the circular drive. "Now that Mathilda has taken care of your future absences, how about we spend the next few days together when you're not practicing with her? I'll take my classes remotely, so it won't be a problem for me to miss."

She flashed him a smile. "I'd like that very much."

〜

Silence hung over the library until the foyer door thudded closed.

"Finally," Sunni huffed as footsteps echoed down the corridor.

"Come in, dear," Ramona said, patting the sofa.

Charles sat by his mother on the sofa's edge, stretching his legs out in front of him.

"Okay, Charles, let's have it," Mathilda said.

He nodded. "After the vanishing spell, while the image of the owl was still there, I had Lottie try to pick up on the negative energy left behind. She was horrified, and I knew she wasn't thinking clearly, so I got into her mind before she could see the vision and blocked it from her view. I regretted doing it initially, but I'm glad I did after what I saw in her mind. There was a murky shadow of a female. She was casting. I couldn't see her face or hear enough to decipher anything, but I did pick up on her intent. This woman is empty and full of hatred, but not necessarily at Lottie. She wants something from her. She's getting frustrated, but she's patient. I got a strong sense that she was planning to hurt Lottie.

"There's also an issue with Gwen and Abbey, Lottie's friends. According to her, there are major personality changes with them. She says they're cold and mean toward her now that she's with us. Lottie thinks they're acting out of jealousy, but Jake Putnam takes it beyond that. He's been watching her, and it has Lottie on edge. I had a run-in with him today. The boy gives off some nasty vibes. I read him but couldn't see his involvement with the owl in Lottie's locker."

"Did you sense any magic in the boy?" Regina asked.

"No," Charles replied. "He's not a witch."

"But he could be working for one," Trina suggested.

"Perhaps," Mathilda said, frowning. "Charles, I want you four to stay very close to Charlotte. Channel each other whenever necessary, and let us know if you suspect anything. She won't think much of you lingering about her. I fear the pendant may be the root of this, but I can't be sure yet."

"What makes you think that?" Charles asked, alarmed.

"It's just a theory. This is the only life in which someone is targeting Charlotte—and the only one where her powers are coming all at once.

She can barely control them this time. Her pendant will get warm if someone actively searches for the hidden moonstone holding Cassandra's powers. They are linked, so watch her closely. Now, you kids head home," Mathilda said. "We'll keep each other informed."

Charles nodded and followed the others out of the library.

"I have a plan," Phil said once the elder coven was alone. "I don't like the idea of Lottie being in town over the summer. Regina and I were talking earlier. Why don't we take the kids through Europe once school lets out? It'll give us a chance to teach them more of the old ways of practice, and Lottie will be out of danger."

"Splendid idea, Phil," Ramona said.

Mathilda hesitated. "I don't know…Charles specifically said it was a woman's voice he heard in Charlotte's mind. I say we locate the woman sponsoring Matthew. He said that she wasn't a witch. What if he's lying to protect her? We've sensed a dark force for some time now. It very well may be her."

"All the more reason to get Lottie out of here," Regina replied.

"You and Phil take the children abroad then," Mathilda said, resigned. "I will stay here with the others and try to learn more about the mysterious Ms. Sullivan."

"It's settled then," Ramona said with satisfying finality. "Now, we must find a way to convince Lottie's parents."

"Leave that part to me," Regina said with a wink.

CHARLES OPENED THE DOOR FOR HIS MOTHER WHEN HE SAW her pull the car into the drive. "I didn't expect you back from Mathilda's so soon."

Ramona placed her keys on the table and settled onto the sofa. "Sit by me, and I'll fill you in on everything."

Charles listened while his mother explained the details of the trip.

"I guess it's a good idea."

"Cheer up, son. This plan is beneficial to you all."

"Mom, I'm grateful, but you have no idea of the darkness lying in wait for Lottie."

"Yes, I do. Believe me. That's why I'm staying behind. We'll take down this threat before you return."

Charles nodded. The plan was a good one, and Lottie would love it. He was sure of it. He took out his phone to message her. *Have something exciting to tell you. Will come by tonight.*

Lottie smiled as she read Charles's text. *Hint?*

His response was immediate. *No.*

Grinning, she shoved her phone in her pocket. Tired of being indoors, she headed toward the woods, pausing to admire some wildflowers growing by the large oak. The air was cool at the small clearing, her favorite place to go when she wanted to be alone, and she took in a deep breath as she settled onto the mossy ground. A twig snapped in the distance, sending a squirrel bounding toward her. Tingles of alarm ran down Lottie's spine. She suddenly felt uneasy, as if someone was watching her. She focused all her energy on the sounds around her. Nothing out of the ordinary stood out, but it was much quieter than usual. She wondered if the protection spell over her house also included the woods. She would make a point to ask Mathilda, but until then, she headed back to the safety of her home.

~

"Damn them," Selene fumed, storming down the hill. She flung her arm outward, sending a blast of energy into a rotted log blocking her way. It splintered at once.

Matthew flinched. "Mistress, you shouldn't be in your true form. What if someone sees you?"

Selene's head whipped toward Mathew, lashing all her fury out on him. He dropped to his knees and grabbed his head, writhing in pain. As she increased his agony, her eyes glowed brightly.

"Please, Mistress...." Matthew begged.

She stopped the assault and composed herself.

"Don't ever assume to tell me what to do. Is that clear?"

"Quite," he rasped.

"It appears the protection spell around Lottie's house is impenetrable—for now. Find me more recruits, Matthew. This time get me witches with some considerable power. I'll get through that spell one way or another."

Matthew cringed at the thought of what would happen when he found recruits.

~

LOTTIE HAD JUST FALLEN ASLEEP WHEN SHE HEARD HER window open. She bolted up in bed, disoriented as fear flooded through her.

"It's just me," Charles soothed.

She exhaled in relief, realizing she had dozed off while waiting for him.

"Look at you; come here." He eased onto the bed and pulled her close. "I'm sorry I scared you."

"It's okay," Lottie said, settling into his warmth. "I didn't mean to fall asleep. What's this exciting news you have to tell me?"

A slow grin spread over his face as he angled himself toward her. "Phil and Regina want to take all of us to Europe as soon as school wraps up. They think it'll be a good way to let us experience some of the old ways of magic."

Lottie's eyes widened. "Oh, my God! Are you serious?" The smile fell from her face as she pondered the trip.

"What is it?"

"I doubt my parents will let me go. That's a huge thing to ask for."

"Regina has it all planned out. She can be quite persuasive when she wants to be. It's one of her talents. Wren can fill you in on those details."

"She'll have to be beyond persuasive if she's going to convince my parents to let me leave the country."

"Trust me. She is."

Chapter Fourteen

"Look at that smile, Randy. She's in love."

Lottie blushed, nearly dropping her bowl. "Mom!"

"Well, aren't you?"

"Yes, but you don't have to blurt it out like that."

"I'm happy for you, sweetie. I like Charles. You two have a good thing going. Very rare at your age."

Her father shook his head. "Can we change the subject?"

"Your dad is in denial. He thinks you're still his little girl."

"She is," he growled.

"You two, good grief. Let the 'little girl' eat her breakfast in peace."

Charles arrived in his usual timely fashion. Lottie grabbed her backpack and headed out under the pretense of attending school.

"Morning," she greeted. "You're looking quite handsome today."

She noticed his calmness, which hadn't been there last night.

"Do I now?" He smiled, running his fingers through his hair.

"You know I love it when you do that."

He smiled wickedly. "I know. Your thoughts betray you."

Lottie shook her head. "So, what do you want to do today?"

"Wren asked us to come over before school. Her mom wants to talk to you about the trip."

"Sounds good."

When they pulled up, Lottie noticed the gleaming, berry-red car with a black top in front of the Wesley's house.

"Wow, whose car is that?"

"It's Phil's Aston Martin. The man has more exotic cars than an exotic car dealership."

"Really? Where does he keep them? His garage isn't big enough for dealership quantity."

"He has an underground garage."

"You're kidding?"

"Nope. You'll find we witches have many secret rooms."

"How do Phil and Regina have so much money anyway?"

"All of the elders are loaded. Phil and Regina are just more extravagant with their spending. When you've been around as long as they have, there are ways of building your fortune. Phil's specialty is objects of interest. I'm sure you've noticed the rare items and paintings throughout his house. He's got a whole room off his garage full of artifacts and collectibles he obtained over the centuries. He sells pieces from time to time. Although, I'm not sure he sells as much as he buys."

Charles pressed the doorbell and stepped back.

"Good morning," Regina greeted. "I made breakfast if you're hungry."

"Thank you," Lottie said, following her to the kitchen.

"Oh, good. You're here," Wren greeted. "Tell Lottie the plan, Mom."

Regina paused to refill her coffee. "Well, I will call your mother today and invite her to lunch. I'll ask her if she will be kind enough to allow you to go with us on some educational trip this summer. I don't know how she can refuse that."

"No, that sounds like a good plan. I hope it works. I think I would die if my parents said no after getting my hopes up."

Regina smiled. "They won't say no, don't worry."

"Mom is golden," Wren remarked. "If she says you're going, you're as good as packed. Now, let's finish up and head out into the woods. I've gotta squeeze in my morning meditation before school."

They meandered out to the clearing, to their spot under the trees. Lottie sat with her back firmly against a tree, soaking up the sun and the energy. She tuned out the others and listened to the pulse of nature around her. Exhilarated, a rush of adrenaline coursed through her. She let herself be free to its will, laughing at the freedom she felt as she released the energy into the earth.

Lottie gasped when she opened her eyes. The clearing was covered in flowers. More sprouted along the outer circle of the trees.

"Oh, Lottie, it's so beautiful," Rowen said, looking around.

Charles picked one of the violets and tucked it in Lottie's hair. She blushed as his knuckles grazed her cheek. "I guess I got a little caught up in the moment."

Charles smiled. "That's a good thing. You do amazing things when you let go."

Sunni glanced at her phone. "We'd better get inside; twenty minutes before time to leave for school.

"I'll be along shortly," Lottie replied. "I want to collect some bloodroot for Mathilda."

"We'll help you, then," Wren said.

When they returned to the house, Lottie let go of the bottom of her shirt—her makeshift basket—allowing the bloodroot to tumble onto the counter.

"Is that bloodroot?" Regina asked. "Wow, I haven't seen that growing here in ages. Where did you find it?"

"In the clearing," Wren replied. "Lottie was at one with her inner witch and had a moment. The whole clearing is full of it."

"Yeah...," Lottie admitted. "I guess it would be a good day to forage."

"Did you call Lottie's mom?" Wren asked, placing a bunch of flowers on the counter.

"I did," Regina replied. "She agreed to meet me today for lunch."

"Good. Keep us posted then."

"I'll do that. Hurry up and get wrapped up for school. Charles, you and Lottie are welcome to hang out here if you'd like. Just stay out of town today unless you want to be seen by Lottie's mother."

Charles gave a salute. "Will do."

Lottie started separating the bloodroot. "I'll bundle these up while we wait for Regina to return."

"I'll get the supplies for you," Wren replied, opening a drawer.

Lottie wrapped twine around the stems of one bundle and set it aside.

"You know there's an easier way, right?" Wren asked. She waved her hand, and the string wound around in a neat knot in seconds. "See? All done, not a minute wasted."

"I like handling the herbs. I find it peaceful."

"If you say so. I don't have the patience for that."

"Right?" Rowen added. "I admire you, Lottie. You have this connection with nature that's amazing but frustrating. Hurry up already; you're making me crazy watching you drag that out."

Sunni grabbed up a bunch of the bloodroot. "Race you."

Rowen glowered toward the group. "Oh, it's on."

Wren flicked her wrists and sent the twine wrapping before the others could start. Rowen jumped in and tried to catch up.

"Hey guys, come on," Lottie whined. "Don't bruise them."

"Ha! You're going down, Wren," Rowen taunted as she finished the last one. "Count 'em."

"Fifteen," Sunni said.

"Nineteen," Wren boasted. "How many do you have, Rowen?"

"Seventeen," she scowled. "You cheated."

Wren frowned. "I resent that, Rowen Maxwell. You're just mad because you lost."

Rowen's eyes widened. She flicked her wrist, causing the rest of the twine to wind through Wren's hair.

"Here we go," Charles muttered.

"Oh, you little *witch*. You know how bad my hair tangles."

Rowen tried not to laugh. "Okay, I'm sorry. I'll get it out."

"No, I don't trust you. I'll do it."

Sunni huffed. "Oh, just stop. Let me. You're not getting the pieces back here."

"And *that's* why I like to handle the herbs—with care," Lottie muttered.

~

"YOU'RE GOING TO WEAR OUT THAT RUG," CHARLES STATED, watching Lottie pace by the window. "Relax. I'm telling you there's nothing to worry about. Regina has a way with her words. One of her many talents is the magic that flows through her speech. No one can resist her when she wields it."

"Well, that's a dangerous talent to have," Lottie said, shuddering at the thought.

"Given to the wrong person, yes," Charles agreed.

Lottie paused her pacing as she waited for Regina to come inside.

"Hello, you two," Regina greeted as she swept through the door.

"You might want to put Lottie out of her misery," Charles suggested. "She's been wearing a path in the rug for the last half hour."

"I'll get right to it, then. Lottie, you'll need to get your passport. You're going to Europe."

Lottie squealed. "Oh, my God. This is awesome. Thank you, Regina. How did you manage it?"

"Your mother is such a nice lady. She was only too happy to let you go. Honestly, the only bump was over money. She had a hard time accepting the all-expenses-paid part."

"I'm sure she did. I'm still trying to come to terms with that part. We're not used to such freedom with finances."

"Get used to it, sweetheart. You're quite the wealthy young woman yourself. Mathilda saw to that over the centuries."

The corners of Regina's crimson-colored lips tightened as Lottie shifted uncomfortably.

"I probably shouldn't have blurted that out. You should talk to Mathilda about it."

"Would you like me to take you by Mathilda's?" Charles asked.

"That would be great. I'd like to hang this bloodroot in her herb cellar to dry."

Charles grabbed his keys from the counter. "Thanks for letting us hang out here."

Regina smiled. "Anytime."

~

LOTTIE STROLLED INTO THE SUNROOM, WEARING AN EXCITED smile. "Look what I have!"

Mathilda glanced up from her gardening magazine. "Bloodroot. Charlotte, how nice. Where did you get that much of it?"

"It came up during my meditation this morning. You should see the clearing at Phil and Regina's. It's beautiful."

"I may have to go over there."

"Can we take these to the herb cellar?"

"Certainly. It will give us a chance to talk before we practice. Charles, make yourself at home."

"Thanks. I'll be in the library."

"I have news," Lottie gushed. "Mom had lunch with Regina today. I'm going on the trip. Can you believe she said yes?"

"That's wonderful. I have something for you, but let's get these hung first."

"What are you going to do with this much bloodroot?" Lottie asked.

"I have a few elderly people I like to look in on. Some are in declining health, and I often bring a basket of goodies to help ease their discomfort."

"How sweet of you." Lottie paused. "Mathilda, I just realized something. How do you do it? Don't people notice you don't age?"

"Actually, dear, I have aged."

"How? You're immortal."

"It's intentional—as much as I hate it. Over the years, I make myself start to look older so as to not arouse suspicion. I own properties all over the world. When my time is up in one area, I leave. After several generations pass for no one to remember me, I come back young and invigorated. Sometimes, I don't come back to the same area for centuries. Once, I altered my appearance totally so that I could stay here. I told the townspeople that I was Mathilda Longhurst's niece. I hated it, though. I didn't like being brunette either, no offense."

Lottie grinned. "So, before I found out we were witches when you told me this castle had been in the family for centuries, you were referring to yourself, weren't you?"

"Right. Before this go-round, I hadn't been back here for over 107 years. Fate brought me back to Akron to meet your mother." Mathilda gazed around with a wistful smile. "I like it here."

"How did you find my mother?"

"I was living in Savannah, Georgia when I became pregnant with you. I stayed there until around five months into the pregnancy. Then I prepared to come back here where I could have my privacy without any of your magic inadvertently showing to well-wishers wanting to see you. That's when I met your mother. After you were born, I returned to Georgia to pick up a few antiques and things I missed. You were asleep when the attack came.

"Someone had let themselves into the bedroom while I was packing up. I sensed you were in danger, and I rushed into the room. Whoever it was must have heard me coming because they were gone when I came in. You were blue and struggling to breathe. I discovered a small cloth in your mouth and managed to get it out before you asphyxiated. Your mother's face came into my mind at that moment, and I knew what I had to do."

Lottie shuddered. "My God. How horrible. Did you ever find out who tried to kill me?"

"Several months before I became pregnant with you, there was a coven of witches in Savannah causing trouble for some of the locals. They started drawing the attention of the authorities. After a grisly murder took place, my coven stripped them of their magic. They had ties to some witches in Charleston, and a witch from that coven acted out the revenge on their behalf. That's why I gave you up. I couldn't bear thinking of anything happening to you because of me."

"And yet here I am, in danger again," Lottie said softly. "Do you think it could be the same person?"

"No. We haven't had any coven issues since that time. You are of age now, fully aware of who you are, and reunited with me. How someone knows it, though, I cannot fathom. We are working hard to find who's doing this evil to you. And we will—make no mistake."

Lottie nodded. She glanced around the cellar at the bundles of drying herbs, ancient-looking mortars, and pestles.

"I can't imagine what it's like for you. Do you like being immortal?"

"That's tough to answer," Mathilda said. "It's difficult to say goodbye to places and part with your children. That's the hardest thing we have to do. But there are so many beautiful places to see, and my coven sisters keep me going, Regina especially. She has such a passion for living. I prefer to be alone, but it's good to know that I have them."

"What does the rest of the coven do when it's time to leave a place?"

"We've stuck together since our beginnings. You children need each other, so we made a pact never to separate."

"So, you were the first immortal witch in your coven. How did it all happen?"

A brief flash of sadness reflected in Mathilda's eyes. "Cassandra gave me this life. She had a use for me at one time and tricked me with her 'gift' in the form of a toast. Once I drank from the chalice, I became as she was. Immortal. I never asked for it, but I couldn't change what I was, so I tried to forgive her after coming to terms with it.

"Cassandra appeased me with her pretty words of being changed, but once I learned of her true nature and saw her dark magic's effects on the earth, I knew I would need the others. I knew the spell and had the means; the rest is history. I granted my coven immortality in exchange for the upkeep of balance. Fortunately, we share deep bonds and love each other. Eternity is a long time for bad blood."

Lottie hung up her last bundle of bloodroot and washed her hands at the sink. Shafts of dim light flooded through a narrow window at the top half of the room, and particles of dust and plant matter floated lazily overhead.

"What was the price of the immortality spell you cast? The sorcerer in your book had to give up his soul and die. How did you manage to live through such a powerful spell?"

"Aelle killed to get his powers. The more he absorbed, the more access he gained to the dark arts. He eventually discovered a way to create the immortality spell when he sacrificed those innocent souls. It was a high cost to him as he didn't realize the price he would pay for their deaths.

"I cheated. Diseases were widespread in the fourteenth century. Those poor souls whom I couldn't save were used to channel my spell. I realized then that my magic was powerful. The fact that the Goddess allowed me to keep such powers after I used those souls for my spell made me realize that she trusted me. I had been given a true gift, so I swore never to use my immortality to harm anyone outside of protecting the goodness and balance within the earth. The others in my coven made the same blood pact. We dispel dark witches whenever necessary. It's the only time we use dark magic. Eliza Duprey is the perfect example of what happens to witches when they meddle in forbidden magic."

"What happened to her?" Lottie asked.

"Ms. Duprey was an heiress in the late 1800s. She killed her family for their fortune and revenge. Her mother was a religious fanatic and never tolerated the gift that her daughter was blessed with, and her father refused to send her away because of the scandal it would cause. So, she was mistreated and ill-used by her family until the day she killed them.

"With her family out of the way, Eliza was free to unleash herself as she saw fit. The good people of Akron were frightened of her, and slowly, she stopped receiving calls and invitations. Her dark nature festered, and she killed anyone who even looked at her wrong. We eventually stepped in and proceeded with a binding spell, but she was strong and lashed out toward Ramona with her magic. Regina struck her down before we completed the spell. We sealed her in her family tomb in Massillon, and you know the rest."

"Wow. I love discovering new things about you, disturbing as they may be."

"I'm very private, Charlotte. You and I are very alike in that way."

"What was my father like?"

"Ah, your father...," Mathilda mused, a smile tugging at her lips. "He was a Celt, a warrior chieftain of the Ferguson clan. He was bold and fearless but a good man. Your father pursued me before I finally relented," she said, chuckling. Her smile turned wistful as she lifted a section of Lottie's dark chestnut waves. "You have his exact shade of hair and look so very like him, but you took after me in nature."

"Did you love him?"

A haunting sadness shadowed the depths of Mathilda's eyes. "I did. Our souls smashed into one another with a fierce intensity. Our time together was brief, however. He would come and go with the wind. War and rebellions took him off after one cause or another. It finally caught up to him, and he died in battle in 1333."

"I wish I could see him. I don't suppose you have a painting of him somewhere around here, do you?"

"I have something better. Come here."

Mathilda placed her fingers on Lottie's temples. The image came at once. Her father stood on a knoll dressed in furs, his long hair whipping wildly about his shoulders. His hair and beard were indeed the same rich shade of brown as Lottie's color. His features were firm but very handsome, and his dark eyes peered down as if looking directly at her.

"Oh, God, that was freaky!" Lottie said, pulling back. "It was like he saw me. He *was* handsome—and quite formidable."

"Yes, he was. More handsome than one man should be allowed."

"What was his name?"

"Duncan."

"I didn't think I'd ever know what he looked like. Thank you for showing me."

"You're welcome. Come on, let's go up to the library. Would you like some tea?"

"Sure."

Marie was gathering some old magazines from the table when they returned.

"Ah, Marie. Charlotte and I would like tea when you're ready."

"Yes, ma'am."

Lottie watched her turn on her heel and disappear from the room.

"How long has Marie been with you? She seems completely devoted to you."

"Marie has been with me since 1558. Her trust has been quite valuable, especially when witches were sought out and tortured. In 1563, she became gravely ill, and I couldn't bear the thought of losing her. So, in addition to healing her, I cast a spell for her immortality. She has remained with me since then and is as loyal as ever. The same thing happened with Dabney and Cook. Dabney nearly died in 1887, and I've had Cook with me since 1472."

Lottie shook her head. "This is—well, I would say unbelievable, but knowing otherwise, I can't say that."

"You'll find trust hard to come by outside of the coven, Charlotte. You must always be careful."

"Speaking of careful," Lottie said. "The protection spell over my house, does that include the woods? I like to go out there and meditate."

"I know you do. It's protected as well."

After Marie poured the tea, Mathilda reached for an envelope on the side table.

"I want you to have this for your trip to Europe. There are also some items upstairs in the armoire for you to take along."

Lottie opened the envelope and stared blankly at the money inside. "I can't accept this, Mathilda."

"Nonsense. I want you to have it. This is your first major trip, and I want you to enjoy yourself. It's your own money from an account that I set up a long time ago."

"Yeah...Regina mentioned something about that earlier."

"Yes, I know," Mathilda said flatly. "Regina admitted her little faux pas to me after you left her house. I have transferred money into that account through the years, and there's plenty more, so don't be afraid to spend it."

Lottie blinked away the tears pooling in her eyes. "You are so good to me."

"I only want you to be happy, Charlotte."

"I am. Thank you."

"I'll bring the money to your house tomorrow. I wouldn't want your mother to find it before I've spoken to her."

"Okay."

THE HOUSE WAS QUIET WHEN LOTTIE CAME IN. HER MOTHER sat at the kitchen table sorting through invoices. She glanced up over her reading glasses.

"Hey, you. How was your day?"

"Good. You?"

"Interesting. Regina Wesley invited me to lunch today. Why didn't you tell me she asked you to travel with her to Europe this summer?"

"I didn't find out until yesterday. And honestly, I never thought that you'd say yes. Sorry, I didn't tell you."

"It's okay. You're excited about it, aren't you?"

"Oh—my gosh, Mom, I'm *so* excited! This is a once-in-a-lifetime trip."

"I know," her mother said, grinning. That's why your father and I said yes. I have always wanted to get out of Ohio, travel, and see the world. I wouldn't dream of taking that away from you. Oh, I almost forgot; Mathilda called me this afternoon. She told me she's paying for you to go on this trip. She also said she has money saved for you and I shouldn't worry about expenses. You told Mathilda about the trip?"

Lottie shifted her gaze to the floor. "I mentioned it to her last night when I called her. That's very kind of her."

"Yes, it is. Mathilda said she'd come by tomorrow to drop off the money for you. She also said she bought some clothes for you to take on the trip."

Lottie noticed a look of apprehension in her mother's eyes. "Don't worry, Mom. Mathilda's not trying to buy me over. She just wants to help. What did Dad have to say about everything?"

"He's not thrilled about any of it, but your dad understands what it's like to want to do something like this, and he knows the trip is important for you. So, here's the deal: I'll need to take you after school tomorrow to get a passport. Have Charles drop you straight home so we can take care of that."

"Okay."

∼

AFTER DINNER, LOTTIE TOOK A LOAD OF LAUNDRY DOWN TO the basement. She returned to the kitchen and saw her father getting out of his van. He looked tired. She opened the door for him.

"Hey, Dad. Bad day?"

"Long day."

"I'm sorry. You want me to heat some food for you?"

"That would be great. I just want to sit here with a drink for a few minutes."

Lottie took a can of soda from the fridge and set it on the table for him.

"Thanks." He took a long gulp and placed the can on a coaster. "I bet you're pretty excited about the trip, huh?"

"Yep."

Lottie sensed her father's heavy thoughts as she filled his plate and put it in the microwave.

"Dad, I appreciate you and Mom allowing me to go on this trip. It means the world to me."

"I know it does. It's hard to imagine you being gone all summer. I'll miss you."

"I know. I'll miss you, too. I'll bring home some awesome souvenirs, though."

He smiled at her. "You make sure you do."

Matthew reluctantly placed the file he held into Selene's upturned palm.

"Those are all of the witches that have assisted with the Paranormal Investigators within the last five years," he remarked as she glanced through the different profile pictures inside.

She scoffed. "Seven is not enough."

"They were the only ones I could find on record."

"Then find more. I'm not trying to do parlor tricks here, Matthew. I am *this* close to getting what I want. I need enough power to ensure nothing goes wrong."

"There are no more listed in the system."

"Then look elsewhere. There was a coven of witches in Defiance when I found you, if I'm not mistaken."

Matthew hesitated. "Yes, but some of them are old acquaintances."

"All the easier for you to lure them here."

Selene gave the file back to Matthew. He stared blankly at it, thinking of his old friends. He knew there would be no saving any of them.

~

Roots protruded above ground and stretched across the forest floor. Lottie had a feeling she was here for a purpose. There was something she needed to find....

~

"Lottie? It's getting late. You'd better wake up."

Her mother's touch jerked her from the mystical forest.

"Oh, I'm sorry, honey; I didn't mean to startle you. That must have been some dream."

"I dreamt about trees with giant roots. It was bizarre."

"Ooh-kay... well, hop up and get dressed. You overslept. Charles will be here soon."

Lottie sighed. "I guess it's going to be a ponytail day."

~

"Where to?" Charles asked, pulling away from Lottie's house.

"I don't know. Mom is taking me to get my passport after school. We'll have to watch the time wherever we go."

"Want to go back to my place and watch movies?"

"Sure. Will your mom mind me dropping in unexpectedly?"

"No, not at all."

Ramona was on the sofa when they came in, her feet tucked underneath her. A small box with a raised lid sat by her side, and she was looking at some old photographs. A trace of sadness lingered on her features that disappeared when she looked up at them.

"Hello, Lottie. What a pleasant surprise. Had I known you were coming, I would have made you breakfast."

"Thank you. Don't worry about me, though. I ate before I left home."

"What are you looking at?" Charles asked.

"Just some old photographs of you. They were in the box where I keep our passports."

"Can I see them?" Lottie asked.

"Certainly. Sit by me," Ramona said, patting the sofa.

Lottie picked up a picture of Charles when he was four years old. She smiled. He hadn't changed much.

"He was such a beautiful child," Ramona bragged. "He still is."

Charles sighed. "Let's not bore Lottie, Mom."

Lottie noticed a miniature portrait painting beside the photos. "Who is this?"

"That is my mother," Ramona replied.

"You look a lot like her. What was her name?"

"Leticia."

"She was beautiful."

"Thank you."

"Lottie and I are going to hang out and watch movies today if that's okay," Charles said, placing his keys on the table.

"Of course. Make yourself at home, dear."

"Thank you," Lottie replied.

She followed Charles up the stairs. At the top, a small, cozy sitting area to the left caught Lottie's attention. The nook was surrounded by built-in shelves, bursting with books and old framed photos. An antique lamp sat on the table, casting soft light onto the wood floors.

"What a great reading area."

Charles grinned. "This is more than a reading area. You're looking at the entrance to my mother's keeping room."

"Oh, cool. It's a great cover."

They walked a little farther down the hall. Charles's bedroom was on the right. Lottie stepped in and smiled. Just as she had always imagined, his windows faced the street side. Natural light poured in. The large tree out front she had dreamt of climbing, reached out, nearly touching the glass. Lottie noticed the bed against the wall. Nothing fancy. Oak, navy bedding, neatly made. A book rested on the nightstand by the bed. She glanced at the title, *A Separate Peace* by John Knowles.

It was satisfying being on this side of his windows, finally getting to see what his inner world was like.

Charles reached the TV remote over to her. "Want to find something on Netflix?"

"Sure."

Lottie sat down on his bed and made herself comfortable.

"Is your mom okay? She seemed a little down when we first got here."

"It's getting close to the anniversary of her mother's death," Charles replied as he settled in beside her. "Every year near the Summer Solstice, she gets a little sad."

"Oh."

Charles moved the remote to the nightstand and pulled Lottie close.

THE DULL HUM OF CONVERSATION FROM THE HOTEL LOBBY went unnoticed as Matthew paced, waiting for the last witch to arrive. He could feel Selene's eyes on him from the bar, further agitating him.

The automatic doors opened, and Mitch Hamilton strode in.

"Matthew, how are you, man? It's been a long time."

"Yes, it has," Matthew replied, giving his old friend a tense smile. How have you been?"

"Well, I got married. And I have a three-month-old daughter to brag about now."

"Congratulations, Mitch. That's great." Matthew felt a sick pit in his stomach at Mitch's words. He looked toward Selene. How could anyone be so cruel?

"So, what's going on with this missing woman?" Mitch asked. "Your message to meet here seemed urgent."

"Shelly worked with me. She's...like us. She was assisting the Munroe-Falls Paranormal Investigators on a case when she disappeared. A fellow witch and I have been trying to locate her, but we're not having any luck. We thought the Defiance coven could assist us and hopefully keep out police involvement."

"I'll do what I can," Mitch said. "How many are here?"

"Seventeen, not including myself."

"That should do it."

They entered the hotel conference room, and Matthew called everyone to attention. "I appreciate you all meeting me here on short notice. I wouldn't have asked you to come if it weren't urgent. One of my co-workers—and fellow witch, Shelly White, has gone missing. I'd like to introduce you to Selene Sullivan. She's been assisting me in trying to locate Shelly."

Selene stood and nodded to the group. "Thank you, Matthew. It was very kind of all of you to come to help your sister witch. Shelly has been missing for several weeks. Matthew and I hope that if we join our powers, we can locate her."

"If you all don't mind taking a drive in the morning," Matthew interrupted, "I'll take you to the last known place that Shelly visited. Feel free to hang out here or at the bar. I'm calling it a day." He stood and pushed his chair back underneath the table, and someone booed jokingly.

Matthew forced a smile. "I'm afraid the long hours are catching up with me. It was good seeing all of you."

He caught Selene's eye roll as he strode out of the room.

~

"Mom, why didn't you let me pay the passport fees?" Lottie asked, getting into the car. "I feel bad that you paid extra to expedite it."

"Honey, it's fine. I wanted to make sure you got it in time. You keep your money for the trip."

"Thank you, but I wish you hadn't done that."

"Have you heard from Mathilda?"

"No. I told her I'd let her know when we wrapped up. I'll message her now."

It was five when Mathilda arrived. Lottie and her mother stepped outside.

"Lovely evening, isn't it," Mathilda greeted.

"Yes, it is," Lottie's mother agreed.

"Lottie, would you like to help me get everything inside?" Mathilda asked.

"Sure."

Her mother held the door open for them. "Do you need help carrying anything?"

"No, thank you, Carol," Mathilda replied. "It's just these two cases."

Lottie could tell that her mother was uncomfortable with Mathilda coming inside by the insecure manner in which her eyes darted around the house.

Lottie brushed past her and led Mathilda upstairs.

"So, this is my room."

Mathilda smiled. "It's very charming, just as I pictured it. You have a nice view of the mountains from your window."

"I do. It's my favorite spot in the house. I sit here for hours sometimes."

"I can see why. Go ahead and open these up and tell me what you think."

Lottie unzipped the first case. It was packed to capacity.

"Look at all of these clothes!" She pulled out a dress and held it up. "I love this. Thank you."

"You're welcome."

Lottie rummaged through the second case. "I don't have to pack much of anything now. These are all so perfect."

"Good. Here is the money. Do you need anything else?" Mathilda asked.

Lottie hugged her. "No, you've more than taken care of me. Thank you, Mathilda."

"You're welcome, dear. I'll go so you can get back to your family time."

"I'll walk you out."

Lottie stood on the stoop with her mother as Mathilda pulled away.

"I don't suppose you'll need to pack much now," her mother stated.

"No, just the basics."

"So, what do you say to takeout and board games?"

"I say yes."

Chapter Fifteen

Matthew glanced in his rearview at the line of cars following him to the Duprey Tomb. His thoughts were wild with possibilities as he drove. He had to thwart Selene's plan somehow.

Fear mounted as he arrived at the end of the secluded dirt road. He knew his fate should he even attempt to divert her. He steered his car into the field, turned the engine off, and watched the vehicles filling in around him.

"Is there no other way, Mistress? Mitch has a new baby—these are people with families—"

"Shut it, Matthew," Selene interrupted. "Or join the ranks of the almost newly departed." She slammed the door, ending the conversation.

Matthew clutched his phone. He considered dialing Ramona, but if Selene knew he was having second thoughts, his punishment would be swift and severe. He got out and shoved his phone into his pocket.

Mitch stood by his car, talking with his wife on the phone as Matthew passed by.

"I will," he said. "Kiss the princess for me. I love you too."

To hell with retribution, Matthew thought. He pulled his phone back out and texted—*HELP* to RL. He quickly deleted the conversation and made his way toward the front of the tomb to join the others.

"This is the last place we know Shelly visited," Selene said, walking toward a simple wooden table she had brought for the occasion. "I have some special items to channel her that I will set up on this altar. Clear your minds as I make ready."

She reached into her bag for the objects for her spell. When she needed to draw on immense power, Matthew had seen Selene use these before. A small bird skull, which he knew to be from a chicken, an odd, misshapen iron circle, too large to fit on a finger but too small to wear on the wrist, and a dagger that appeared centuries old. Matthew felt intense discomfort looking at them. Something foul permeated the air every time she took out these items.

"Please, join hands," she said, taking her place beside Matthew.

He turned to her with pleading eyes. She squeezed his hand painfully.

As the last member closed the circle, Matthew felt the power from Selene's magic rush around the perimeter. The others became locked in the spell, unable to move. Selene pulled her hand from the woman beside her and walked to the center. Matthew remained where he was.

"Let go, Matthew."

"I want no part of this. It's wrong."

Selene waved her hand and dispelled Matthew from the circle. He flew backward and landed hard on the ground; the breath nearly knocked out of him. She sealed the broken circle with a band of dull, murky energy and quickly turned to the table. Reaching for the dagger, Selene punctured her palm with the blade, then took the skull in one hand and the ring in the other. A line of blood streaked down to her elbow and onto the ground with a loud hiss as she raised her arms toward the group. Her words were mixed with many voices as she shouted: *"Release unto me...."*

At once, everyone's eyes flew open, white and glassy as they stood frozen, linked with Selene. The elements jolted awake. Dark, angry clouds gathered, and thunder cracked. Lightning flashed in the sky as the power of each witch streaked out toward Selene. Her eyes glazed, and she began to levitate off the ground.

Matthew jerked his phone out frantically but found it was suddenly dead. He could only watch, helpless, as his old friends were stripped of their powers. As the last of the magic left their bodies, they became like empty hulls. Lifeless. The wind slashed away at skin and bone. Torrents of dusty particles swirled around, taking the remaining few still standing until nothing was left of anyone. Then it stopped. The particles gently scattered throughout the field, erasing any trace of their existence. Slowly, Selene lowered to the ground. She stood motionless, still transfixed in the spell.

"Mistress?"

She didn't respond. Matthew walked cautiously toward her.

"Mistress?"

Her eyes flashed, no longer white like before. Now, they were completely black and terrifying to look upon. Matthew stumbled backward in shock. His first instinct was to run to his car. Just as he was within reach of the door, a force jerked him back to the tomb.

"Going somewhere?" Selene asked.

"I, um, you frightened me," he stammered.

"You should be frightened. You disobeyed me. And you know what that means. Punishment."

"No, please...I got scared. I won't let it happen again."

Selene reached out her hand, and Matthew began to jerk. His screams of agony echoed across the field as his body shifted form. His bones popped and snapped one by one as he transformed into the black wolf.

"I did warn you," Selene said with a cruel smile.

She waved her hand, and pieces of metal from the cars scattered across the field along with the wind until they, too, were gone. The gravesite looked undisturbed once more.

"Come," Selene said to the creature that had once been Matthew. He whined in submission and followed close by her heels.

"Good boy."

∽

R AMONA LOWERED HER BOOK TO HER LAP, DISTRACTED BY the chime of her phone. She picked it up off the table and turned it over.

—HELP

She dialed the number back and waited. An odd distorted ring, followed by ominous-sounding whispers, came through the phone, and it went dead. She quickly dialed Mathilda.

"Gather the others. I'm coming over. I believe Matthew is in grave danger."

~

"I 'M GOING TO ASSUME THE REST OF YOU ALSO FELT THE disturbing tip of balance," Regina stated. Her red-bottomed heels clicked loudly on the floor as she came in behind the others.

"You are correct, sister," Ramona said. "I got a text earlier that simply read 'help'. I didn't recognize the number, but it was Matthew; I sensed it. When I tried to dial him back, the sounds on the other end were unnatural and disturbing—they were voices not of this world. Whatever it was is not something we've dealt with since the time of Aelle."

Mathilda pulled down on the sconce by the fireplace.

"Given the magnitude of this imbalance, I think we had better begin."

She closed the heavy wooden door to her keeping room behind everyone, sending a hollow echo reverberating throughout the space. Going over to her cabinets, she took out an ancient amulet belonging to Aelle, the foot of a chicken covered in a millennium of old bloodstains, an etched dagger, and a bronze bowl, green with age. She joined the others in the pentagram and sat everything in the center.

Isobel stared at the items. "It's been a while since we've had to use these."

"It's been a while since evil forces of this magnitude have required it of us," Mathilda replied, placing the chicken leg and amulet in the bowl. She pricked her finger with the tip of the blade, squeezed a few drops of blood over the contents, then passed the dagger to the others to do the same.

They chanted in the language of their ancestors as the energy of the elements was channeled into their circle. The flames on the candles shot up and suddenly went out.

"Did you see that?" Regina asked. "Eliza Duprey's tomb. I saw it clearly in my mind."

"I did," Mathilda replied. "We had better get over there right away."

When they arrived, Mathilda walked out into the middle of the field. She stayed there for a moment, soaking in her surroundings. She bent over, scooped up some loose dirt with her right hand, and closed her eyes. "It cannot be...."

"What?" Ramona asked. "What do you see?"

"A sacrifice took place here. Seventeen witches were stripped of their power and turned into the very earth that I hold."

Isobel gasped. "Anyone we know?"

"No. But Matthew was here. His role in this tragedy is hidden from me. But I do know with certainty that he met with an unfortunate fate —not death, but an agony so great that he wished for death."

Trina shivered. "We have to find him,"

"I agree," Ramona said. She redialed Matthew's phone. It went into a fast, busy tone and then disconnected.

"You look deeply troubled, sister," Isobel remarked. "What are you thinking?"

"I'm wondering where Selene Sullivan came from and who she's working for," Ramona replied. "I've considered everything... another descendant of Aelle's, someone possibly finding one of his written spell-books buried deep in some hillside— I've even pictured Cassandra rising like the Phoenix."

"We all know that two of those ideas are impossible," Mathilda said. "I, too, considered the possibility of someone finding some hidden text of Aelle's. However, I'd say the probability of that is slim. We destroyed most of his books after we bound Cassandra; what we kept is safe in my house. I suggest we get back to the circle right away. We must find Matthew."

"I'll see what I can find out at the Paranormal Investigators Office and meet you back at the house," Ramona stated.

"Good," Mathilda replied. "And Regina, why don't you go with her? Your talents may be needed to coax something out of the staff."

"Of course," Regina replied. She pulled out her phone. "I'd better have Phil notify the children. It's going to be a long night."

~

LOTTIE GRABBED A BOTTLE OF WATER FROM THE FRIDGE AND went upstairs to her room. She had a message from Charles on her phone.

-Elders are meeting at Mathilda's. Fill you in when I know more.

She tried not to worry as she put her phone down. Charles would have mentioned if anything was wrong. Instead, she organized her backpack for her final week of school. She unzipped it and dumped everything out on her bed. Notebooks, pencils, a novel, and a piece of a black ribbon tumbled out. A shiver went through Lottie when she saw the silky fabric. She quickly picked it up and put it in an empty bowl on her nightstand.

"Burn."

A flame danced over the ribbon, sending thick black smoke throughout her room. Lottie opened her window and watched as the fire went out, and the ashes were all that remained. Grabbing a small jar of cotton balls, she quickly shook them out and tapped the ashes into the empty jar before making her way out to the woods.

The scent of pine needles and wet leaves were like a tonic to Lottie's rattled senses. Grabbing a stick, she gouged it into the ground and dug a small hole. As she dumped the ashes from the jar and covered it with the earth, empowerment swept over her, erasing the fear. She placed her palms on the ground, noticing the energy radiating into them.

"Thank you," she whispered to the goddess.

A smile crept across Lottie's face as she got closer to the house. It was nice getting to do magic without destroying something in the process.

"You must be at one with nature," her mother acknowledged as she stepped inside. "You glow when you come in from your walks. I guess that's a side effect of being a witch?"

Lottie shrugged. "I suppose. I love being in the woods. It's so peaceful."

"It is pretty quiet up here on our little hill, isn't it? Just look at that sunset. So, what would you like to do tomorrow? Dinner out? Movie?"

"Actually, Mom, I just want low-key, hanging out here at home."

"That sounds good. How about a pot pie for dinner?"

"And a cake—chocolate."

"You got it."

LOTTIE TWISTED THE HANDLE CLOSED ON HER NAIL POLISH bottle and sat back in her chair, blowing on her nails. It was nearly midnight. Her eyes were heavy, and they threatened to close.

She quickly stood up before she fell asleep, wondering if Charles was awake.

I'm awake.

Show off.

You okay?

Yeah. Just bored and pacing. I almost fell asleep waiting for my nails to dry.

My mom still hasn't gotten home from Mathilda's. It's pretty dull around here, too. Would you like some company?

Sure.

Be there in a bit, then.

Lottie cleaned up the nail polish mess and ran a brush through her hair while she waited.

I'm here. Is it safe to come up?

All safe.

Charles rose in a quick, fluid motion. He pressed a kiss on Lottie's cheek.

"How do you get here so fast walking?"

He flashed a crooked grin. "With a little magical assistance."

"You'll have to show me sometime."

"How about now? Wanna go for a walk?"

"Sure. Let me grab my jacket and a blanket. I want to take you to my sacred place in the woods."

"It's a good thing you don't have neighbors next door, or this might be a little hard to explain," Charles said after they floated down from her window.

"I know, right?"

The woods were alive with nighttime sounds. The smell was different, too. During the day, the scent of leaves and pine was dominant, but the earth ruled under the blanket of darkness; her aroma was distinct and thrilling to the senses. Lottie inhaled deeply, breathing in the coolness mixed with moss and rich dirt as if searing this scent into her very being.

"How far out are we going?" Charles asked.

"Just up ahead."

They followed the path until it opened up into the moonlit mossy clearing. Lottie smiled.

"Here we are."

"Very nice. I see why it's special. The moss is great."

"It is. Makes for some good grounding beneath my feet."

She spread the blanket and settled next to Charles with a contented sigh.

"Isn't it beautiful?"

"Yes. Very," Charles replied, his gaze on Lottie.

"I meant the moon."

His lips twisted up into a smile. "I know you did."

He placed a kiss on the edge of Lottie's lips. She turned and kissed him back—more passionately than she intended.

He moved his hand to the back of her neck, pulling her closer. Lottie's heart raced wildly. She eased away and rolled onto her back, regaining her senses as she gazed upwards.

"It really is so beautiful. I've never been out here at night before."

The stars twinkled brighter as if the sky had moved closer to the Earth. She saw things she had never noticed—clusters of stars and galaxies.

"You did this, didn't you?"

Charles smiled. "Maybe."

"Can anyone else see it?"

"Nope. Just you. I'm very focused. I can envision what I want and cloak it from humankind simultaneously."

Lottie shook her head in awe. "You have an amazing gift."

"So do you. We all do. You should see Wren create a spell on the fly. And Sunni can make you see things that aren't there. Rowen has an amazing talent for healing. There's nothing we can't do, especially when we combine our gifts. That's why we do so well together as a coven."

"I don't think I've found my talent yet."

"Ah, you're different," Charles said, raising onto his elbows. "You were born with a purpose, to find the dark powers. You're strong, Lottie, and you have this connection with the elements that none of us have. Mathilda has it. I guess that's why you're like that. You don't even realize the capabilities you have. You will, though. I'm still finding things out about myself that I didn't know I could do."

Lottie shook her head. "I can't believe this life I have come into. It's amazing, to say the least."

"It is," Charles agreed. "We should probably get back. Want me to show you my version of speed walking?"

"Yep."

He stood and stepped; then, he was out of sight in a blur.

Where are you?

I'm at your house.

No way!

He suddenly appeared in front of her again. "Way," he said, giving her a quick peck on the lips. "And now you know how I get here so fast."

When they came out of the woods, Lottie noticed something move by the garage.

"Charles, there's someone in the shadows over there."

He peered toward the garage. "It's just Phil."

Lottie's smile faded when she saw Phil's expression.

"What's going on?" Charles asked.

Phil let out a heavy sigh. "There was a witch sacrifice at the Duprey tomb. Seventeen of them, in fact."

Lottie felt sick.

"Do you know who's behind it?" Charles asked, echoing her thoughts.

Phil gave a curt nod. "Selene Sullivan, the woman who sent Matthew to aid the investigators. Regina and Ramona retrieved a photograph of her from a file at the Paranormal Investigator's office. However, they learned that it wasn't her true form. They're still in Mathilda's chambers trying to break the cloaking spell."

"How do they know the image of Selene is false?" Lottie asked.

"When they tried to focus on her photo, the image began to swirl and shift out of form, but it kept returning to the image this woman cast for herself. Given what happened at the Duprey tomb, this changes things. I hate to be the one to tell you, kids, but the trip is off. I'm sorry. I know how much you were looking forward to it, but this evil has to be dealt with."

Charles nodded. "What about Matthew? Was he in on it?"

"It's hard to say. The coven sensed his energy at the tomb, but he wasn't part of the sacrifice. Something happened to him; they know that much. A locator spell may help, but the coven won't break as long as they can harness the energy from whoever caused it. Once they do, they'll try to find him."

"Are we in danger?" Lottie asked.

"I don't think so, but until I hear from Regina, I want you both to stay here and look out for each other. Charles, make sure you're gone before Lottie's parents wake."

"Thanks, Phil. Keep me posted."

"I will."

Lottie sat down on the bed and kicked off her shoes.

"Oh, my God, Charles. How awful. Seventeen witches. I'm scared. What if someone comes after our powers?"

"They won't. Whoever it is would've already tried it. Besides, our coven is too strong for anyone to get to us."

"I hope you're right."

"Come on, get in bed. I'll take the chair."

∽

IT WAS ALMOST NOON WHEN LOTTIE WOKE. SHE remembered Phil's visit, and a flood of emotions swept over her. The thought of all of those witches dying scared her more than the sadness over their deaths. She wondered what the elders had discovered.

Charles?

Yeah?

Have you spoken to your mom?

She came in a couple of hours ago, exhausted. She couldn't talk.

Is she okay?

She's resting now. I'll find everything out after she gets up and let you know.

What am I going to tell my parents about the trip?

I don't know. Say there was a death in Regina's family. A cousin or something.

Okay.

Lottie thought about calling Mathilda, but if Ramona was exhausted, the others probably were as well. She flung the covers back and went downstairs.

"I smell bacon," she said, pushing through the swinging door into the kitchen.

"I just put some on," her mother replied. "I was going to surprise you with breakfast in bed, well lunch now, but since you're down here... Surprise."

Lottie gave a weak smile. "Thanks. I'm starving."

"I'd say so. You slept through pancake time, you know."

"Yeah, I was up late last night, texting Wren. Her mother had a death in the family. The trip is canceled."

"Oh, honey, I'm sorry. I know you must be so disappointed. Was it a close relative?"

"A cousin. They were pretty close."

Lottie's father came into the kitchen dressed for work. He kissed her on the head and grabbed a piece of bacon.

"What's with the long faces?"

Lottie bit her lower lip as the tears welled up.

Her dad set his plate down. "What's going on?"

"Lottie's trip was canceled," her mother replied. "Regina's cousin passed away last night."

"I'm sorry," her father said. He opened his arms, and Lottie fell into them. "Are you okay?"

She wished she could tell him how she really felt— terrified, confused, sad, stalked by a depraved witch.

"I'm fine, Dad. I'm disappointed and exhausted from staying up late the last few nights."

"You take it easy today, then. I'm going out on a couple of calls. I'll check on you later."

"Okay."

"I'd better get this mess cleaned up," Lottie's mother said, pulling a dishcloth from the drawer. "Is there anything you'd like to do today?"

"I don't know. I'll call Wren to see what's happening and go from there."

"Okay. Millie is prepping an order for me at the shop today, so I'm here all day if you decide."

Lottie's thoughts were on the Elders as she showered and made her bed. She picked up her phone and messaged Wren.

-What's going on?

-Don't know yet. Mom's in the shower.

She dropped into her chair with a sigh. Her phone rang. *Finally.* "Hello?"

"How are you, dear?" Mathilda asked. Her voice sounded strained.

"I'm okay. What about you? I heard you had a rough night."

"I'm doing better after my rest. It's been a very long time since I've had to go into that kind of channeling. I figured you'd be worried, so I thought I'd invite you for a late lunch to fill you in."

"I'd love to. Let me make sure it's okay, and I'll call you back."

"Mom?"

"Out here."

She followed the sound of her mother's voice to the landing outside the kitchen door.

"Do you care if I go to Mathilda's? She invited me over."

"That's fine. Do I need to take you?"

"You can. I'll have Mathilda drive me home."

~

LOTTIE NOTICED RIGHT AWAY THAT MATHILDA LOOKED tired. There were purple shadows beneath her eyes, and she looked pale. Lottie wondered what the coven had gone through to take such a toll on Mathilda's usual flawless appearance as she followed her to the side garden.

Mathilda gestured to a chair. "Have a seat. Cook will send everything out shortly."

Lottie sat down and poured a cup of tea.

"So, what would you like to ask? I know you have things weighing on you," Mathilda said, reaching for the teapot.

"Were you able to find Selene Sullivan?"

"No. We tried to locate her, but she fought us as harshly as we pushed to get through. We finally decided to break and try our focus elsewhere on a weaker link."

"What did she gain by killing all of those witches?"

"An overload of power. But the question remaining is, why does she need that much power?"

"Were you able to reveal her true form?"

"No. Selene has protected herself very well. But don't worry, we'll get to her soon enough."

"What about Matthew?"

"We don't know what became of him. We'll have another gathering to try and sort it out."

Marie came out to the garden with Cook and helped put lunch on the table. Lottie waited until they went back inside before continuing.

"I told my mom that the trip was canceled due to the death of Regina's cousin."

"Very creative. I'll let Regina know so she won't be caught off guard should your mother send condolences. I'm truly sorry the trip had to be put off. Once we get rid of this threat, perhaps we can reschedule."

Lottie nodded.

"Don't look so deflated, dear. It isn't the end of the path for my coven. I promise you we will find both Matthew and Selene. We will put things right once more."

∽

A SHIMMERY HALO OF CLOUDS THREATENED TO BLOT OUT the moon. Lottie tossed in her bed as shadows moved behind the shades. She suddenly jerked awake. A strong sense of wrongness set off an alarm in her head. She closed her eyes, instinctively reaching out with her mind. She sensed a presence.

Charles, someone is here.

I'm on my way. Stay inside.

She watched him come into the light and opened her window.

"What happened?" he asked.

"I woke from a dead sleep, fully aware that someone was watching me."

"Did you hear anything or see anyone?"

"No, but I sensed their presence somehow. It felt wrong. How did someone get through Mathilda's spell?"

"I don't know. You get some sleep. I'll stay with you until morning."

Lottie nodded. "I'd better text Mathilda."

She placed her phone back on the nightstand and slowly fell asleep, comforted by Charles's vigilance.

∽

THE OLD LOCK GAVE WAY AS SELENE TURNED THE KEY, AND the heavy iron door, warped with age, swung slowly on rusted hinges, flooding the blackened room with light. She raised the back of her fingers to her nose as dust particles rushed in on the draft. They swirled furiously along the back wall before being sucked back to the entrance.

The shrill creaking from the hinges penetrated the silence, jarring Matthew to consciousness. He lay naked on the floor, covered in filth. Squinting, he put his hand up to shield the light.

"Have you learned your lesson?" Selene sternly asked.

His tongue felt heavy in his mouth as he struggled to speak. "Yes, Mistress."

Selene threw a cloak at him. "Good. Get up. We have work to do."

He staggered to his feet and wrapped the cloak around himself, horrified and disgusted by the grime beneath his fingernails and coating his skin.

She thrust a vial toward him. "Here, drink this. I'm moving things along, and I need you alert—and Matthew, if you're a good boy, the transformations won't hurt in the future."

The liquid was bitter, and it burned as it went down. Matthew's senses slowly sparked to life. He cursed the day he ever agreed to help Selene so many months ago. He recalled how she suddenly appeared outside the school where he taught in Defiance. At the time, she had told him she was a witch and needed help finding someone, but he soon learned of her darker intentions, and by then, it was too late. Her threats were enough to yoke him to her, though he often wondered if she had spelled him to stay. He hated her for it, for everything. Dropping the vial, he followed behind her, his emotions numbed by the memories.

~

CHARLES RUBBED HIS EYES AND SAT UP IN BED. THE SOUNDS of daytime were too invasive to sleep through. He pulled on a T-shirt and ran his fingers through his hair.

A soft knock came at his door. "Are you dressed, Son?"

"Yeah, come in, Mom."

Ramona stepped into the room and frowned. "Oh, sweetheart, you look tired. Maybe you should stop these late visits to Lottie's. Let Phil resume the task."

"I don't mind. I can't sleep much anyway because I worry about her. It *would* be a good idea to have Phil take shifts with me. I left Lottie's house sometime after one-thirty, and shortly after that, she sensed someone watching her. I shouldn't have left."

"Charles, don't be so hard on yourself. You can't continue at this pace."

"I'm fine, Mom. I can catch a nap later."

"So, nothing was seen or heard?"

"No. When I got there, everything seemed normal. Lottie was shaken up over the fact that someone had broken through the protection spell. I want to take her to Chagrin Falls today to get her mind off everything."

"I think that's a fantastic idea. I'm meeting Mathilda and the others in a bit. That will allow us time to go to Lottie's house once her parents leave and check things out for ourselves."

"All right. I'm going to shower. Keep me posted if you figure anything out."

~

LOTTIE WOKE AND, BY HABIT, GLANCED TOWARD THE EMPTY chair where Charles had slept. She longed for the days when they could wake up together. Her phone chimed, breaking her thoughts.

-You awake?

-Yes.

-How do you feel about a day trip to Chagrin Falls?

-Sounds good.

-I'll pick you up in an hour if you can go.

Lottie heard her father's van start and rumble down the hill. She got out of bed and walked over to the window. There was a raven perched on the roof of the garage. It seemed oddly out of place. Its large, glassy eyes looked her over. *Go away, Creepy,* she thought. "Wind."

A sudden gust came, and the raven took flight.

"I thought I heard you in here," her mother said.

"Where did Dad go?"

"He said he needed to pick up some supplies. Apparently, the wind knocked some shingles off the garage roof last night."

"Did it?" Lottie said thoughtfully. She wondered if whoever had been watching her at night had damaged it.

"I think I'm going to ride into Kent today to shop. Would you like to come with me?"

"Charles just texted. He wants to go to Chagrin Falls. Can I go with him?"

"So, you'll go with Charles and not your mother?"

Lottie frowned.

"I'm kidding. You can go. Just don't be too late getting back.

"I won't."

~

"LOOK AT YOU," CHARLES GREETED.

She smiled and twirled around in her pale yellow sundress. "I figured I'd wear this dress today since I no longer need it for the trip."

"Did you sleep well?" he asked.

"I did. Were you able to rest at all?

The corner of his mouth lifted slightly. "Your snoring kept me up."

Lottie punched his arm. "I do not snore!"

"Ow, I'm kidding. I slept enough. Don't worry about me."

"So, what have you planned for us?" Lottie asked.

"There are some neat shops and restaurants in Chagrin Falls that I think you'll enjoy. Mom and I used to go there a lot. It's not as exciting as Europe, but I want to get you out of town to distract you from everything going on."

"It sounds great."

Lottie watched out the window blankly at the passing scenery for most of the drive until Charles turned onto a quaint street with rows of shops on both sides. She smiled, looking around as he found a parking space in front of a floral shop.

"What do you think?"

"It's perfect."

"Wanna grab some lunch? There's a bistro nearby."

"Sure."

They placed their order and went outside to sit at one of the small tables.

"I'd better let Mom know we made it," Lottie said, reaching into her bag. "Oh, I must have left my phone in the car."

"I'll go get it for you."

"Thank you. Mom will freak out if I don't keep in touch."

"No problem, be right back."

"You're awesome."

"I know," he joked.

Lottie sipped her water and watched the people strolling in and out of the shops. She reveled in the safety and simplicity of the moment, so much so that she was taken off guard when prickles suddenly rushed up her spine. As before, it was followed by the awareness that someone was watching her. She looked around at the different faces, but nothing seemed amiss with anyone. Something drew her attention to the tree in a small grassy area opposite the street. Nothing out of the ordinary there, either. Then she saw it—the raven. Somehow, she instinctively knew what to do.

Reveal.

Black wings flapped in a flurry of motion, swirling and contorting as the raven shifted out of its form. Then it vanished. Lottie's brows furrowed in frustration.

Charles sat down in the vacant chair across from her. He held a bouquet of roses in his hand. The smile fell from his lips when he looked at Lottie. "What's wrong?"

"This morning, at home, I saw a raven on the garage roof. It creeped me out a little, but I didn't think much about it. While you were getting my phone, I felt someone watching me again. I saw a raven in that tree over there. I attempted a Reveal. It was human."

"Did you see who it was?"

"No. Whoever it was vanished before they completely turned."

Charles quickly slid his chair back. "I'm taking you home. I should never have left you alone."

"No, Charles, I don't want to go. Besides, they're gone now. You got me flowers," she pointed out, changing the subject.

His jaw tensed. "I did."

She leaned over and kissed him. "Thank you. I love them."

He gave a small attempt at a smile and glanced across the street. "I'm going over to check where you saw the raven."

Lottie watched Charles cross the road. He reached out and touched the tree where the raven had changed its form, quickly pulling away as if burned.

What is it?

Come here.

She grabbed her things and headed over, stopping short of the tree. Something felt very wrong here. Darkness gripped her heart. "Oh, no."

"What?" His eyes were on hers, searching.

"Remember all of those nightmares I told you about? That same evil presence from my dreams was here. It left a strong energy behind."

"Yes. I feel it, too."

Lottie shivered despite the warmth. "Who could be watching me?"

"I don't know," Charles said, gazing at the tree. "Let's pack our food and head back to my house. I want to tell Mom about this."

~

REGINA GLANCED AROUND LOTTIE'S YARD, RUBBING HER arms. "Do you feel that? The energy here is vile. There's no other word for it," she added with a look of disdain.

"I sense the same negative energy that I felt when we touched Selene Sullivan's photo," Trina remarked.

"As do I," Mathilda agreed. "Right off, I'm picking up on the masking spell she uses, but there's something else." She bent down and placed her hand on the ground. "She's not trying to harm Charlotte. She wants something from her, and she's having a devil of a time getting what she wants because of my protection spell over Charlotte."

"You're right," Regina said. "There is an overwhelming feeling of want here." She paused for a moment. "You don't suppose she's after Lottie's powers, do you?"

"No," Mathilda replied. "I've been sensing her frustration for some time. However, there isn't that feeling of an imminent threat against Charlotte. We must find Matthew. He can lead us to Selene; then, we'll discover what this is about."

"I'll swing by The Paranormal Investigators office," Ramona said. "Perhaps he's been in contact with them."

~

CHARLES DROVE IN SILENCE. EVERY NOW AND AGAIN, HIS JAW would tense, so Lottie left him to his thoughts.

When they arrived at his house, she sat anxiously on the sofa while he explained everything to his mother.

Ramona turned to Lottie. "Give me your hands, dear."

Lottie reached out, waiting as Ramona delved into her.

"I'm able to pick up on the energy you felt. Have either of you told Mathilda yet?"

"No. I drove straight here," Charles answered.

"Let's head over to Mathilda's now. I'll message the others to meet us there."

Charles closed the passenger-side door for Lottie and got in the back seat. "Did you figure anything out at Lottie's house earlier?"

"Yes and no," Ramona answered, meeting his eyes in the rearview mirror. "We know for certain that Selene Sullivan is the one who broke through the protection spell."

"Can she harm me now that she's gotten through?" Lottie asked.

"She isn't trying to harm you. She wants something."

Lottie frowned. "What could she want from me?"

"That's what we're trying to figure out. Our locator spells aren't showing us where she is, so we're focusing on finding Matthew instead. Once we get him, we can extract the information we need to locate Selene."

Once they arrived, they went inside to relay everything to Mathilda.

"Sorry, I got held up," Trina said. "What's going on?"

"Someone followed Charlotte to Chagrin Falls," Mathilda answered. "She saw a raven twice today. She attempted a Reveal, but whoever it was disappeared before they changed. Ramona and I both have delved into Charlotte. The presence she felt there had the same dark energy we encountered in our channeling. She also mentioned the evil that sometimes appears in her nightmares was what she felt today."

Trina sat back against her chair. "So someone has been invading her mind for some time now."

Mathilda nodded. "It seems so."

"We had all better take turns watching Lottie's house," Isobel suggested.

"I have a better idea," Regina said. "I think she needs to move in with you, Mathilda. No one can get to her here. You know I'm right."

Mathilda scoffed. "Her parents would never agree to that, and we can't very well tell them about what's happening. They would take Charlotte and run.

"We can always cast a spell to make Lottie's parents forget her," Regina said half-jokingly.

Mathilda's jaw dropped. "I would never do such a thing to Charlotte. It would crush her. You know that."

"Then we'd better figure out a way to make it happen," Trina said. "I'd be interested to see if Lottie's watcher follows her here."

"So would I," Regina said. She pushed open the French doors and called for Lottie. "Go ahead and tell her," she urged as Lottie stepped inside.

Mathilda pressed her lips together and raised a hand to her forehead in exasperation.

"Tell me what?" Lottie asked.

"Trina and I think you should move in with Mathilda," Regina said challengingly.

Mathilda gave her a scolding look. "As I stated before, but I will reiterate for Charlotte's sake, there's no way we can do that without telling her parents why. It's unsafe to involve them. Selene would eliminate them if she found out they knew of her. We simply cannot involve them."

Regina threw up her hands. "She's being *followed*, Mathilda. Until we find Selene, she's not safe."

Lottie watched their heated exchange. "I have an idea."

All eyes turned on her.

"I think it's time I get to know my biological mom." She smiled at Mathilda. "I've wanted to for a while now anyway. It will hurt my parents, but at least they'll be safe with me out of the house."

"Charlotte, are you sure you want to hurt your parents like that?" Mathilda asked.

"No. I don't, but it's the only way. If I remove myself, they can be safe from whoever is trying to get to me."

"What if it doesn't work?" Charles asked. "What if they say no?"

"Let me try before we think about what's next."

"I'll take you home, then," he said.

Her parents were finishing dinner when she came in through the kitchen. The soft glow of the antique pendant light over the table cast a romantic setting. Lottie noticed their chairs were pulled closer together than usual and felt guilty for intruding.

"How was your outing with Charles?" her mother asked. "You guys have fun?"

"Yep. Did you enjoy your shopping?"

"I did."

Lottie went over to the sink and poured a glass of water. Her mind reeled with the complexity of her situation. She hated this. She took a deep breath and turned around.

"I'm glad I have you both in the same room. I want to ask you a huge favor."

Her father turned his attention to her. "Go on."

"How would you feel about me spending the summer with Mathilda?"

Her mother's brows climbed as she sat against the back of her chair. Lottie continued before they had a chance to interrupt.

"I'd like to get to know her better and enjoy being at her house. Since the trip to Europe was canceled, I thought this could be a consolation adventure; plus it will give me a chance to work on controlling my magic without being distracted by schoolwork."

"Lottie," her mother interrupted in a slightly exasperated tone. "I'm not going to let you spend the whole summer with Mathilda. Maybe a couple of weeks."

"But why? I was going to be gone anyway. It's the same thing."

"No, it's not. I said no, and that's the end of it."

Lottie turned to her father. He was trying to stay out of the drama by turning all his attention to his apple cobbler. She would try begging. Her father had a soft spot for that.

"Dad, please. I've been wanting to spend some time getting to know her. I've been so bummed over the trip, and this will be fun for me."

Her parents exchanged glances.

"I still have so much I need to learn," she continued, almost desperate now. "Please?"

"Lottie, what's this all about?" her mother asked.

"Just what I said. I want to get to know Mathilda better."

"Sweetheart," her father struggled to find words. "We want you here. We want you home with us."

"I know, Dad. But this is important to me. I wouldn't ask if it wasn't." Her eyes were on him, pleading. She sensed him weakening. "I need to do this. I've had such a hard time since I found out about the adoption and then found out I'm a witch. The visits with Mathilda aren't enough. I never have enough time to finish conversations or ask questions—"

"Don't you dare play on your father's sympathy, young lady? I know what you're doing. You're not going, and that's final!"

Anger coursed through Lottie. She began to veer from her mission. Instead, she felt like an angry, irresponsible teenager. Her fingernails dug crescents into her palms.

"Fine," she snapped, slamming her cup on the counter.

"Whoa, whoa, whoa. What's this tone I hear?" her mother asked.

Like an opening dam, all the fear gushed out, desperate and angry. "You don't like her. That's what this is about. You hate it every time I go over there; I can see it in your eyes. You hate the fact that Mathilda's my mother. My *real* mother."

The sharp gasp that came from her mother snapped Lottie's mouth shut. Regret was immediate, but it was too late now.

Her father pounded his fist on the table, causing her to jump. "All right, that's enough! You will *not* speak to your mother like that. Get up to your room."

Lottie choked back a sob and ran out of the kitchen.

Charles's voice sounded in her mind as she topped the stairs.

Are you okay?

No.

I'm so sorry, Lottie.

Not as sorry as I am. I let it get out of control. I said things I shouldn't have.

Give them time to process it. They'll forgive you.

I doubt it.

They will. That's what parents do.

I hear them talking. I'll get back to you.

Lottie swiped a hand across her eyes and pressed her ear against the door.

"I'm sorry, Carol. She didn't mean it."

"I know. It doesn't make it hurt any less, though, does it?"

"No, but Lottie's hurting, too. She's been through a lot and handled it incredibly well. I can understand her request. I think we ought to consider it."

"Randy! You can't be serious."

"Let me ask you something. How *do* you feel when Lottie visits Mathilda?"

"I...what does that have to do with anything?"

"Seriously, how do you feel?"

"I don't like it, okay? Is that what you want to hear? I'm afraid Lottie will choose her over us."

"She won't. Lottie loves us. *You're* her mother. Listen, I'm not trying to make you the bad guy, but we have to see it from Lottie's point of view, too. I don't think what she's asking is too unreasonable. I believe if you put your feelings for Mathilda aside, you'll agree with me."

"I doubt that."

"Carol, if we try to make her stay, she'll only resent us for it. It's only through the summer. She would be gone anyway had the trip to Europe worked out. I say we let her get whatever this is out of her system. She'll be over it soon enough and back with us where she belongs."

Her mother sighed.

Lottie stepped away from the door and sank into her chair, leaving her parents to work out the rest of their fears in private. She felt horrible. She gazed out the window, watching the moon inch across the sky, when a knock came at her door.

"Can I come in?" her mother asked.

"Yes."

A flood of guilt swept over Lottie again as the scene replayed through her mind.

"Mom, I'm sorry. I didn't mean to say those things earlier. I don't know what got into me."

"It's okay. Your emotions have been messed with a lot in the last few weeks. Throw in teenage hormones, and there you have it."

Lottie wiped a tear away with the back of her hand as her mother crouched down by the arm of the chair. She wrapped Lottie in a hug.

"Honey, it's okay. Don't cry."

She felt free to let go of the pent-up emotions in her mother's arms. Tears streamed down Lottie's face. She didn't bother to wipe them.

"I'm sorry. I think it's safe to say I'm highly emotional." She took a breath, regaining her composure.

"So, Dad and I talked. You can spend the summer with Mathilda."

Lottie's eyes widened. "Really?"

"Yes," her mother said, wiping the remaining tears from Lottie's cheeks. "I let my fears and jealousy of Mathilda interfere with considering your request."

"Thank you, Mom. You don't know what this means."

"So, when do you want to go?"

"How about tomorrow after school? Mathilda said I could come any time."

"That's short notice, not to mention you still have another week left in school."

"Please, Mom? Finals are already over, and it's not like I have to prepare for anything major."

"Finish out the school week here with us. At least give me one more week with you. Then you can go next weekend for the whole summer."

Lottie sighed.

"Sweetheart, it's only a week."

Lottie worried about what could happen in a week, given the horrible things that had been going on, but she knew her mother wouldn't relent.

"All right," she agreed.

Her mother smiled and patted Lottie's knee. "Come on. Let's go have some ice cream."

"Sounds good. Let me text Mathilda, and I'll be right there."

-Good news. I can stay for the summer. Bad news. I can't come until next weekend.

She stared at the screen until Mathilda's reply chimed.

-Don't worry. We'll watch the house as planned, and I'll see you next weekend.

Lottie went down to the kitchen and scooped some cookies and cream into a bowl.

"How about some good clean TV comedy?" her mother asked, putting the ice cream back into the freezer.

"Sure."

Once settled on the couch, her mother switched the channel to *The Golden Girls*. Lottie rolled her eyes as the all-too-familiar theme song started.

Her mother sang the opening line embarrassingly loud.

"Mom, really? Golden Girls?"

"Sing it," her mother urged.

Lottie mentally groaned but joined in.

Her father wandered into the living room and grinned. "Good to see my two favorite girls getting along."

"Finish out the song, Randy."

Silence.

"Way to belt it out, Dad," Lottie teased.

"I don't sing. You two enjoy your ice cream. I'm going up to bed."

"Night, Dad."

Lottie rinsed out her bowl and said goodnight to her mother. As she got ready for bed, the horrible words she had said earlier came rushing back to her mind. She had never spoken to her mother in such a hurtful manner. The look on her face was something Lottie wouldn't soon forget.

Are your parents in bed? Charles's voice came.

Yes.

I'll be there in a bit.

Lottie opened the window once she saw him.

"How did everything go?" he asked.

"I'm moving in with Mathilda for the summer."

"Was your mom okay with it?"

"Yeah, Dad helped her see reason. We finished the night with ice cream and a couple of episodes of *The Golden Girls*."

Charles gave a crooked smile. "I'm glad you guys ended on a good note."

"Me, too."

"Okay. Try to get some sleep. I'll keep watch."

Lottie gazed at his profile. The glow from the garage light below highlighted his nose and cheekbones while shadows hollowed out the rest of his features.

"Charles, aren't you tired? Staying up late to watch out for me has to be taking a toll on you."

"I've been napping before I come over, don't worry about me. I'm fine."

Her gaze lingered briefly, then she turned off the lamp and rolled onto her side. She wondered what life would be like with Mathilda. Would Selene try to come after her there? Would her parents truly be safe? Her eyes grew heavy, and her thoughts fell away.

Chapter Sixteen

Wake up, Lottie. I made all your favorites—and chop-chop," she added with two quick claps. "It's our last meal with you for a while." She winked and slipped out of the room.

"Be right down," Lottie called after her mother. She yawned and got out of bed, stepping around her luggage on her way out the door.

"So you're leaving at noon, huh?" her father said as she joined him at the table.

"Yeah. Will you be home?"

"I have an errand to run, but I'll be home before you go."

"Good. I would hate to leave without saying goodbye."

Lottie pinched off a piece of biscuit and noticed the sunbeams pouring in through the small window above the sink. She always loved the little things in life, like sun rays and breakfast with her parents. She would miss them dearly, but leaving was for the best. She would do anything to keep her family safe.

A little after eleven, her father's van rumbled up the drive. Lottie smiled. He was true to his word. She grabbed her pillow and favorite blanket and carried her things down the steps, blowing puffs of air at the hair hanging in her face.

"Here, let me get that," her father offered.

"Thanks, Dad."

A flash of something yellow in the corner of her eye drew Lottie's attention to the kitchen. Her mother rubbed the cleaning cloth over the coffee maker with rigorous detail. She paused to tug at the yellow glove on her left hand.

"Oooh-kay...." Lottie muttered.

"Your mother's trying to keep busy," he whispered. "She cries every time she's idle when she thinks about you leaving."

Lottie set her things on a chair. "I think it's clean, Mom."

She put the cloth down. "I believe you're right. Are you all set?"

"Yep."

"Do you need anything before you go?"

"No, I'm fine, Mom."

"Can I convince you to stay home if I promise no more *Golden Girls*?"

"Nice try, but I did have fun with you last night."

"I did, too, honey."

When Mathilda drove up the driveway, Lottie noticed tears in her mother's eyes. She smoothed non-existent wrinkles at the front of her shirt as a distraction.

"Don't cry, Mom. I'll be back. We can get together over the summer, too."

"I'll hold you to that."

"I'll carry your bags out," her father said.

"Thank you both for allowing Lottie to spend the summer with me," Mathilda said, opening the trunk of her car. "I'll look after her well. And you are always welcome in my home if you ever want to visit her."

Her mother nodded. "Thank you." She placed a kiss on Lottie's head. "You take care, sweetheart. Let me know when you want to get together."

"I will. Thanks again for letting me go."

Her father wrapped his arms around her. The familiar scents of the garage and aftershave comforted her.

"If you decide you want to come home, just call me. I'll drop everything."

"I will, Dad. I love you guys."

She got into the car and waved to her parents as they drove away. A hitch caught in her throat as they went down the hill. She didn't want to leave, and yet she did.

"How are you doing?" Mathilda asked.

"I've had so much to deal with lately that I don't know how I feel."

"Once we get you settled in, you should feel better."

Anticipation coursed through Lottie as she considered the freedom she would have with her magic once she moved in with Mathilda.

When they arrived, Dabney dutifully opened the door for Matilda and carried Lottie's things inside.

The sound of an engine drew her attention toward the driveway. She smiled when Charles got out of his car. "What are you doing here?"

"I thought I'd come to see you." He wound his fingers through Lottie's and pressed his lips to hers. "Need help with anything?"

"Care to grab my nail polish box?"

"Sure."

Marie waited by the door to Lottie's bedroom. She gave a slight nod. "I'll help you unpack, Miss."

"Actually, Marie, I'd like to do it. But thank you for the offer."

"Very well." She turned on a muted swish to go down the hall.

"Let me help you, at least," Charles suggested.

"Okay, but we're doing it the fun way."

He raised an eyebrow, amused. "What do you have in mind?"

Lottie grinned as she unzipped her bag. She swiped her hand, and the closet door opened.

"Shoes, to the closet," she said primly.

"Oh, okay, my turn," Charles said as Lottie's shoes glided past. He flicked his fingers, and the luggage case opened. He eyed the contents. "Shirts on hangers, jeans on the shelf, socks in the drawer," he said quickly. Clothes flew everywhere.

"Hey, no fair. You got them all."

Charles looked in the case again. "Not everything." Mischief danced in his eyes as he flashed her a devilish grin.

Lottie peered in and gasped. "No way," she commanded.

"Bras out," he teased.

"Bras, stop!" she shrieked.

Mathilda stepped into the room as a bra flew past. "What's this?" she asked, brows raised.

Lottie burned with mortification.

"I thought Marie was helping you get settled in."

Lottie quickly gathered her undergarments, which had abruptly dropped to the floor. "Sorry, we got a little carried away unpacking."

Lottie thought she saw the corner of Mathilda's lip twitch.

"Is there anything you need?"

"No, I'm okay."

"Make yourself at home, Charlotte. If you do need anything, let Marie know. Cook will have dinner ready at six."

"Thank you."

Lottie burst into laughter when Mathilda left the room. "Well, that was fun."

"Yes, it was," Charles agreed. He pulled her to him. "I'm glad you're here. I won't worry about you as much, plus I'll get to see more of you." He cupped her face, brushing a thumb over her cheek as he kissed her.

"I like the sound of that. Thanks for helping me."

~

LOTTIE SLID INTO A CHAIR AT THE DINING TABLE PROMPTLY at six.

"Good, right on time." Mathilda unfolded her napkin and placed it on her lap. "Did you get everything in your room set up to your liking?"

"I did."

"I've been doing some thinking. Since you're staying here now, I should probably do something to make the place more teenage-friendly. I've decided to convert one of the smaller studies into a game room."

"Really? I'd love that."

"I have someone coming Monday morning to look at the space. You,

Charles, and the girls get together, think of what you'd like to put in there, and let me know."

"Awesome. I'm sure we'll come up with some cool ideas."

"You and Charles sure have gotten close," Mathilda acknowledged. "You know, in your last life, you two were married by now," she added casually as if remarking about the weather.

Lottie nearly choked on her bite. "Married? We were *married?*"

"Oh, you've been married many times. You have been deeply in love since you set eyes on each other in your first life together. It's been like that in every lifetime. When the time is right, it will happen. You'll see."

Lottie tried to hide her shock by turning her attention to her meal. She kept to the solitude of her bedroom the rest of the evening, consumed by thoughts of what Mathilda had told her until she grew tired. She picked up the phone to call her parents before going to bed.

"Hi, Mom."

"Hi, sweetie. Good to hear your voice. Are you all settled in?"

"Yes. What did you and Dad do today?"

"Dad was in the garage all afternoon, no doubt, staying busy to keep from missing you. Kind of like me, scouring the kitchen all day."

"I know. I miss you guys, too. I'll call you next week or so to get together."

"I'd like that."

"Well, I'd better go. I'm pretty tired."

"Okay, I love you, baby."

"Love you too, Mom. Tell Dad goodnight."

Lottie sank back into the bed with a sigh.

You're quiet tonight. Is everything okay?

Yeah, just processing some information Mathilda hurled at me.

What information?

We've been married—many times.

Yes, I know.

You knew? And you didn't tell me?

I figured we'd talk about it sooner or later.

I'm always the last to know about everything.

Don't feel bad, Lottie. I'm sure Mathilda will fill you in on more now that you're living with her.

I suppose so. I'd better get to sleep. I'm exhausted.
Okay. See you tomorrow.

~

"WHAT DO YOU MEAN SHE'S *GONE?*" SELENE RAGED.

Matthew winced at her words. "I did as you commanded. I waited to see who would show up to guard the house, but no one ever came. I thought it was odd, so I kept watch. I waited all night but never saw Lottie once. Her energy is just...gone," he added warily.

Selene paced wildly across the room. "They think they're so smart. Bring me that mirror," she demanded, abruptly stopping her gait.

He rushed over with it, afraid of what she might do if he didn't hurry. She yanked it from him and placed it on the table, then muttered a word in a language he didn't understand. The mirror shattered immediately. Matthew stepped back instinctively, warily watching Selene's shoulders' sharp rise and fall as her rage built. He could sense the hatred pouring from her as she glared at the jagged shards of glass still attached to the mirror's edge. In a flash, she grabbed it by the stand and flung it against the wall, her cry of rage muting the crash of metal hitting brick.

"Block me out," she said, regaining composure. "No matter. I've waited this long."

~

THE CURTAINS DRAGGED ACROSS THE ROD, JERKING LOTTIE awake. She raised onto her elbows, gaining her bearings. "Oh, Marie, you scared me."

She paused by the bed and offered a contrite nod. "I'm sorry. The mistress asked me to rouse you for breakfast. What would you like?"

"I would like pancakes, please."

"Will that be all?"

"With a lot of syrup," she added.

"Very good," Marie replied. "The mistress asks that you join her in fifteen minutes," she added with a firm gaze.

Lottie sighed. It was apparent Mathilda ran a tight ship. "Tell her I'll be down shortly." She slipped on the house shoes by the bed, smiling as she thought of her mother's ugly pink ones, and went straightaway to the breakfast room.

Lottie grimaced at her disheveled appearance upon noticing Mathilda sitting elegantly at the table, immaculate as ever in her pale yellow blouse. It looked like a hoard of hair and makeup artists had descended upon her to achieve such perfection. Mathilda was one of the most beautiful women Lottie had ever seen.

Noticing Lottie, she poured tea in the cup across from her. "Good morning, dear. I trust you slept well?"

"I did," Lottie replied. "What time do you get up around here anyway?"

"I'm up by five every day. I meditate, go for a walk, and commune with nature. A witch gets her best grounding in the early hours."

"If you say so."

"Have you decided what you'd like to have in your game room?"

"No, I messaged the others to come over in a little while if that's okay."

"Very good. Have you spoken to your parents?"

"I called Mom last night."

"How are they taking the fact that you're with me?"

"They miss me, of course, but they're okay."

"Maybe you can invite them over for dinner one night."

"That would be great."

~

Lottie stepped out on the portico as Wren finally arrived behind Rowen and Sunni.

"Watch yourself," Rowen whispered. "Wren is grouuuchy."

"Why don't you shut it, Rowen?" Wren snapped, slamming her car door. "You're way worse when you have to get up early."

"See?" Rowen pointed out. "So, which room do we get?" she asked, bouncing into the foyer

"Come on. I'll show you."

Lottie filled everyone in on the details as she led them down the hall.

"*This* is small?" Rowen asked, taking in the room.

"Dude, we could do a ton of stuff here," Wren remarked. "I see a row of gaming PCs lining that wall," she gestured toward the left.

"I know, right?" Sunni agreed. "Maybe we can get Lottie on board with playing Ori and the Will of the Wisps."

"Sure," Lottie said. "As long as you agree to play air hockey with me. What about you, Charles?"

"Definitely gaming computers," he replied. "And a pool table would be cool."

"Okay, so anything else?" Lottie asked.

"Ms. Pac-man," Mathilda added.

Lottie turned toward the doorway, surprised by her response. "*You* want a video game?"

"I'm not completely devoid of fun, Charlotte. I'll give Mr. Johnson your requests and let you know what we come up with."

Lottie smiled. "Thank you, Mathilda. This is really nice of you."

"Yeah, thanks for including all of us," Sunni added.

"You're welcome. You kids are welcome to stay here if you'd like."

"I have to get going," Charles said. "I'm helping Mom with some yard work."

"Thanks for coming over," Lottie said, kissing his cheek.

"You guys wanna go to the mall?" Rowen suggested.

"Fine with me," Sunni replied.

Lottie looked toward Mathilda.

"Go ahead, dear."

The mall was empty when they arrived except for a few walkers. Employees were busy opening up their stores as they made their way past the windows.

"Let's go in here," Sunni said, veering into a store. "I wanna try on that top by the front display table."

Lottie noticed a white dress on a mannequin. She took one in her size, a pair of sandals hanging nearby, and headed toward the fitting rooms.

A shock of red caught Lottie's attention as she turned the corner. Christy stood in front of the mirrors, her waves of thick, red hair framing her delicate features and tumbling down her back. Her brows knitted as she inspected the angled view of herself.

"Christy, hey. How are you?"

"Oh, hey, Lottie! Pretty good. Janet told me I could pick out a few outfits for summer. I think I'm digging this blouse."

"Definitely. I've always thought you looked good in green."

"Thanks. So, what's going on with you?"

"Not much, really. Wren, Rowen, and Sunni invited me to shop with them today. What about you? Do you have any plans for summer break?"

"Not anymore. Janet was going to take us to California to visit her cousin, but now she's decided against it. She can't bring herself to leave her little haven here."

"I'm sorry, Christy. Do you still have my number?"

"Yep."

"If you ever want to get together, let me know."

"Thanks. Well, I'd better get out of here. I told Janet I'd hurry."

"So, are you getting the dress?" Wren asked when Lottie came out of the fitting room.

"I think so. How are things with you and Bryan? Are you guys getting deeper?"

"I don't know. I like him, but I'm not sure if I want a serious relationship. He's still more on the friend side."

"With benefits?" Sunni asked.

"Don't be crude," Wren scolded. "It's not like that."

"Lighten up. I'm just kidding. Go home and take a nap and get happy."

∼

"You'll be interested to know that Matthew is still in the area," Ramona said as she poured a glass of wine. She sat down on the sofa by Isobel.

"How did you find that out?" Regina asked.

"One of my random visits to the Paranormal Investigators' office paid off. Nancy Withers told me he came in yesterday, packed up his things, and quit without reason."

"Interesting," Mathilda said. "Did you discover anything else?"

"No, but I sense that he's still around."

"Yes, but where?" Isobel asked.

"I don't know, but I bet we can find him," Ramona replied. "This is the pen he used to sign his resignation letter."

Trina smiled. "Let's have a bit of fun then, shall we?"

Mathilda set a map of Akron and surrounding areas on the table and placed the pen on top. She joined hands with her sisters and whispered, "Show us the way."

The pen sprang to life, twitching but not cooperating.

"Show us the way," they said in unison.

The pen started spinning. As it went faster and faster, the grandfather clock in the library gonged. Mathilda looked up. The clock's hands sped forward, hour after hour, gonging briefly in between until eleven hours had passed, and then it stopped.

"Well, well," Regina said.

Mathilda slid the map closer and circled the area where the pen had stopped. "It appears that Matthew is going to be somewhere in this vicinity eleven hours from now."

"Finally," Trina said. "Maybe we can get some answers."

THE FLASHING TELEVISION WOKE LOTTIE. SHE TURNED IT off and rolled over. She heard voices coming from downstairs and crawled out of bed, following the sounds to the library. She could sense magic as she went into the room. "I'm going to assume you guys aren't here for a cup of soothing bedtime tea."

Regina smirked at Lottie's comment.

"No," Mathilda replied. "Ramona has discovered that Matthew is alive and well. He went by his office, packed up, and left without giving a reason."

"Why? Where has he gone?"

"We don't know exactly. Ramona was kind enough to bring us this pen from his desk."

"Ah, what did it show you?"

"A general area of where he will be in the future."

Lottie frowned. "But nothing now."

"Come over here, Charlotte." Mathilda placed the pen on the table. "Let's see if you can detect any missing details."

"Okay." She closed her eyes and wrapped her fingers around the pen. "I saw him sign some papers at the Paranormal Investigator's Office and then walk out the door, but that's as far as I got. Why can't I see past that point?"

"Selene must be cloaking him. He's not strong enough to cast a spell of that nature on his own."

"His energy is still within town limits," Ramona added. "We just need to figure out where it's the strongest and try pinpointing it."

"Yes," Mathilda agreed. "We're hoping if we find him, we find Selene."

Lottie nodded, hope spreading over her features. "Okay, that's a start."

"We'd better call it a night," Regina suggested. "Phil and I have a date night planned at home."

"Very romantic," Trina said.

Regina smiled. "It will be."

"So, how do we proceed?" Lottie asked.

"You leave that to us," Mathilda replied.

"I just want this to be over."

"I know you do. The fact that we discovered that Matthew is still in town shows that Selene is weakening. We'll find him."

THE SUN TOUCHED EVERYTHING IN THE GARDEN. LOTTIE leaned back onto her elbows, watching the flowers dance in the breeze. All at once, the sky grew dark, and strange clouds formed and shifted, splitting off into the shape of two eyes. The eyes watched her. A low growl took her attention from the sky. Standing along the perimeter of the grounds

was a large black wolf. Its teeth bared as it tried to get past some unseen barrier but could not do so. It turned and ran back toward the woods, but its golden eyes were still glowing, watching her.

~

LOTTIE BOLTED UP IN BED. "MATHILDA!"

The hall lamp flickered on as Mathilda rushed into her room. "What's the matter?"

"I had a nightmare. There were eyes in the sky watching me. Then this wolf was there. It was trying to get past something, but it couldn't. What does it mean."

"Someone knows you're here."

"My parents—"

"They're safe. Don't worry. Phil checks on them every night. Charlotte, you're safe here, I promise. I'll make you something to help you get back to sleep. Can't have you waking up with dark circles under those pretty green eyes." She patted Lottie's leg and left the room.

Lottie decided not to tell Charles about the dream until tomorrow. At least one of them could get some sleep undisturbed.

~

LATER IN THE MORNING, MATHILDA CAME INTO HER ROOM with a tray in hand. She sat it on the side table and opened the curtains, flooding the room with light. "How did you sleep?"

Lottie squinted at the sudden brightness. "Better once your brew kicked in."

"I brought you some breakfast." She placed the tray across Lottie's lap. "I've been thinking. I'd like to take you to my chambers for some dark magic. I've thought about it thoroughly and decided it's the best route to take after that dream of yours. It can be terrifying for someone inexperienced in the dark side of magic. That said, if you don't want to participate, under no circumstance should you. What are your thoughts on the matter?"

"I'll do anything to get this darkness out of my life. What do I have to do?"

"Well, my coven and I, we'll put you in the center of the pentagram and use you to channel the darkness you encountered in your nightmare. The channeling will send you into the dream. It would be as if you were truly there. The images you see may be the same, or things could be much worse. I'm not going to sugarcoat it, Charlotte. It can be terrifying. That's why I've also asked Charles to join you in the circle. His connection with you is strong, and his presence in the ritual will help you stay more in touch with us without feeling trapped in the dream. You don't have to decide now—"

"I'm in. I want this over with."

"Very well. Eat your breakfast. I'll notify the others when you're ready."

～

CHARLES LOOKED MORE CONCERNED THAN EVER AS HE CAME down the hall.

"Hey," Lottie greeted.

He paused in front of her, taking her hands in his.

"Mom filled me in on everything. Lottie, are you sure you want to do this? It could get pretty ugly. I've seen my mom after one of these sessions. It's exhausting."

Fear inched its way into her heart as she thought of how the dark magic affected Mathilda and the others. She couldn't let these thoughts deter her.

"I'll let them explain everything. I won't do it if it seems too much for me to handle. Besides, I'll have you."

"That you will."

Lottie took a deep breath as she walked the length of the corridor behind the fireplace. She focused her eyes on the old wood floor, wondering how often Mathilda had walked this same path. In the keeping room chamber, the elder coven was preparing the circle.

She attempted to smile. "Okay, let's get this over with."

Mathilda took her hand. "Here's the plan. You and Charles will go into the circle. We'll begin with our ritual and start the spell. Once locked in, you'll lose all awareness of the five of us. As this is your nightmare, you'll think that it's actually happening. That's where Charles comes into play. He'll find you and remind you that you're in the spell. What you hear and see might be very disturbing. We're channeling the darkness that caused the nightmare so that it will be from that point of view.

"Charles, you must find Charlotte as soon as you enter into the realm of her dream. You were not part of it, so you'll have to get to the rose garden at my house."

He nodded. "I will."

Mathilda turned her attention back to Lottie. "What do you think? Are you sure you want to go through with this?"

"Yes. Charles will find me. I'll be fine," Lottie said.

"Very well. If at any point before the spell locks in, and you change your mind, we'll break the circle and end it."

Lottie reached for Charles's hand, and they stepped into the pentagram on the floor. Ramona's eyes were on Charles. He met her gaze and nodded.

"Go ahead and lie down," Mathilda said. "We'll speak English so that you'll know where we are in our incantation should you want us to stop. When we get to the point of calling on the spirit realm, that is when you will be channeled."

Lottie rested her head on the floor and squeezed Charles's hand.

"Let us begin," Mathilda said.

At her words, the atmosphere changed. The air thickened, and a tangible, electric current rippled over Lottie's skin. Flames shot up on all the candles surrounding the room as the coven joined hands.

Regina began. "We, your faithful Guardians, call upon Earth. We ask that you bring stability to this circle. Keep your servants grounded in what we seek."

Ramona was next. "We, your faithful Guardians, call upon Air. We ask that you bring wisdom to this circle. Keep your servants connected with what we seek."

Isobel began next, "We, your faithful Guardians, call upon Fire. We ask that you bring strength to this circle. Keep your servants steadfast in what we seek."

It was Trina's turn. "We, your faithful Guardians, call upon Water. We ask that you bring willpower and intuition to this circle. Keep your servants receptive in what we seek."

Lottie took in a deep breath. Fear started taking root, seeping out of her pores as a cold sweat. Charles squeezed her hand. *We do this together.*

Just find me.

Mathilda's voice finally came, clear and firm, "To the Spirit Realm in this circle, we ask that you now guide us to the purpose of what we seek."

Lottie and Charles were cast into the dream.

The sweet smell of the rose garden filled Lottie's senses. She inhaled, a smile touching her lips, as she stretched out onto the grass, opening her limbs to the sun. Suddenly, the sky grew dark, choking out the light. She sat up, watching the clouds shift and swirl above her. One of them split in half and formed the shape of two eyes. Strange and demented voices surrounded her from all sides, and a horrible darkness gripped her. Scrambling to her feet, she rushed for the safety of the house.

Reaching the door, she found it locked. She ran to the front portico entry and turned the handle, which was also locked. She beat on the door. "Mathilda, let me in."

The wind was fierce now, and Lottie struggled to stand. She froze as she heard growling behind her. Careful not to make any sudden movements, she turned around.

A large black wolf stood at the edge of the property. Its yellow eyes seemed to glow as it watched her. Terror squeezed Lottie's heart. She beat on the door once more.

"Mathilda! Please let me in."

She glanced back. The wolf now stood in the middle of the garden. Its teeth bared as it growled. She sprinted away from the house toward the driveway. She could wave someone down to help her if she could reach the road.

With each step, the growling got closer. Lottie ran faster, choking on sobs. The wind beat her hair wildly around her face, making it impossible to see where she was going. The sounds of the wolf's thundering paws drew even closer. Hysteria rose from the terror. Unable to control her movements any longer, she tripped and skidded hard along the pavement. The wolf was almost upon her. She scrambled to her feet once again and started running. She turned right as the wolf jumped at her.

Her scream was cut short.

Someone had grabbed her. Her screams drowned out their voice. But then clarity could be heard in their words.

"Lottie, Lottie, it's me, Charles. I'm here. Lottie!"

She gained a sense of reason once more. "Charles? What's going on?"

"We're in a spell. Remember? The coven locked us in the spell. You're okay. It's only the nightmare."

She glanced around, wary. The wolf was gone, and so were the eyes. The fierce wind had died down to barely a breeze. Everything she saw was cast in gloom. All the beauty that once belonged here was now gone. The garden was in a state of ruin. The flowers, all withered and dead, were the only things reminding her of where she was.

"Come on," Charles said. "Take my hands. It's time to go back."

Lottie jerked awake. She raised onto her elbows, shaking with relief. "We made it back. Thank God we made it back."

"How are you, Charlotte?" Mathilda asked.

"Shaken up and very happy that it's over."

"Marie, bring the potions, please."

She carried two glass containers over. Mathilda gave one to Lottie and the other to Charles.

"Drink this. It will give you a sense of calm and revitalize you."

"How long were we out of it?" Lottie asked, turning up the contents.

"Nearly twenty minutes."

"It felt like an eternity. Did you find anything out?"

"You and Charles go rest for a bit. I need to wrap things up in here, and then I'll fill you in."

"Okay."

Charles reached for Lottie's hand as they stepped out from the corridor and back into the comfort of the library. "Are you sure you're okay?"

"Yeah. The ordeal was horrible. The first time I had the nightmare, the wolf couldn't get through the protective barrier, but in the spell, it was in the garden— it chased me."

"Come with me."

"Where are we going?"

"To the rose garden."

The warm sun and the familiar sweet scent of the garden greeted Lottie when she stepped outside. She shuddered, recalling every detail that happened in the spell.

"See, just as it should be," Charles said, easing up behind her, wrapping her in his arms. "Let's do some grounding. I know I could use a reboot."

Lottie sat facing him and drew in a deep, cleansing breath. With each exhale, she sent all the black energy she felt into the earth. Her peace had returned by the time Ramona opened the French doors to call them inside.

Settling in on the sofa, Lottie turned her attention to Mathilda.

"Matthew is involved," she said. "He is a shifter. He was the wolf you saw in your dream."

"Oh, my God," Lottie replied. The weight of the words sank in, leaving her fingers trembling. "He tried to hurt me in my dream."

"He can't hurt you," Mathilda assured. "We're going to find Matthew and learn his part in all this."

Lottie nodded and gazed at her hands, vaguely noticing a chip in her nail polish.

"You kids should get out of the house, go have dinner or something," Regina suggested. "It will be good for you both to get your minds off everything you've been through today. Phil and I will trail you to keep an eye on things."

"I think that's a great idea," Charles agreed. "How about Bricco? Maybe we can catch a movie afterward. You up for it?"

Lottie was grateful for Regina's suggestion. She had to get out of this place, away from the rose garden and the memory of the wolf. "Bricco is great. I'm craving Italian."

～

REGINA TAPPED A SHINY RED FINGERNAIL AGAINST THE steering wheel while waiting for Mathilda to answer her phone.

"What's happening?" Mathilda asked.

"You were right," Regina said. "The area you circled on the map where Matthew's pen stopped was dead on. He followed Lottie and Charles to Bricco. Ramona and I are watching the kids, and Phil is watching Matthew."

"Very good. Keep your eyes open for an accomplice."

"Will do. Hey, gotta go. Phil just messaged me. He's on the move."

Regina hung up and read the text. "Phil says Matthew has left his car and to channel each other from here on."

Ramona glanced around the parking lot. I don't see him."

Regina focused her mind on her husband. "He's around the side of the building going toward Matthew. You go around this way and head him off. I'll stay here and watch the kids."

"Keep your thoughts clear," Ramona said, easing out of the car. "It's hard to say where this will go."

Phil kept a slow pace giving Ramona time to catch up.

Do you see him? he asked once she rounded the corner.

I do. Distract him if he reaches you first.

Matthew paused to peer in the windows.

"Have you eaten here before?" Phil asked, skimming over the menu posted by the door.

Matthew turned at Phil's voice. "I, um, I haven't. I was thinking about going in. I thought I'd take a look at the menu first. Anything look good on there?"

"The shrimp linguini is quite tasty," Ramona said from behind.

Matthew stiffened when he saw her. A look of fear etched over his features as he slowly backed away.

"Don't do it, Matthew," Ramona warned. "I don't want to hurt you, but I will."

A blank look crossed his face, and he turned, looking for an easy escape. He winced when the pain began, grabbing at his head.

It will get much worse if you don't come with us.

"How did you get into my head? What do you want?"

"We just want to talk to you, Matthew," Phil assured.

Matthew glanced nervously across the parking lot.

"Looking for someone?" Phil asked.

"No," he lied.

Phil turned his mind to Regina. *We have him. How are the kids?*
Fine. Be careful. I'll stay where I am.

Phil ushered Matthew around to the passenger side of his car. "Get in."

Matthew shifted in his seat, his eyes wildly darting around the parking area.

"Why do you keep looking around?" Phil asked. "Are you waiting for someone?"

"No."

Phil turned to Ramona.

"He's telling the truth. I'm going to ask you some questions, Matthew, and I want you to give me honest answers. If you don't, I'll know. Are you alone tonight?"

"Yes."

"Why are you here?"

"I just wanted to have dinner."

"Matthew...." Ramona chided.

He grabbed his head again. A sob escaped him, and he began to cry uncontrollably.

"Stop, make it stop! I can't do this anymore."

"Do what, Matthew?" Ramona asked.

"She made me do it. I told her I was against it from the beginning. She hurt me...."

"Who hurt you?"

Matthew rocked back and forth in the seat. He suddenly looked like a small child, lost and afraid.

"The Mistress," he finally answered. "She said the next time, I would be lucky to survive it. She makes me change."

"Change, how?"

"The black wolf. The first time, it was easy, but then she got angry and made it hurt. My bones broke. I just want to die," he sobbed.

"Who is your mistress?"

Matthew's eyes widened in terror, and he shook his head no, over and over.

"You can tell us, Matthew," Ramona urged. "We need to know where she is."

He shook his head again, more violently this time.

"I want you to do something then. I want you to think of your mistress in your mind. Can you do that, Matthew?"

He nodded his head, yes, seeming even more childlike than before.

"Very good. Close your eyes and clear your mind. Just breathe."

Matthew sat focused for a moment. Suddenly, his face turned red, and he started to convulse.

He slumped over, giving up his last breath. Two lines of blood drained from his eyes. Two more from his ears, dripping in muted plops onto his lap.

"No!" Ramona shouted.

"Did you see her?" Phil asked.

"No, I was so close. An image started forming, but Selene severed their link at the last second." Ramona shook her head as she gazed at Matthew. "She had a death spell over him, set to take effect should he ever attempt to reveal her, and he didn't even realize it."

Phil pinched the bridge of his nose, letting out a deep sigh. "We have to find her."

"We will. We have to take care of Matthew first." Ramona waved her hand, and Matthew disappeared from view of anyone but them. "Let's go tell Regina."

They drove around to the back of the building and parked beside her car.

"Are the kids okay?" Phil asked.

"They're fine," Regina replied. Her eyes lingered on the passenger seat. "What a shame; look at the terror on his poor face."

"We need to go take care of his remains," Ramona said. "Follow us to the forest reserve. Isobel and Katrina will take over here."

Phil drove the winding road and pulled over into a densely wooded area. Regina parked behind him and got out.

"You two grab his feet," Phil said.

Regina grunted as she struggled to carry Matthew. "My God. When was the last time we had to do this? These heels will be rendered useless after this."

"Don't complain, sister," Ramona chided. "Shoes can be replaced."

They stretched Matthew out on the ground below an ancient-looking tree.

"*Patefio,*" they said in unison.

The earth rolled back at the tree's base, allowing the roots to lift out of the dirt. They wound themselves around Matthew and pulled him to the ground. Then, the earth shifted back over the hole, undisturbed once again.

❦

"So, did you enjoy the movie?" Charles asked.

"I did," Lottie replied. "I appreciate you taking me out. I needed the distraction."

"Good. Speaking of distraction, why don't we all go to the lake tomorrow?"

"That would be great. I'll need to run it by Mathilda and my parents."

A gentle breeze tickled Lottie's skin. She rubbed the goosebumps on her arms. "There's a strangeness to the energy tonight. Do you feel it?"

"A little. It's probably the effects of the spell we went through earlier."

"Maybe."

"A good night's sleep should do the trick. Come on, let's get you back."

❦

Regina gulped down the contents of her glass. "I needed that," she said, filling it again.

"You're certain Lottie and Charles were oblivious to the ordeal?" Mathilda asked.

"Yes, completely unaware of the situation. Phil went back to join

Trina and Isobel at the theatre to keep an eye out should Selene or some other accomplices show up."

"I don't believe Selene will be any more trouble tonight," Ramona added. "When she severed her link with Matthew, I felt her recoil. Her power is weakening, and she's taking a step back to regroup."

"That poor man. What he must have endured under her control." Ramona leaned forward, tucking a section of hair behind her ear. "The woman is cruel. She was making Matthew transform into a wolf. She didn't even make it easy for him. He felt every bone break as he shifted."

Regina shuddered. "It's too awful. At least he is free and at peace now."

∼

WHEN LOTTIE RETURNED FROM HER DATE, SHE NOTICED A light was on in the library. The sounds from the television echoed down the hall.

"What are you doing up so late?" she asked, stepping into the room.

"Waiting for you," Mathilda said, switching off the remote. "Sit down; I need to talk to you."

Lottie felt the weight of the words as she sat alongside her.

"What is it?"

"Matthew is dead," Mathilda began.

"Dead? How do you know?"

"We were able to track him. Matthew followed you and Charles to the restaurant tonight. Phil, Regina, and Ramona went there to keep an eye on him and managed to talk to him alone, but unfortunately, Selene had placed a death spell on him should he betray her. It killed him before Ramona could extract any useful information."

A knot of fear settled in Lottie's stomach. "Oh, my God." She sank against the back of the sofa. "So where is Selene now?"

"We still don't know. Killing Matthew drained some of her stolen power. Ramona said she felt enough of Selene's presence in his mind to reveal she has taken a step back."

Lottie suddenly recalled Charles's plans.

"Charles wanted to go to the lake tomorrow with the others. Are we safe to go?"

"I doubt Selene will try anything so soon, but to be safe, one of us will go along and keep a presence in the vicinity."

Chapter Seventeen

Sunlight poured into the secluded clearing by the lake. Lottie smiled when she saw Wren and Rowen dancing. She grabbed her bag and blanket while Charles carried the chairs.

"It's about time you got here," Wren teased.

"Hey, not everyone drives like a maniac," Charles replied. He leaned the chairs against a tree. "I'm going back for the picnic basket."

Lottie spread the blanket out and kicked her shoes off.

"This heat," Rowen complained. "I vote we go swim."

"You go ahead," Lottie said. "I want to be right here on this blanket in the sun." She leaned back with a contented sigh.

"Suit yourself."

Charles pushed an umbrella into the ground near Lottie.

"Let me know if you get too hot. I'll open it up."

"Thank you." She watched Rowen go over to a large tree and pull back the rope that hung from a sturdy branch. Her scream shattered the silence as she swung out over the water, only ending when she plopped in.

Charles shook his head and smiled at Lottie. "Wanna swing out with me?"

"Oh, I don't know. I don't like the thought of being dropped into a body of water."

"Come on. It'll be fun. I'll be right there with you." He held out his hand to her.

"Ugh...okay, but you'd better not let go of me."

Lottie followed him to the tree while Sunni and Rowen cheered them on.

Charles pulled the rope back. "You ready?"

"I guess so."

"Hold on to me."

She wrapped her arms around him and closed her eyes.

"Here we go."

Lottie squeezed her legs tightly around his as they swung over the lake. Charles let go of the rope, and she screamed before splashing in the water. She untangled herself from him and pushed to the surface.

Charles popped up after her, smiling. "Well?"

"I guess it was fun."

"You guess?" He splashed water on her face.

"Oh, you shouldn't have done that, Charles Lachlan."

"Mercy, I call mercy," he begged.

"You got lucky. I was going to let you have it."

"I know. I could feel your revenge."

The sun peaked overhead, signaling lunch. Lottie took a sandwich from the basket Charles brought and passed it to him. She opened the other one and took a bite.

"Mmm. This is really good."

"I made it myself."

"Did you?"

"Charles thinks he's Guy Fieri," Rowen mocked.

"The only difference is I'm much better."

"Ah-ha, ha...." Rowen laughed sarcastically."

"So, what's going on with you and Bryan?" Sunni asked, tossing a bag of chips toward Wren. "Are you two official or what?"

Wren dumped a few chips onto her plate. "I'm not in any hurry to rush a relationship."

"The boy is hot, Wren—like smoking. Feel free to send him my way if you can't commit." Sunni threw her hands up at Wren's stony gaze. "Chill. I'm joking."

The clearing darkened significantly as a massive, puffy white cloud moved in.

"Oh, man," Rowen whined, looking up.

Lottie swiped with her hand, and the cloud moved past the sun."

"Awesome! Thanks."

They cleaned up and headed over to the edge of an old boat dock. The water bobbed and sloshed around the beams from Sunni and Rowen's splash battle.

"Dudes, you're getting us wet," Wren shouted.

"You *are* at a lake," Sunni pointed out.

"You guys are out of control," Lottie joked.

She noticed the nod Rowen gave to Sunni and the grin that spread over their faces from their wicked intentions.

"Don't do it," Lottie warned.

Her words went unnoticed. She stood and wiped the water from her eyes. "You know this means war, right?" Her lips twisted up as she turned and faced the lake.

"Uh-oh," Sunni said. She quickly tried to wade out of the water with Rowen close behind, but the current sucked them back as it gathered into a massive band rising eight feet overhead. Sunni's scream was cut short as the water tumbled over them both.

"All righty, then," Wren muttered to herself.

Sunni adjusted her swimsuit and staggered onto the grass. "Impressive," she said.

Lottie flushed. "Sorry, I guess that was a bit much."

"You *think?*" Rowen said, peeling her hair away from her eyes.

"Remind me never to make you mad," Charles teased.

"I'm going to my blanket," Sunni said, trudging up the bank. "Do not disturb."

Lottie followed along. She smeared more sunblock on and noticed her friends stretched out in silent contentment.

"I think they have the right idea," she said, turning to Charles.

"Me, too. Here, let me get the umbrella up. Can't have you getting sunburned."

She snuggled against Charles and let her eyes close.

~

"Ow!" Lottie woke disoriented.

"What is it?" Charles asked.

"I thought I felt...no, it's nothing," she said, her fingers lingering at her chest.

"Lottie, tell me."

"I don't know, really. It felt like my pendant was hot for just a second. I thought I got burned, but it's not hot now. I must have been dreaming."

"Are you sure?" Charles asked. His eyes, deep with concern, held hers.

"No, I think I made a mistake. Too much sun and magic."

Lottie noticed the others exchange worried glances amongst themselves. "I know what you guys are thinking, but look." She lifted her pendant away from her chest. "It's fine, see?"

"Why don't we pack up and head back?" Charles suggested. "It's getting late."

Lottie gathered up what she could and headed around the lake.

"Do you think her pendant activated?" Wren asked, stepping close to Charles. "Mathilda told us it would get warm if anyone searched for the moonstone."

He raked a hand through his hair, keeping his gaze on Lottie. "I don't know. For her sake, I hope not."

Lottie pulled her shoes off and massaged the side of her foot. "Do you care if we stop at my house before heading to Mathilda's? I want to get my Vans. These are rubbing my feet."

"Sure."

Her parents were on the bench swing under the old oak tree when they pulled up the drive. Her mother threw her head back, laughing at something her father said. She gave a teasing shove to his arm. The sight of them together like this warmed Lottie's heart.

An endearing smile sprang to her lips as she exited the car.

"I'm glad you guys are home. I'm going to grab a different pair of shoes."

"Go ahead, honey," her mother said, laughter still dancing in her eyes.

A twinge of homesickness swept over Lottie when she went to her room. Reaching for the closet door, her bracelet snagged on her swim coverup. "Great." She took it off carefully and freed it from her cover. She grimaced as she caught a glimpse of her reflection in the mirror. Her hair was a mess. She raked a comb through it and went to grab her shoes.

The sound of her mother's giggle brought another smile to Lottie's lips as she stepped outside.

"Ah, oldies but goodies," her mother said, looking at the shoes Lottie now wore.

"Yep."

"There are cookies on the stove. Why don't you run back in and take some with you?"

Lottie considered it, but she wanted to get to Mathilda's, strip out of her swimsuit, and shower. "I'll pass— this time," she said with a wink.

"I'll check in with you in a few days," her mother replied.

"Okay, love you guys."

CHARLES HELPED LOTTIE GET HER THINGS INTO MATHILDA'S house.

"Thanks for a fun day."

"I'm glad you enjoyed it," he said, kissing her cheek.

Her phone rang as she closed the door behind him. "Hey, Mom. What's up."

"I just wanted to let you know you left your bracelet in your room. Your father and I will ride out and bring it to you."

"You don't have to do that tonight."

"It's fine. I know how much you love wearing it. Besides, your father wants to get ice cream."

"I'll watch for you, then."

Lottie ran upstairs to get a shower before her parents arrived. When their car came up the driveway, she stepped out under the portico and met them at the car.

Her mother rolled down the window and held out the bracelet. "Here you go."

"Thanks. You guys going anywhere else after you eat your ice cream?"

"I thought I'd take your mother the scenic way home around the mountain."

"Wow, you guys are adventurous," Lottie said flatly.

Her mother scowled. "I'll have you know, that's the best place to see the sunset, missy."

"Chill, Mom. Teenage sarcasm. Be safe and enjoy the ride."

Her mother pressed a kiss on Lottie's arm. "We will."

"Goodnight, Dad. Love you guys."

Her mother blew a kiss as they pulled away. Lottie returned it and darted in to say goodnight to Mathilda before turning in for an early bedtime. Settling under the covers, she studied her pendant, trying to recall what happened when she woke at the lake. It did seem like it had burned her, but she couldn't be sure. Too exhausted to think about it anymore, she resolved to mention her concerns to Mathilda in the morning and deal with it then.

~

"CHARLOTTE? WAKE UP, DEAR."

Mathilda's voice sounded strange. Lottie opened her eyes. A dim light from the hallway cast a golden glow around Mathilda's silhouette.

"What time is it?"

"One a.m."

An alarm went off inside of Lottie. "What's wrong?"

Mathilda lowered her head. When she finally spoke, tears were in her eyes.

"Oh, honey, I don't know how to tell you."

Lottie trembled with fear. "Mathilda, what's happened? Tell me."

The few beats of silence were dreadful.

"It's your parents," she finally said. "They were in a terrible accident. Their car went off the road...."

"What?" Lottie shrilled, bolting upright. "Oh, my God! No." She searched Mathilda's eyes, desperate for any signs of hope, but found none.

"Charlotte, they didn't make it. I'm so, so sorry."

Lottie shook her head in protest. "No, you're wrong! You're *wrong*!" she shouted, demanding a different response.

A tear spilled down Mathilda's cheek, and Lottie knew what she'd said was true. Her body went numb inside.

They didn't make it.

The words were brutal. Lottie smacked her hands against her head — once, twice, three times, wishing she could somehow make the nightmare disappear. As the sobs wracked her body, she felt darkness consume her. It crawled around inside, wiping away all reason. Mathilda spoke to her, but she couldn't hear anything except sorrow. She clamped her hands over her ears and screamed.

All the lights in the bedroom and bathroom flashed on and off and then exploded. Shards of glass flew everywhere.

"Charlotte! Lottie!" Mathilda's voice snapped her out of the blackness. She crumpled in Mathilda's arms, shaking with sobs.

"I never should have come here," she whimpered. "I never should have come...."

"Honey, I called Charles. He's on his way."

Mathilda cradled Lottie in her arms. Silent tears streamed down her face as she rocked her daughter.

SHE HEARD HIS FOOTSTEPS POUND UP THE STAIRS AND INTO the corridor. Her arms reached for him, desperate.

"Lottie...." He rushed over to the bed and gathered her up. "I'm so sorry. What can I do?"

"I don't know...I don't know," she wailed.

"Stay with her tonight, Charles," Mathilda said, slipping out of the room.

"Thank you."

He settled farther down into the bed and pulled Lottie close.

MORNING CAME. LOTTIE WOKE, SCREAMING.

"It's okay," Charles soothed.

Tears filled her eyes as the memory of last night's events refreshed again.

"Can I get you anything?" he asked, smoothing his fingers over the back of her hand.

"No. Nothing." She swiped the tears from her cheek. "Thank you for staying with me. I went somewhere bad last night before you got here. I don't ever want to feel that way again." Her lower lip trembled as she fought to contain her grief. "Oh, Charles. My parents, my mom...."

He pulled her in his arms.

"I should have stayed longer. I should have taken the cookies, sat with them, and not rushed off. I'll never see them again." She pressed her hands over her eyes and took a deep breath.

"Mathilda didn't give me any details about the accident last night. Do you know what happened?"

Lottie shook her head no, squeezing her eyes shut against the tears.

There was a knock at the door. Charles walked carefully around the glass to open it.

Mathilda stepped into the room. "How are you, Charlotte? Can I get you anything?"

"No. Thank you." She noticed Marie standing near the door. A pitied look replaced her usual stony features.

"Charlotte, I hate to disturb you, but would you mind letting Marie clean up in here? I don't want you to get cut on the glass."

Marie swished past Mathilda toward the bed.

"I'm deeply sorry for your loss, Miss Charlotte. I will be quick."

"Leave it," Lottie said.

Marie gave a start. "Excuse me?"

"I said leave it," Lottie reiterated firmly.

She saw Charles's surprised reaction but ignored him.

"Charlotte," Mathilda said gently. "I know you would rather not leave the comfort of your room, but we must clean up in here. This glass is dangerous."

"I don't care. I'm not leaving."

"Lottie, what is this?" Charles asked.

"My parents are dead, Charles. They're dead because of me. I deserve to sit in discomfort for what I've done."

"Oh, Charlotte," Mathilda said. Tears pooled in her eyes, and she moved toward the bed.

"Get out," Lottie said. *"Get out!"*

Mathilda flinched at the outburst. A tear streaked down her face, and Lottie began to sob. Mathilda rushed to the bed and wrapped Lottie in her arms.

"I'm sorry," Lottie said against her chest. "I didn't mean it."

"My darling girl," Mathilda said, smoothing her hair. "I am so very sorry for your loss, but your parents' deaths are not your fault. Do you hear me?"

Lottie nodded placatingly beneath Mathilda's chin, but nothing she said would make Lottie accept anything less than the blame.

Mathilda reached for a tissue and wiped Lottie's face.

"I promise to do everything I can to help you through this difficult time—starting with this room. My dear, we have to clean up, you understand, don't you?"

Lottie nodded, relinquishing her stubbornness to punish herself at least. She paused by the door, casting a contrite glance across the room. "I'm sorry, Marie."

～

A PALE LIGHT FILTERED THROUGH THE VEIL OF CLOUDS, glinting against the silver chaffing dishes on the table by the window. Mathilda lifted a lid off one, filling the breakfast room with the smell of sausage. She took a plate and turned to Lottie.

"Would you like some pancakes, too?"

"I'm not hungry," Lottie answered.

"Will you please eat a little something, some fruit perhaps?"

"No."

"Have a little breakfast with me," Charles said gently. A sweet smile touched his lips, bringing her out of total despair. She had to be strong. Her parents wouldn't want her like this.

"I'll try some pancakes," she said.

After they ate, Charles stepped outside to phone his mother. Lottie watched him pace, feeling the pull of the question weighing on her mind.

"Will you tell me what you know about the accident?" she said, turning to Mathilda.

"Of course," Mathilda replied. She placed her coffee cup on the saucer and met Lottie's attentive gaze. "Someone traveling over the mountain saw your parents' car upside down and dialed 911. A police officer went to your house to notify you, but since you weren't there, another officer on the scene went through your mother's belongings and found my name and address written on a piece of paper. He came by last night to inform me of their deaths. According to his report, there were no signs of foul play. They simply went over the side of the mountain. I went to identify their bodies and to see if he was missing anything. I sensed no involvement of magic."

Lottie stared into her hands. She took a calming breath. "Did they say what caused the wreck?"

"They think your dad got distracted and lost control of the car by how the tire marks veered off the road."

Lottie nodded, allowing the information to sink in.

"I want to see them. Where are they?"

"They're at the morgue. I don't mind taking you, but are you sure you want to see your parents that way?"

The image of her parents' lifeless, damaged bodies flooded Lottie's mind. She tried not to cry, but the overwhelming images shut down the shreds of control she desperately clung to. She reached for her napkin and gave in to her grief.

"Oh, you, poor girl," Mathilda said, pulling her into a snug embrace. "Is there anybody you'd like for me to call?"

"No. My mom's only sister died when I was young, and the only relative Dad has is his aunt Margaret. She's in a nursing home in Florida with Alzheimer's. I wouldn't want her to know."

"I understand. We'll need to make arrangements. I will help you with everything."

Lottie cut her short. "I can't do this right now. Can I please be alone for a while?"

"Of course, dear. I know this doesn't mean the same coming from me, but I love you and am here for you. Go upstairs to my bedroom and get some rest. I'll check on you once Marie is finished in your room."

Lottie pulled Mathilda's throw over her face and fell into a deep sleep. When she woke again, Charles sat in a chair by the bed.

"Have I been sleeping long?"

"A few hours. How are you?"

"I feel like I've been hit by a bus."

"Are you up to going downstairs? The covens are here."

"I don't know. I'm not sure I'm up to talking to anyone."

"They're worried and want to be here for you, but if you aren't ready to see anyone, I can go down and let them know."

Lottie sighed. "I know they do. I'll go get ready?"

Charles gave a reassuring smile. "Take as long as you need."

Lottie walked down to her bedroom. Marie had everything back in order. All of the lights were replaced with new bulbs and there was fresh bedding. She took a quick shower and returned to her room to get dressed. There on the nightstand was the bracelet from her parents. Tears stung her eyes as she recalled the night they gave it to her. She took a deep breath, put the bracelet on, and went down to face everyone.

The dining hall was full of concerned faces. Everyone got quiet as she walked into the room. Wren was the first to approach. "Lottie, I'm so sorry about your parents."

"Thank you."

Charles put his hand in hers. She felt his strength and closed her eyes.

Thank you. I needed that.

"How are you, Lottie?" Phil asked.

"Numb."

"Please let us know if there is anything we can do for you," Regina added.

Sunni and Rowen hugged her and gave their condolences.

So many voices: "I'm sorry. I'm sorry. I'm so sorry, Lottie...." It was too much.

Choking back a sob, she ran from the room. She flung herself across her bed and allowed the tears to come.

Sometime later, a soft knock came at her door. "Can I come in?" Charles asked.

"Yes." She wiped her nose and sat up as he settled in beside her.

"Are you okay?"

"No. I don't believe I'll be okay for a long time."

He pulled her close. "I know this doesn't sound possible right now, but time will heal you. This is the hard part. Don't feel bad for needing time to grieve."

She felt his love and support radiate into her.

"I don't know what I would do without you."

Mathilda stepped into the room. "Everyone has gone home."

"I'm sorry. I didn't mean to run out on them."

"They understand. They sent their love."

"Thank you."

"I know you don't want to think about this, but we need to make the funeral arrangements."

Lottie stared wide-eyed as panic coursed through her. "I can't. I'm not ready."

"I know you think you can't do this, but you can," Charles said. "We'll help you through this process. You're not alone."

Lottie wiped the fresh tears from her eyes. "I know. I just never thought I'd be doing this. Why? Why did this happen? They didn't deserve to have their lives cut short."

Mathilda sat on the bed and covered Lottie's hand with hers. "Life is a mystery. There's joy, pain, love, and unfortunately, you've had to deal with death. Their love and memory will be forever etched in your heart. They're not gone. Not as long as you carry their love with you."

"Just let me get through this night. I can't think about it tonight."

Mathilda nodded. "Okay. Do you want to come down for dinner?"

"No. I'd rather stay up here."

"I'll bring something up for you. Charles, would you like some food?"

"If you're sure it's no trouble."

"Not at all."

Lottie folded herself over her knees and buried her head in her arms. She imagined her parents' wreck. Were their bodies recognizable? A sob escaped.

Charles pulled her over onto his lap and kissed the top of her head. "I'm so sorry."

She sniffed and let out a jagged breath. "I keep thinking about my parents and wondering how badly they were damaged. I don't think I could bear to see them like that, yet I feel horribly guilty that I would even consider not seeing them."

"Lottie, you have nothing to feel guilty about. Mathilda identified their bodies. You can always choose to have a closed casket service. You don't have to put yourself through that. Remember them how they were, sitting on the garden swing. That's a fine memory to carry with you, as they were."

She swiped a tissue across her nose. "Thank you. I needed to hear that."

Marie brought up their food and left them to their solitude.

"I'm glad you're eating," Charles said.

"I'm trying. Nothing tastes right anymore."

When she finished, Charles put their plates on the tray and set them on the table outside the door.

"You look tired. I'll go and let you get some sleep."

"Don't go. I don't want you to leave me."

"Let me talk to Mathilda. If she says it's okay for me to stay over again, I'll go home, get some things, and come back."

He pulled the covers up over her. "I love you. I'll be back as soon as I can."

She nodded and grabbed her bracelet from the nightstand. Hugging it tight against her chest, she cried herself to sleep.

The following day, Lottie woke with a bad headache. She glanced around the room, but Charles wasn't there. Mathilda must have said no to him staying over.

She got out of bed, went into the bathroom, and rinsed her face, cupping cold water over her swollen, puffy eyes. Her stomach growled. Food suddenly seemed appealing. *Maybe this is progress,* she thought.

Lottie put on her robe and headed out into the corridor. Charles was coming up the steps as she went out.

She gave a weak smile. "Hi."

"I'm sorry I wasn't in your room when you woke. I stayed in one of the guest bedrooms last night. You were sleeping soundly when I came in, and I didn't want to bother you."

Lottie nodded. "Have you eaten?"

"No. I wanted to wait for you."

She felt his eyes on her as they pulled their chairs to the table.

"Are you okay?" he asked.

Lottie mulled over his question. *Define okay?* She felt different. Everything in the world seemed wrong now. It was as if she was somehow detached from her body, watching this whole nightmare from afar. Glancing up, she met his eyes, full of love and concern, and felt guilty for not wanting to have an in-depth conversation.

Her voice was distant when she finally answered. "Fine. Just hungry."

Mathilda poured a cup of tea and passed it to Lottie. The silence around the breakfast table was prevalent as they ate.

After she finished, Lottie placed her napkin on the table and stood. "I'll go up to get ready. Will you drive me to the funeral home?"

"Of course," Mathilda replied.

"Would you like me to come along?" Charles asked.

"Yes, please," Lottie replied.

Mathilda pushed her chair back. "I'll get changed and meet you down here when you are ready, then."

The water from the shower beat down upon Lottie, stinging her eyes. She felt empty. She felt nothing. Everything she did afterward was a process, going through the motions, feeling dead inside.

The silence on the ride to the funeral home was stifling, but no one did anything about it. When they arrived, Charles went around the car to get the door for Lottie, but she opened it herself and quickly walked ahead of him.

"Don't worry, Charles," Mathilda soothed. "She's trying to deal with this the only way she knows how."

"I know. It's killing me to see her this way."

A man with startling blue eyes greeted them at the door. He bore a shocking resemblance to a young Chris Pine. For some reason, his youth and good looks made Lottie boil with anger. A petty voice said he should be older and gaunt, and she resented him for this fault.

She was cold and emotionless throughout the process. After it was over, Lottie thanked the man and quickly stood. "I'd like to leave now."

"Is there anything else you'd like to do?" Mathilda asked.

"No. I just want to go ho— to your house," she corrected.

Lottie went straight up to her room without a word when they returned. She sat on the edge of her bed, staring at the floor, feeling utterly lost.

Charles came in and sat beside her. "I know I keep asking, but are you okay? You've been so quiet, and I don't know what to do for you."

She glanced at him, then back to the floor. "I don't know. I feel strange," she replied. "Just empty and hollow."

"Would you like to be alone?"

"I think so. I'm not very good company today."

"I understand. If you need anything from me, please let me help you."

"I will."

After Charles left her room, she changed clothes and decided to go for a walk. Maybe being outdoors would help her feel better. It usually did.

Stepping into the garden, she inhaled deeply, breathing in the scent of roses. She noticed they were in full bloom now. She ran her fingers across their satiny petals as she walked along the path, letting her hands trail behind her. Suddenly, a sharp stinging replaced the smoothness of the blooms. She watched the bright red dot on her finger from the thorn prick grow larger until it rolled off the tip and onto the ground. Her blood was warm and flowing, and her parents had no blood, no warmth, no life.

The pain made it real. Another dot started to form again. "Heal." At her command, the blood dried up, and the skin repaired.

She stretched out on the grass and let the sun warm her body. Clouds floated overhead. She moved her fingers and formed shapes in them. Closing her eyes, she became acutely aware of the ground beneath her. Her parents would soon be in the earth, and she would be....

"Not alone. Don't say it," Charles said behind her. "Can I join you?"

"Sure." She continued forming shapes in the clouds.

"I know you feel alone, but you're not."

Lottie paused her movement and sighed. "I know. I'm sorry. I appreciate everything you are doing, Charles. Please don't give up on me. I just need to be sad."

"I will never give up on you. You be as sad as you want to be."

He looked up as Lottie flicked her wrist. "Is that a bunny?"

"Yeah. Try one."

He wrote in the air with his finger.

I love you, Lottie, formed in the clouds. She turned and, without speaking, said, *I love you, Charles.*

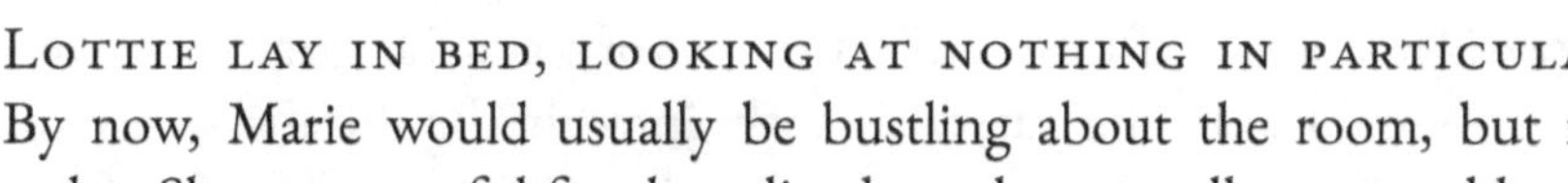

LOTTIE LAY IN BED, LOOKING AT NOTHING IN PARTICULAR. By now, Marie would usually be bustling about the room, but not today. She was grateful for the solitude as she mentally prepared herself for her parents' funeral service.

After a long shower, Lottie stood in front of the mirror, looking at the expanse of black on her body. The dress set the mood. Bleak. She put on her bracelet and pressed it to her heart. "I'm so sorry, Mom, Dad." She grabbed a tissue and caught the building pool of tears before they spilled.

She missed her mother so much, the embracing of her arms, the comforting words, and her father's reassuring presence— always there and always ready with a kind word for her. Her body shook with racking sobs. She wanted to go home. Home to where her parents are— were. The reality of her future without them was too harsh to contemplate. She reached for fresh tissues, wiped her eyes again, and shoved some more in her clutch.

Her mother would be proud. *"A woman should always come equipped,"* she would say after shoving her purse with a stash of tissues. Lottie managed a weak smile at the thought. She crossed the room toward the door and went down downstairs.

After pouring a cup of tea, Lottie headed to the solarium. She took note of the thick layer of gray clouds as she stood by the windows gazing out at the lawn. She was glad for the overcast day. It seemed appropriate. She heard footsteps and turned.

"Sorry I'm late," Charles said, slipping his arms around her. "I made a stop before coming over." He reached into his suit pocket and pulled out a strand of pearls.

Lottie gasped. "My mom's necklace."

"I hope you don't mind that I let myself into your house to get them. I thought you might want something from your mother today."

"Oh, Charles. Thank you." She draped the necklace around her neck and fumbled with the clasp.

Noticing her struggle, Charles lifted her hair away and took over. "There. You look beautiful. How about we go eat breakfast?"

"Sure."

Lottie's finger traced with the rim of her cup as she nibbled at a pastry. Her stomach churned. The thought of seeing her parents' caskets was unbearable. As she gazed absently into the liquid abyss, her tea started boiling and bubbling toward the rim. Charles covered her hand with his. Her attention diverted, and the bubbling stopped.

What is it?" he asked.

"I don't know if I can get through this," her voice broke.

"Lottie, I won't leave your side for a moment. Draw from my strength. I'll help you."

"What if I lose control like this," she gestured toward her cup. "What if someone realizes that it's me making it happen?"

"You leave that to the coven. They've already considered it. You get through this day however you need to, and don't let the fear of your magic showing distract you."

~

LOTTIE STARED NUMBLY OUT THE WINDOW ON THE WAY TO the cemetery. She wasn't aware they had arrived until Dabney opened the door for Mathilda. She stepped out and turned to Lottie. "You can do this. You're stronger than you think you are."

Lottie nodded, took Charles's outstretched hand, and let him guide her toward the gravesite. Seeing the elder coven gave her slight comfort. Her coven, however, looked as sad as she felt. She tried to smile, but her lips refused to cooperate. She noticed some of her parents' friends and co-workers but couldn't bear to make eye contact. She turned away, walked over to the caskets instead, and gazed down at the closed lids. The thought of never seeing her mom and dad again was too much. The tightness in her chest doubled, and breathing was a struggle. Right on cue, the wind ripped through the trees. Charles squeezed her close to him.

At Mathilda's nod, the coven members focused on Lottie. Suddenly, the wind calmed, as did Lottie. She turned away and buried her face into Charles's shoulder.

After the service, several men who knew her father came over to offer their condolences. Her mother's employee, Millie, was last to approach. Lottie noticed her eyes were puffy from crying.

"Oh, Lottie. I'm so sorry. Is there anything I can do?"

"Thank you, Millie. Just being here is enough."

Millie wrapped her arms around Lottie. "Let me know if you need anything at all."

Lottie stood quietly as the caskets lowered to the ground. Her heart sank further with every inch they descended. She bent down and scooped up a handful of dirt. Her hand tingled with negative energy. Odd. She took a deep breath, threw some over the caskets, and put the rest in the tissues in her clutch. Later, she would see what she could make of this dark energy she felt.

Charles and Mathilda embraced her. Their love radiated, lifting her. Lottie smiled and let their love heal her. "Let's go home."

~

THAT EVENING, MATHILDA BROUGHT DINNER TO LOTTIE'S room.

"Did Marie go on vacation or something?"

Mathilda smiled. "No, I wanted to talk to you." She poured a cup of tea and placed it on Lottie's side table. "I've been thinking. You are considered an orphan, and there are laws regarding minors in situations such as yours. I've spoken with my attorney, and he has prepared adoption papers. I know this is sudden and not what you want to hear right now, but we need to get something in place for the sake of the law and your well-being."

Lottie stared blankly at Mathilda.

"What are you thinking?"

"I don't know," Lottie replied. "I haven't had time to process anything."

"I want to take care of you, Charlotte. I want you to be happy. I hope you're not upset with me for doing this without talking to you first. John suggested we go ahead sooner rather than later to ensure you get into a stable situation. I agree with him."

"I'm not upset with you. It's just one more thing I never thought I'd have to deal with."

"I'm sorry, Charlotte. Would you like to go by your house to get anything today?"

"No. I'm not ready to face the house yet. I need more time."

"You take all the time you need, and when you want to go, just let me know."

Lottie thought of her house. What would happen to it? She knew her parents had savings, but they had never discussed the details with her. And their belongings... What would become of everything? She shuddered as fear of the unknown swept over her. She would have to talk to Mathilda about what to do, whether she liked it or not.

Chapter Eighteen

Lottie woke the following morning with another headache. She saw her clutch on the nightstand and remembered the dirt she had taken from her parents' gravesite. She reached for it and opened it. On top of the tissues was a small letter. She hadn't noticed it being there yesterday. She pulled it out and froze at seeing the black ribbon tied around it. Her fingers trembled as she unfolded it and began to read.

Do I have your attention now?
What luck getting both of your parents together.
Very well-orchestrated, don't you think?

Lottie dropped the letter to the floor. The room seemed to swirl around her as the words sank in.

She let out a heartbroken cry.

"Charlotte?" Mathilda rushed into her room. "Are you okay?"

"*Why!*" Lottie screamed. "Why is this happening?"

"What do you mean?"

Lottie pointed to the floor.

Mathilda bent over and picked up the letter. "Oh, no."

Lottie took a deep breath and leaned back against the headboard. "I feel sick."

"Marie," Mathilda called out.

"Yes, Mistress?"

"I need my herbal tea made up for Lottie immediately. Make sure you put ginger in it."

Mathilda placed an extra pillow behind Lottie's back. "Lie still. I'll get a cool cloth from the bathroom."

She returned and placed it against Lottie's forehead. "Where did you get this letter?"

"I don't know," Lottie sobbed. "It was in my clutch when I opened it this morning."

"Thank you, Marie," Mathilda said, taking the cup from her. She waved her hand over the rim. "Drink this. It will soothe you."

Lottie sipped the brew. Its warmth spread through her as the potion started to take effect. Her eyes closed, and the cup slipped from her hand. Mathilda took it from her and gave it to Marie.

"Let me know when she wakes."

"Of course, Mistress."

Mathilda went downstairs and dialed Ramona. "I need you to gather the coven immediately— Charles, too. Charlotte found another letter this morning. Her parents were murdered."

"Oh, my God. How is she?"

"Not good. I gave her a sleeping potion. I'm going to go set up if you'll notify everyone."

～

WHEN CHARLES ARRIVED, MATHILDA TOOK HIM ASIDE. "STAY near her. She's going to need you now more than ever. I'm going to my keeping room with the others. Send Marie to fetch me if Charlotte isn't any better."

He nodded.

Mathilda placed the letter beside the ornate gold stand mirror in the center of the table. A black candle flickered lazily beside it. She joined hands with her sisters and started the ritual.

"Forces of darkness, I call upon you. Show us the purpose of your evil in this letter."

The flame on the candle flickered wildly, and a thick black smoke snaked upward. Whispered voices came from the mirror, and a clouded fog swirled around in it. An image began to form, blurred at first, but then the mist cleared, revealing a massive moonstone. The flame on the black candle streaked over to the letter. It burst into flames, and the mirror shattered. Everything was silent.

"My God. That was the moonstone," Isobel said. She stared at the mirror in stunned disbelief. "I never thought I would see that thing again."

"Sisters, we've just discovered Selene's true motives," Mathilda stated. "She is searching for Cassandra's powers."

Regina nodded. "Her behavior over the past few months certainly points to that."

"Lottie's pendant hasn't been disturbed," Trina pointed out.

Mathilda sighed and leaned back in her chair. "No. But it's only a matter of time. I'd better go up and check on her."

CHARLES RESTED HIS ELBOWS ON HIS KNEES, TAPPING HIS steepled fingers as he watched Lottie stir from her sleep. She pushed herself up a bit and glanced around the room. "Where's Mathilda?"

"She's in her chamber with the elders. She told me about the letter. Lottie, I'm so sorry."

She nodded, trying not to cry.

Mathilda came in with another tea and gave it to Lottie. "This will clear your head."

Lottie took a sip and rested the cup between her hands. "What did you find out?"

"Selene is searching for the moonstone with Cassandra's powers."

Lottie's fingers flew to her pendant. "It did."

"What do you mean 'it did?'"

"Remember the day I went to the lake?"

"Yes."

"While we were there, I felt my pendant get hot— well, I thought I did. I had fallen asleep and woke to the feeling of it burning me, but it was only for a moment, and it didn't happen again."

Mathilda flinched. "Charlotte, why didn't you tell me this?"

"I meant to, but the accident happened the same night, and I forgot."

"Of course. I'm sorry, dear. Have you noticed any changes in it since the day at the lake?"

"No. What's going to happen?"

"Pay close attention to your pendant. I feel it's only a matter of time before it fully activates. When it does, we'll cast a locator spell. That will give us a rough idea of where the stone is, and once we know where we're headed, we'll use your pendant to do the rest of the work as it is linked to the moonstone. We must find and destroy it before Selene gets her hands on it."

Lottie's phone chimed. She reached for it and read the text. "It's Wren. She invited me to come over to get my mind off everything."

"I'd like to keep you here, safe for a few days while we sort this out."

"I'll be safe at Wren's house."

"I know, but now that we know Selene is after Cassandra's powers, I want you here with me."

"She's right," Charles added. "It's best for you to be here for now."

Lottie stared dumbly at them both, unaware that her fingernails dug crescents into her palms. She didn't want to be restricted. She felt as if she had been confined for weeks. There were too many emotions running through her to respond rationally.

"Fine," she snapped. "I'd like to be alone for a bit if that's not asking too much."

"Charlotte, I'm truly sorry. I know this is hard for you—"

"Can I please just be alone? I need time to think."

"Of course," Mathilda said. "I have a couple of errands to run anyway. I'll check in on you later."

Charles kissed her head. "I'll head home to eat lunch and return a little later."

~

LOTTIE STARED PAST THE BED FOR SOME TIME, HER thoughts on her parents. Selene murdered them. It had to be her. She no longer felt the crushing despair. Now, a wave of seething, vengeful anger took over. She got out of bed and gathered some items for a spell. Opening her clutch, she took dirt from the tissues and poured it into a pouch before stuffing it into a bag. She tossed the bag over her shoulder and headed for the woods, keeping to the dense coverage of trees until out of view from the house.

Kneeling by a gnarled oak, Lottie rummaged through her bag for the candle. She dumped some dirt from the pouch into a bowl and shoved the rest of it into her pocket. Her attention was honed and focused, as sharp as the blade tip that pricked her skin. With each drop of blood that fizzled and burned over the dirt, she thought of Selene.

"Reveal. *Reveal!*" Lottie screamed. Blinded by rage, she was unaware that her pendant was hot. *"Who are you?"*

A bolt of light came from the ground and hit Lottie's pendant, flinging her back into the tree. A vision of her parents' house came into her mind as she fell into blackness.

Lottie winced at the throbbing pain at the back of her head. She wondered how long she had been unconscious. She noticed a burn on her chest in the shape of her pendant. There was no mistaking this time; it had been activated. She quickly collected her things and ran toward the house.

Mathilda was still out running errands when Lottie returned. She would have to tell her about the pendant later. For now, she had to get to her parents' house first. The urgency that was felt from the vision couldn't wait. She considered having Dabney drive her, but she feared without Mathilda's permission, he'd refuse.

She picked up the phone, called a cab, and gave specific instructions to be picked up at the end of the drive so that none of the house staff would delay her intentions. She tossed her bag under the bed and slipped out the side entry.

When the cab arrived, Lottie got in and gave the driver the address. Her thoughts were wild as they drove toward her house. It would be the first time she had been back since her parents' death. She wondered why she felt drawn to go there now. Nothing from the vision was specific; Lottie just felt a compelling need to be there.

Her senses were heightened as the cab turned onto the driveway. Something was off. It was as if darkness had descended over the house, erasing all traces of the goodness that once dwelt here. She paid the driver and walked to the door, trying to shake the ominous feeling.

Lottie lingered outside momentarily, recalling the last time she'd been here. The memory of her parents waving as she and Charles drove away would forever be etched in her mind.

Fighting back the tears, she put her key in the front door lock and stepped into the living room. She wasn't expecting the dimness that greeted her. The curtains were never drawn. A slight movement over by the window caught her eye. Suddenly, the curtains were yanked open, forcing light into the room.

Lottie's mouth gaped open. "Christy? What are you doing here?"

A smile spread across her face, but not a smile that Lottie had ever seen. It was more like a sneer, sending shivers down her spine.

Christy sauntered over to the sofa and climbed up on the back of it.

"Oh, Lottie. Poor, stupid Lottie. First of all, it's not Christy. It's Cassandra. And you're here because I summoned you."

Just hearing her name sent tingles of fear shooting through Lottie. *Cassandra is alive.* No elder coven member had ever spoken of Cassandra as still living. Lottie stepped backward toward the door, which slammed shut behind her, making her jump.

"You can't leave now," Cassandra said. "Don't you want to know what I have in store for you?" She said the words in a tone one would use when speaking to a small child.

Panic shot through Lottie as she realized no one knew where she was. *Charles, where are you?* Something was wrong. She no longer felt connected with him. She reached for her pendant.

"It's no use, Lottie. When I activated your pendant, I rendered it useless, at least for a while anyway."

Lottie frowned. Cassandra must have inadvertently blocked her link to Charles.

"Oh, dear, you look a bit dismayed," Cassandra remarked. She eased off the back of the sofa and jumped up and down on a cushion before her feet thudded hard against the floor.

Lottie gritted her teeth in anger when she saw the dirty shoe prints on the fabric, recalling how her mother loved that piece of furniture.

"Let's have a little talk, shall we? Some quality girl time," Cassandra said, whirling around. "I've been searching for you for a very long time, and my search led me here to this wretched little town," she scoffed. "I must say, dear old Mathilda did well. She had you veiled, protected... all kinds of magic where your identity was concerned. But as you can see, I found you, didn't I?"

"How?" Lottie asked, her voice shaky.

"That day in the cafeteria, of course. You revealed yourself to Charles. You stupid girl, you released your magic. Every good witch knows never to release magic without a masking stone—Oh, wait, that's right. You didn't have witchy Mother Dear guiding you at the time."

Lottie's heart raced as Cassandra paced in front of her. There was a wildness to her eyes that made her seem very unstable. She could sense the dangerous energy radiating from her.

Lottie inched her way toward the steps, questioning her sanity. *Idiot!* Everyone always runs upstairs in the face of danger.

Cassandra's laugh brought her attention back. "Considering running upstairs?"

"No."

Lottie knew Cassandra expected her to run. In a blink, she levitated toward the second floor, but before she reached the top, Cassandra waved her arm, flinging Lottie against the lower landing wall. She groaned, unsure if her elbow was broken or badly bruised.

Cassandra strode over casually. She gazed at Lottie, the corners of her lips edging up as she lifted her foot and applied pressure to Lottie's elbow. By gods or goddesses, she somehow stifled her cry.

Cassandra smirked, seemingly impressed by Lottie's resolve. "I sensed your power the first time I met you on the bus. I knew you were a witch before you did—in fact, I was planning to take your powers, but when you and Charles reconnected, I realized then that you were the daughter of Mathilda and the one I had been searching for."

She lifted the pendant and let it drop to Lottie's chest. "I knew that death spell I cast on your lot would finally pay off. It gave me the ulti-mate revenge on Mathilda and her beloved *'sisters'* and gave me a way to keep you around to find my powers."

Lottie sat up, rubbing her elbow. "What do you want from me?"

"Don't you worry, my friend. You'll find out soon. It's broken, by the way. You should probably do something about that."

Lottie kept her anger in check. She rubbed her palm over her elbow three times, gasping sharply as the bone corrected itself.

"Now, where was I?" Cassandra said, tapping her chin. "Cafeteria, right. Once I found you, I wanted to have some fun— after all, I had waited centuries; I deserved a little fun. I needed a story. A poor adopted girl seemed good enough to keep you from suspecting me. Then came the followers. I took control of your weak little friends, Gwen and Abbey—and let's not forget Jake."

"It was you... You turned them against me."

"Um, *yeah*. I needed your friends to focus on me. And how else was I supposed to get cozy with you? Honestly, Lottie.... So, after taking over your friends, I created yet another persona for myself as the eccen-tric Selene Sullivan. It enabled me to gain access to the Paranormal Investigators to see if they knew anything about what I was doing. Of course, that meant getting rid of Shelly so Matthew could take her place to keep an eye on them."

The enjoyment Cassandra seemed to gain from recounting the story was unsettling. She resumed her pacing and continued with her tale. "Initially, I tried to get into your head, but Mathilda's stupid protection spells made it impossible. When that didn't work, I tried getting your attention any way I could—the cat that ran out in front of your mom's car, what a thrill that was. Lucky for me, I'm immortal." She suddenly laughed. "You should have seen your face—and you, crawling around on the ground. That was priceless. But you just didn't get the message.

"You all thought I was trying to discover who you were, but my purpose was to make *you* realize your true identity. That's why I scratched you. The magic revealed your name in blood. The ugly truth was finally out for all to see. It did get you back with your pendant, and that's the point of my motives. I knew if I could get around the veil, I could activate it. The only real problem was all those witches hovering around you. Maddening. Especially Charles. So, I figured if I got him out of the way, maybe I could reach you since your focus wouldn't be on him anymore. I have to say, that crash was really something."

Anger rushed through Lottie. She struggled to conceal it.

"Don't be mad. I was kind enough to see that you weren't harmed. You know, I honestly thought I had Charles. I didn't expect you to save him. You were stronger than I thought. So, you see, you left me with no choice. I had to kill your parents. Their demise finally led to what I wanted; your world shook up, giving me access to your mind."

Cassandra chuckled. "If you'll think about it, it's kind of your fault that they died. You should have cooperated."

The fear and rage exploded from Lottie. "You bitch! I'll kill you!"

Cassandra's eyes widened. "Oh, my. How frightful for me. Oh, wait — that's right. You can't. That immortal thing."

Her mocking tone and the way she reveled in rehashing her evil deeds went beyond cruel.

"What do you *want*?" Lottie shouted, feeling defeated.

"Well, it's simple. I want you to find the moonstone. The source of my powers, hidden away somewhere." Cassandra turned abruptly, her eyes wild. "*I want it, Lottie.* I've been trying to reach you for centuries. I'm tired of living off these temporary powers. They pale in comparison to my own," she said disgustedly. "But they sustained me and kept me hidden from dear old Mathilda. She would have instantly recognized my magic, and I never would have had the fun I've enjoyed these few months."

"That's why you sacrificed all of those witches. How could you?"

"Oh, don't judge. Didn't you just threaten to kill me? So now that your pendant is activated, you will lead me to my powers."

Lottie raised her chin. "And if I don't?"

Cassandra's eyes narrowed. "You'll be sorry if you don't. You think you've felt pain? That's nothing compared to what I'll do to your precious Charles. As we speak, my loyal followers are watching him. Someone is standing by, just waiting to do my bidding. I can guarantee he won't survive the next *accident*."

Lottie thought of Jake Putnam, Gwen, and Abbey and wondered if they could carry out such a task.

"That's right, Lottie. Those little fools at the lunch table that you ditched as friends don't even realize they're locked in a spell linked to me. One word is all it takes, and they'll carry out my mission. It's the same with the others— Rowen, Sunni, Wren. You all thought you were so smart when I've had you right in my grasp the whole time. Now move!"

Cassandra shoved Lottie through the kitchen door toward the woods behind her house. Thorns ripped into her legs as she stumbled through the dense brush farther away from her home. Her heart raced as Cassandra urged her even deeper into the woods. When they went over the ridge, Lottie saw a car waiting on the road below—a man she had never seen before got out and nodded to Cassandra.

"Ronald, Lottie. Lottie, Ronald—my new lackey. Get in," she demanded. Cassandra's eyes roved hungrily over Ronald's muscular form, and a smile tugged at the corners of her lips. "Ronald, here, is a fine replacement for Matthew. Much more accommodating," she said, grinning. He met her eyes in the rearview and winked.

Lottie turned away from their disgusting interaction, shuddering as she recalled Matthew's death.

Cassandra chuckled. "It was a horrible way to go. I can assure you that he was in agony to the end."

Lottie's blood ran cold. She didn't know if Charles and the others were safe. She had to be careful if she wanted to save them. She paid close attention to every detail as they drove.

The car turned into the cemetery and stopped in the old section. Lottie shuddered. She hated this part of the cemetery. There was an odd feel to this place.

"Get out," Cassandra ordered.

Lottie stepped out of the car. There, amidst the graves, was a makeshift altar. She took note of the knife perched atop a large headstone and felt a deep fear that went beyond panic. Cassandra clearly had a plan. Lottie reached for her pendant. Maybe the spell had worn off by now. Before she could even think of contacting anyone, Cassandra yanked it from her neck with an invisible magic grip. Lottie rushed toward her in reaction, but Ronald pulled her back.

As Cassandra picked up the knife, Lottie braced herself for the worst.

"Relax. This isn't for you—at least not yet." Cassandra walked over to the altar and sliced into her hand with the knife. She placed Lottie's pendant against the blood and let the drops fall over a blank paper.

Her words were in the ancient language Mathilda used but were much more sinister. "Reveal," she commanded in English.

The drops of blood joined together and began to form into a map. Lottie focused on it, storing the image in her mind.

Cassandra smiled. "Well, well.... It looks like we're going to Wiltshire, England."

Lottie's mind raced. *Wiltshire!* How would anyone find her if she was out of the country?

Cassandra spoke more strange words. The blood lifted from the paper and into Lottie's pendant. She gave a twisted smile. "I linked myself to your pendant. If you try anything while you're wearing it, I'll know. But just to be sure, I'll hang on to it for now in case you're stupid enough to try channeling anyone along the way."

Cassandra made a spiral motion with her hand, and the chain was repaired. She put it over her neck and pushed Lottie into the car, slamming the door shut. "Take us back to Lottie's house, Ronald. She'll need to get her things."

Lottie thought of Charles. *Please be okay.*

~

Cassandra's knuckles dug into Lottie's back as she nudged her down the aisle of the plane.

"Right here," she said, gesturing for Lottie to sit in the window seat.

Lottie slid in, helpless and angry. Looking up at the sky, she closed her eyes. Dark clouds formed, thickening. If she could cause a delay in takeoff, maybe Charles would find her.

"Don't even think about it," Cassandra said. She swiped her hand, and the skies cleared.

Tears stung Lottie's eyes. She stared at her pendant around Cassandra's neck, nearly choking on fury.

"Chill out, Lottie. The pendant will only find the moonstone when you're wearing it. I'll give it back when we arrive."

She hoped someone would find her before it came to that.

~

"CHARLOTTE, ARE YOU IN HERE?"

Mathilda opened the door when Lottie didn't respond. She went downstairs to ask if any house staff had seen her.

"No, Mistress. It's been hours since we last saw her," Marie replied.

"Notify me at once if you see her. Something's wrong. I can feel it."

After she checked the gardens, Mathilda went inside and grabbed her phone.

"Charles, is Charlotte with you?"

"No. Why?"

"I can't find her."

"I'll be right over."

Charles arrived as Mathilda was finishing up with a locator spell.

"My bond with Lottie is broken," he stated. "I can't connect with her. Were you able to find her?"

"No. She isn't wearing her pendant, and my spells aren't reacting at all with her energy. I need to get the center stone from my keeping room. Come with me."

Charles followed Mathilda into the dark chambers behind the walls of the main house. With one snap of her fingers, the candles along the walls lit.

Mathilda reached into a velvet-lined box and pulled out the large pentagon-shaped moonstone, the center stone connecting the five points to the pendant that each of the younger coven members wore. She placed her hand over it and murmured something too low for Charles to hear. She looked up at him. "The link has been severed. Charlotte's pendant was fully activated. We must find her right away."

They spread out to search the grounds. Charles paused by the gnarled oak. "Over here," he called out.

Using her magic, Mathilda was at the tree as soon as he said the words.

"She was here," Charles stated.

"Yes, she was," Mathilda agreed. "There's a trace of dark magic here. I'm going back in to search her room."

Mathilda glanced around Lottie's bedroom, noting everything for a clue of her whereabouts. She saw a strap sticking out from under the bed. Reaching down, she pulled the bag out and dumped the contents on the bed. "The candle was lit, and there's a bit of dirt from the cemetery."

Charles picked up the bowl. An image of Lottie's parents' house jolted into his mind, along with the same murky image he saw when he got into Lottie's head after the incident with the dead owl.

"She went to her parents' house. Someone lured her there."

"Quickly, let's go," Mathilda said. "I'll follow you in case we need to split up."

When they arrived, Charles exited his car and ran to the door. "It's unlocked," he said over his shoulder. He rushed in. "Lottie?"

"She's gone, Charles. I know who took her." Mathilda said. She went back through the house, searching for something.

"Who has her?"

"Cassandra. I felt her presence the moment I walked in. She wants her powers back."

"How is she...?" Charles's eyes widened in horror. "She'll kill Lottie!"

"Not until she has the moonstone."

"So, Selene was working for Cassandra all this time."

"No, Selene *is* Cassandra. She's been using the persona to get to Charlotte."

"Why is she no longer masking her presence, then?"

Mathilda plucked at something on the sofa. "Got it."

"What?" Charles asked.

"A strand of Cassandra's hair—and to answer your question, she no longer feels she has to hide. She has Charlotte and the pendant, and now her energy has to be spent locating the hidden moonstone."

Mathilda lit a candle on the table and put the hair in the flame. A clear image of what happened came to her. "They went through the woods and to the road below, where a car awaited. Cassandra performed a locator spell with Charlotte's pendant. They're going to Wiltshire, England. Charles, we have to leave now. There's no time to lose. Meet me at the airport as soon as you can. I'll call to have my plane ready for takeoff."

~

THE PLANE WAS FUELED AND READY BY THE TIME THE ELDER coven arrived. They all boarded and sat pensively.

Charles gazed out the window, his jaw clenched in worry.

"Son, we'll find her," Ramona assured.

"Before or after Cassandra is finished with her?"

"Don't put any negative energy out there. Trust me. We all need to work together if there's a hope of finding Lottie."

He raked a hand through his hair. "I know, Mom, but how is this happening? I thought Cassandra was bound and dead."

"You will have to ask Mathilda. It's not my story to tell. All I can say is that her power *is* gone. She's been using stolen magic. She must have found some gullible witch to transfer their power to her, no doubt tricking them by repeating a language the poor soul couldn't understand. Cassandra has great knowledge of Aelle's dark spells. Once she had acquired magic, she would have had to steal more before the temporary powers left her."

Charles shook his head. "What Lottie must be feeling."

~

LOTTIE BRACED AS THE PLANE SCREECHED DOWN THE runway. She was tired, hungry, and worried sick over Charles. If she could just get to her necklace... The burn on her chest tingled. The pendant! It seared into her skin. A part of it was with her. She touched her fingers to her chest.

Charles, I don't know if you can hear me. Cassandra found me. We just landed at Heathrow, England. The moonstone is hidden somewhere in Wiltshire, and she wants me to use my pendant to find the exact loca-tion. She has followers— Gwen, Abbey, and Jake. They're watching our coven. Please, be careful. And Charles, if something goes wrong, I will find you again in the next life. I love you.

"What are you doing?" Cassandra asked.

"What? Nothing," Lottie stammered.

Cassandra eyed her suspiciously. "When we get off this plane, you will do exactly what I say. Do you understand?"

"Yes."

"Good. Stay close."

It took longer than expected to disembark. Lottie was grateful for the delay. It gave her time to think. She filled her thoughts with the hope that Mathilda had acquaintances in the UK who would come to her rescue.

As they stepped out of the plane, Cassandra squeezed Lottie's arm. "If you even think of running, I will kill that woman pushing the stroller behind us as your first punishment."

"You wouldn't dare," Lottie whispered. "There are people everywhere who would see you."

"People have heart attacks every day, Lottie. No one would think anything about it. Her death would be on your hands."

Lottie swallowed her anger. She followed Cassandra through the baggage claim area, thankful to stretch her legs. They approached a man holding a sign that read Baxter. Cassandra stopped in front of him. "You will drive us to Wiltshire."

"Yes, ma'am," he replied in a flat voice. He dropped the sign he had been holding, then turned and walked out of the airport. Lottie wasn't sure what had just happened.

Cassandra scoffed. "Come on, stupid. Good God, have you ever used your magic for anything other than useless do-gooder crap?"

She ignored Cassandra and followed behind the man. He led them to a car, opened the door, and drove out of the airport.

Lottie waited until Cassandra wasn't focusing on her before trying to reach Charles. She slowly moved her hand to her chest and pretended to look out the window.

I hope you can hear me. We just left the airport and headed to Wiltshire. Cassandra has my pendant. She's linked herself to it. When it acti-

vated, it burned me. That's how I'm able to reach you. So far, she doesn't realize it. I'll try to keep in touch.

~

"OH, THANK GOD. LOTTIE'S OKAY," CHARLES SAID. "I JUST heard her voice."

"What did she say?" Mathilda asked.

"She said they just landed and are driving to Wiltshire, where the moonstone is hidden. She told me to be careful. Cassandra has followers watching my coven."

"Can you reach Charlotte?"

"I tried. I told her we were on our way and to be strong."

"We're nearly there," Mathilda said. "They don't have much of a lead on us. Let Charlotte know this."

"I will."

"See, we'll find her," Ramona reassured him.

Charles sat silently for the remainder of the trip, trying to reach Lottie.

I'm coming for you. Please be strong. I will find you.

~

LOTTIE HEARD CHARLES'S VOICE. SHE WAS CAREFUL NOT TO show any emotion. If Cassandra knew she could communicate with him, there would be hell to pay—literally.

The car stopped at an old pub in Avebury. The front sign depicted a red lion with white claws and tongue. The words RED LION were carved underneath. Lottie got out and stretched. She was thankful to walk after the long flight and drive.

"Time to take a walk," Cassandra said.

Lottie tried to keep her expression calm and think of a way to stall. "I need to use the bathroom and eat."

"Nice try. No."

"Listen, I'm telling you now that if I don't eat, you'll have a problem. I get sick very easily. I won't be any good to you if I'm vomiting every other minute."

Cassandra let out a frustrated sigh. "Fine. A quick break, and you'd better not be lying."

When they walked into the pub, Lottie asked where the bathroom was.

Cassandra followed her to the door. "Straight out, Lottie."

She went in and locked the door. She put her hand to the burn.

I'm at a pub in Avebury—the Red Lion. I'm getting food and stalling. I don't have much time. Are the others with you?

Yes.

Do you have water near you?

Yes.

Have Mathilda link us. I'm running water as my element. The only way I'm able to reach you is by touching the burn. It's getting harder to do that. Cassandra is suspicious.

"Hurry up, Lottie," Cassandra called.

"Almost finished."

Hurry, Charles.

"Now, Lottie!" Cassandra demanded.

"Okay, I'm coming. I'm rinsing my face."

Okay, it's done. Mathilda linked us.

Lottie splashed water on her face and unlocked the door. Cassandra gazed intently at her.

Lottie leaned against the door, feigning weakness. "I feel sick. I really need to eat."

~

"How long will it take before the linking spell works?" Charles asked impatiently.

"It should start any time, but you need to relax, or you'll delay it," Mathilda replied. "You'll see through Charlotte's eyes where they are, what's happening, and the surroundings. Just clear your mind."

They headed to where the cars were waiting to drive them to

Avebury. Charles put his bag in and stopped. "I see her. They're at a pub. Oh, my God. Christy Adams is with her."

"That's Cassandra. What else do you see?"

"The building looks old. It's white with a brown thatched roof. I see huge stones outside near the pub."

"I know where they are. Quickly, everyone into the cars," Mathilda implored.

~

LOTTIE FINISHED HER FOOD AND TOOK ONE MORE DRINK.

"You're finished," Cassandra demanded. "Get up."

Lottie took her time. She sensed Cassandra's irritation as they headed out the door.

Cassandra took the pendant off and gave it to Lottie. "Put it on. Remember, my blood is in the stone. If you as much as attempt a spell or try to channel anyone, I'll know."

"I won't."

"Good girl."

Lottie put her pendant on. As soon as it touched her skin, it felt warm.

"Well?"

"It's warm," Lottie replied. She closed her eyes. "I see trees." She walked to the right and stopped, feeling it grow cooler.

"Get with it, Lottie."

She turned and walked the other way. The pendant began to feel warm again. "It's this way."

"Good, hurry up."

~

"THEY'RE WALKING," CHARLES STATED. "LOTTIE SAW SOME trees in a vision. There were roots all along the top of the ground. She's walking in that direction."

"We've been there before," Mathilda replied. "Hurry, they're not far."

~

IT HAD GROWN FULLY DARK. THE MOON SHONE OVER THE landscape, guiding the way.

"It's close," Lottie remarked. "The pendant is burning me." She saw a section of trees ahead. "There. Among the trees." As they approached the grove, Lottie flinched from shock. Reaching across the earth were massive roots. She had dreamt of this place.

The closer they came to the trees, the hotter the pendant got. It was almost unbearable. Lottie lifted it away from her skin.

"I feel it," Cassandra said, inhaling deeply. "My powers are here."

Lottie tried to think. She could no longer talk to Charles now that she was wearing her pendant. She didn't know how else to delay.

"I know you're stalling. Get the stone. Now."

"No."

"No?" Cassandra questioned. "You *will* do what I say."

"No, I won't," Lottie replied. She felt the rage inside of her taking over. "You killed my parents. You're going to pay for what you did."

Charles's voice came—*Wait, Lottie. It's not that easy.*

Cassandra smiled. "You forget something, Lottie. My blood is in the pendant, weakening you. And now, I will take every bit of your power away." She stretched out her arms and began pulling the magic from Lottie.

"You don't have the stone yet," Lottie struggled. "If you take my power, I can't find the moonstone."

"Oh, it's here. I can feel it. I'll get it myself."

Lottie had a sudden awareness of the pouch in her pocket. The dirt from the spell she'd cast earlier was still there. She grabbed what was left and blew it into Cassandra's face, breaking her concentration.

Her heart raced as she sprinted away. She slipped behind a large tree and tried to calm her breathing.

"Big mistake," Cassandra called. "I'm patient, and I have time. You, on the other hand, do not."

Lottie focused all of her energy on locating the stone. The ground got hot beneath her feet. She dropped to her knees and frantically dug between the roots. She glanced over her shoulder just as Cassandra came around the tree. She stretched her hands forward and let out a force that sent Lottie flying back. Cassandra started digging for the moonstone herself.

Trembling with anger, Lottie stood and reached out her arms. The earth quaked. Roots ripped up from the ground. At her command, they wrapped themselves around Cassandra.

"I bind you, Cassandra, from harming me and anyone I love. I bind you, Cassandra, from harming me and anyone I love...."

Cassandra's musical laugh confused Lottie.

"Nice try, but only an original witch can bind me, and there's not one here now, is there?"

"I wouldn't say that," Mathilda's voice rang out from the darkness.

Cassandra's triumphant look turned to shock. "You! There's nothing you can do. It takes all five of you."

"Yes, it does," Regina's voice came from behind Lottie.

Cassandra's eyes darted wildly.

"You should be worried," Mathilda said, stepping out from the dense cover of trees.

Charles rushed over to Lottie. "Are you okay?"

"Yes, I am now."

He pulled her back a bit, keeping her tight against him.

Mathilda joined hands with her sisters.

"No! *No!*" Cassandra screamed.

"Five witches to gather. Five witches to steal. Five witches to bind. Five witches to kill," they chanted.

Cassandra became trapped where she was. She struggled to move.

"This time, we finish it," Mathilda said. "Charlotte, toss your pendant in the center of our circle."

Lottie did as she told.

"Were you able to locate the moonstone?"

"Yes, it's over in the grove."

"Very good. Go and fetch it."

She ran to the place where she had felt the powers. She uncovered the stone beneath the roots of one of the beech trees. It was massive, and she struggled to pull it free. The way the moon reflected off of it was mesmerizing. She felt drawn to its seductive power. Everything around her seemed to disappear as she gazed at it.

"Bring it here, Charlotte." Mathilda's voice snapped her out of the trance. "Place it beside your pendant."

Cassandra's violent screams were unnerving as the coven began their spell. Each of the elders added something they had gathered from the earth within the circle.

"We bind you, Cassandra, from harming us and all others. We bind you, Cassandra, from harming us and all others. We bind you, Cassandra, from harming us and all others."

Mathilda looked skyward. "We draw from the power of the full moon." Still holding hands, they raised their arms upward and chanted together. "Take the evil within this circle. Reap your harvest, destroy the source."

Fierce winds blew in from all four corners of the land. Lottie's hair whipped around, stinging her eyes. Charles pulled her close, shielding her.

The wind drowned out Cassandra's screams as the moonstone glowed with a bright silvery light, gathering the powers she had stolen into it. Electrical currents came from the ground, and the sky cracked with thunder. The currents drew toward the moonstone and Lottie's necklace. All at once, a bolt shot out of her pendant, striking Cassandra dead. The moonstone exploded with a blinding force, shooting a bright beam across the land. Then, everything went calm.

A dim light hovered over Cassandra's lifeless body. Mathilda held open a small antique vessel, and the orb floated over it as the body disintegrated into the earth. She bent over, scooped up some of the debris, and dumped it in a small box.

"Balance has been restored," she said calmly. She reached for Lottie's pendant. "Here you are, dear. Safe and sound."

Lottie was stunned at what she had witnessed. She threw her arms around Mathilda. "Thank you."

"I'm so glad you're okay. I'm proud of you, Charlotte. You were courageous."

Lottie glanced at the spot where Cassandra had just laid moments before.

"Mathilda, why did all of you allow Cassandra to live the first time you bound her? From what you've told me, she was even more evil in those times."

Mathilda let out a sigh. Her expression was sad and distant, as if recalling a painful memory.

"She was my half-sister, the daughter of Aelle, my father, and his mistress. I didn't tell you before, because I knew that she lived. If Cassandra had found you and learned that you knew of her, she would have realized that you were the one to find her powers. I couldn't risk that—although she realized it on her own, and the result was just as I feared."

Mathilda rested her fingertips against her brow and shook her head. "In all of these centuries, there has never been any sign of Cassandra. I never once sensed her. I didn't know that she'd been stealing powers. But, in her day, she was quite powerful and knew the proper way to conceal herself from us. I read Cassandra's mind tonight," Mathilda said, looking up. "The first thing she did when she obtained power was to mask herself from me. She managed to stay completely blind from my view, growing stronger. She never tried to search for the moonstone until she had developed enough energy to be powerful enough for this one task— and she finally succeeded. I wanted to believe that she could be good. I thought with her powers stripped, she couldn't hurt anyone. I should have known better."

"Mathilda, I'm so sorry. I had no idea."

"It's okay. I realize now there was no hope. There was no light in her at all. I feel at peace now."

Epilogue

SIX YEARS LATER

"C ome on, Lottie," Wren fussed. "Everyone's waiting."

"Okay. I'm coming."

Lottie took one last look in the gilded floor mirror. She adjusted her veil and straightened her necklace. Her mother's pearls rested against her skin, giving her comfort. "It's a good day, Mom. I love you, Dad. I know you're watching."

"Lottie!"

"Coming." She opened the door and stepped out into the hall.

Wren smiled. "Wow…You look beautiful."

"Thank you. Have you seen Charles?"

"No, but Dad says he's as cool as a cucumber."

"He would be. I'm impressed that I'm not nervous."

"Well, it's no wonder. All you two have done since Cassandra witch-napped you is talk of getting married. You've had plenty of time to work out the nerves."

"True."

A radiant smile spread over Mathilda's face when Lottie entered the solarium. "Are you ready?"

Lottie returned her smile. "I've never been more ready for anything in my life."

She took Mathilda's arm and stepped out into the garden. The orchestra paused, and the singers Mathilda hired began to sing *I Was Married* by Tegan and Sara. The guests stood and turned toward Lottie, but she only saw Charles. His eyes were on her, drawing her to him. Each step down the aisle felt like floating. They stopped at the arch, and Mathilda released her to Charles.

Phil smiled warmly at them and whispered, "Here we go again." He winked and turned his attention to the guests.

"We gather today to celebrate the bond of marriage between these two souls. May our love and happiness surround them as they say their vows."

Charles turned to Lottie. His smile nearly took her breath away. His eyes rested on hers as he took her hands in his.

"I, Charles, take you, Charlotte, as my wife. From this moment, I promise to take care of you, to keep you safe from harm and love you as long as my heart beats. And should sorrows come, I will carry you. For all eternity, I am yours." He slid the ring on Lottie's third finger against the raised, clear green prasiolite and diamond engagement ring he'd had fashioned from her favorite stone in Mathilda's keeping room.

She wiped a tear away and gazed into Charles's eyes. What she felt at that moment was so intense and heavy with love. His eyes bore into her as their souls blended. She felt his deep and eternal love and began.

"I, Charlotte, take you, Charles, as my husband. From this moment, I promise to love you as long as my heart beats, to comfort you through any sorrows this life may bring, and even though death may separate us, my soul will be with yours for all eternity." She put the ring on Charles's finger.

Phil smiled and lifted their hands. "You have given these rings to one another as a promise of your love. It pleases me to say that I now pronounce you husband and wife. Charles, you may kiss your bride."

Lottie giggled.

"Come here, wife."

He pulled her gently to him. As their lips touched, Lottie felt drawn into him somehow. Their individuality disappeared as her connection to him was as one being. A rush of adrenaline coursed through her body as she realized they were indeed one. "I love you, Charles," she whispered.

He placed one more kiss on her lips. "And I love you, Lottie," he whispered back.

"Ladies and gentlemen," Phil announced. "I present to you, Mr. and Mrs. Charles Lachlan."

Breathless, Lottie turned toward the guests. She smiled at Gwen and Abbey, who beamed at her. She was pleased they had no memory of their time linked to Cassandra.

As she took her first few steps down the aisle with Charles, each coven member tossed Stephanotis petals at them. Perfect, Lottie thought, recalling the symbolization of the flowers—happiness in marriage.

~

THE MUSIC FROM THE RECEPTION FADED AS CHARLES AND Lottie danced their way toward the privacy of the side garden. The sounds of nighttime surrounded them as the last remnants of the sun melted away. Lottie rested her head against his neck and watched the fireflies flit along. She sighed in contentment.

"I'm so happy, Charles."

"I'm glad. I'm going to do everything I can to make you happy, Lottie."

She thought her heart would burst with love for him. She closed her eyes and leaned into him as they danced to the rhythm of nature.

I love you; I love you, I love you... she silently said.

Charles kissed her. "Forever."

~

AFTER ALL THE GUESTS HAD GONE, LOTTIE WENT UP TO change out of her gown. Marie was dutifully waiting to help. With nimble fingers, she unbuttoned each tiny satin-covered button down Lottie's back.

"There you are, Mrs. Lachlan."

"Thank you, Marie, but would it be okay with you to still call me Miss? I've gotten rather used to it."

For the first time since Lottie had met Marie, she smiled. It was a lovely smile.

"Of course, Miss."

Lottie stepped out of the gown and put on the pale green dress she had hanging outside the armoire.

Charles knocked on her door as she finished up. "Can I come in?"

Marie took her wedding gown, opened the door for him, and left with a soft swish of fabric.

"How is my beautiful bride?"

"Wonderful. And you, husband?"

He kissed her before responding. "Wonderful."

"This day was perfect. It doesn't seem real—and it's the first time I've had you all to myself."

Charles gave her a wicked grin and pulled her toward him.

"Knock-knock," Mathilda said.

Lottie groaned. "You—me—this moment, later...Come in," she called.

"If you two would be so kind as to join me in my keeping room, I have one more wedding gift for you."

Lottie looked at Charles with raised eyebrows.

He gestured toward the door. "After you."

The elder coven had smiles plastered on their faces as they walked into the room. Lottie noticed Rowen, Wren, and Sunni all wore the same confused expression.

"Have a seat, everyone. As you are all well aware, the curse that Cassandra placed over you has left each of you trapped in human form, vulnerable to everything that goes along with it until death. Now that Cassandra is dead, her curse no longer has a hold on you."

"We're free from the curse?" Lottie asked.

"Yes," Mathilda replied. "You can finally be at peace when it's your time to pass on, if you wish, or continue as you always have: living, dying, and coming back. I can recreate Cassandra's spell for you if you want it her way. Or you can choose my way: I'm offering you immortality. I can grant you a life that never ends. But you have to decide if this is truly what you want. Eternity is a long time to have regrets. You don't have to decide now—"

"Yes!" Sunni shrieked.

"Me, too," Rowen added.

"I'm in, too," Wren said. "You guys couldn't survive eternity without me."

"Charlotte, Charles, what about you?" Mathilda asked.

"Can I have a minute to talk with Lottie?" Charles asked.

"Of course. Take your time."

He led her outside to a garden bench. "So, what do you think? Could you stand an eternity with me?"

Lottie fidgeted with a twig she found. "I want nothing more than to spend the rest of my life with you, Charles. Eternity is a very long time. What if we get bored with life or run out of things to do and places to go?"

He covered her hand with his, calming the nervous fidgeting.

"We don't have to do this if you aren't sure. I'll support your decision. If you choose immortality, then I will choose it. If you want this human form, I'll remain as I am. As long as we're together, that's all I want."

"Me, too. What would you choose?"

"You tell me, Lottie. What would you choose?"

She fixed her eyes on his. "How I have felt about you since we met has been the most amazing thing I've ever experienced. After we got to know one another, I longed for you when we weren't together, and when I finally got to be with you, every time I saw you, it felt like my heart would burst. The feeling of falling in love is like nothing else. A part of me wants to discover you over and over again, but when I think of the car accident... Charles, if I ever had to go through that again, I don't think I could stand it. So, I vote for all of eternity with you."

A smile spread over his features. "Then I happily accept immortality. To wake up with you every day without ever having to worry about losing you is all I want."

Lottie clasped her hands together in excitement. "Okay. Let's go tell the others."

Lively, conversation echoed through the room when they returned. Lottie felt confident with her decision once she saw how happy the others were. She loved each of them as her family, and she knew they would all flourish as long as they stayed together.

"It's about time," Rowen said. "So...?"

"We've decided not to accept your offer, Mathilda," Charles said.

Lottie frowned. *Um, what are you doing, Charles?*

Having fun at their expense.

"*What?*" Sunni shouted. "You can't! We have to do this together. You can't leave us now."

"Relax, Sunni. I'm just messing with you."

"Charles Lachlan, you jerk!" Wren slapped him hard across the arm. "Ow!"

She turned and wrapped Lottie in a hug. "I'm so happy. I couldn't have stood an eternity without you, Lottie. You too, you big jerk."

Charles winked at Wren. She rolled her eyes.

"God, you married him, Lottie. Good luck."

"Since you all agree, we can begin," Mathilda said.

Lottie suddenly had a thought. "Can I talk to you in private, Mathilda?"

"Sure."

Lottie stepped out into the corridor and closed the door behind them.

"What is it, dear? You look worried."

"This is a bit awkward...."

"Tell me."

"Well, Charles and I just got married."

"Go on."

"What if we want a child someday? Will I be able to conceive once the immortality spell is cast?"

"Cassandra's curse prevented you and Charles from ever conceiving, but with it broken, I can alter that. However, I must make something clear before we go through with everything. I can cast the spell for all of you to have a child when you're ready. But I warn you, Charlotte, the babe will not be born immortal. She will be as vulnerable as any other human child. She will have strong powers as a witch, but she can die. Are you sure you will want to go through life as a mother grieving her child? I can tell you it is the hardest thing you will ever face."

Lottie thought over Mathilda's words. She had been through so much loss already, and she survived. Having the love of a child— even only for a short time was better than none at all.

"Yes. I want a family one day."

"Very well, then. No one should be denied the gift of family."

"Thank you, Mathilda. I love you."

"You sweet girl, I love you, too. Come on, let's join the others."

Mathilda made sure everyone was still in agreement as Lottie rejoined her coven.

"Ramona, please give me the vessel on the table."

Ramona carefully lifted the ancient relic from the table and handed it to Mathilda. She placed it at the center of the pentagram. "Each of you stand at one of the points."

Mathilda began her spell. At her words, the vessel began to shake. The lid rattled until, finally, it was forced off, shooting a blinding beam of light across the room. The energy became densely tangible.

A tingling sensation radiated around her abdomen as Lottie lifted off the ground. Warmth crept through her body, and she became aware of a powerful energy crackling through her veins as the transformation completed. A gust of wind entered the circle, and slowly, she lowered to the ground. Lottie put her hands to her stomach. She smiled at Mathilda and mouthed the words, "Thank you."

"Is it done?" Wren asked.

"Yes," Mathilda replied. "You are free to leave the circle."

"Oh, my God!" Sunni squealed. "I can't believe it. We're immortal! Now what?"

"Life as usual," Isobel replied. "You go to college, live your lives."

"What about potential spouses?" Wren asked.

"You say nothing. Not one word," Regina replied. "Relationships end. You absolutely say nothing."

Lottie glanced over at Wren. She quickly turned away.

"Regina is right," Mathilda said. "If any of you girls are lucky enough to find a true companion, we'll go from there. Phil is an example of what I am speaking of. Regina had never shared a single detail of her true nature with him, even though she knew he was also a witch. As time passed by, she grew certain of her feelings toward him. He proved to be trustworthy, so he was allowed into our circle. He was granted immortality and made fully aware of our role as Guardians, and though he isn't one, he has devoted his life to the cause. You must carry on as always, never speaking of your life to anyone outside of the coven. If you ever find yourself certain of a relationship, we guarantee that we will consider it. You'll find we are very supportive of true love."

"That sounds fair," Rowen said.

"I guess so," Wren agreed.

"Does Bryan rank as true companion material?" Lottie whispered.

"I don't know. Considering the whole eternity thing, it's definitely not something I plan to rush into."

"I don't blame you," Lottie replied. "Time does have a whole new meaning now, doesn't it? When you find your soulmate, you'll know. Fate won't steer you wrong."

"Lottie," Mathilda interrupted, "I believe we've kept you and Charles long enough. I spoke with Dabney earlier. The cottage is ready for you."

"Thank you," Charles replied. He reached for Lottie's hand. "Are you ready to go?"

"Yes. I sent all of my luggage over with Marie earlier."

Charles turned to the elders. "Thank you for all you have done. Your love and support are everything to Lottie and me."

Mathilda smiled. "We're all so happy for you both. Don't hesitate to ask if you need anything while you're away."

Lottie gave Mathilda one last hug. "I love you. This amazing life would be nothing if you weren't part of it. Thank you for everything."

"You're so welcome. You and Charles, be safe as you travel tomorrow."

"We will." Lottie turned back to Mathilda again. "What was in the vessel earlier?"

"A soul powerful enough to grant immortality."

Lottie shuddered as she thought of Cassandra.

~

THE SOFT LIGHT SHINING FROM THE WINDOWS OF THE GUEST cottage cast an enchanting glow on the ground below.

Charles placed a kiss on Lottie's cheek. "Brace yourself," he warned.

"For what?"

He scooped her up effortlessly and carried her across the threshold.

She giggled. "Honoring tradition, I see."

"Always."

He put her down and took her hands in his. "I know this isn't what we planned, spending the night here at the cottage."

"It's perfect. I'm glad we decided to delay the flight until morning. Flying to Martinique tonight wouldn't have worked anyway. I had no clue Mathilda was going to do the immortality spell."

"None of us did. I'm glad you're okay with the decision. I just wanted our wedding night to be spent alone, with no turbulence or flight attendants."

Lottie glanced toward the bedroom. She noticed her luggage along the wall and her nightgown hanging from the armoire. Her heart raced when her eyes fell on the bed. She and Charles had agreed to keep their hands off each other the month before the wedding, and she had missed his touch.

Charles grinned as he followed her gaze to the bed. "Remember, Lottie, I can read your thoughts when we connect."

She flushed under the heat of his gaze. Like magnets, he closed the distance between them, pulling her close and kissing her brow, then her cheek, before moving along her jawline.

Lottie shuddered, kissing him with all the love she felt within. He slipped the straps of her dress over her shoulders, inching it below her waist. She felt it pool at her feet and shivered at the air moving over her skin.

Charles intensified the kiss as his hands explored her body. Lottie tugged his shirt over his head, then trailed her fingers across his skin before she worked to open the button of his pants. She urged them lower, and he whispered a laugh at her anticipation. He lifted her onto the bed and slid in beside her. "You are so beautiful."

His lips moved to her neck. She shivered and pulled him closer, feeling the intensity of the moment, and she allowed herself to get lost in it.

"I love you, Charles. I love you...."

～

THEY LAY TOGETHER AS THE MOONLIGHT STREAMED IN, bathing them in soft shadows and light.

"It's beautiful, isn't it," Lottie asked.

"Yes," Charles replied, gazing at her.

"The moon!"

"I know, I know."

"Thank you. For remembering me, for loving me, for marrying me."

He held her close. "Thank you, Lottie. You're the one who found me."

She fell asleep with a smile, Charles's arms wrapped tightly around her, and an eternity of love ahead.

～

Two a.m.

Lottie awoke to the sound of crying. She quickly got out of bed and ran into the other room. Bending over the side of the crib, she picked up her baby and gently kissed her cheek.

"Don't cry, Althea. Mama's here. Shh...."

Lottie settled into the rocking chair and snuggled her daughter close. She suddenly felt her mother's presence. "She's beautiful, isn't she, Mom? I hope you don't mind that I gave her your middle name that you hated."

"Is she okay?" Charles asked, stepping into the room.

"Yes, she's just fine. Aren't you, baby girl?"

～

LOTTIE WOKE FROM HER DREAM WITH A START. SHE WASN'T sure whether she'd had a vision of the future or just a dream. She felt

Charles beside her and smiled. Snuggling closer to him, she drifted back to sleep.

<h1 style="text-align:center">Acknowledgments</h1>

I would like to acknowledge Highlander Press. Thank you for taking me on. I have enjoyed the process and will treasure the wealth of information you provided.

To the 2024 Spring Cohort: I am grateful to have gotten to know all of you in our classes. Your kindness and support will stay with me. I wish you every success in your writing journeys.

To Amanda: Thank you for helping me through the editing process and for all of your suggestions. I appreciate your insight.

To Debby: I am eternally grateful to you and for the time and energy you put into my book. Thank you for believing in me and for holding my hand through so many moments. Your wisdom and insight have helped me tremendously.

For my husband: I love you endlessly. I will forever be grateful to you for your support. Thank you for allowing me to be as I am and enduring all of my quirks and silliness. And thank you for supporting my Reese's Cups habit.

For my kids: Thank you for your patience through the years of writing. You are both amazing and I love you. Never give up, always be curious, and believe in yourselves.

For Mary, my biggest cheerleader, my sister-cousin, my protector against cicadas--I love you! Thank you for your support and for keeping me supplied with plenty of cat memes and whacked humor.

Lastly, thank you to those who supported me in the very beginning with the awful first draft. Jana, Kat, and Mrs. Amanda, your encouragement were so important in those early days.

ETERNAL ENCHANTMENT

PREQUEL TO THE KNOWING

KIMBERLY PATTON

Excerpt from
Eternal Enchantment

KIMBERLY PATTON'S FORTHCOMING BOOK

"As stars above, as air between, as earth below, your soul shall keep."

CHAPTER 1

The forest was alive after the long hush of winter. New life had finally pushed from the earth, growing denser between each sunrise and carrying a vibrance that thickened the hazel branches and the verdant canopy of the towering giants above. Several finches chased one another overhead, and somewhere in the distance, a thrush sang a graceful melody. Mathilda Longhurst kept to the rough-trodden path, still wet with morning dew. She paused, taking in her surroundings. Everywhere her eyes fell, droplets hung from leaves, shimmering in the sun like thousands of sparkling diamonds. Her heart swelled with love for this place. Her place. All of nature was her home.

As she walked deeper into the forest, nature responded to her presence. Like magnets, the leaves pulled to her when she brushed past them. A deer lifted its head momentarily, unperturbed by her sudden appearance, before returning to the vegetation pushing through the blanket of dead leaves. Mathilda smiled, recognizing the light in the creature's eyes, the same light she recognized in herself and everything before her.

A fluttering sound below a thicket drew her attention. Bending down, she saw an injured blackbird thrashing wildly upon the forest floor. Pushing her long honey-golden hair over her shoulder, Mathilda reached beneath the thicket and gently cupped the bird between her hands.

"What happened to you?" she softly said.

She closed her eyes, and a scene began to unfold in her mind. She saw the bird flying for its life from a hawk. They swooped and dipped in rhythm through the branches until the blackbird plunged low and crashed through the scrub.

"You poor thing," she soothed. "Here, let me make you better."

She pulled out the injured wing and blew a gentle breath over it. The bird fluttered, regaining its strength.

"There, all is well. Be careful of predators, little one." Mathilda kissed its head and released it into the sky. She shielded her eyes from the sun and watched it fly out of sight.

"Rescuing the injured ones again, I see?"

Mathilda smiled at the familiar voice behind her. "Yes, Mother. I found it under the thicket with a broken wing."

The sunbeams streaking through the trees highlighted her mother's head like a shimmering crown. Unlike other women, she wore her hair unbound, and long, golden waves, nearly the same shade as Mathilda's, cascaded to her waist.

"You are a compassionate girl, Mathilda," her mother said, smiling warmly. "And your powers are growing stronger. The Goddess grants you the healing talent that most witches covet. Keep your innocence and peace with the earth. Others will try to corrupt you for their own gain. You must never allow such a thing. Wisdom, caring, and a giving heart, my dear child, are what give you your strength. Now, come," she said, gently cupping Mathilda's chin. "We must finish our preparations for the Beltane celebrations. You must be ready for Hecate to grant you her gifts."

Mathilda followed her mother back down the path toward home. As they approached, she noticed a raven pulling at a reed from the thatched roof.

"*Maelen!*" her father bellowed.

"I am here, Aelle," her mother quickly replied, rushing into the house.

"Do something about that wretched bird upon the roof. I cannot think with that thing scratching about."

"Yes, husband." She reached for the broom by the door and beat it against the stone facade, scaring the raven away.

Mathilda looked toward her father, and the familiar feelings of anger and fear replaced the blissful state she had obtained from her morning in the forest. She searched her mind for the memories of when he had once been kind to her and her mother. They were harder and harder to recall the more vile and hateful he became.

He went about the room searching for something, his potions, written spells...then, in a fit of anger, he overturned the table, sending potion bottles crashing to the floor, splintering into shards of broken glass. Mathilda's mother rushed over to clean up the mess.

"*Leave it!*" he roared.

"Come, Mother," Mathilda said, beckoning toward the bedchamber. "Let us make preparations for the festival."

Settling into a chair, she took her needle and thread and began to stitch the band onto a sleeve.

"Why do you stay with him, Mother?" she said, keeping her voice low. "We should leave. I doubt Father would even notice."

"Oh, but he would," her mother said, glancing up from her work. "As soon as he needed something done, he would notice. I will not leave. This is my home. Besides, he will be off to the bed of the woman, Gundred, soon, leaving us in peace."

Mathilda cringed. "Why do you allow him to leave your bed? I know you; there are spells you keep that would put Father in his place."

Her mother paused, needle in hand. "Did it ever occur to you, daughter, that I do not want your father in my bed?"

Mathilda kept silent at that. She thought of the many nights that she would watch her mother slip off into the darkness, no doubt to the arms of Fulk. Her mother often gave him smiles that seemed too familiar.

Mathilda remembered seeing Fulk at last year's Beltane festival. The way he touched her mother when he thought no one was looking. They were looking. However, no one dared to speak of it. Everyone loved her mother. She was a great healer and compassionate to all. But as much as they loved her, they equally feared for her. Feared what Aelle might do to her or Fulk if he ever found out. He was powerful and ruthless in his cruelty, and everyone knew he was no longer married to Maelen in body or mind. He had been visiting the bed of the witch, Gundred, for as long as Mathilda could remember. Gundred was cunning and manipulative but not strong in power, though she had a burning desire to become more powerful than any woman of her kind. She practiced the dark arts and used Mathilda's father to gain more power through his knowledge of spells.

There were rumors of a child between their union; however, Mathilda had never seen proof of any such child, and neither she nor her mother dared ask Aelle. He forbade them to even speak of Gundred. There was a darkness in him that grew stronger by the day. Mathilda could sense it. She hated the fear he brought from her mother. If only they could be free of him.

"Ow!" Mathilda put the needle down and wiped the drop of blood from her finger.

"What is it, child?" her mother asked.

"I was thinking of Father. He is so spiteful."

"Yes, but do not waste your time fretting over him, Mathilda. He brings out the worst in anyone, and I will not have you darkening yourself over him. Now pick up that needle and pay attention to your work. You have a dress to finish." She pressed her own needle into a sleeve, smiling. "You will be the most beautiful maiden at the festival by far."

Mathilda smiled warmly and returned to her sewing. "Mother?"

"Yes?"

"What gifts will the Goddess bestow upon me?"

"I know not. Each maiden is different. The Goddess looks into every witch, granting her additional gifts according to her deeds and strength of powers. Of the five of you, your powers are far stronger. Your gifts will be unique, my child."

Mathilda thought of the four other girls who would be participating in the coming-of-age ritual with her. Each one approaching or in their eighteenth year, like Mathilda, and all maidens from surrounding towns and villages near Northumbria. Regina was the only one that Mathilda could remember in detail from past festivals. She was from a wealthy, titled family and very beautiful, with a livelihood about her that drew everyone in.

Ramona, she knew well enough. She lived deep in the forest away from the village. She was a beauty of dark hair and eyes with fair skin, and had a certain Romanesque look to her features. Mathilda remembered that Ramona had a keen skill for reading into the mind of a person. She also had a stony personality and rarely let anyone too close. Mathilda wondered what gift could possibly be bestowed upon her. The others, she could not readily recall their faces as it had been many years since she had seen them.

She finished the last stitch on the band of her sleeve and put the needle down.

"Let us see it then," her mother said.

Mathilda stretched the dress across the bed and inspected it. The dye from the woad was an even shade of pale blue. The warp and weft weaving were tight, and the small floral embroidery band at the sleeve and hem was straight and tidy. The matching belt was embroidered with the same floral pattern and not overly embellished to keep the sumptuary laws per the status of the lower classes. Her family once had the means to afford some of the luxuries allowed to the middle classes from her father's work as a master stone carver, but in his pursuit of the dark arts, he abandoned his occupation. It was now because of her mother's talents as an herbalist, weaver, and dressmaker that occasionally allowed them the means for some niceties within the law.

"Very good, Mathilda. You are almost as good as I am. To the untrained eye, this dress is finished. But I see a loose stitch at the hem. Repair that, and you are my equal."

"Yes, Mother."

Mathilda repaired the stitch and looked beyond the bedchamber door.

"Listen," she said. "It is quiet. Father must have left us."

They peered into the main room.

"And so he has," her mother said brightly. "Shall we go into the forest to gather our offerings for the festival?"

"Yes. I will fetch my basket."

Mathilda noticed the broken potion bottles and their contents still on the floor. She sighed and went to clean the mess. Reaching for her father's mortar and pestle, she gasped sharply as her fingers grazed the stone bowl. A darkness slammed into her mind, and her knees buckled. Feelings of pain, suffering, and death engulfed her. Whatever it was that her father was about was of no good.

"Mathilda? Child, what is it?" her mother asked, crouching by her side.

A tear streaked unnoticed down her face. "I do not know. I touched Father's mortar and pestle and was filled with darkness. I sensed evil and suffering. What does it mean?"

Her mother touched the pestle and made a hissing sound. "Come with me. I want to show you something. Quickly, now"

Mathilda got to her feet and followed her mother into the forest.

The sun had climbed over the trees, slipping behind a mass of clouds when they stopped along the edge of a large clearing. Mathilda felt at peace here. The landscape looked mystical, and it was filled with the sounds of birds and humming insects. Her mother closed her eyes and whispered something under her breath. A haze-like atmosphere fell away as a magical veil was lifted, revealing a little cottage. Mathilda gasped as she watched her mother walk toward it. It was perfect, she thought—no enchanting.

"You must tell no one about this place," her mother said over her shoulder. "Do you understand?"

Mathilda nodded.

It began to rain as they drew closer to the cottage.

"Hurry inside," her mother urged. "Light the candles."

Mathilda raised her arms, and flames danced on wicks, bathing the room in warm, golden light. Her gaze swept over the room. There were apothecary jars and herbs along the ledges and walls, and magical items, books, and totems lined a small chest in the corner. A table sat near a window to the right of the hearth, and baskets of various sizes hung from the ceiling above it. Her mother took a jar of herbs and a fat candle from the ledge, along with her husband's tainted mortar and pestle, and walked toward a door at the back of the room into a small sleeping chamber. Mathilda watched as she pulled back the rushes, revealing a deep, blackened etching of a magical circle marring the stone floor.

"Sit quietly and watch," her mother said, settling herself on the floor with her items.

Reaching into the jar, she sprinkled a pinch of herbs over the candle and spoke a single command: "You will yield your secrets unto this faithful Guardian." At her words, the flame on the candle shot up. Suddenly, she convulsed and slumped over.

"Mother!" Mathilda cried. She rushed over and gently touched her face. "Mother, are you well?"

"Yes," she replied, stirring slowly." She raised herself onto her elbows.

"What did you see?" Mathilda asked.

"Your father is completely overtaken with darkness. The Goddess is no longer with him. He has found a way to obtain vast power, but it required spilling the blood of an innocent that he gained this strength."

Mathilda's eyes widened. "Who...?" she said, breaking off in a shaky voice.

"A peasant girl," her mother answered sadly. "It was her spirit that communed with me just now. She told me that your father is working on something terrible, but we were separated from each other before she could say more." She paused, shaking her head. "That poor child was only twelve years of age. I never imagined Aelle could do such a thing. Something has to be done," she said, rushing to her feet. "I must send word to the other Guardians. Quickly, child, my parchment...."

Mathilda found the quill, ink, and parchment and sat them on the table. Her mother hastily wrote a few words and rolled the parchment up. As she tied a crimson ribbon around it, she whispered something.

"Mother, what is going on? Who are these Guardians?"

"I had planned to tell you everything on your eighteenth birthday, but we do not have time to wait until the end of May. Now, listen closely, Mathilda. I belong to a coven of five witches who guard against the usage of magic for dark purposes. You already know them as my old friends, although it has been many years since we were all in each other's company as it is growing dangerous for us in these times. We rarely come together except to celebrate at occasional feasts and pay homage to the Goddess or in situations like this, when we must protect the innocents from dark magic.

"Our coven is an age-old lineage that goes back beyond memory. My mother was a Guardian, now myself, then you. The girls that will be going through the ritual with you are the daughters of my coven sisters. As part of the ritual, each of you was to begin receiving from us the full knowledge of the Goddess from our traditions, in addition to her gifts of powers. I am telling you this now because of your father. You *must* protect yourself at all costs. Do nothing to anger him. If he were to lash out at you and harm you, the line would be broken.

"Now, I want you to take my letter and place it in the hollow of The Druid Tree and return home immediately. Here," she said, reaching overhead. "Take this basket and fill it with herbs along the way for the festival. As many as you can. I do not want to rouse your father's suspicions about where we have been. I will be along shortly."

"What will you do?"

"I need to raise the veil to conceal this place and then, like you, get a gift for the Goddess. Now run along. We will discuss this again soon."

Mathilda took her basket and went out into the woods. Her mind reeled from her mother's revelation. How careful she had been meeting with her sisters. Brief encounters at gatherings, hushed words exchanged with peaceful features to mask their true intentions of meeting. She wondered what they would do about her father as her feet led her to find the great white oak, known as The Druid Tree. She came across it behind the intersection of The Three Paths. Its massive size alone was a thing of wonder. The branches gnarled and twisted outward as if carrying a wealth of knowledge in those ancient arms. A hum of energy embodied the massive tree, calling to Mathilda as if it were a sentient being. She plucked the letter from her basket. Standing on her toes, she reached up as far as she could to place it in the deep hollow. Once she was sure it was tucked in unnoticed, she set off again.

A loud screech stopped her in mid-stride. Whirling around, she saw a long-eared Owl fly off with the letter clasped in its talons. She had heard of these winged messengers assisting witches from her mother's lore but had never witnessed one until now. Mathilda watched it fly off with silent wings and hurried back through the forest, gently plucking the best herbs and berries she could find along the way.

When she returned home, her mother was already there, sweeping up the rest of her father's mess. The mortar and pestle were neatly replaced on the ledge.

"Has Father returned?"

"No, he has not. Did you have any trouble finding the Druid Tree?"

"No. An owl took the letter from the hollow."

"Good."

"What do we do now?"

"Wait for a sign of response."

"How will we know what the sign is?"

"Listen for the cry of the owl's return. You will hear its call nearby when a response has come. I see you filled your basket," her mother remarked, inspecting the bounty. "These look free from blight. They will make a fine offering."

"And did you find a suitable offering as well?"

"Yes. Come, I will show you."

Mathilda followed her mother into the larder at the back of the house, where the herbs and food storage were kept. It was built lower down into the earth to keep the room cooler for food preservation. Above the table, two plump rabbits hung by their feet.

"They will make a fine offering," Mathilda remarked.

"Indeed, they will."

"Maelen!" Aelle's bellow startled them both. Mathilda clenched her jaw as anger flowed through her.

"Remember what I told you," her mother whispered, pinning Mathilda with a firm gaze. "Do not anger him. I am here, husband," she called out.

He stomped into the entrance of the larder "I am hungry," he said.

"I have the herring over the pot and—"

"I will have those," he said, pointing to the rabbits.

"But they are for the Goddess," Mathilda replied.

"Shut your mouth, girl," her father hissed.

"No matter, child," her mother interrupted. "I can find more in time for the celebrations." She took the rabbits down from the hook.

Mathilda looked on in hatred at her father. Her mother placed a hand gently on her arm.

"Come, help me with these. You and I will eat the herring tonight."

~

Mathilda stabbed angrily at her fish. She focused on the repetitious sounds of her own chewing to drown out the angry thoughts of her father. She watched him finish the last of the meat. He gulped down the rest of his mead and wiped the back of his hand across his mouth before stalking out of the house.

"Well, he is gone for the evening," her mother said lightly.

"I hope he never returns," Mathilda replied.

"My dear, please do not say things like that. You are not a hateful person."

"You are right. I am sorry, Mother. What will you do about a gift for the Goddess? The eve of Beltane is tomorrow."

"You let me worry about that. Now, let us clear this mess and then off to bed. You will need your rest for the festivities."

~

Mathilda lay in bed, listening to the sounds of the nighttime creatures. As she drifted off, she heard the call of the owl. Shortly after, her mother's footsteps could be heard walking out into the night.

To Be Continued

About the Author

Photo credit: Marjorie Stallard

Kimberly Patton is a devout lover of cats, overcast autumn days, and the deep, shadowy places of woodlands. She resides in Virginia with her husband and two children, where she spins tales that rivet readers. Learn more at <u>kimberlypattonauthor.com.</u>

instagram.com/authorkimberlypatton

About the Publisher

Highlander Press, founded in 2019, is a mid-sized publishing company committed to diversity and sharing big ideas thereby changing the world through words.

Highlander Press guides authors from where they are in the writing-editing-publishing process to where they have an impactful book of which they are proud, making a long-time dream come true. Having authored a book improves your confidence, helps create clarity, and ensures that you claim your expertise. Learning how to leverage your author business takes your experience to a whole new level.

What makes Highlander Press unique is that their business model focuses on building strong collaborative relationships with other women-owned businesses, which specialize in some aspect of the publishing industry, such as graphic design, book marketing, book launching, copyrights, and publicity. The mantra "a rising tide lifts all boats" is one they embrace.

facebook.com/highlanderpress

instagram.com/highlanderpress

linkedin.com/highlanderpress

tiktok.com/@highlanderpress